We
All
Love
the
Beautiful
Girls

ALSO BY JOANNE PROULX
Anthem of a Reluctant Prophet

JOANNE PROULX

We
All
Love
the
Beautiful
Girls

VIKING

an imprint of Penguin Canada, a division of Penguin Random House Canada Limited

Canada • USA • UK • Ireland • Australia • New Zealand • India • South Africa • China

First published 2017

LIBRARY AND ARCHIVES CANADA CATALOGUING IN PUBLICATION

Proulx, Joanne, author
We all love the beautiful girls / Joanne Proulx.

ISBN 978-0-7352-3288-4 (paperback)
ISBN 978-0-7352-3289-1 (electronic)

I. Title.

PS8631.R6815W4 2017   C813'.6   C2016-907174-X

Cover and interior design: Jennifer Griffiths
Cover image: Ian Ross Pettigrew/Getty Images

Printed and bound in the United States of America

10 9 8 7 6 5 4 3 2 1

Penguin
Random
House

For my kids: Simon, Sophia,
Elise. Cody, Brady, Behn.

Into a fragile world pour your
strength and goodness.

In memory of my friend
Renate Mohr, master of life
and impermanence.

And always, forever, Martin.

None of that. Not allowed. Be good.

ALICE MUNRO, *"Vandals"*

January

The 14th

I love her. Everything. The way she smells. Tastes. Feels. *Jesus.* The way she feels.

The first time. It was an early-morning thing. I was coming out of the bathroom. Jess was in the hall. We were both still half-asleep. I don't know why she was sleeping over—she wasn't babysitting, we were way past that, I can't remember, it wasn't that unusual, she's always been at our place a lot. She put her hands on my shoulders and backed me into the bathroom, kicked closed the door. The whole thing lasted about fifteen seconds.

You took advantage of my morning wood, I say, later, months later, when I've regained my ability to speak.

Lucky boy, she says.

Lucky boy.

We're lying in my bed this time, a map of the world pinned to the wall above us, a million other places we could exist. I'm rubbing the lace on her bra, trying to take things slow, so she knows that I can. The lace is scratchy against my thumb.

Doesn't this bug you? I ask.

Not really. You get used to it.

I kiss her, there, beneath the lace, so now it's scratching my cheek.

She puts her hand on my belt buckle, gives a little tug, and I can't help it, I moan just thinking about what's next.

Your parents would be mad if they knew, Jess says. They expect more from me.

More than this?

She laughs. Her lips are gorgeous. Her teeth white and perfect. Perfect. She undoes the top button of my fly. And Eric, she says. He'd be very mad.

My jaw tightens, back teeth clenched. Yeah, I say. Whatever.

She undoes another button. And whatever you do, you can't tell Eli. Because he'd tell Eric. For sure.

I know, I say. I'm not stupid. I know Eli.

Jess lifts her head off the pillow, opens my mouth with hers, slips her tongue inside, long black hair sweeping my face, the smell of summer in winter.

I like it with you, she says. She works the last button loose and slides her hand inside my jeans. With you I don't have to be a porn star. With you, I can just be myself.

Her hand. Jesus, I love her hand.

The 21st

Mia and Frankie are well into an impromptu photo shoot when Frankie asks her if Michael, her husband of nineteen years, is the first guy she really loved. Mia tells the girl no. Without lowering her camera, she tells her how the first boy had been trembling when he whispered he loved her on the stone bridge that crossed Black Bear Creek.

"Actually?" Frankie says. "Trembling?"

"Like a leaf in a storm. We were young. Fifteen." He'd walked her home for weeks before he worked up the nerve to hold her hand.

Mia rotates the ring on her lens, snaps the girl sharply into focus. A beauty. A lioness. Broad shoulders, amber eyes, beautiful lips, crazy, springy hair—the deepest shade of red. Behind her a wall of old north-facing windows, winter creeping in around the puttied edges.

What Mia doesn't tell Frankie about the night on the bridge is how that first *I love you* collapsed her life before into a trinket. How one beat back her heart had been a quiet thing, hung in her chest like an un-struck gong. Instead, she dips her camera so she and the girl are eye to eye. "Hot chocolate?" she says. "A cup of coffee?"

"Nah." Frankie flips her phone over on the settee. "I'm good." The blue rectangle shines bright on the purple velvet, the fabric dark as a bruise in the low northern light that floods the front of the studio and lets Mia shoot without a flash.

Frankie puffs a stray curl away from her face. Over the last couple of years she's grown out her hair and found some magic product to tame it. Today, her curls lie long and loose, only a hint of wild, and there's a new gleam at her nostril—the nose ring she hasn't told her parents about. It's the reason she came to the studio, to show Mia first and build up the courage to go home. Mia's already reassured her that the new piercing looks good—and it does—and sure, her parents might be upset, but they'll get used to it. Although honestly, Mia's not certain they will.

"So." Frankie glances up from her phone. "What happened with the trembler?"

Mia tells her how she loved the boy back, so unguardedly, so completely, so willingly, and the tragedy of him being a fundamentalist Christian who didn't believe in premarital sex. How intense it all was, the two of them falling deeper and deeper into a frustrating fumble of love.

"God," Frankie says, "that sounds horrible."

"It was." Mia is surprised by the camera's tremor. She presses the body more firmly against her brow; old-fashioned, she knows, but she rarely uses the screen. "After three years," she says, "all I wanted to do was, well, you know, fuck."

"*Mia!*"

It is their best moment together, and Mia has caught it, the girl leaning so joyously toward her, laughing, her body draped over her knees, the ring in her nose a gold glint in the soft grey of the studio windows.

And then, after she's sitting straight again, she asks so shyly, "Well, did you?"

"No," Mia says. "We broke up. He was pure when he left me. Both of us pure and broken-hearted and terribly, terribly horny."

"That's a sad story." Frankie's shoulders lift as she laughs.

"The saddest part," Mia says, "was afterwards we could not find a way to be friends."

Frankie stares off out the window at the sternness of a Canadian winter. In her hand, her phone tumbles, darkened screen flipping to dusty-pink case.

"How about you?" Mia asks. "You met anyone special?"

The girl casts a long stare into the camera. Light framing light, she lets Mia in, the shutter clicks, a flicker of black, and Frankie snaps back bright at the centre. She brushes her nose, and her auburn mane quivers. "No," she says. "Not really."

The 30th

Michael unfolds the scrap of paper he's drawn from the bowl. "Frankie," he reads, and she flashes him a peace sign. Sitting on the floor of her family's slope-side chalet, leaning up against one of the old leather couches, her cheeks are red from being outside all day. Like everyone else she's in her après-ski wear: woolly socks, long johns and a baggy sweatshirt, *Mont Orford* embossed across the front. Michael sees no sign of the nose ring Mia mentioned, which probably means Frankie lost that fight.

"I hope you've learned to draw," she says.

"No, I hope *you've* learned to draw," Michael teases back. They've always been easy together. On the chairlift that morning, bobbing in the air thirty feet above a slope of glittery white, their skis brushing the tips of snowy evergreens, she'd asked him to just, blah, be quiet for a bit. A few seconds later, with her face tipped to the sun, she said it felt like she was communing with God.

Finn picks his mom's name from the bowl, leaving Frankie's parents, Helen and Peter, as the third team, which isn't ideal. Peter can't draw to save his life, and board games make Helen cranky, especially when she's paired up with her husband. Regardless, everyone's pretty mellow as they settle in around the table and set up the board, well fed on spaghetti and meatballs—Helen's recipe, always wonderful—and muscle-tired after a good day on the hill: bright blue sky and decent snow and a fairly mild minus ten, which is about as good as it gets in the Eastern Townships in January.

The teams select their markers. Michael and Frankie get stuck with a stray chess piece, a knight. The game's old, the little hourglass also missing, so Finn pulls out his iPhone to use as a timer.

Peter places a red marker on the board. "Think we're going to get the management contract for the Soho?"

"Yeah," Michael says. "I think we're good."

"Premium condo building. We'll make big money."

Mia rolls her eyes. "Can you please not talk business tonight?"

"Fine with me," Michael says, and picks up the die. "Who starts?"

"We have to get off P." Frankie has the rule card in her hand. "Person slash place slash animal."

Helen holds up a bottle. "More wine?" Mia raises her glass.

"Can I have some?"

"You're seventeen, Francine," Helen says. "The drinking age is nineteen."

Finn glances up from his phone. "Eighteen in Quebec. And we're in Quebec."

Helen sets down the bottle, doing her best to look stern, which isn't easy for her. "Then next year you both can have a glass."

"You and me"—Finn high-fives Frankie across the table—"rockin' the clubs in Orford."

Peter jimmies the first card from the box. "Are we starting here or what?"

"HOW DID YOU get tinsel out of that?" Michael plucks the paper from Mia's hand. "He drew three squiggly lines."

"Are you two cheating?" Peter leans over, trying to see what Finn's drawn.

"Definitely cheating," Frankie says.

"We don't need to cheat. We're just good."

"Yes we are," Mia says, in her most pleasantly obnoxious game-player voice.

"I swear you two can read each other's minds." Michael looks at the paper again, those three anything lines, feeling unsure, disconcerted.

"NO ACTIONS!"

"Come on, it's right there." Michael cocks a thumb over his shoulder, at the chairlift behind him, framed by the picture window. "Does it say no pointing? Where does it say no pointing?"

"It's *Pic*tionary." Finn picks up the lid and shows it to his dad. "The Game of Quick *Draw*. First Edition."

"I'm fine with pointing," Frankie says. "I mean, it's hanging right behind his head. It seems almost wrong not to use it."

"I like your thinking, partner." Michael gives her a wink. "Someone should get you a glass of wine. Maybe a nose ring while they're at it."

"Would you stop," Helen says. "Michael, you are a s-h-i-t disturber."

He reaches across the table and squeezes her hand. "You know the kids can spell now, right, Helen?"

"Just move your stupid piece, you cheater," she says, finally letting herself laugh.

"HOW IS THAT a giraffe?" Helen stares at Peter's drawing in disbelief. "It looks like a horse. Oh my gosh, we're never getting off the first square."

Peter elongates a line, stretching his stick horse's neck. "There. Now it's a giraffe."

Helen tuts. "My kindergarten students draw better than that."

"Yeah? Well, they're not on your team tonight, are they?"

"Everyone knows giraffes have long necks, don't they? I mean, isn't that what defines them? Their long necks?"

"FRANKIE, YOUR HAIR. I can't see what you're drawing. Skirt. Dancer. Skirt?"

She stabs at the paper with her pencil and gives Michael an exasperated look.

"What? Dress? Oh, oh"—he snaps his fingers, his eyebrows lift—"tutu."

"Yes!" Frankie whinnies as she moves her marker onto the same square as Finn and Mia's and rubs it saucily against their playing piece.

"Are you hitting on our little blue thing?" Finn asks.

Frankie whinnies again and rears up her little plastic horse.

"WE'RE THINKING ABOUT going to Whistler for Family Day weekend." Helen drops the game pieces into the tray. "You guys interested?"

Michael and Mia exchange a glance. They definitely do not have the funds for a trip like that.

"Whistler!" Finn says. "We should so do it."

"We've never gone together," Frankie says. "It'll be sweet."

"Isn't it kind of expensive," Mia says, "to fly across the country for only a couple of days?"

Peter looks up from folding the board. "We're just tossing the idea around. We haven't decided anything."

Helen's jaw drops. "I thought I was supposed to book the tickets."

Peter slots the board into the box. "Finn, can you hand me the lid? We were just going to talk about it, Helen."

She shakes her head. "I thought we already had."

"So, what?" Frankie says. "We're not going, then?"

"LOOK."

Finn's first to notice the snow falling outside, so dense the night sky has lightened to grey and the evergreens bordering the runs have disappeared in the flurry along with the looping string of chairlifts. Michael slips his arm around Mia's waist and tucks her into his side. She smells good, a fine blend of wood smoke, red wine and fresh air. For many reasons, he's happy that they have their own room at the chalet tonight, that Finn and Frankie have moved out of the bunk beds and onto the living room couches where they can watch old movies on late-night TV.

Helen frowns out at the storm. "We'll need more food if we get snowed in."

"We're not getting snowed in," Peter says. "We have work on Monday."

Frankie bumps her shoulder into Finn's. "Powder in the east."

"Who needs Whistler?" he says. "We can be happy right here."

February

The 26th

Friday night, there's a knock at the door. Michael and Mia, stretched out on the floor in front of the fire trading sections of last Sunday's *Times*, a half bottle of shiraz standing on the carpet between them, both groan.

"You expecting anyone?"

Mia shakes her head.

"Probably someone collecting for something," Michael says. "They always come on Fridays, when they know we're at our weakest."

"Charity people—heartless bastards."

"You went out for Heart and Stroke."

"Don't remind me. Most of the neighbours were so unhappy to see me, cap in hand. God, and *Randolph*. The millionaire on the corner—"

"With the Aston Martin."

"—dropping change into my hand. Nickels, dimes, the occasional quarter." Mia shivers. "I've been wishing a heart attack upon him ever since. Or a stroke. Either would be fine." She leans a little closer and lowers her voice, as if there's a chance whoever's on the front porch might overhear her. "He doesn't deserve the tree on his lawn."

An enormous maple, at least two hundred years old, Mia's always been crazy about it. Even Michael, not a huge tree connoisseur, is impressed by its size, the fact it grew so large in the city.

They lie still, listening for the dull thud of boots on snow-packed porch stairs to release them back to their papers. Instead, there's another knock, this time louder, more insistent.

"Shit," Michael says. "You get it."

"No, you."

"No, you."

"I'll blow you if you get it."

"Deal." Michael slaps Mia's ass as he rolls up off of the carpet. He knows that after another couple glasses of wine, they'll probably both fall asleep in front of the fire. Still, he likes the sexual banter, likes the fact that after nearly two decades of marriage Mia still says the words and, from time to time, graces him with the deed.

He goes to step away, but Mia slips her hand under the hem of his jeans and gives his ankle a squeeze. "Lucky," she says.

Which is exactly what he'd been thinking. By the end of the work week, all he wants is to be home. When they're invited out for dinner, separated by people, he misses having her to himself. At a party, it's always Mia who catches his eye. Her vitality, her youthful heart. He'll wait for her to feel him watching. Then from ten, twenty, thirty feet, their eyes will lock, hold, as love rises sly into the room.

Front door open, Michael can't quite process the man shuffling from foot to foot on his porch, in a tuque and puffy down jacket, each breath an icy fog. Michael's used to seeing Stanley tugging at his tie in their boardroom, trying to explain to him and Peter why even though sales are up, their property management companies aren't making the money they once did. Stanley showing up at his house on a Friday night, even with his briefcase clutched to his chest, is way out of the norm.

Michael puts a hand on Stanley's back and guides him into the front hall. "Come in before you freeze to death."

"Sorry to drop in like this." Stanley places his boots on the mat beside the door, then unzips his jacket, revealing an impressive paunch, fallout from long hours behind a desk and too many client lunches. "I saw your Jeep in the driveway."

"You want something to drink?"

"This is a professional visit," Stanley says, "but if you're having one."

Mia's still on the floor by the fire, but now she's sitting up, cross-legged with a pillow on her lap. "Mia, you remember Stanley. Stanley, Mia, my wife." Michael knows he doesn't have to clarify the relationship, to add the title, but he likes to lay claim. Mia's always worn her hair long, but this week she had it cut into a short bob, the bangs high on her forehead. On an older woman the haircut would be severe, on a child it would look like a mistake, the scissorwork of an unskilled parent, but on Mia the effect is gamine, showing off her straight, dark eyebrows, her moony eyes. She looks like a ripe tomboy from the Isle of Man, a French schoolteacher who prefers cafés to classrooms.

"Our boys were on the same team a few years back, weren't they?" Mia says, repeating a neighbourhood mantra, forget Kevin Bacon, everyone one ice sheet removed.

Stanley nods. "Finn's not playing this year?"

"Nope," Michael interjects. He bends and picks the wine bottle from the floor. "Concentrating on his marks." Which is only partly true. Finn will be applying to universities next fall, so sure, his marks are important, but playing hockey a couple of times a week hadn't hurt his grades; Finn's always done well at school. But when he turned fourteen, fifteen, the sport turned rough. Even in their no-hitting house league the boys had started raising their elbows and slamming each other into the boards, trying out their bigger bodies, throwing around their new strength. Finn had been one of the biggest kids on his team—close to six feet tall and naturally muscular—but still he started hesitating going into the corners, looking over his shoulder, shying away from really fighting for the puck. Michael wasn't sure if anyone else noticed, but he sure did.

At one mid-season game against a team of farm kids from Quebec, a brawl had broken out, every guy on the ice grabbing hold of an opponent, jerking them around by their sweaters, trash-talking each other in both official languages. Finn had been the only kid to skate away. Michael had felt relieved, although standing in the brouhaha of hollering parents, he's not proud to admit he'd also felt a stab of embarrassment. There was a code in hockey, unwritten rules governing sportsmanship and honour, and his boy wasn't playing along. Watching Finn hanging on the boards by the bench, the word *pussy* had floated into his head, although Michael had pushed it away fast.

When it came time to sign up this year, Finn had said he was going to stick to shinny, that he preferred pickup games on outdoor rinks with only his gloves and his skates and his stick.

"Daniel still playing?"

"Only thing that gets him off the computer." For the first time since he walked in, Stanley risks a smile. "Made the A team again this year."

"Good for him," Mia says as Michael heads for the bar at the back of the room.

They bought the house before Finn was born and had extended the legs on an old pump organ they'd inherited from Mia's grandmother, added a matching rosewood extension, complete with a built-in fridge and a discreet stereo system. They'd painted the walls a rich ruby red, and Mia had hung velvet curtains and an antique mirror behind the bar and a Fortuny lamp—hand-painted Venetian silk; Michael hadn't even asked how much it cost—overhead, so what had been an awkward, unused end of a long living room now had the lusty warmth of a Parisian salon.

"You still taking those pictures?" Stanley asks.

"I am."

"That one you took of Daniel a couple years back. My wife just loves it. You just, just got him somehow, you know?"

"Well thanks, Stanley," Mia says. "He's a lovely boy."

Michael pulls the curtains against the cold and clunks a fresh glass onto the bar. The kid is a puck hog. Fast, but he never passes. Always tries to go end-to-end, which worked okay when the boys were younger but rarely once they all figured out how to skate. Michael pulls the cork and motions to Stanley. "Shiraz okay?"

Stanley nods but stays put at the front of the room. "I have some papers to go over." He reaches up and scratches his neck. "We'll need better light."

"It's brighter in the kitchen," Mia says, flashing Michael a wondering look. "You could use the table in there."

Michael has no desire to sit in the kitchen. He's comfortable behind the bar. "Should I call Peter for this?" he asks, rather gruffly. "He's the finance guy."

"No." Stanley shakes his head. "You shouldn't. You definitely shouldn't call Peter."

THE PARTY'S A RAGER. And like all things Eli, his basement is killer. Rich kid. Rich parents, currently in Costa Rica. Everyone drunk on their left-behind booze.

If anyone tries to talk to me, I pretend I can't hear over the music, which is loud—Eli's at the coffin, two decks, two laptops, professional six-track mixer. Tonight, I'm not into it. At all. What I'm into is drinking—tequila shots, beer, more tequila. You know, whatever. What I'm feeling is the bass from the upstairs party. Like hammer blows from above.

Frankie and this other girl, Brooke, from my physics class,

straddle arcade motorcycles in the corner. Eli's dad got them cheap from some place that was going under, gave them to Eli and Eric last Christmas. I got a hockey stick and some socks. The girls swing into the curves—the bikes tip, their asses tip—but I'm not really paying attention. Until game over, Frankie slides off the bike.

I got owned, she laughs, stumbling against my leg, drunk or pretending to be. She sits on my knee, holds up her phone and leans in for a selfie. I tell her she's heavy and bounce her off. She gives me a bitchy look as she walks away.

Like I care. Tonight, I only care about the upstairs party, the music. Which is irritating. And distracting. Very Fucking Irritating and Distracting.

I haul myself off the couch, head over to tell Eli I'm leaving. But he's totally oblivious, in his five-hundred-dollars-a-pop headphones. He finally sees me and frees up one ear. You okay? he shouts over the music. Travi$ Scott. "Goosebumps." Tonight I hate the fucking song. You in a shit mood, or what?

I'm fine. A bit wasted.

Crash here. In my room. Just don't puke in my bed. His pupils are small, the whites red. He's been upstairs with Eric. Eric and Jess.

I'm not gonna puke. I'm fine. I'm going home.

Come on, man. Stay here. I'll call your mom. Make some shit up. He tries to throw an arm around my shoulder, but I shrug it off.

Frankie elbows her way in, flashing smiles and cleavage as she leans into Eli, making some bogus musical request, shimmery and happy, pretending I don't exist. Eli smiles loosely back—he's always been into her, she's given him nothing so far—his face lit blue by MacBook, his stupid fucking smile.

When he's stoned, he looks just like him.

I'm going, I say.

I'm halfway up the stairs. Eli calls over the music. Finn!

I trip.

Hey, Finn!

I trip again.

WHEN MICHAEL CALLS HER, his voice sounds strangled, as if Stanley's got him by the throat in the kitchen. They've been in there a while—obviously their time together hasn't been pleasant. Reluctantly Mia downward-dogs her way off the living room floor, finds the remote and with a click shuts off the fire. She and Michael have always agreed she wouldn't get involved in the business. And despite her financial acumen—ten years as a corporate banker—Peter never argued. Nothing more emasculating than a wife hovering over her husband's shoulder, he'd laughed. Especially one as number smart as Mia. But there'd been no bonuses at the company this year or last, and recently Michael has been making noises about her taking a look at the books.

Let him and Peter work it out. She's had enough of men and their money. She knows that in every business numbers get fudged, games get played, and honesty and integrity aren't typically at the top of anyone's list.

She pushes hard through the swinging door. Michael and Stanley are sitting side by side, watching as she makes her way across the kitchen. If it weren't her husband and his accountant at the table she'd laugh; the two men are the embodiment of white-collar scared shitless. Normally with his easy smile and beautiful skin Michael looks like a man just back from sailing. But tonight his face is the colour of chickpeas. His lips are white. And Stanley's hot and red as a second-degree burn. Two full glasses of wine stand forgotten in the spread of papers between them.

The radio, permanently tuned to the CBC, is playing an old Q rerun, the host interviewing Joni Mitchell. Mia turns it off. She also shuts off the hood fan left on after a dinner of homemade lasagna, so all is quiet, the air undisturbed but for the lingering smell of burnt cheese. Mia takes the two steps down to the garden room. The dining room. A new addition to an old home. A bank of windows overlooks the yard; Michael likes to stretch out on the long bench seat beneath them after dinner. The outside lights are off, so the windows reflect back the room, making it feel encapsulated, as if beyond the glass the world has stepped soundlessly back. The deck, the trellis, the snowy yard, the crabapple's twisted branches. The cedar fence flattened. The house behind them, converted to a triplex years ago now, much to the chagrin of the neighbours—Jess and her mom live on the second floor. All of the houses, all of Old Aberdeen crept away, the handsome bridges fallen. They'll wake tomorrow alone in a new wilderness, a white flatness running to every horizon, the river a rush in the distance.

The image is not entirely unpleasant. When Mia was a new mother, she had a recurring dream of watching the house burn. Smoke gushing out the windows, flames shooting from the roof, the heat pressing into her where she stood in the middle of the avenue. And instead of feeling panicked, she'd feel relieved, joyous even. She'd wake flushed and excited, as if she'd been liberated into a glorious second chance, although even in her dreams she was careful; she always held Finn in her arms and stood Michael squarely beside her before burning her life to the ground. At least that's the way she remembers it now.

Mia circles the table and takes the chair next to her husband, so she's facing away from the windows.

"Explain it to her," Michael says, his voice pinched.

Stanley squares papers neatly in front of her, ready to back up all his bad news with official documentation. A corporate search, his fingerprints clammy along the edges. "During the last restructuring," he tells her, "the splitting of one company into three, Peter wrote Michael out."

"What?"

"He wrote him out."

Company records slide across the table, an amendment to the shareholder agreement with Michael's signature at the bottom. Mia does her best not to flinch. Stanley explains how Peter had things drawn up so he was the sole owner of the Conrad Management Group, eliminating their negotiated sixty-forty split with a few scratches of a pen. Formed a new company—Peter Corp.—*Peter Corp!*—into which, after flowing from one company to the next, consulting fees totalling close to half a million dollars were funnelled annually.

"How could this happen?" Mia directs her question at Stanley. She doesn't look at Michael. It is enough seeing his signature on these pages.

"Michael always left the financials to Peter." Stanley taps a short stack of documents beside him, the ones Mia hasn't yet seen. "He never really read the paperwork."

"We're friends," Michael says. "We've known each other since high school."

"He's been withholding information," Stanley says. "Purposely making things difficult to figure out. I just work with the in-house numbers I'm given. I'm not paid to ask a lot of questions. But for the past few years, things just haven't added up. I've done more than I should."

Mia stares across the room at the fridge. Finn's last report card, a notice from school about an upcoming ski trip, a dental appointment reminder, the fine details of their lives held up by glossy magnets. She wonders what, if anything, Helen knows about this.

"I'll call Peter tomorrow," Michael says. "Get this whole thing straightened out."

"I wouldn't do that if I were you," Stanley says, his eyes skittish. "I'd get in touch with a lawyer first thing Monday. First thing, you hear?"

———

UPSTAIRS, I STAY close to the wall. I try not to look over. I try not to look over at her. Leaning on the counter, her back to me. Two steps and I'd be grazing the sliver of skin showing above her jeans. Running my fingertips along it. Like just casually, on my way by.

Eric's standing beside her. Not touching her. *Not touching her.* Lucky, stupid prick. The first time I came over, he dumped the dog's water bowl on my head. I was, like, six. He's been selling weed to half my friends since grade eight. On the breakfast bar in front of him, a big blue bong, a lazy cloud drifting overhead. Upstairs crowd. Downstairs crowd. Except for the dedicated stoners, we don't really mingle that much.

I make it through unnoticed. In the aftershock of the journey, my heart's hammering, confusing a stroll through the kitchen with a blind stumble across a minefield or something. Idiot. Idiot heart.

I dig through the pile of winter jackets on the couch, locate mine—neon blue, so it's easy—rip it from the pile, grab one black glove, then another, it's not mine, I whip it back into the fray, if it wasn't so fucking cold I'd just ditch, do a couple laps of the block, punch a tree, sober up, go home.

And I don't even see her at first. I'm still rifling through the pile, but I *feel* her come out of the kitchen. I *feel* her moving along the hall. I turn my head and she disappears into the bathroom. She's wearing a pink sweater that I know to be incredibly soft. I drift over, like smoke I drift over, press myself against the wall and listen to her pee—even this I love—the toilet flush, water running as she washes her hands. When she comes out, the smell of soap, I know it's stupid, but I don't care, I grab her around the waist.

She lets out a little scream before she sees it's me. Finn, she hisses, twisting away. I reach for her again, but she traps my hands in hers, holds them down and away.

I stare at her as hard as I can.

Stop it. She squeezes my fingers, tight, so I know she's not fooling around.

What?

Just stop. You're drunk. You wouldn't do this if you weren't.

She has a velvet ribbon tied around her throat. Black. Black on creamy brown. Thai. No, Indonesian. Or maybe half. I'm not sure—Jess never talks about her dad.

I like your necklace thing, I say.

Thanks. A quick, cautious smile.

Can I touch it?

No.

Can I?

No.

I pull one hand free, wave it around a bit, let it do a little victory dance, before I reach up and run my index finger slowly along the ribbon.

Soft, I say. Like you.

Finn. She steps away. Glances toward the kitchen. No one's watching. She tilts her head to one side. I tug a dangling black end. The bow collapses. The ribbon falls from her throat. I take my time wrapping it around my fingers. I can do all this because I'm drunk and I don't care.

Are you leaving? She nods at my jacket.

Yeah, but I can't find my glove.

She takes my hand and leads me to the front hall. Wait here, she says, pressing down on my shoulders, collapsing me onto the stairs. I'll find it for you.

She's back in a minute, my glove on her right hand. I pull her down beside me, thankful when she doesn't resist.

You okay? she asks.

No. My knees jumping, radioactive. I was losing it downstairs. I sound so sucky, like a two-year-old, but I can't help it.

Finn.

It's been six months.

Really? Are you serious?

Yeah. Six months today. Every second, of every minute, of every hour, of every day. I bump her shoulder. Your fault. You started it.

I shouldn't have.

But you did.

She takes my chin and turns my head toward her. It's just that you're so gorgeous. So gorgeous and so nice.

Come to the bathroom with me, I say.

She raises her hand, makes my glove deliver the warning, an obedient puppet. Be good, Finn.

I will. In the bathroom. You know, the bathroom.

Finn, she says, I can't. Her face is two inches from mine, her breath is warm and weedy, her lips are—

HEY!

Like a kick in the fucking head hey and Eric standing in front of us, his hands on his hips. You babysitting or what?

She's off the step, *poof*, gone. Finn's not feeling great, she says, all trippy and fast.

Ahh, Eric says, poor Finn.

I think about hiding the hand with the ribbon, but I don't. I let it hang there between my knees. He'll see it if he looks. I want him to see it.

I thought maybe you could drive him home.

Yeah, I say, in the Porsche. Or the Caddy. Jess and I'll sit in the back.

In your dreams, he says, glaring at me, glaring so he looks like some kind of animal, a wolf maybe, a wolf that trots sideways from the woods, kills more than its share, disappears back into its piss-marked territory, panting, with blood on its teeth. Just one of the Kelly boys.

When he grabs Jess's hand, a sting of vomit hits the back of my throat. Come on, he says, I want to show you something. He pushes past me, his knee slamming into my shoulder. She slips by like I'm not even there. They climb the stairs together. The one I'm sitting on quakes.

Even then, I can't help myself. I'm a fucking masochist. I look up. I watch. They round the banister and start down the hall, he's in front, she's one step behind, her hand wrapped in his and my glove on her other hand and her ribbon wound round my fingers and his room, *his room* at the end of the hall.

MICHAEL'S IPAD CLATTERS onto his bedside table. "You mad?"

Mia opens one eye. All she wants is to sleep, but Michael is staring down at her, double-chinned from this angle, and still weirdly pale. He looks like he needs a transfusion, although she's the one who spent most of the night alone in the kitchen, going through the financial statements, tracking the money from company to company, drawing up a cash flow statement, finishing off the wine.

"Mad?" Mia considers his question. "I don't know. I don't know what I am."

"If it's true, I'm going to kill him."

"Who?"

"*Peter*," he says. "Who else would I be talking about?"

"Oh. Well, it's true."

"And *you're* not mad about it?"

Michael might be asking the question, but he's the one who's furious. She wouldn't have expected anything else. For a normally well-balanced human being, Michael does not do well when things go wrong. Whenever a hockey coach yelled at Finn, or Finn got hurt, or wasn't where he was supposed to be at the allotted hour, Michael's temper would flare. Once when Mia was rear-ended on her bike and ended up sprawled on the pavement, Michael had raged at the driver, an older man, close to seventy, who'd been as shaken as she was. Mia had limped over and calmed Michael down, but once she'd separated him from the driver, he'd started in on himself. *He should have been riding behind her, he should have seen the car coming, he should have warned her about narrow roads and careless drivers, he should have, he should have, he should have.*

Tonight his anger tires her. She has no desire to placate him. A stubbornness settles over her. And it's probably just the wine, but she's having a hard time taking the whole thing seriously. She *knows* it's serious, a million and a half dollars is serious, but money, Peter, his greed—at the moment it all feels so cliché and melodramatic. "I guess I'm mad at myself for being too lazy or unwilling or complacent or complicit or whatever I was to look at the books before. I mean, in retrospect, it seems negligent."

"We all agreed you'd stay out of it."

"Which seems stupid now. I mean, we know what kind of man Peter is. In some ways, he was just being true to his nature."

"Jesus Christ, Mia. I'm glad you can be so philosophical about it."

"It's business," she says. "He had no duty to protect us."

"No duty to protect us? He *lied* to us, Mia. He *stole* from us. They're our best friends, for Christ's sake." Michael yanks one of the pillows out from behind his back and throws it to the floor.

"Men who lust after money. They'll screw over their own mothers for a buck. We were naive to think friendship would change that."

"So it's our fault, then? Is that what you're saying?"

"No, that's not what I'm saying." Mia sits up, cross-legged on top of the covers, her sleepshirt hammocked over her knees. "But we probably should have expected something like this. We have a fairly lax attitude toward money, and we've climbed into bed with a man who doesn't. Hoping his greed would be big enough to keep us all living in style."

"Are you fucking kidding me?"

"No," she says bluntly. "I'm not fucking kidding you."

"I worked my ass off for fifteen years building that business. *I* brought in every client. *I* closed every deal."

"I know. And every successful company needs men who work their asses off and one sick, greedy bastard to make sure the focus of all that work is directed toward one thing and one thing only. Making money. Peter's that guy." She catches the swoop of cotton T-shirt stretched over her knees and pins it to the mattress, covering her fleshy folds, the dark points of entry. "You don't care enough about money to be a successful entrepreneur."

"Oh, fuck. Is that your professional opinion?"

"Yeah. It is."

"You're such a hard-ass, aren't you?" Michael is now sitting fully upright in bed.

"You don't last ten years in corporate banking by being soft. I'm a much kinder photographer."

"Are you?"

Mia snorts disdainfully and flails her way under the covers. Michael *knows* it bothers her that no one would ever describe her as kind. Smart, yes. Honest, yes. Moral, yes. But her opinions can be harsh. She has high expectations of herself and the people around her. She does not easily forgive. When she had Finn, she surprised herself by being such a loving mother. She'd never babysat, never even liked kids. But she's always adored Finn and is her best self when she's with him. She gets along well with teenagers in general, loves their energy and their unrest, the possibilities, so many different lives they might live. She is patient with the elderly and almost no one else. Most women find her intimidating: too confident, too assertive, too much. Other than Helen, whom she fell in with so easily—their husbands' partnership, kids the same age, Helen's sweet nature—Mia doesn't claim many women as friends.

"You want to know what I'm mad about, Michael? You signing that amendment to the shareholder agreement without consulting a lawyer. Writing *yourself* out of the companies. You want to tell me how that happened?"

Michael collapses back onto his pillow as if he's just been deflated. They lie side by side in a heavy quiet, interrupted only by the soft thump of Michael banging his own forehead. Mia snaps off her light. Turns on her side so her back is to him and stares into the darkness, letting herself hate him just a little.

"It was probably on a Friday," he says, finally. "At lunch. We used to do paperwork then."

"Your famous Friday lunches at the Mekong. Peter getting you drunk and taking advantage." *Like a fucking schoolgirl*, she thinks. Nineteen years. Nineteen years of marriage to this man. Mia reminds herself most of them have been happy. That on good days, they love being together. That every day, they love Finn. That the last word she said before Stanley showed up was *lucky*.

"I'll call David on Monday," she says. "He's the best lawyer I know. And the *kindest*." Behind her, Michael sighs heavily. "He'll work it out. What you have to do is . . . Michael? Are you listening?" With the slow roll of his body the mattress gives, then his breath warms the back of her neck, a disturbance she does her best to ignore. "What you have to do is find every document that directly states or implies that you and Peter are partners in the business. Preferably documents that he signed. That way we can probably get him on fraud."

"I'm sorry," he says, after another long pause. His hand slides up her thigh, under her shirt, and settles on her hip. She slaps it away, more forcefully than intended. With a frustrated huff, Michael lurches to his side of the bed. Ten seconds later his iPad grey-glows the room. Mia closes her eyes, but still finds the light annoying. A common complaint, an old argument, one she has no energy for now.

"What about Finn?" Michael asks. "When's he coming home?"

"His curfew's one thirty. You know that." She should get up and find her phone in case he tries to get in touch. It's downstairs—somewhere. The front hall table? The pocket of her coat? She can never keep track of the damn thing. "I'm tired." And she is, suddenly and desperately so, every thought sluggish, every bone heavy. "You wait up for a change. I worked all night. I'm off duty."

FUCK YOU, ELI, my friend, fuck you who pulled up a stool and pushed the bong toward me even though you know I don't, and I did, I put the chamber between my lips and inhaled, and the drunken freakoid rage receded like you said it would when you found me smacking my head against the wall. I inhaled again, I coughed, it was funny, everyone laughing, everything funny, *hey, Finn's finally partaking*, the bong reappeared, reappeared, and I laughed when she slipped her hand in my back pocket. I turned and she was like, whoa, right there, *aren't you hot in that jacket, Finn?* and I was, I was so hot, my blood like rocket fuel, and fuck it, I leaned in and kissed her like I knew she wanted me to, wanted me to for the last five years. And I got so into kissing her, my hands on her butt, one glove on, my other glove upstairs, gone, shit I didn't want to think about that, so I kept kissing her, people guffawing, get a room . . . Who were those people, Eli? I didn't know, I didn't care, I wanted to go and she knew it. Then you, all loud, like ground control to Major Tom, *Where are you going, Finn? Hey, Finn!* as she pulled me up off the stool and led me out of the kitchen and into the laundry room and closed the door and dropped to her knees and it was so mind-fuckingly amazing I let her do it, sweat running down my back, and my hand in her hair, it felt so good, I didn't care who she was, I didn't want her to stop.

MICHAEL LISTENS AS Mia's breathing slows and deepens, feels her body fall still on the bed. The chart of hockey standings he's been feigning interest in for the last five minutes—the Canadiens are in second place in the East—blurs on the screen in his hands. He relaxes back against his pillows, exhales, thankful Mia's finally asleep. With her awake, he'd been holding himself motionless, too tense to even risk a sideways glance.

Michael rotates his head on the pillow to loosen up his neck. Fucking Stanley. Fucking *Peter*. And Mia, his lovely wife, turned into a complete banker bitch. He lets his iPad drop to his stomach and closes his eyes for a second. When he opens them again, it's quarter after two.

Christ.

Sleepy and disoriented, he stalks through the house flipping on one light after another. Finn's bedroom is empty. His bathroom. TV room, living room, kitchen, shit, shit, shit. By the time he reaches the basement, he's wide awake and the house is lit like summer.

He yanks his phone from its charger on the hall table, tries calling. No answer. He texts him. *Where are you? It's late.* No answer.

Finn. You should be home. Come home NOW. In the chill blaze of their front hall, it takes Michael half a dozen tries to get the capitalization right. He stares at the small screen in the palm of his hand, waiting for three small dots to tell him that Finn is responding, willing a text bubble to bloom a reply.

Where are you can you answer me

Come home.

A current of cold air sweeps across Michael's ankles; the fire's off, the thermostat programmed to drop at night. He should probably go back upstairs and wake Mia. She has everyone's number. She'll know where he is. Some party somewhere. But the disdain in her voice when she'd told him to wait up for Finn, as if it was something he could actually manage, still rankles. Not to mention the way she slapped away his hand.

Finn?

I'm not mad. Just come home
Can you get in touch please
Finn? Are you okay?
Finn?

I AM A SPOTLIGHT, spotlit, the only thing that's glowing. My eyelids a radioactive blood orange, a pink-jelly sunset snapped to black, everything quiet and calm. I exhale and open my eyes and *whoa! like, just whoa!* Above me the pale city stars, I have never seen anything so beautiful in my entire life. Except for the moon, *fuck! the moon,* a sickle of pure silver light, all the stars switching places, the trees sliding across the sky. The whole yard spinning, then faster so I press my heels into the snow and turn my head and hold on to the moon. And I'm scared—*get up*—but also sort of laughing, feeling my body heat reflected back by the snow, amplified, so warm it's keeping me safe, Inuit and igloos, I am one with my northern brethren in their homes of ice, I totally get it, the insulating properties of snow and I know there's probably an equation for it, Mr. Elms could write it on the board, *It's simple, kids, it's Physics 101,* why my fist burns in a hotspot of snow, my hand melting into the snow and the snow melting into my hand, the boundary between snow and flesh disappearing, the boundary between everything beautiful and everything beautiful melting away, my body gone, my heartbeat floating . . . slow . . . slow . . . slow . . . into the universe . . . and everywhere, everything love.

Love.

I feel it. I am it. Every neuron fires into that awe.

From some great distance I see myself getting up to build an igloo, but it's so nice here, so nice being so cold and so fearless, I was so hot before.

———

THREE A.M. MICHAEL grabs his hat and coat, shoves his feet into a bulky pair of Sorels and stomps out the front door. He has no patience for scraping the tough web of ice from the windshield or letting the Jeep idle to warm. He sinks into the collar of his coat and hustles up Springfield on foot, like the last man on Earth, shadowed by darkened homes and naked maples—one on every patch of lawn. Icicles big as children hang from the corners of the roofs, giant daggers of ice; one fell and sheared the side mirror off Mia's Jetta before Christmas, leaving a stump of shattered plastic in its wake.

The spongy creak of packed snow, the grind of sidewalk grit marking time, Michael trudges up the snowy street, in the heart of Old Aberdeen. A neighbourhood of good schools and decked-out parks—tennis courts, soccer fields, speed skating ovals, baseball diamonds—and of course, gracious avenues of red brick homes with leaded windows and big wraparound front porches. Kids riding bikes in summer, ringing friends' doorbells, playing pickup in the winter, and regardless of season, the streetlights their cue to get home. Like the old days. Like it was when Michael was a kid, growing up in Beaconsfield, an anglo enclave in Montreal. Only nicer. And pretty much a hundred percent English.

Although Michael doesn't often think in these terms, Old Aberdeen is actually an island, a long, narrow strip of land only a ten-minute drive to downtown. The western tip—where his buddy Peter lives, on an estate-sized lot in a house overlooking the water—cleaves the Aberdeen River into two streams. The northern passage is man-made, a stone-walled canal that in fact created the island a hundred and seventy years back. The canal ferries boats safely past a rough section of the river, although along the island's southern shore, not all the water runs fast. Interspersed with the rapids are long stretches of slow, sliding calm that freeze every winter, although even this far north, it's not something you can count on anymore. The canal is still usually solid enough for skating—city crews monitor the conditions carefully—but it's gentlemanly, real Hans Christian Andersen, and sticks and pucks aren't allowed. So far the winter has been a bitter one—tonight is no exception—and Old Aberdeen is well surrounded by hand-shovelled rinks and foot-thick ice.

Michael pauses when he reaches Main Street, empty at this dead hour. His thin leather gloves were a bad choice—two minutes outside and his fingers are already aching. He pinwheels his arms, like a speed swimmer warming up for a race, encouraging blood back to the tips. He looks left up Main. The bagel shop. Past the bagel shop, a few new hipster bars and restaurants serving craft beers and questionable cuts of meat—places Finn couldn't get in and would have no reason to visit. To the right, Eli Kelly's riverside home. Eli's father, Don, slapping Michael on the back at the door, sloppy drunk, insisting on a nightcap. And his wife, Dorothy, worn down but still flirty, a dark, leathery tan.

Michael turns left. Across the street, sun and sand shine from a bright-lit billboard, the undulating taunt—legs hip waist breasts—of a bikinied girl against a blue Cuban sea. All-inclusive. All yours for only $999.

He could buy a lot of that with half a million dollars. Or a million and a half—Stanley said it's been going on for the last three years. So to hell with a week in the sun. A loop through Southeast Asia would be nice. Thailand, Vietnam, Japan. A dip down under to Australia. He and Mia have always talked about showing Finn a bit of the world.

Christ, Finn. It's so unlike him not to check in. He's always been a thoughtful kid. Confident, but laid-back. Rarely gets mad, rarely raises his voice. Doesn't do drugs, if what Mia's told him is right. He's come home noticeably drunk only once. Fighting a slur, he'd tried to tell her about his night, but she sent him to his room, said she didn't like talking to him when he was in that condition. "Aw

Mom," he'd said. Michael had been lying in bed, the door open to the hall, and he'd heard the shame in Finn's voice, how much he hated disappointing his mother.

Michael begins to jog, awkwardly. His boots are clunky beasts, tough leather and felted wool, footwear pried from an unearthed Neanderthal's desiccated feet. He jogs past boutiques and coffee shops, a pet store pushing hand-knit sweaters and rubber booties for dogs, the Italian deli where an organic tomato can set you back three bucks. The air sears his lungs—it's like breathing dry ice—but he keeps on running, suffering the hard ache in his chest, deserved punishment for anyone without enough sense or luck to stay inside so deep on a winter's night.

What else? He distracts himself with everyone's favourite game. What to Do with the Money? A ski chalet in the Eastern Townships. Definitely a cottage, nothing big, nothing fancy, just a wedge of pine-scented forest, a couple hundred feet of frontage, lake water like warm velvet at midnight, a million stars overhead.

Peter and Helen have all that. Claimed the cash came from her parents as part of some tax-saving deal, assets tipping from one generation to the next without the grief of anyone actually dying. Most summer weekends, he and Mia and Finn are invited up to the cottage. In winter, it's the chalet in Orford. He supposes all that's over now. They'll be making other vacation plans. Other plans, period.

Michael thought he knew the deal with Peter. Like Mia said, the man was born lusting after money. He stretches the truth and bends rules to get more of it. Michael's seen him do it countless times at work. Hell, he watched him pluck twenties from his mother's purse back in high school, helped him smoke the pot he bought with the stolen bills. Still, Michael had somehow convinced himself that Peter's greed would never trump their friendship. Hundreds of teenage parties, hockey games, baseball games, dozens of girls.

And later on, hadn't Peter shown up at Mia and Michael's door, suitcase in hand—not once, but twice—after finding out that his then fiancée had been cheating on him? Hadn't he lived with them for months? They were *close*, for Christ's sake. And Peter wasn't stupid. He knew he needed Michael to soothe the staff and charm the customers while he took care of the dough.

When the company had started to take off and they sold their first few franchises, it was Peter who insisted they formalize their arrangement. Michael hadn't even wanted a shareholder agreement. They'd always worked on a handshake-is-my-word basis and there'd never been any trouble between them.

Except for the incident with the boat. A two-hundred-horse bowrider, wraparound white leatherette seats trimmed in navy, surround-sound stereo, built-in cooler. He'd only had it a couple of weeks when their bookkeeper, Jill, all six feet two of her, had marched into Michael's office, closed the door and told him about the unauthorized $35,000 withdrawal from the company's main account on the same day Peter purchased the boat. Michael wasn't sure if he didn't totally believe her, didn't want to believe her or simply didn't want to confront his friend, but he never said a word. Told Jill to leave it alone. She stomped around the office for a few weeks until Peter found some excuse to let her go.

He never told Mia about it. Hadn't wanted her to worry or think he didn't have things in hand. And if he's honest, he hadn't wanted her to force him to, well, rock the boat, because he knew it was something she wouldn't let lie. He wonders what would have happened if he'd confronted Peter then—this was ten or eleven years back, now—if the company would have blown apart or if they'd have come out the other side on more even ground.

His throat anaesthetized by frigid air, lungs pruned by cold, Michael wheezes his way through Kettleman's parking lot. Choking back a cough, he peers through the front window, streaming with condensation. Booths of kids, ski jackets, flushed faces, saggy tuques, he searches for but can't find the right combination. The neon blue of Finn's jacket, the pocket of brown hat, the jut of dark brown hair.

He yanks open the door, stumbles into steamy heat, young noise and yeasty wafts of baking bread. A deep, wood-burning oven runs fifteen feet across the store's back wall; the bagels are fed into the oven on wooden pallets the length of a grown man. Like a crematorium, Michael can't help thinking every time he sees it.

College kids who've outgrown worried parents hang along the counter beside the oven. The bearded guy who begs change outside Metro hunches over a shaky metal table by the front window— drafty, second-class seats in winter. In one of the middle booths Michael spots Tristan, a friend of Finn's, with two girls whose backs are to him. It isn't until he's standing at the end of the table that he recognizes Frankie. Her curls are hidden beneath a floppy tuque, her eyes glassy and unfocussed. He gives her a stiff nod. "Francine."

"Hi, Michael." A red flush creeps up her neck. She holds herself a little straighter and starts fiddling with the straw in her cup. No one else says hello or glances up from their phones.

Frankie looks drunk. Tristan looks drunk. The blond girl—they all look drunk.

Despite his joking at the chalet, Michael can't get used to it. The fact that the kids are drinking. That they're out this late. That Finn is AWOL and Frankie is apparently wasted and now has a hoop through her nose. He stifles his fatherly instinct to bawl her out. To drag her from the booth by her nose ring—wasn't she supposed to have gotten rid of it?—and march her on home. Any other night he'd have done it. Any other night.

"Have you seen Finn?" He directs his question at Tristan, who slowly turns his way.

"Finn?" he says, all bleary-eyed and amused. "Hey, Frankie, have *you* seen Finn?"

Frankie's golden ski-tan turns pink.

"Have you seen him?" Michael's voice is harder now, louder.

"He's probably still at the party," the blond girl says.

"What party?"

Eyebrows raised, she flashes him an incredulous look. "Eli's."

Shit. He should have woken Mia up before he went out looking. She would have known about the party.

Tristan reaches across the table and nudges Frankie's shoulder. "In the laundry room," he says. "Right, Frankie? Right?"

"Don't." She bats a hand vaguely at Tristan, at the straw standing erect in the cup in front of her. For a second Michael thinks she might cry.

"Tristan," the blond girl says, "don't be an asshole."

Michael's halfway out the door when he stops. "Francine!" he hollers. And waits until she's looking. The frigid air seeping in from outside, the raised voice, have everyone muttering. "Shut the fucking door!" one kid yells. Michael ignores him, and the rest of the irritated chorus. He and Frankie make eye contact across the bagel shop. "You should go home."

"I'm staying at Brooke's," she calls, as if that explains everything.

"Well then get yourself there. It's late," he says, letting the door slam shut behind him.

THE KELLYS' FRONT PATH looks like it hasn't been cleared all winter; end of February and the walkway's a ragged trough of frozen footprints, melted and thawed a dozen times over. Despite his chunky boots, Michael can feel the jagged edges of ice as he picks his way up the path. With every twisted step, he thinks *lazy*, he thinks *stupid, careless people. Rich pricks*, he thinks. *Assholes.* He wonders how many people Don Kelly screwed over to pay for this place.

Michael actually hates the house. When the Kellys bought the property a few years back, they had the original Tudor demolished and threw up a palace of glass, a James Bond beach house spliced into a Victorian neighbourhood. Tonight, the house is a scream of light, nothing turned off, nothing shut down. Through the glass of the front door, free-floating wooden steps fan gracefully up the foyer wall, like something in a modern art museum.

Michael steps onto the porch. Leaked from inside to out, he can both hear and feel rap music pounding into him like the home's own erratic heartbeat. To his left, a floor-to-ceiling window showcases the living room. The white leather sectional, empty now like the rest of the room, could fit twenty people. Beer bottles and red Solo cups clutter a glossy coffee table. From the arch of a chrome lamp, a video game controller dangles like a gutted forest creature.

Michael knocks, but only waits a second before he tries the handle. He isn't surprised when the front door swings easily open. And he doesn't even bother shouting for Finn—the music, the absence of people—it isn't worth the effort. He finds no one in the marble bathroom. No one in the laundry room. Only stacks of beer cases and boots and hockey bags, and a chalkboard with "Be good!" written at the top and a long-distance number scrawled below. Michael shouldn't have worried about running into either Don or Dorothy; he'd forgotten they spend most of the winter in Costa Rica, a credit card or two left behind to ensure their precious boys have everything they could possibly need—other than a bit of parental guidance.

In the kitchen, a haphazard pyramid of dishes teeters in an industrial-sized sink. Domino's boxes litter the counters. The long kitchen island is the only surface that's clean, with a water pipe standing alone at its centre. Smoky blue belly, long, delicate neck, a medusa of darkened tubes, it stands on the granite counter like a signpost confirming kids travelled beyond rolling papers and pot.

Upstairs the music loses its power. Michael starts calling for Finn, but the ceilings are high, every angle sharp, every surface hard—glass, metal, stone. His voice sounds thin and hollow, as if he's searching for his son in an abandoned mausoleum. He ghosts his way along the hallway, trying every door—glancing around the empty rooms, fingering the icy phone in his pocket. He'd found Mia's cell in a clutter of papers on the front hall table and propped it against her bedside lamp, ringer on full. Just in case. But his plan is not to wake her. He'll find Finn. He's here somewhere. He'll find him and bring him home. They'll deal with him together in the morning. At least one of them will be well rested.

Michael puts his shoulder to the oversized door at the end of the hall, the bottom edge resisting the thick carpet. Inside, a light from the ensuite cuts a swath across the room. Adrenaline slams through him. On the bed, two kids sleep in a tangle of sheets; he's sure one of them is Finn. Banded by bathroom light, the torso of a girl—flat brown belly, a scrape of ribs, high breasts, one sculpted shoulder—and a boy. *Shit*, now that his eyes have adjusted he can see the kid, compact and muscular, is nothing like Finn. It takes a minute for Michael's heart to slow to a dull, flat thud and for his limbs to lose their tingle.

"Hey," he says, loudly. "Hey."

The boy doesn't budge. The girl whimpers, reaches up, one arm twisting, slim and beautiful, before dropping back onto the bed with a fleshy slap.

"Hey, wake up. I'm looking for my son."

Michael flips the switch inside the door, flooding the room with light. The bed is the size of a squash court. Its headboard climbs halfway to the ceiling, a black leather monolith. He takes in the scatter of clothes at the foot of the bed: a pink sweater, lacy red underwear, a bra with red cherries, a pair of jeans peeled inside out. A black glove. It looks like Finn's but any black glove would. Michael steps forward and picks it off the floor. If he were alone, he'd put it to his nose and inhale, see if he could pick up a scent.

He clears his throat. "I'm Michael Slate." He keeps his eyes off the girl. "Finn's dad. I was told he was here."

The boy squints across the room, looking baffled, indignant. Even with his face screwed up, Michael recognizes Eli's brother, the feral good looks that easily cut to mean. "Turn off the fucking light," he says, scrambling the sheet up.

"I'm looking for Finn. I was told he was here."

"Finn?" The boy says the name as if he's never heard it before.

"Yes, *Finn*. Finn Slate."

"Go ask Eli," he says.

"I can't *find* Eli. I can't find anyone. I'm looking for Finn."

"Yeah," he says. "I got it." The boy's eyes sweep the room. He jabs his chin at the corners. "Do you see him?" His movements are exaggerated, impatient, performed for the benefit of an idiot. "Seriously, if you wouldn't mind turning off the fucking light on your way out, that would be great."

A couple of long strides and Michael is at the bed. He smacks the boy with the glove, a quick, weightless slap across first one cheek, then the other, fighting back the urge to grab him by the throat. If the kid had ever dared talk to Michael's father that way, well, he would have done it.

The boy bats the glove away and swings his legs off the bed. "What's your fucking problem!" He drags the sheet onto his lap, uncovering the girl.

Long black hair. Full lips. And all the rest. It's a shock to see Jess lying in this bed, with this boy, like tripping over her, spaced out and panhandling for change, on a grubby downtown sidewalk. *Christ, why does this night just keep getting worse?* Jess should be twelve years old, wearing pink flip-flops, a Kermit the Frog T-shirt, a pair of faded jeans. She should be perched on a stool in the kitchen, talking to Mia, or stretched out on the living room floor reading Dr. Seuss books to Finn. She should be smiling at him from behind the cash at Metro or better yet, jumping out of the crabapple tree into their yard, like she did when they first moved in and Michael hadn't yet pried a couple of boards off the fence to make a passage, so she wouldn't get hurt making the leap.

"I could sue you for that."

Michael looks down at the boy. "What?"

"Hitting me. You fucking hit me."

The glove in Michael's hand. "Go ahead," he says. "Call the cops. They'll love the bong in the kitchen."

An injured moan from the far side of the bed has both of them staring. Jess inches herself up, or tries to. Her elbows buckle and her head hits the mattress before she stumbles to her feet and staggers naked into the bathroom. There's a thump, followed by the sound of hollow retching.

"Nice," Michael says, shaking his head at the boy.

"It's not my fault she got trashed."

"But you thought it was a good idea to bring her up here?"

"She was the one who dragged me upstairs."

"Yeah, I bet."

"Whatever. She's my girlfriend." The boy—Eric, his name's Eric—lunges for the jeans on the floor, a pair of boxers settled inside. He misses and rocks back onto the mattress, still clutching the sheet to his waist. Michael kicks the clothes toward him and starts slapping his own leg with the glove.

Finn was here? Yeah. *You saw him here?* I said he was here. *When?* Earlier. I don't know. *What condition was he in?* What do you mean? *I mean was he drunk?* Yeah. *How drunk?* Very. *Very drunk?* Yes. *Jesus Christ.* The boy smirks as he zips up his jeans. *When did he leave? Who was he with? Where did he go?* I don't know. I don't know. I don't know.

In the bathroom, Jess begins to vomit.

When she's through, Michael goes in and flushes the toilet. He has to step over her, curled up on a plush white bathmat, one cheek resting on the cool tile floor. He grabs the cleanest-looking towel from the rack, wipes her face with one corner, and does his best to cover her up while Eric watches from the doorway.

"Jessica. Hey, Jess. It's Michael. Your neighbour. You okay?" He keeps his voice even, holding back judgment, the stiff edge of impatience.

Her eyes blink slowly open. "Michael," she says, one corner of her mouth creeping up.

He gives her shoulder an easy rattle, pushes away all recognition of warm, young skin, the way the towel is slipping off her breasts. "You okay?"

She squeezes her eyes closed. Her jaw muscles pulse. Michael can see she is probably going to be sick again. "Jessica? Jess. Do you know where Finn is?"

"Finn." She gives Michael a sudden radiant smile, a drunken laugh. Her breath is foul, biting. "I just love Finn."

IT'S OBVIOUS FROM his narrowed eyes and the snarly twist of his lip that Eric thinks Michael is a complete moron. "They always party downstairs." With the gentlest of kicks, with one big toe, Eric glides open a sliding door to reveal a descending staircase.

Even Michael can't believe he overlooked this door, just down the hallway from the kitchen. He'd thought it was a closet, hadn't even considered the possibility that it might open onto anything but a rack of coats. Unlike all the century-old homes in the neighbourhood, with their squat, damp basements—more dungeons than rec rooms, most often accessed via witchy exterior doors— this modern marvel would have an incredible lower level. Michael hasn't moved, but he can already see Finn asleep on the floor in front of a wall-wide TV, or sprawled on a leather couch, or worst case, worst case, passed out on the floor of a bathroom, fully clothed and two floors down, but otherwise in the same condition as Jess. At this point it would be a thrill to clean him up and take him home.

Eric shoves his feet into a pair of running shoes, flicks another switch, and a half-acre of snow-covered yard appears from the black beyond the glass of the back door. In the centre of the soft-lit yard, a kidney-shaped indent, like a gigantic footprint, delineates the off-season pool. On the right, a cabana, window-deep in drifted snow. Eric yanks open the door and tramps across the unshovelled deck. Apparently done with Michael and the search that hasn't ended, he unzips and begins adding to one of the pitted ponds of frozen boy piss that trench the deck's edge.

Michael can't help staring at the grey glow of the backyard, like a still from an old Hitchcock movie. The trees that line the back fence look flattened—filigreed silhouettes stamped onto a cold-sharpened sky. The snow itself appears illuminated, as if it has a hidden power source and is giving off its own light. The dent of the swimming pool is darker, the block of the cabana darker still. But it's the electric-blue shimmer emanating from the snow at the cabana's far corner that holds his eye. The only shiver of colour in a mono-chrome landscape, it's like a mirage, there one second, gone the next. An electric-blue shimmer riding the crust of the snow. Then gone. Then back.

Michael crashes out the door and tumbles across the deck, falls into the yard, slips in his socked feet as he trips toward that shimmer. Finn is sunk deep in the white. It's his sleeve Michael had seen, propped up a little higher than the rest of him, barely breaching the lip of snow that encases him. Michael stumbles closer, Finn's whole jacket now a bright blue scream in the spotlight that hangs, snow-dipped, from the eaves of the cabana.

Michael drops to his knees beside his son. He hovers over him, afraid to reach out, afraid to touch him. The boy's eyes are frosted shut, his skin otherworldly. Michael has to force himself to move, to bend, forward, like a spastic robot, to turn his head and press an ear to Finn's icy lips. In his panic he is not certain there is breath. He is terrified of its absence. He pulls away, presses two trembling fingers to his son's neck, beneath the jaw, so cold it's like touching death. Frantic, he grapples for Finn's wrist, bare, no glove—the glove upstairs—the hand dark and fisted. With his fingertips he listens for a pulse, but all he can hear is the bang of blood in his own ears.

The zipper on Finn's jacket gives way in jerky bursts. Michael slips his hand inside and his soul explodes with the small warmth at Finn's chest. He slides his hand in deeper, presses his palm flat and hard against his son's ribs. Michael holds himself motionless—the world suspended, time stretched thin—and offers himself up, offers up anything, everything, in exchange for one beat of this heart.

"MIA." A HAND on her shoulder. "Wake up."

A small circle of light, the bedside lamp, darkness beyond—still night. She lets her eyes slip thankfully closed.

"Mia." Michael. His hand gripping her shoulder. "Wake up."

She squints against the light. Michael. In his hat and coat. "Where are you going?"

"Get up," he says. "Get dressed."

The clock on the bedside table glows 4:37. She remembers Stanley. Peter. Does this have something to do with Peter? Her head is swimmy with sleep. It is Michael's boots that finally hold her attention, the snow melting onto the carpet beneath them. He has worn his Sorels upstairs.

She pushes herself off the warm mattress. The down comforter falls away. Even in winter, they sleep with the window open; the air in the room is chill.

"Michael . . ." She is afraid to say it. "Where's Finn?"

"Get up," he says. "Get dressed."

In the car Michael tells her what happened. She's heard stories like it before. Drug addicts, the homeless, passing out in the snow. Stories that have nothing to do with her or her family. When Michael finishes, he loops back and repeats the whole thing again, almost word for word, so she's heard it twice by the time they pull into Emergency. The important thing, he stresses as he parks the Jeep, the important thing is that the paramedics found a heartbeat. Slowed by the cold, like patients cooled before surgery, but beating, his heart had been beating. Mia does not find this reassuring. Of course Finn's heart was beating. How could it not be beating?

There is no wait. The triage nurse checks her screen and informs them that Finley Slate has been taken directly to the trauma bay. They push through a pair of heavy swinging doors. Utilitarian grey. Michael reaches for Mia's hand but she pulls away. She cannot be touched. He cannot touch her.

A balding doctor in green scrubs leads them to a windowless waiting room. Fluorescent overheads cast a cold, clinical light. The room is empty except for a row of back-to-back vinyl chairs and one depleted vending machine, its empty corkscrews gleaming. The doctor talks, he tells them things.

Mia interrupts. "Can we see him?"

The man frowns, shakes his head. The mask dangling from one ear swings. He is wearing running shoes. White. There's a circle of blood on one toe, a single drop. Is it Finn's? Michael hadn't said anything about him bleeding. She wishes she'd brought her camera, that she was holding it in her hands. She tilts her head, changes the angle on the triangle—Doc Martens, Sorels, white sneakers—centres it on the glossy red dot. She blinks the triptych of footwear into memory, a snapshot of fear at ground level.

Two nurses pass in the hall, leaning into each other, whispering. One of them throws back her head, her laughter loud and guttural, a harsh foreign language. Mia focuses on the doctor. Superficial injuries, he says, and she exhales. Temperature-controlled mattress. Warm saline administered intravenously. To prevent blood rushing from his core to his extremities. A risk of ventricular fibrillation. The shutting down of vital organs.

A slight flicker in the doctor's eyes is the only acknowledgment that·Mia has placed a hand on his arm. "We need to see him," she says, squeezing his wash-softened sleeve. "Please let us know when we can see our son."

MICHAEL GIVES MIA'S BOOT a gentle knock. "No socks."

She peers into her Doc Martens. Beneath her calf-length tights, a gap of pale skin.

The doctor has been gone for thirteen minutes. Mia is sitting in the chair beside Michael, facing the looted vending machine—three packages of Ritz crackers and cheese, one Mounds chocolate bar. On the wall, a big clock ticks, its second hand jumpy.

"I've got some in the car. In my ski bag," Michael says. "I'll go get them." He stands. "It's something I can do."

From behind, he looks almost normal pushing through the grey swinging doors. Left alone, she tracks the second hand's stilted migration around the face of the clock and stares through the glass of the vending machine at the menacing metal spirals.

It takes Michael six and a half minutes to return with the socks. They are somehow warm. When she asks, he tells her he tucked them under his shirt on his way back from the car.

March

The 1st

Finn's smile—radiant and smug and slightly stoned—is driving Michael nuts. He knows the boy's on morphine, but still, he seems particularly spaced out. When the nurse comes to change his dressings—wetting layer after layer of bandages with sterile water before peeling them away from his feet, his hand, his wrist, bandages stewed with dead flesh, every colour of blood and pus—Finn turns toward the window and closes his eyes, but that dopey smile never wavers. Not even when Cathy—it's Cathy on night four of this hell—plump, freckled, with a butt so broad it stress-tests the limits of her polyester uniform, starts debriding the wounds. Debriding— using surgical tweezers to tear chunks of necrotic tissue from Finn's toes. Michael feels every goddamn tug.

Superficial injuries my ass, he thinks. When he works up the nerve to glance at Finn's feet, he experiences a moment of vertigo, feels like he's staring into the eye of a swirling comet, a deep spin of pulpy flesh. And the shocking bluntness that now ends Finn's right arm? Every time Michael looks at it, bandaged or otherwise, he imagines the drop of a guillotine, the swing of a machete, the thunk of an axe; the whole thing leaves him breathless and weak-kneed.

Superficial injuries? *Christ.* What the hell is superficial about losing part of yourself?

Michael flinches every time Cathy pokes her needle-nose tweezers in too deep, pricking the heart of a wound, pale pink tissue once protected, now exposed, nothing holding in from out. From his chair by the window, the sour odour that creeps toward him as the bandages come off—it's as if some small creature has died in Finn's bed—conjures up the package of rotting chicken Michael once found, slipped from a shopping bag into the trunk of Mia's car, parked in the driveway for the better part of a hot summer week while they'd been up at Peter and Helen's cottage. He'd had to replace the carpeting in the trunk and have the whole car detailed, but even then the smell of death hung on, and he sold the vehicle the following winter, when the odour was tempered by cold.

"Dad."

Michael jumps. *Christ, have I been muttering?* He can't be sure. But it doesn't really matter. He knows what Finn's seeing: him in the chair, tense, miserable, face shrouded and tight, a cut-out of his own father twenty years prior, hunched over his dinner plate after a day when nothing had gone right at work and everyone else at the table quiet, knowing enough to let him alone.

Michael runs finger and thumb along his brow, stretching out the lines, trying to wipe the darkness away with a shaky hand.

"You should go home and get some sleep," Finn says.

"Don't worry about me. I don't want to leave you alone."

Cathy looks up from rewrapping Finn's foot, the toes blistered and swollen to three times their regular size. "I'll be here for a while," she says.

"I know," Michael says. "That's why I'm staying."

"*Dad.*"

Cathy is frozen mid-wrap, holding the length of bandage taut and high. On her left hand, above the gauzy white tether, a diamond shines. Her lips are pinched into a scowl, one eyebrow has flown up, but after trading stares with Michael, she lowers her eyes—perhaps she also grew up with an angry old man—and resumes looping the bandage around Finn's foot, moving up the sole, closing in on the blistered toes.

"You want me to go?" Michael says to Finn. "I'll go."

"I don't *want* you to go. It's just . . . well, I know this stuff bugs you. And I'm fine."

"You're fine?" Michael is up out of the chair, striding to the bed, gripping the side rail. "Look at your foot," he says. "Does it look fine to you? Do those toes look *fine*?"

Finn's eyes do not leave his father's. His smile flickers but does not fade. The smell is sharper near the bed, thicker, mouldy cheese and rotting meat; Michael wants to give the bed, and in it his injured, amputated son, a good rattle, but instead he turns to the nurse.

"Why the hell aren't you wearing gloves?"

"I'm allergic to latex." She blushes. "I've got an exception."

"And you think that ring's a good idea? You think that's hygienic?"

She nervously spins the small stone around with her thumb, vanishing the diamond into the palm of her hand. "I just got engaged."

"So you get engaged and my son gets a superbug?"

"I wash up between pa—"

"Is that the gold standard around here? Give that ring a little splash and on to the next poor sucker?"

Eyes downcast, Cathy and Finn study their own chosen corners of the room.

As the door swings shut behind Michael, a whoosh of air escapes the room, and with it Finn's apology to the nurse. *Sorry about that . . . you can leave it on, I don't care.* And before he even reaches the nurses' station, he wants to go back, to make amends, to be a better man, a better father, to say the things he cannot say. He punches the button on the wall, summoning the elevator, frustrated it hasn't already arrived.

The 2nd

Mia nudges pale eggs and two rigid strips of bacon around Finn's plate, guessing at what he might eat. Five days in the hospital and he is noticeably thinner, a boy who had no extra pounds to lose. Yesterday, he had plain toast for breakfast and sipped on a cup of soup at lunch, leaving the spoon untouched.

When Mia looks up from the plate, Finn is staring at her hand. She scrambles it away, curls her fist in her lap and smiles weakly, embarrassed by the grace of her movements, the ease with which she can manoeuvre a fork.

"Where do you think it is?" he asks.

"What?"

"My hand."

Her spine stiffens. "Your hand?"

"Yeah. Where do you think it is?" His smile is too big for this conversation, his eyes too bright, so she is careful with her reply.

"I don't know, Finn. Where do *you* think it is?"

"Somewhere kind of beautiful," he says. "Like at the top of a mountain or something."

Mia had spoken with the doctors before the amputation. She knows all about incinerators and ash, vacuum-sealed biohazard bags lumpy with knobs of knucklebone, industrial green dumpsters with weighty tamper-proof lids.

"Remember that bowl at Blackcomb?"

"Yeah . . . I do." They were the first ones up after the avalanche blasting had finished. The three of them trekking the narrow pass, skis over their shoulders, reaching the summit to stand exuberant on the lip of the back bowl, above the timberline, the world spread before them, cast in a fresh, new white. The air cold and thin, the sunstruck snow cupped deep in the valley beneath them, their futures fated, uncut and powder-perfect. Michael had her camera in his backpack. The light was tricky, but still she got some good shots.

"I think it's somewhere like that." Finn radiates an expectant high-wire energy, a fragile joy that seems somehow wrong on the face of an injured seventeen-year-old boy. He looks so vulnerable in his hospital bed, so torn wide open, yet so glorious. Like one of those religious nuts you can almost believe in, Mia thinks, a soul recently converted.

"Or you know," Finn says, "chilling at the cottage."

Peter and Helen's cottage. The lake a hoop of silvery blue, waves lapping the dock, making a splish-splashy music. The soft bump of the boat tied alongside, a flit of dragonflies, the lonesome call of a loon. Mia closes her eyes and a sigh escapes her, a tidal rise and fall of her chest.

"On the dock," she says, trying out the words. "On one of the recliners."

"*Exactly.*" Finn nods. "Like, just taking a breather."

The recliners are old and weatherworn: once-red cushions faded to pink, wooden frames softened to a seaside grey. And Finn's hand, his beautiful, long-fingered hand, there, on one of the cushions. This is what he is asking of her. To seal the wrist cleanly shut so there are no raw edges. To reimagine the skin not reddish black like it was that night when Michael and Mia were finally allowed in to see him. On the cushion, the skin is lightly tanned, the nails clean from a weekend of swimming. She knows that hand so well, has held it in hers on a thousand trips across a thousand streets and on into a hundred different parks. She has washed it, dried it, pushed back its cuticles to reveal rising moons of white. Wrestled the thumb with her own. Positioned the fingers correctly along the handle of a spoon, the shaft of a pencil, the strings of a guitar, so her son could eat, draw, play music.

His lost hand on the chair. The skin is still boyish but its size and strength are that of a man. It's too small on the long cushion, there is not enough of it, of him, but otherwise the picture feels okay—the first thing in days that has.

Mia reaches past the uneaten food and lifts Finn's other hand from the sheet.

"You okay?" she asks. "Not hitting the morphine a little too hard?"

"I'm good, Mom."

"Really?" A flutter in her chest. His answer feels impossible.

"Yeah," he says. "I'm fine."

She rests her head lightly on his good hand, his only hand—suddenly exhausted, she's barely slept in days—and lets him hold her up for a while.

TOO IMPATIENT TO wait for the elevators, which are always packed and slow, Michael undoes his coat and finds the nearest stairwell. He climbs at a steady pace, one that complements the logic of his thoughts and the slap of his boots on the stairs. Today, he has to cool it. Stop getting mad. His footsteps echo off the concrete walls. He lightens his step, bends his knees, works his ankles so the echo softens.

Outside Finn's room, he pauses. Through the small window in the door, its glass cross-hatched by wire, he can see Mia pulled up close to Finn's bed. The dopey smile doesn't seem to faze her. They are talking easily, but seriously, something Michael can't seem to manage with anyone at the moment. She lifts Finn's hand from the bed and leans her forehead to it. Another thing Michael can't manage. He can't remember even touching his son since the night in the Kellys' backyard.

He can almost feel the weight of Mia's head on Finn's arm. Their elbows press into the mattress as if into his own chest. They prop each other up, a shelter of flesh and bone. Staring through the small square of wire-strung glass, Michael swallows down the saliva that's collected in his throat, swallows down his fear and his frustration and the sense that he's missing out on something so big it's beyond him.

"Are you going in?"

Michael jumps. Cathy, the nurse with the ring, is standing in the hallway behind him, unsmiling, avoiding eye contact, a pleated paper cup of pills in her hand.

"No," he says, flustered at having been caught at the window like some pervy peeping Tom. "Not yet."

"Can you let me by, then?"

MAYBE IT'S THE night noise of the hospital or the swing of the door that wakes me up. Or maybe I just feel her watching me. All the lights are off, the window black, but it doesn't matter. I can see her perfectly. Standing by the bed. We stare at each other for what feels like a really long time. I can't even begin to explain the catastrofuck I am inside. She paralyzes me by taking off her jacket. Her green polyester Metro shirt. Her jeans. Nothing on underneath. Legs like columns of summer tan, a neat strip of pubic hair.

She pulls back the covers and slides in beside me. Presses her hand to the middle of my chest. I'm pretty sure she can feel my heart ricocheting off my ribs.

Relax, she says, I'm almost a nurse. Then Sorry, she whispers, resting her forehead against my shoulder. I'm so, so sorry. We stay like this, her hand on my chest, her head on my shoulder and me unable to speak, until really slowly she climbs on top of me, her legs straddling my hips. This is what we do, I tell myself. This is what we always do. But I can feel her being careful of my injured parts.

When she kisses me I don't stop her. Even with the rotting stench and the oozing bandages, her tongue moving in and out of my mouth, a soft collision of teeth, kisses like slippery fingers, long and wet they undo me, until finally, finally, I put my hand on her back, low down, in the hollow.

Touching her makes me shake.

When she slides my dick inside her, I don't move at all, except for the shaking, shaking away flesh-and-bone defences, shivering me down to rawness, to truth, to her on top of me saying, shh, shh, don't cry, Finn, don't cry, and I don't, can't, say anything, can't tell her shut up, to stop, to leave me alone, to leave him, to come every night, to never leave me.

I hold the arm motionless on the mattress, pretend-forgotten, exiled from all action. Finally I just close my eyes. Make myself over as one perfect hand on the small of Jess's back, a dick moving inside her and then the shaking stops, and she is all there, she is all mine, and she's the one shaking, shaking and shimmering over me like some crazy-gorgeous dream of before.

AFTERWARDS I TELL HER. That night? In Eli's backyard? It felt like it does when I'm with you. She turns her head away when I say it, so I don't say anything about love or sacrifice.

The 3rd

The papers Stanley left on the kitchen table are now stacked on Mia's desk, a whitewashed antique table, drawerless, impractical, but pretty. Her office is the same: a converted second-floor sun porch with drafty wraparound windows. Six months a year Mia has to wear fingerless gloves to even work out there. Since renting the studio she uses the office infrequently, to pay bills, to do their income taxes each spring. Today, the snow-covered branches of the old maple brush up against the windows, transforming the room into a glittering winter tree fort, a contender for one of the beautiful places a boy might leave a hand.

She has come to the office with the intent of emailing David, the lawyer she should have called Monday if she'd been in any state to follow through on Stanley's advice. Instead, she gives the stack of papers a push. They spill sluggishly across the desk: with a few adjustments it could be the cover shot for an article on the risks associated with equity partnerships, the myriad ways one man can rip another man off.

She watches two squirrels spiral around the trunk of the maple like frenzied wind-up toys. Male or female, young or old, in a game of chase or in a frantic mating ritual, Mia doesn't know. The squirrels bounce into the tree's snowy branches, disappear in a puff of white. Only one emerges. Body stretched and claws extended, it leaps three feet of sky onto an electrical wire and scurries away down the street—a scoundrel, a survivor, a high-wire escape artist.

Mia stands up quickly; she can no longer bear the cold.

In the hallway, she absently opens the linen closet and is overcome by the stacks of sheets and towels. In Finn's room, she folds a crumpled pair of jeans into a neat denim packet and sets them on the bed. Picks a sock from the floor, and then, without really thinking, makes a fist and stretches it onto her hand. Her knuckles bump across the toe. Three black bars of an Adidas logo stripe her palm. Although she's alone in the house, she kicks closed the bedroom door.

She shakes out the jeans, then refolds them. Pinches the waist between her breast and her socked forearm. The empty legs dangle down limply. With her good hand, she draws the waist across itself, then brings the legs up in a loopy fold and tosses the pants back onto the bed. She wouldn't get hired at Abercrombie, but it's not too bad a job.

In Finn's bathroom, Mia opens the top drawer of the vanity: toothbrushes, toothpaste, a container of dental floss—impossible—a nail clipper—also impossible—and a comb. She takes a toothbrush and balances it on the lip of the sink. Unscrews the toothpaste cap with her teeth. Spits it onto the counter. When she tries to squeeze a minty blue slug onto the bristles, the toothbrush tips into the sink.

Hard. She yanks off the sock. Everything's going to be hard.

MICHAEL DRIVES BLINDLY through the city trying to calm himself down. Another night at the hospital, another night of bandage changes and dopey smiles, another night of trying to talk to his out-of-it son. Michael asking questions, Finn barely giving answers, more an interrogation than a conversation. On autopilot, Michael startles the Jeep to a stop at a red light without a clear recollection of how he'd arrived at that particular intersection—farther from, not closer to, home. He ends up in the downtown core, where half the buildings he passes are ones he brought into the Conrad Group. The office tower at 300 Slater with its leaky tar and gravel roof. The beer store on Hunter that continually got tagged with graffiti. The apartment at 101 Somerset, where tenants on the fourth floor rented two adjoining apartments then knocked through the wall and started a grow-op. When he'd opened the door for the police, the walls had been running with water, and they'd been nearly knocked flat by the smell of the weed, which he'd joked about harvesting for himself and Peter.

Heading east on Somerset, Michael passes under the ornate Oriental arch and, easing off the gas, glides the Jeep slowly past the Mekong. With its darkened windows, muted decor and the old hand-painted sign replaced by a trendy black awning, it's a little classier than the rest of the joints in Chinatown. He and Peter did a lot of business over the Mekong's spring rolls and pot stickers and too too many Tsingtaos. Michael thought getting sloshed on Friday afternoons, flirting with their waitress, letting things slide sideways for a while was one of the perks of being your own boss. *Jesus.* What an asshole.

He U-turns away from the Conrad offices where he'd

inadvertently been headed. His front bumper crunches into a snow-bank, he throws the Jeep into reverse and fishtails back into his lane. He doesn't even want to think about that office tonight. What a sucker he's been. A sap. There were two messages from Peter on his cell this morning, asking what, if anything, he and Helen could do to help out. He'd sounded nervous in both of them, probably wondering why a week on—has it been a week? It feels like ten—his old friend hasn't called him back.

Michael swings into a residential neighbourhood, but there the snow-narrowed streets and the red brick houses remind him of his home and his street and how he'd jogged so slowly along it last Friday night while his son lay freezing to death in the Kellys' backyard.

He arrived at the hospital with a blood alcohol level of .18. They'd found THC as well—so much for Mia's claim that Finn didn't do drugs. My god, what had he been thinking? And where was Eli? Or Frankie? Or any of his other friends? Had no one, *no one*, been watching out for him? They're all so connected, with their texts and their tweets and their stories, did everyone just take the fucking night off?

Behind the wheel, Michael slips into a complete reboot of the hours Finn was missing. He's done it a hundred times, sitting in the orange vinyl hospital chair by the window, splicing minutes and diverting time. The doctors estimated the duration of Finn's exposure at approximately two hours. Michael can make them never happen. Stanley doesn't come over and fuck up their life. He and Mia don't argue. He does not fall asleep. Mia waits up for Finn as usual, and they start the search an hour earlier. Flesh does not freeze solid in sixty minutes. Hands do not die.

So one hour. If he'd turned right at the end of the street rather than left, skipped the bagel shop and headed straight to the Kelly house, that would have saved another fifteen, twenty minutes. If the front door had been locked and he'd been forced around back, if he hadn't taken so goddamn long looking around the house, if he hadn't stumbled over Jess, if, if, if.

Michael shudders behind the wheel. He is both a fool and a failure. His business with Peter is finished. Finn's hand is never coming back.

MIA IS JUST out of the tub when Michael walks into the bathroom. It isn't even nine o'clock. When she asks why he's back so early, he tells her curtly that Finn had fallen asleep so he came home for some rest. Since Finn's been in hospital, neither of them has slept more than a couple of consecutive hours, and most of those have been in the flattened visitor's chair. They're both exhausted, although, at the moment, Michael seems edgy, his energy dark, leaning back against the counter, gripping its marble lip.

Mia doesn't even try to engage him in conversation. She lifts one foot onto the tub and begins rubbing down her thighs. She takes her time, alert to the heaviness of his stare, then the sudden shift as he pushes himself away from the vanity. Still, the last thing she's expecting is for him to yank away her towel, shove her against the wall and force his knee up between her legs.

"Michael," she warns.

He drops the towel to the floor and leans heavily against her, so she is pressed up against the wall. She doesn't struggle. Sex between them is rarely gentle, but Michael has never hurt her.

"You do what I want," he says, and her heart jumps.

When he pins her arms, she twists from his grip and slaps him.

They end up on the floor, Mia scrambling backwards, crab-crawling along the tile, trying to get away, playing at trying to get away, before Michael grabs her ankle and yanks her into place beneath him. Expended, she falls still and waits for him to push into her, she is expecting it, bracing for it, wanting it, the fierce thrust, the stabbing penetration, but for a long few seconds, he lies motionless on top of her, making her feel the full weight of his body, the threat of his cock hard against her leg.

The 4th

The nurse unwinds the bandages.

And the surgeon, the axe-man, leans in and takes a look. He flips my arm around a bit, flexes my elbow, pokes at what's left of my skin. Smiles. So I figure he likes what he sees.

I glance down. I do not like what I see. What I see is a fucking shock.

Healing well, the doctor says. He rattles the chart from the bottom of the bed. Starts scratching away with a pen. Incision is closing up nicely. The flaps—both palmar and dorsal—and thus the skin coverage wasn't what we wanted, it's not a clean closure to be sure, but we saved the wrist and that was our goal. We were also able to attach the wrist flexors and extensors to the remaining carpal bones, which will enhance your motor strength. By preserving the full forearm length, you'll have a nice long lever arm to lift the terminal device, which is excellent. If we have to, we can do a graft in the future, but from what I've seen today, I don't think that will be necessary. Which is again excellent.

He bangs the chart back into the cage at the end of the bed.

You're young. He smiles, a mouthful of yellow country teeth. And the young heal quickly.

His gloves come off with a rubbery snap. Jocelyn, re-dress the residual limb and we'll give the prosthesis a go.

The nurse hustles over, clattering a cart behind her. All the usual gear on top—bottle of sterilized water, gauze, silver antibacterial stuff they cut with scissors and press onto my oozing spots, tweezers they use to torture off my dying skin.

While the nurse does her thing, the doctor squats down beside the cart and starts laying the stuff from the lower shelf on the bed.

A lace-up plastic sleeve. About the length of a forearm. A cable contraption bondage thing, black, some sort of Velcro harness. A two-pronged hook . . . like something you'd dig in the garden with. Or wear on Halloween.

The doctor shows me how the harness connects to the cable, how the cable attaches to the hook, how the hook attaches to the plastic sleeve. He seems excited as he slips two rubber bands around the metal claws and talks lateral pinch and prehensile tension. He pulls the cable. The claws open around a disposable cup on the bedside table. He releases the cable. The rubber bands snap the claws closed. The cup collapses with a plasticky crunch.

Ah, well, he says, you get the idea.

I try to breathe as the nurse pulls a cotton stocking cap over the blunt, bandaged end of my arm. As the doctor laces the sleeve onto my forearm.

How does that feel? he asks. Is that good?

He finally stops and takes a look at me.

This is a temporary terminal device, he says. It's not cosmetic. It's simply to get you used to . . . Studies show the earlier the prosthesis is introduced, the less psychological distress is observed. The earlier the better. Normally we would have fit you with a temporary socket in the operating room immediately following the amputation, but given the extent of the surrounding tissue damage . . . Well, we've already talked about that.

He picks up the hook and hisses at the nurse. Parents?

Father was here briefly this morning, she whispers. His mother's coming this afternoon.

Great. Has the psychologist been in?

I don't know. I'm not sure.

Well find out.

Nurse gone, the doctor fits the hook onto the sleeve. It butts up against my sewn-up flesh, my sawed-off bones. I drop the arm. The claws stab into the mattress.

For now, the doctor says, just operate the cable with your left hand to get the feel of it. Tomorrow we'll attach it to the shoulder harness and let your back muscles do the work.

The doctor holds out the cable. Finally just sets it on the bed.

MIA COULD LIE DOWN on the settee at the front of the studio, but instead she stretches out on the floor. She's still wearing her hat and scarf, but the red-and-black-checked lumberjack coat she's had since she was pregnant with Finn is pillowed under her head. Soft northern light streams through the front windows, and overhead a chandelier glitters—one of a pair she scavenged from a restaurant renovation. Beneath her the hardwood is sun-warm and buttery smooth, polished soft over the years by troops of pink-slippered feet. Before Mia, the studio—a ten-minute walk up Main, close to the canal in the increasingly hipster part of Old Aberdeen—was home to Miss Stacey's School of Dance. If Mia had been able to carry another child to term, if she'd been lucky enough to have a daughter, she might have taken classes here.

Her leather backpack, heavy with Stanley's unwelcome gifts, sits next to her camera on the high wooden table that runs almost half the length of the room. In the laundromat on the ground floor, the washers and dryers are going, and the air in the studio is moist and smells deliciously of soap. She inhales deeply and closes her eyes. The hardwood thrums with a gentle energy, a low-frequency vibration that shivers through the building and her body on the floor.

You do what I want. Good god. Mia wonders what had been going on in Michael's head right then. Forcing his knee between her thighs. Pinning her to the wall. His hands tight around her wrists. She can't pretend she wasn't into it. Slapping him felt good, damn it.

For a sliver of an hour, she didn't have to be calm or sensible or in charge. No one's mother. No one's wife. No real risk of harm. One word and it would have ended. But there was release in the fight, relief in the submission. And something else. Excitement. A flicker of the primal. When Michael lay so still and heavy upon her, Mia had understood that beyond the moment, the man overpowering her was capable of overpowering others. There was strange comfort in that.

The telephone rings into the room. Mia turns her head, watches the light pulse on the black rotary phone. Except for her camera equipment and her iMac, everything in the studio is retro, which is exactly what she'd wanted. Not just a studio but a retreat. Not just a retreat but a retreat into a simpler time.

The ringing stops and the answering machine clicks on. "Mia?" She waits, breath held, upon the floor. She can feel Helen waiting, too.

"Mia? Gosh. Where *are* you? I've tried your cell a dozen times, left messages at the house. I dropped Frankie off at the hospital, oh, I don't know, a half-hour ago. We weren't even sure they'd let us in, but we didn't have any trouble. Anyway, Finn looked good. Better than I expected. He seemed happy to see us. A little upset, maybe, I don't know." Helen sounds confused, almost desperate, her voice an octave too high. "Can you please get in touch? I know it's a tough time, but I really want to talk to you. You know Peter and I will do whatever we can to help out. Just let us know what you need. Listen," she says, "I'm going to come by the house. If you're not there I'll leave the casserole on the porch. It's the chicken one with the mushrooms that you like. I also have wine and a baguette. I fig-ure you need a little TLC, but everything should be fine on the porch. Except the grapes. I could use the key in the frog if it's not completely buried. I'll put everything in the fridge. Geez, I wish you'd call me or answer your cell. Did you lose it again? Maybe you're home. Sleeping. I don't know. Anyway, I'm coming by. Okay? If you're not at the house, I'll check the studio. Mia? I love you. Can you please call when you—"

The long beep of the machine finally cuts her off. Mia lies unmoving on the floor until a poorly balanced load in one of the washers downstairs turns the thrum in the floorboards into a quake. As she stands, her body feels brittle and inelastic, like a fruit dried too long in the sun.

Before she empties the papers from her backpack, she checks the door to make sure it's locked. Makes a mental note to remove the key from the belly of the ceramic frog they keep on the windowsill by the back door of the house. Then she erases Helen's message from the answering machine, and before she can falter, calls her lawyer friend David.

His secretary puts her straight through. He's happy to hear from her, and no, no, he's never too busy for her.

She explains what's happened with Peter.

"Bastard," he says. "Not surprised."

She tells him about Finn losing his hand.

"Wow. Poor kid. That's a drag." He says he'll swing by on his way home and pick up the paperwork, read it over tonight, off the clock. He tells her not to worry, he'll take care of everything, and she is suddenly crying on the phone, relieved and overwhelmed and exhausted and sad for them all.

"Heyyyy. Miiiia." Crying wasn't allowed at the bank. "Let me worry about this crap with Peter. I've seen it a thousand times. It's what I do, all right? You just worry about Finn."

She manages to snuffle up an embarrassed thank-you, and the phone is already halfway down when she hears a faint "Mia!" and presses the receiver back to her ear.

"You know"—David's voice is tricky—"I wouldn't have pegged you for a crier."

"Oh, fuck off." She has to laugh.

"Ah, there's the girl I know," he says. "Hang in there. I'll call soon."

AVOIDING THE ELEVATOR, a habit he's picked up at the hospital, Michael jogs three flights of stairs and pushes through the heavy metal fire door. He woke up feeling rested and surprisingly clear-headed. He's going to do this quickly, get in and get out as fast as he can.

Sandy, the red-headed receptionist, looks up from her computer as Michael yanks open the glass door to their suite of offices. Poised and welcoming, her face drops as Michael blows by, and in their cubicles, the property managers fall silent. His admin, Bev, is already standing up—she's seen him, everyone's seen him—but she remains behind her desk as he strides across the room.

Bev's worked for him for fifteen years. She thinks she knows him almost as well as his wife; she's said as much. Their eyes catch long enough for him to know that she feels his gravitas, the hard, reduced scope of him, and that she's staying behind her desk for a reason.

Michael orders her to get him a box and slams his office door. He jerks open the top drawer of his file cabinet and digs out a handful of folders, flips through them quickly, before either stacking them on his desk or dropping them to the floor. Unanswered phones jangle, the entire staff on hold. They look uneasily from Michael's office to Peter's. He knows they know Finn lost his hand in a stupid, drunken accident. They're probably expecting Peter to get in there and talk to him. Probably can't understand why he's not.

Michael saw him. Parked behind his big desk next door. If he had any doubts that Peter sensed something was up, they're gone now.

A rap and Bev steps into the office. She makes room for the box on the desk, then backs away, almost to the door, grasping the handle behind her. Michael strangles his laptop with its power cord, rams it into the box and starts tossing file folders in on top.

"How's Finn?" Bev says, quietly.

"Not good." From the credenza behind the desk, he grabs a framed photograph of himself and Mia taken at last year's Christmas party and stuffs it into the box. Throws in a stapler, a small gold clock—a gift from the staff, some celebration or another. He's forgotten what he's supposed to be looking for, what Mia had said they would need. Documents signed by Peter? It was Friday night, and now it's what, Friday again? In between one and the next, his son managed to lose his goddamn hand.

And last night with Mia. Christ. After a few decades together you do what you do to spice things up, but that was something else altogether. Tense, agitated, he'd watched her drying herself off, the towel slipping back and forth between her legs. Six inches shorter and a good fifty pounds lighter; Michael knows the numbers, understands the perversity of the math. But last night he saw opportunity in the differential and his cock had stiffened. Mia's foot up on the tub, the dark gleam between her thighs, her sex so open to him.

"How can I help?" Bev asks.

"You can't." He scoops some folders from the floor and tosses them into the box. He doesn't know where any of the pertinent paperwork is. Never has. Never will. That was never his job. He plays his tongue along his bottom lip, cut on the inside from Mia slapping him. If he's unsure about the rest of it, he knows she enjoyed that part. One hard slap for fucking things up with Peter, for falling asleep on Finn.

In the end, it had been easy to control her. Easy to pin her arms and force her legs apart and fuck her right there where they'd landed on the bathroom floor. He isn't sure what she'd been thinking, only knows that she'd responded, that she'd been wet when he thrust inside. And afterwards, she hadn't seemed upset, just quiet and slightly shocked, like him.

"I'll get things organized if you want to work out of the house for a while."

"I'm not working out of the house." Michael grabs the box. "Pack up the rest of the files. The shareholder agreement. The incorporation documents. All of it. Have it sent to my place." Mia can figure it out at home.

Bev is still holding tight to the door handle. "Can you please— We're all so wor—"

"Just open it," he says, and she steps aside.

OTHER THAN JESS, Frankie's the first one to come to the hospital, and the last time I saw her she'd been on her knees in front of me. Other than a lot of snow, her hair is probably the last thing I touched with that hand. So even though I'm keeping my arm perfectly still under the sheet, I can tell she's nervous. Fiddling with her phone and kind of rambling about the big melt at Orford, making jokes about global warming wrecking the ski season, LOL.

I'm sorry. I just kind of blurt it out. About what happened at Eli's, I say. In the laundry—

Finn. Seriously. Forget it. *I'm sorry.* And her cheeks go all blotchy and red.

I feel super shitty about—

Finn don't. Just, just . . . don't. I was drunk. You were drunk.

And high.

Yeah, and *high*, she says, and for the first time she sounds sort of mad.

It was . . . it was a completely fucked-up night. Obviously.

Obviously. Don't worry about it, she says. It was stupid. It was nothing.

You sure?

Yes. Can we just not talk about it anymore? It's so awkward. Frankie throws her phone into her giant purse and starts rustling around inside.

Sorry, I say, again. I feel like shit about it.

Her hand goes still in her purse. I left right after, she says. With Tristan and Brooke. I thought you left, too.

Everyone thought I left. I should have left.

I should have made sure you were okay. I should have walked you home.

It wasn't your fault. What happened had nothing to do with you.

I still feel terrible about it. Everyone feels terrible.

It was my fault. It was all me. I was stupid.

She pulls a pack of gum out of her bag, takes a piece, offers me one. I shake my head—don't want to deal with the wrapper one-handed.

Eli asked me to go to a movie with him, she says. On Friday.

Really? You should go.

He wanted to come see you but apparently your dad said he couldn't.

My father kind of goes insane when things mess up.

Yeah, no kidding. She starts lightly tapping the rail. Anyway, I'll probably go. To the movie.

You should definitely go.

You think so?

Yeah. Eli's always been really into you.

Huh. And it wouldn't bug you or anything?

No. Why would it bug me?

Just . . . I don't know . . . nothing.

Then more silence for a while and neither of us looking at each other. Finally I give Frankie a wonky smile. I can actually feel how whacked it is, so stiff and big it doesn't even begin to fit my face. Can I ask you something?

Sure.

It's sort of weird. It's sort of—

What? she says.

And I pull back the sheet. We both stare at the hook, that fucking clunk of inhumanity, tamed by two rubber bands.

Can you take it off? I say.

Her eyes flicker to mine, a flash of alarm. *What?*

Take it off, I say.

Shouldn't you maybe get a nurse—

It's fine. They said if it was bugging me . . . it's fine.

She leans in, her hair hiding her face. Starts loosening the lace.

Like this?

Yes.

I don't want to hurt you.

You won't.

She wiggles the unlaced sleeve off and sets it on the table by the bed. The hooks are facing up, giving the world the metal finger. The cables hang over the edge of the table, turning slowly, first one way and then the other, just barely brushing the floor.

Frankie smooths out the stocking cap, then runs her hand lightly down my forearm. Through the layers of cotton I can feel her fingertips moving toward the end.

It doesn't bother me, she says. I want you to know that. She cups her hand lightly over the rounded end of the bandage. You can still ski and everything, she says. You can still—

I yank my arm away. The doctor said everything's good. The doctor said I'm doing really well.

Yeah . . . you look good. The ping of her cell gives her an out. She frowns, texts, tells me that blah, she's gotta go, she has a chemistry test tomorrow. She loops the straps of her purse over her shoulder and starts buttoning up her coat.

Frankie . . . can you . . . I stare at the thing on the table. Her eyes follow mine.

What?

Take it.

She frowns.

I don't want it in here.

Won't you need it later?

They're going to get me a better one. A lot better one.

Yeah, I was wondering . . . But shouldn't you . . . Won't you get in trouble?

Fuck, Frankie! Just put it in your bag.

MICHAEL PLACES THE BOX on the floor outside Peter's office. For a moment he hangs in the doorway, suspended on the threshold. Peter's planted behind his desk. Michael knows that cautious, calculating smile, can see him looking for an opening, something safe to test the waters.

"I called your cell a thousand times," he says, but he doesn't get up. "There was no answer at home. I left messages. Helen and I both did. We wanted to come to the hospital, but when you didn't call back . . . Christ, Michael, Helen and I are . . . Frankie . . . we're all just sick about what happened to Fi—"

"Don't." Michael spits the word through clenched teeth. "Don't even say his name." Four steps and he's looming over Peter's desk.

"Michael," Peter says, rigid in his soft leather chair, "what's happening here?"

"You tell me." Michael lets his gaze wander the room, lets the unpleasantness settle in and the blood creep from Peter's collar. He takes in the business-achievement awards on the walls, the motivational posters Mia loathes. When she redid their offices, she wanted them gone, but Peter held on to a couple. *Better Actions, Better Outcomes. Brave Now. Dare to Soar.* That one's got an eagle, wings spread of course.

Casually, Michael plucks a picture from the corner of Peter's desk. Mia had set her camera on the picnic table and used a timer so they're all in it. Frankie and Finn elbow-high and pudgy in bright bathing suits, Mia and Helen squinting smiles into the sun, the men pretending to christen the bow of Peter's new bowrider with a bottle of Champagne they'd chosen to drink instead on their maiden voyage around the lake. A family sunset cruise, Diana Krall purring from the built-in speakers, Peter taking it easy behind the wheel. Later, after they'd put Finn and Frankie to bed and the women had a Scrabble board and a bottle of wine between them, Michael and Peter had gone back out. They took turns opening up the engine, the thrill of two hundred horses at play, splitting black water, laughing and whooping, tearing across a lake struck with moonlight, giving the shore shit with the power of their wake.

"You know," Michael says, glancing up from the photo, "you used to look kind of cool, with your hair long like that, but now it's all thin and stringy. You should definitely get it cut. I'm thinking it's unprofessional. I'm thinking it's bad for business."

"Is that what you're thinking?" Peter's face flushes. Even his wide centre part turns pink. "That my hair is bad for—"

"And you should probably stop smoking all that pot. It wouldn't look good if people found out what a stoner you are."

Peter is up out of his chair.

"Down, big boy," Michael says. Peter glances nervously out at the office—he's paranoid about keeping his drug hobby a secret at work—where everyone is suddenly heads-down in their cubicles.

Peter is a couple inches taller than Michael, broad shouldered, but soft beneath his dress shirt. A belly. It's another thing Michael could razz him about—the man is vain. Needy and vain. Wants to be liked, but turns most people off. Michael has never been intimidated by Peter. There is a weakness to him that is more than physical. Michael always thought people sensed the flint of greed around which he is built and kept their distance. Now he thinks it must be all the lies Peter tells that prevent him from ever standing on solid ground, his whole foundation shifting like beach sand in a low wind. Peter has to be ready to adjust, reposition, depending on what bullshit he's told whom. It doesn't make him a comfortable person to be around. Michael doesn't know how he and Mia did it all those years, although the ski chalet and the cottage and all the booze certainly helped. And the business, of course. The hope of making it rich in tandem. And Helen was always a doll. And then Finn and Frankie came along.

Michael shoves the picture at him. "You remember this?"

Peter crosses his arms over his chest and takes a sudden interest in the carpet beneath his feet.

"It was an awesome day, wasn't it?"

"Yes. It was."

"Great friends, right?"

Every wrong Michael's relived over the last four days, every vengeful thought he's had, converges inside him. Even Finn's accident feels like Peter's fault. Michael should grab him by the stringy hair and slam his face into the wall, should have slammed his face into the wall the day Jill told him about the money he stole to buy the boat.

"Stanley talked to me," he says, through gritted teeth.

"Stanley? Stanley doesn't . . . Stanley shouldn't have—"

"Yes, he should have. He should have talked to me three years ago." Michael takes another look at the picture, then grins up at Peter, a hard, sardonic grin. "You're a lucky man to own a boat like that. I wish I had a boat like yours."

Peter slowly spreads his arms, striking a gentle Jesus pose. "We can get you a boat if you want one," he says, carefully.

Michael smashes the picture on the corner of the desk. Smashes it again. With a flick of the wrist, he launches what's left across the desk. Inside the battered frame, their families spin across the rose-wood and drop over the edge.

"I don't want a fucking boat."

MIDNIGHT, MIA AND MICHAEL devour the casserole. They split the bottle of wine. Pérez Cruz, from Argentina. A familiar favourite. An old standby. Like the chicken-and-mushroom casserole. A slice of Gorgonzola from Nicastro's to go with the baguette, and fresh green grapes for dessert. All of it waiting for them when they got home from the hospital. All of it delicious, regardless of its source, or maybe because of it, Mia isn't sure. It's the best meal—the only meal—they've eaten in days. Bellies full, they slowly climb the stairs. Doors locked, tonight they'll sleep like the dead.

The 5th

"You ready for a rookie?" Cathy, the Cabbage Patch kid of a nurse, winks at Finn.

He lays his head back on the pillow and closes his eyes. "Go for it, Mom."

Cathy holds a gauze pad beneath Finn's foot. "You'll want to soak the dressing to make sure it doesn't stick coming off." The bandage is splotched with dried blood and crusted with fluids. As Mia pours sterile water onto the dressing, the nurse prevents the excess from spilling onto the bed.

"Cold?" she asks.

"Uh-huh." Finn's Adam's apple bobs, but his head remains turned toward the window.

The nurse hands Mia a pair of tweezers she's picked from a stain-less steel tray and explains how after Finn is discharged a home-care nurse will come twice a week to check on his progress. "But most of the ongoing wound care will be up to you and your husband," she says.

Me, Mia thinks, it will be up to me. In the latex gloves, her fingers feel clumsy and thick. She tugs at the tape securing the dressing. Sodden, it peels away easily from the top of the foot, but as she unwinds the bandage, the gauze remains caught up near his toes.

"More water." This time Cathy pours, while Mia holds the absorbent pad. Still the bandage sticks. "Sometimes you just have to give a little tug," Cathy says, crinkling up her nose.

Through latex and tweezers, Mia can feel the damaged tissue lifting along with the dressing. She flinches, Finn flinches, and the bandage finally gives way. With it comes a sharp reek that she does her best to ignore.

"That first one's not easy. But you'll get used to it."

Mia drops the sullied bandage, its bits of torn-away flesh, into a small plastic bucket the nurse holds out. Sure she'll get used to it.

"You okay?" she asks Finn, holding tight to her tweezers.

He nods. "How about you?"

"Good." She smiles, and like him, tries not to see the fresh blood seeping from his feet, his pulpy, blackened skin.

"MIA?" CATHY LEANS over the counter at the nurses' station. "Dr. Sullivan asked you to stop by on your way out."

"I was just going to grab a coffee." Sit down. Work the kinks out of her neck. Take a couple deep breaths. Collapse.

"He should be in his office now. It's best if you go straight away," she says. "His schedule is crazy. Here, I'll jot the directions down."

As her hand moves across the paper, her diamond throws off light, a small solitaire that reminds Mia of the one Michael gave her, which she no longer wears because the band irritates her skin.

"Beautiful ring," she says, and the girl extends her hand, pudgy and soft, offering a better look. "When's the big day?"

"July twenty-third."

"Well, good luck."

Cathy slides the small square of paper across the counter. "By the way, you did great in there," she says. "And Finn's a great kid. All the nurses think so. Such a cutie. I'd say hot if you weren't his mother."

"Ha. Thanks. It's been a tough week for everyone." Mia studies the directions. She'd expected loopy writing, little circles over the *i*'s, but instead Cathy has drawn a neat schematic of the hospital basement, the elevator shafts, the numbered corridors, the operating theatres, an *X* marking Dr. Sullivan's office, like treasure on a map.

"Listen," Mia says, "I'm a photographer. I'd be happy to shoot your wedding next summer."

"Really?"

"For free, of course. For all you've done for Finn." She roots through her purse for a business card. "I haven't done a wedding in a while, but you can check my website—it's out of date, but you'll see my work."

"Well, thanks," Cathy says, blushing. "That would be great. I mean, I'll have to talk to Toma about it, we'll look at your site, but, well, money's tight."

Mia slides her card across the desk, a small peace offering to the girl who, with sharp instruments, is caring for her son.

DR. SULLIVAN PEERS over the dark frame of his glasses when Mia knocks. Although his door is open, he seems annoyed by the intrusion, his gaze sharp. It takes a moment for him to place her. "Ah, Mrs. . . . . Mrs. . . . ." he says. "The BE amputee's mother."

Mia's jaw drops.

"Sorry," he says curtly. "Below-the-elbow. I'm good with cases, lousy with names." He flips his wrist, checks his watch, then points to the empty chair on the other side of the desk. "We're having some issues with your son. I'll be with you in a minute," he says, and returns to the file in front of him.

"Finn," Mia says, still standing in the doorway. "His name is Finn Slate. Finley, actually. We were going to call him Blank but decided against it at the last minute."

The doctor gazes up over his glasses. "Funny." He nods at the guest chair. "Now, please take a seat."

His office is modest for a surgeon's. Windowless, neat. A huddle of framed diplomas on one wall, leather-bound reference books on the shelves behind his large metal desk. In the corner, a skeleton stands ramrod straight, its bones knitted together by fine wire. Two small coffee cups and a human skull top a high file cabinet.

"I've always prided myself on my handwriting," Dr. Sullivan says, still addressing the page. "Not like the chicken scratch of most of my colleagues. Too busy, too important to take the time to cross their *t*'s and dot their *i*'s. Nonsense really. All pretense."

She would photograph him from below. An unflattering angle. Highlight the softening jawline, the loose waddle of skin pouched between the protruding cords of his neck. Exaggerate his nose, the flare of his nostrils, ask him to smile, show off his snaggle of old teeth. With the money he makes, it is hard to imagine why he hasn't had them fixed. A different generation. A different era. It's hard to picture him young and loose. He was never young and loose. He was never a boy.

Dr. Sullivan gathers the papers on the desk and closes the file. He immediately begins thumbing through a stack of identical manila folders, sneaks one out, an orange plastic SL tab clipped to its edge. "Right hand," he mutters, scanning the first page, "preservation of full forearm. Successful reattachment of flexors and extensors to carpal bones, right, right, right, excellent, excellent." He glances up. "Is he a leftie?"

"He is now," Mia says, and his eyes settle on her, unblinking, humourless. "So his handwriting won't be so hot," she says, "like most of your colleagues."

The furrows between his brows deepen. If he threw in a seed and some soil, he'd have a flower between his eyes by spring. "It will come. If he works at it." He trails a long finger down the page, then snaps the file closed. "For the most part, we've found your son to be a rather stoic patient. And generally speaking"—he smiles cautiously—"we're very pleased with his progress. He's a strong young man—"

"He was a hockey player. House league A. Right wing."

"Yes, I—"

"And a skier. Downhill. He used to race but it got to be too much with the hockey. Summers, he longboards. Mostly around town, but also out at the Hills. Have you ever seen the kids out there?"

"I've hiked in the provincial park many times, but no, I've never come across any skateboarders." He glances again at his watch. "Now Mrs. Slate, we introduced a prosthe—"

"I've dropped him off a few times. And I tried photographing them, but ended up in the forest, taking pictures of trees. They go so fast down those hills. It's crazy. I thought he was going to get hurt, you know? I thought he was going to kill himself." Mia is suddenly close to tears.

"Mrs. Slate." He pushes back from the desk and removes his glasses—dark, square, nerdy, hot now with the hipsters, although the doctor's are probably original vintage. "Did you hear about the bonfire last night, out on River Road?" Beneath his white lab coat, a brown sweater vest, woven leather buttons up the front. The finely checked shirt underneath is done up to the neck. "Apparently it was a real winging until some bright light took it upon himself to throw a can of gasoline into the fire, which exploded with quite a pop. Seriously injuring four boys. I spent my night in surgery with them. One after another after another. I am one of the city's only trauma surgeons. Please believe me when I say I understand that an injury to a child is hard on a parent."

"And the child."

"Obviously, Mrs. Slate. Whatever we feel, they feel a thousand-fold. And these boys, because most of them are boys, most of them privileged, this is Old Aberdeen after all"—he places his hand on the stack of files—"come in night after night with blood toxicology that would make you cringe, and I do my best to patch them up. I can't say I understand it, them, but I do my best." He sets his glasses on top of the stack of files, so for a second Mia has the sensation there are two people watching her instead of one. "When we were kids, I don't recall my friends and I being quite so hell-bent on killing ourselves. We had the war for that purpose."

"The war?"

"Vietnam. I'm American. Crossed the Detroit-Windsor border in '68. Had just received a full scholarship to Harvard Medical when I got my notice. Three months later I started at McGill." He stretches up out of his chair. He's a tall, long-legged man. Two long strides and he's at the filing cabinet.

"Can I offer you a coffee?" He opens the top drawer to reveal a small espresso machine. "Technically not allowed, but the stuff in the cafeteria is intolerable. My partner got me this little beauty last Christmas. A Nespresso. From France, I believe. The capsules cost a bundle and they're hardly environmentally friendly, but the coffee!" He pops a small purple capsule into the machine. "Long or short?" he asks as he reaches past the skull and picks up a cup. "I take it straight so I have neither cream nor sugar."

"Long," Mia says. The machine begins to wheeze and rumble. A slip of vapour undulates from the drawer like a charmed snake, along with a heady aroma. "I take it black as well."

"Perfect," he says, wiping down the second cup, carefully, with precision, a thorough disinfection rather than a quick swipe. "I have no regrets," he says, "about the war. I hurt no one. I compromised nothing in myself." He glances over. Without his glasses, she can better see the soft brown of his eyes. "And I enjoy Canada. Country's a little wilder and a lot colder, but I've always felt the people, the politics and the healthcare system are more my style. I'd make significantly more money in the U.S., of course, but, well, as they say, money isn't everything."

She would shoot him in profile. Just a slight pouchiness to the neck. He has a fine nose. Good posture. "Have you been back?" she asks. "To the States? I mean, can you?"

"Carter granted us full amnesty in '77, his second day on the job. I've returned several times to visit family and whatnot, but, well, Canada's home. We've got a cottage on Big Yirkie. You know it?"

"Our friends"—she clears her throat—"have a place on the lake. The Conrads?"

"Don't know them, but I've seen the name on a mailbox. They're on the main road in?"

"Yes." The doctor closes the drawer and picks both cups from the top of the cabinet.

"We plan to retire up there. Sooner rather than later, although the hunt for my replacement has thus far been excruciatingly slow." Dr. Sullivan hands her a coffee, then gently elbows the door closed behind her. "Can't have anyone picking up the scent," he says. "Could start a stampede." Back in his chair, he raises his cup to her. "A little civility in the midst of the madness."

She stares into the cup, at the mocha-coloured crema within the round of white bone china that warms her hands. She feels the energy leaving her body, dripping from her wrists like blood. Her arms tremble from the weight of the cup. She wonders where Michael is at this moment, why he isn't here.

"Biscuit?" A sleeve of cookies slides across the desk. Arrowroots. Dr. Sullivan leans forward and gives the sleeve a rattle. The back of his hand is heavily veined, the skin mottled and purplish, but his nails are short and clean, his fingers strong and finely shapen, as if sculpted by a careful god.

Mia works a cookie loose.

"Take two," he says, and one old brown eye winks. "And another for Mr. Slate. He'll probably be tired when he gets home from the quarry."

This elderly man, his bald, beautiful head, his crummy teeth exposed as he chuckles over his lame Flintstones joke, his surgeon's hand stretching across the desk, the sleeve of simple cookies, this is the shot she would take.

MICHAEL PICKS AN eight-by-ten from the high wooden table in Mia's studio. A gorgeous picture of Frankie, and a recent one from the looks of it—the nose ring's made the shot. "I hope you're not going to give them this," he says, tugging at his collar, trying to let in some air. His gloves are stuffed in his pocket, but he hasn't unbuttoned his coat. The studio is always humid and smells of soap, even when the laundromat is closed.

Mia glances up, a black Sharpie in one hand. "Give who what?" They've been at the hospital all night, it's after eleven, but perched on a stool with her winter gear piled on the table beside her, Mia looks more awake and relaxed than she has all week. She's always been happy at the studio, such a change from her bland little box at the bank. Her office was on the executive floor but her windows didn't open. She said the lack of fresh air almost killed her. That, and all the men.

Michael holds up the picture. "This. Don't give it to Peter and Helen."

She frowns. "Well, I might give it to Frankie."

"And she'll give it to them."

"Oh, come on. She has nothing to do with this."

Michael sets the photograph down. The slight blur to Frankie's shoulders suggests movement, but her face is sharp, her delight in perfect focus. Mia must have been telling a joke, or teasing her about some boy. "You know, she was there that night—at Eli's party."

"And?"

"I'm just saying. She was there."

Mia frowns up at him. She's supposed to be making a sign for the door. So far she's drawn a box around the perimeter of an empty page. "I think there's some wine in the back," she says, setting her marker down.

"Christ, I thought you were only going to be a minute."

"I am. But still, I'd like a glass. You want one?"

"No. I want to get going."

At the makeshift coffee station—a stainless steel Ikea unit along the back wall—Mia uncorks a bottle of red and returns with two glasses. She offers one to Michael.

"I told you I don't want it."

Mia nudges his hand with the glass. "Let's be nice to each other, shall we?" Her manner's light, coaxing. She'd also talked him into playing backgammon tonight at the hospital, although Finn had barely seemed to notice how easily Michael won all three games. The small dose of competitive spirit he'd been born with seems to have been vanquished along with his hand.

Mia sets the glass on the table and practically sashays across the room in her fitted, low-slung jeans and her soft grey sweater. Michael had woken up feeling slightly off—no, way off—and has yet to recover. He'd dreamt about finding Finn in the snow. The panic on mental repeat. The terror playing all night long. How to explain what it was like to touch his icy body? To fail to find any sign of life?

He tongues the cut on the inside of his lower lip. The way he's feeling now, he can barely believe he had the energy, or the balls, to play it rough with Mia the other night. He thinks he might be depressed, that this is what depression feels like. Or maybe he's in some sort of low-grade shock.

"I talked to the surgeon today." Mia dims the lights, then curls up on the settee, angled in the corner by the floor-to-ceiling windows at the front of the room. "Dr. Sullivan. Mr. Rogers with a scalpel. He called Finn stoic."

"What Finn is, is a bad decision maker." Michael yanks his gloves from his pocket and tosses them onto the table. They land on the photograph, partially covering Frankie's freeze-frame laughter, which feels suddenly personal, somehow directed at him. "Boys his age, their frontal cortexes aren't fully developed. Which is why they have parents. To protect them from themselves. To keep them from getting hurt."

"We're good parents, Michael."

"I feel like we have to try harder," he says. "That we can't afford to make any more mistakes." In the front window, his reflection appears bulky, misshapen by his navy woollen coat. His eyes look small and dull. Like a man you could rip off, he thinks. A man stupid enough to lose his child, to lose his capable wife.

His hand trembles as he reaches for his wine glass. "Yesterday. I went to the office."

"Oh, yeah?" He can hear some of the air going out of her. "And?"

"Peter was careful." He twirls the stem of the glass slowly in his fingers. The only sound in the room the soft slide of glass over wood.

"Did you get mad?"

"I broke a picture."

"Only one? That's not so bad."

He takes a long swallow of wine, feels its warmth in his belly. "You know I no longer have a job." He sets his glass back down with precision. "That I won't be getting paid. That we'll have very little money."

"We can throw a couple mattresses on the floor up here. Wash up downstairs. Tumble ourselves dry."

"I like the house," he says. "Our bedroom. Finn down the hall."

Mia's head is now dropped onto the arm of the couch, much of her levity gone.

"How is he going to manage?" Despite the wine, his throat is dry, his words come up pinched.

"I bought him some of those one-handed flossers."

"Oh then, he's all set." He feels a choke building in his chest. He sniffs. Bangs the toe of one boot against the heel of the other.

"Michael," Mia says. "Come here."

Sitting on the floor, he unbuttons his coat and leans back against the couch, his head close to Mia's knee. He concentrates on the light reflector across from him, a metallic umbrella blooming atop a skeletal base, like a flimsy satellite. "I can't talk to him like you can," he says. "I've never been able to talk to him like you."

"Finn adores you, Michael. You've always been good to him." She gives his shoulder a squeeze. "All those hockey practices."

"You went to the games."

"Yeah," she says, "but only to talk to the parents."

The studio is slashed with light and the wet slap of tires churning through slush—a car charging up Main. The silver umbrella flashes; the shadow of the tripod spider-slides across the wall. Once the car passes, the glow from the chandelier feels like darkness, the quiet a vacuum that settles in the cavity beneath Michael's ribs. He has to measure his breathing to get the next words out. "It was close. I thought we lost him."

"I know." Mia's fingers brush his collarbone, a soft, steady rhythm. "But we didn't."

He lets his head drop back onto her knee. "Once my father

jumped into freezing water to save me," he says. "He'd taken me fishing at the Ooze—this river an hour or so out of Montreal. It was late fall, probably off-season, but he never paid attention to that. I fell in. He was wearing these hip waders. When he jumped in they filled up and he was pinned to the bottom. He managed to get hold of me and put me on his shoulders so my head was above water. Somehow walked me back to the dock. I don't know how long he was under, trying to get his waders off. It felt like a long time. When he finally got out, he lay on the dock, coughing and spitting up water. I was scared to death. Seeing him like that. Thinking he was going to kill me. Afterwards, he yelled at me, but it was pretty mild. I got in more shit for fooling around at the table."

"I always liked your dad," Mia says. "He was a gruff man, but he was always sweet to me."

The things his father hit him with over the years: his hand, his belt, the shaft of a hockey stick once, when he ran in front of a car. It was a different time. Michael might have inherited his father's temper, but he's never laid a hand on Finn.

"I wish I'd known your mom."

"I barely remember her. I only really remember Janice." His father married her six months after his mother died of cancer. A year or so after the aborted fishing trip. They had another four kids together but they were so much younger than Michael. Janice was good to him, but he'd always felt like an outsider, as though there wasn't a lot of room in the house for him. Last time he saw any of them was years ago now, at his father's funeral. "My dad stripped me naked in the truck. Cranked up the heat and threw an old blanket over me. We stopped at this little bait and tackle shop on the way home and he bought me a hot chocolate." He remembers how his dad's hand shook when he handed him the styrofoam cup.

"How old were you?"

"Maybe five or six."

"Ah," Mia says. "So small."

He was. All the way back to Beaconsfield, he'd concentrated on not spilling his drink and keeping the blanket from slipping off and holding back his tears, which would have angered his old man.

Michael reaches up and presses Mia's hand to his shoulder. "Hey," he says, then clears his throat. "You did a good job on Finn's bandages today."

In the window, he watches her roll her neck first one way, then the other. "Thanks." She pulls her hand from beneath his. "It was hard."

The 6th

Can I tell you something, I say to my mom, surprised that my voice sounds completely normal.

Of course. And she shifts my jacket to her other hand.

She's just signed me out. Thanked all the doctors, goodbyed all the nurses. She's got my backpack and my jacket and a fistful of amputee literature and she's holding the door to my room. Technically I'm ready to go. I've got the jeans on that she brought me, the shirt, my Vans. I got dressed in the bathroom. It wasn't that bad, but you know. The buttons on the shirt. The laces on the shoes.

I have to tell you something.

Okay, she says, but I just keep holding on to the rail, and my gut is quivering, like if you put your hand on my stomach you could actually feel it quivering. The bandages are fresh, clean and white, but there's that smell, the smell that's coming from me.

My mom wanders back to the bed, looking worried. Do you want to sit for a minute?

No. It comes out loud.

She sets my backpack down and puts her hand on my back and says, like so calmly, You know you can tell me anything, right? Anything at all. And she starts doing this really light figure-eight thing on my back that she's done ever since I was a kid and I try to relax and concentrate on her hand on my back and I try to think about breathing and her breathing beside me—my non-hand on the rail next to my good hand—we just breathe together for a while.

I want to tell her things. I want to tell her what really happened to me in the backyard. I want to tell her about Jess. That she only came to the hospital that one time. That I could never touch her with some fucking hook strapped to my arm. That I'll never touch her with some reeking, mutilated stump. I want to tell my mom about love and fearlessness and how it felt when I was lying in the snow that night and how it feels to be walking out of here right now.

I'm not the same as I was, I say. I'm different now. My knuckles white on the rail. Her hand warm on my back. But it's good, you know? I'm good. Like I understand things I didn't understand before.

Like what things?

Like big things. Like what's important. Like what really matters. I glance at her. She's frowning, her mouth all tight. And I need for you not to worry about me.

Okay.

Promise me.

What?

Promise me you won't worry.

Okay.

Say it.

Jesus, all right. I promise not to worry.

I need you to let me figure things out by myself.

Okay, Finn.

After that, she doesn't say anything for what feels like a really long time, and I just keep holding on to the bed and then she leans in, so her face is close to mine—look at me—and our eyes are hooked in deep in that place where it's impossible to lie and she says, I love you. I love you so much. And I know this is hard but you're going to be fine. And then she picks up my backpack. The dark green Herschel one I use for school. Come on, she says. Let's get out of here.

It's a minute before my hand comes up off of the rail. I take a few steps and then I stop and glance down and my mom sees this, she sees this and she bends down and does up my shoes—loop, swoop, pull, loop, swoop, pull like she taught me when I was still a little two-handed kid. Then she opens the door and I walk out into what is now my life.

MY LIFE. I'm not ten steps out of the room when it pulls back and smacks me in the head. My mom's beside me when Cathy hustles out from behind the nurses' station with a Ziploc bag in her hand.

You sure didn't have much with you when you were admitted. She gives the bag a bit of a swing. Sandwich-sized, my name in Sharpie ink on the side. Nearly empty except for something looped and folded at the bottom. A slim black velvet snake.

I grab the bag and jam it into my pocket, rush for the elevator, forget the way my toes are screaming in my shoes, forget the way my mom is gawking.

I jab the button on the wall. My mom hustles over, my backpack hanging off her arm. She hikes it up onto her shoulder. She's carrying everything, the backpack, the amputee literature, the neon-blue jacket that probably saved my life—my dad told me the story.

I grab the jacket.

Thanks, my mom says, trying to make eye contact. I watch the numbers light up over the doors. I'm crushing the feathers in the jacket, squeezing out all the air.

Are you—?

Don't.

What was—?

Nothing.

My mother sighs. The elevator bings. We step inside. Even with all my gear, my mom manages to wave at the nurse.

I'll be in touch, Cathy calls.

July twenty-third. I have it on my calendar, my mom says before the doors slide closed.

My stomach floats as the elevator drops and a deep electric funny-bone pain shoots through my hand and on into my fingers, but I don't even look down. I ignore the burn in my nowhere hand. And the velvet ribbon riding so close to my hip.

June

The 13th

Since the weather's warmed up, tonight like most nights, Michael grabs the baseball bat from the front hall closet—abnormally tidy thanks to Mia's recent decluttering binge. He grips the neck lightly as he strolls up Springfield Avenue, in shorts and a T-shirt. Mid June and every tree's in leaf, every garden a waft of pollen and perfume. Ahead, one of the neighbours wrestles a sprinkler into place on his lawn. Last year Michael would have stopped to talk drainage, potholes, speculated on the havoc being wreaked on the sewer pipes by the roots of Randolph's giant tree. Tonight he nods curtly—he has no interest in answering questions about Finn or his new stay-at-home-dad routine—and marches past, the swing of the bat matching the casual back and forth of his arm.

At the river, spring's bursting, blossoming, blooming sex scent is undercut by a swampy reek. Belly-bloated, eyeless fish, a gelatinous muck of decaying plants and sticks and candy wrappers, one broken-jawed beaver—winter's slaughtered stew rots along the bank, marking the high tide of the spring runoff. A pair of black swans, released every year in late spring and recaptured each fall, paddles into a scruff of cattails, skittering up a cloud of gnats. Michael turns away from the stench and the bugs, the phony birds paid for with his precious tax dollars, the glimpse of strip mall on the far side of the water, and shifts the bat to his other hand.

Just across River Road, the Kellys' garage doors are open, the ass end of their luxury fleet gleamingly on display. The family might not be great at lawn care—grass so long it's falling over—or looking after other people's kids, but they sure know how to do cars. The fins on the butter-yellow Caddy shine like sci-fi rockets, and in that same box of light, the Porsche also looks very well tended.

Michael leaves the Kellys' and crosses a foursquare of soccer pitches, one off limits on account of a snapping turtle who laid her eggs between its goalposts, where the grass has been worn down to sandy soil. A sturdy circle of chicken wire surrounds the nest, and a posted note warns people to stay back.

He skirts the field, sticking close to the water. Three old Asian men fishing off the rocky bank grin and bob their heads as Michael passes. What they catch, he has no idea. He wouldn't eat anything out of that water. Sewer runoff. People pollution. Dead beavers.

One of the old men, in rubber boots and a white bucket hat, nods at his bat. "Baseball!" he calls out happily.

"Fishing!" Michael calls back and keeps right on moving.

Ahead, past the playing fields, a high concrete overpass ferries six lanes of traffic across the river. The overpass divides Old Aberdeen into east side and west. The western slice of the island is smaller, but more prestigious. Big properties. Big houses. Peter lives on a wooded acreage that backs onto the water. Although it's a detour, some nights Michael passes by before looping home—just to check the place out. Thus far he's resisted the cliché of taking his bat to the Conrad mailbox at the end of the laneway, although he has taken a leak on its post.

Beneath the overpass the air is cool, the rush of traffic muted, and most of the concrete, the supports, the abutments, the wing walls, is bright with paint. The city has declared the bridge a graffiti-friendly zone, and as long as the "art" doesn't creep onto the upper level, the city leaves the kids and their spray cans alone. The walls are covered with tags—bulging, blocky, head-high letters geometrically puzzled together and bordered in black. These stylized signatures quickly come and go, but the epic intergalactic battle scene between bubble-helmeted warrior apes that dominates the upper half of the abutment has been there since last fall, as has the metallic grenade, big as a watermelon that threatens the bridge's main support column.

Tonight, there are only a couple of kids smoking weed down by the water, getting inspired or getting lazy. They see Michael see them and do nothing to hide the spliff.

"Yo," says one kid in a wife-beater and jean shorts so long and baggy he looks like he's wearing a skirt. Behind him, the water broils; the river, narrowed and shallow, runs fast under the bridge. In August, when the water's low, rocks puncture its surface, rounded down over thousands of years, but fixed, unmoved by the hard drag of the current.

Michael gives the boys a stiff wave, clutching tight to his bat. "Just checking out the work," he says, nodding appreciatively at the surrounding blur of colour. He wonders what they'd say if they knew that his company, his former company—which he doesn't miss, the only thing he misses is the paycheque—made a third of their annual revenues cleaning graffiti off banks and bus stops and apartment blocks and park benches and boxcars and the underside of bridges.

The boy throws wide his arms. "Everyone's welcome at the gallery, man," he says, and the other boy snickers.

"Wanna puff?" The boy leans in to take a toke, an ember sparking in the dusk.

Michael has always loved the smell of pot, and it reaches him now, the sweet, musky scent. For a second he thinks about strolling over, putting the joint to his lips, pulling the smoke in deep, holding it, holding it, until his lungs burn and his brain loosens and his body starts to relax. Over the years he's smoked on and off, with Peter, Peter's stash, but it's always been a casual thing, never a claws-into-him habit.

"No . . . yeah, thanks. I'm just going to hit a few balls." Michael waggles his bat and taps the bulge in the side pocket of his cargo shorts, knocking a ball lightly against his knee. "Okay, then. Cheers," he says. "Cheerio." A word he's never used in his life.

Both boys bend at the waist and laugh.

Beyond the overpass, Michael veers away from the water. Through a field of wheaty grasses, he follows a narrow footpath to the dark dirt of a baseball diamond. Except for the path, there's no obvious access to the diamond, no parking lot, no paved pedestrian entry. The diamond is rarely tended by the city and is too remote and in too rough a shape to be used for any kind of league play. The outfield has been recently cut, but the lights are aslant, the padlocked equipment shed at a kinky angle, the chain-link backstop pouchy and sagging at the top.

Michael stands in the dirt of home plate, and with the bat resting on his shoulder, works a ball from his pocket. Small as an orange in his hand, the ball's leather is yellowed and its stitching frayed. He tosses it into the air, sights it, swings. A solid crack and the ball flies straight over second base before landing well out in centre field. Michael pulls another ball, this one a softball, from his other pocket. He catches it low, pops it up, and its whiteness disappears into the darkening sky. Michael follows its vanished arc, imagines the ball's split-second hang at the apogee, its inevitable fall back to earth.

Satisfyingly, it lands right where he expects it, ten feet beyond third base, just inside the foul line. Michael doesn't mind hunting down the balls. It gets him moving. Extends his time out of the house. If he were home, he might be watching Finn struggle to use a spoon or tie his shoes. If he were home, he might be channel surfing, a bleakness settling in, unable to concentrate, getting exhausted from working the remote. Or he might have fallen asleep in front of the TV and be having the nightmare again, wake up terrorized, his fingers still searching for a pulse on his dead cold son. Being out is definitely better. And retrieving balls from cool grass sure beats sitting in some slick lawyer's office being told just how royally your best buddy has screwed you over while the guy doing all the talking ogles your beautiful wife. Or watching said beautiful wife "tidying up the house"—stuffing clothes and sheets and pots and dishes and practically every other thing they've bought and paid for over the last twenty years into bulging green garbage bags that she drops off on her daily run to Value Village. Michael takes little comfort in the fact that she hasn't yet ransacked her shoe collection or dared touch his side of the closet. He doesn't know what she's doing. Making a point? Embracing minimalism? Shedding the skin of their old life?

In the kitchen that morning, she'd turned her head when he tried to kiss her. When they do have sex, which has become a rarity over the last few months, it is more a battering apart than a coming together. Michael fucking her hard from behind and finishing quickly. It's the only way she'll allow it.

She thinks he should be looking for work. He, however, wants the whole shitshow with Peter straightened out before he starts calling up contacts. He needs a solid story in place, one that casts Peter as the asshole rip-off artist, while leaving no room for anyone to question his dupability, his credentials or his value to their organization. This is something Mia doesn't seem to understand. When he does start looking again, he cannot appear weak.

Michael picks the hardball from the damp grass in the outfield. He likes the fit of the ball in his hand, how securely his fingers grip it. He likes the feel of the old bat too, its weight, the smooth, polished handle. He played a ton of pickup as a kid and early on he'd bought his son a glove. They'd thrown the ball around in the back-yard, but Finn had always been pretty half-hearted about it. He preferred hockey, he preferred skateboarding, soccer, pretty much any sport in which Michael lacked expertise.

He jogs back to home plate and picks up his bat. Hits the balls, retrieves them, again and again, meditation via mindless, repetitive motion, the rush of distant traffic on the overpass, the burble of the river all calming background noise.

He's just set the bat down when a ball whizzes past his head and slams into the backstop with a metallic whomp.

"Yo, Cheerio!"

Michael turns just in time to shoot out his hand as the other ball flies at him. The hardball hammers his palm and fingers, dense cork and cowhide, soft flesh and slim bone.

The boy with the baggy shorts shuffles across the infield, churn-ing up a low cloud of dust.

"I didn't see you," Michael says. He fights off the urge to drop the ball and massage his hand.

"Sorry, man," the kid says. "Fucking dark out here." He grabs Michael's old Louisville Slugger off the backstop and in the next instant is pounding the lock that secures the shed. The padlock holds but the screws mounting the hardware pull away from the rotting door frame. The kid works the hinge loose, takes one step back, flashes Michael a grin, then kicks open the door.

From the depths of his giant front pocket, he fishes out a cell phone and follows its rectangle of light into the freshly vandalized shed. The high clatter of wood, something hits the floor with a thud. The kid yells but Michael can't make out the words. From inside the shed comes a spring-loaded snap, and a high electric whine sizzles overhead. A second later, the infield blooms with light, the night-damp dirt coming up a warm, earthy red. The corners of the outfield remain shadowed and the light over left field flickers epileptically, but the rest of the field glows a rich stadium green.

The kid stands in the doorway, obviously pleased with himself, and Michael smiles back. The kid's teeth are surprisingly straight and white, but between the bottom of his shorts and his puffy red high-tops, he looks underfed—like Finn—his shins like sticks stripped of their protective bark.

"If you think that's sick," the boy says, "you'll wanna check this out."

The 22nd

It takes forever for Mia and Michael to escape the Thompson Art Centre's underground lot. Trapped in a labyrinth of idling vehicles and concrete posts, Michael lays on the horn whenever a car from another tributary tries to edge in. With every blast, Mia stiffens but withholds comment. And she closes the vents too late, the air in the Jeep already foul with exhaust by the time they exit the garage into a warm, drizzly night.

They follow Queen Elizabeth Drive, two lanes of rain-glossed asphalt winding alongside the walled waters of the canal. The lighting's bad, the street overhung by leafy branches, so the drive home feels needlessly dangerous; long stretches of shadowy darkness between streetlights, slick pavement, and Michael driving too fast.

Mia taps a knuckle on her window and stares out at the houses blurring past. On this side of the canal, closer to downtown, the homes are still tall, red brick Victorians, but they sit tightly together, most with barely enough room for an adult to squeeze through to the backyard. Some of the bigger homes have been converted to apartments, and the occasional high-rise condo towers over its neighbours.

There's been talk of increasing density and allowing bigger developments in Old Aberdeen, but thus far the residents, well organized, well educated, and well versed in municipal bylaws and zoning restrictions, have fought down every proposal, Mia amongst the vocal throng. At the bank, she'd lent to plenty of real estate developers—all greed and no graciousness, monetizing every square inch of space they could lay their hands on, neighbourhood charm nothing but a selling point in their glossy sales brochures.

"You like the show?" Michael asks.

A modern dance, lithe, shape-shifting beings from the East, a huge column of rain centre stage, bodies wet and churning, a company of perfectly fingered hands, not a broken nail in sight, let alone a misshapen limb.

"It should have been simpler," Mia says. "More dance, less production. That rain."

"I enjoyed it."

He didn't. He'd been squirming in his seat, seemingly desperate to get away, although he'd stayed put during the intermission, no doubt to avoid the slim possibility of running into one of his old business buddies in the lobby. God forbid he work up the courage to tell some macho modern dance enthusiast the truth about what happened at Conrad or inquire about a job.

Michael fiddles with the wipers, clears a sheen of fog from the windshield. "I don't understand what's taking so long."

"What's taking so long?"

"I know they said Finn needs time to adjust to his new body image, body pattern, whatever, but I thought the earlier he got a prosthesis, the better. Didn't the surgeon also say that?"

"Yes." They've been over this.

"So next appointment go with him."

And over this. Michael hounding her to intervene, to fix it, to make Finn get a prosthesis. God knows what he'd do if he found out about the twenty-five hundred dollars they owe for the one that went missing. "Finn doesn't want me talking to *his* psychologist. I don't even know if that's allowed. He's nearly eighteen," she says. "I'm trying to pull back a little."

Michael gapes at her. "You think this is the right time to pull back?"

"Yeah," she says. "I do." She stabs at the button to lower her window, finally remembering to clear the taint of exhaust. A cool mist drifts into the car as they whiz through the city. Despite the wet conditions, packs of die-hard joggers, the odd cyclist, take advantage of the pathway bordering the canal. Mia hasn't exercised in months. A city of half a million people and all of it almost perfectly flat. She should outfit herself in Spandex and take up cycling . . . or join Michael at his ratty old diamond, lose herself in the sweet release of smacking a ball with a bat.

She settles back in her seat and takes a long pull of moist air, in through the nose, out through the nose, yoga style. She isn't proud she followed him—once—but given all the crap going on with Peter and the fact her husband takes a bat out with him every night, she thinks she had a right.

Down by the river, she'd watched him hit to some scrawny boy in gigantic jean shorts. A boy running for balls in the poorly lit outfield. A boy who wasn't Finn. Crouched in the long grass that separates the graffiti bridge from the ball diamond, in a thick chorus of crickets, that's what Mia had been thinking. That it should have been Finn and Michael out there playing, although even at the time, she knew she was being maudlin and romantic. Finn never liked baseball. Even as a kid, he'd come into the house out of sorts after playing catch with his father, put off by Michael's constant chirping and the speed with which he insisted on throwing the ball. Even if he could, Mia can't imagine Finn picking up a glove now.

The drizzle turns to rain. The wind gusts up. When she closes her window, the slap of wipers fills the car—neither of them has thought to turn on the radio. She glances over at her husband, stiff and unhappy behind the wheel. "Listen," she says, "I'm just off three months of wound care. Why don't you take care of Finn's rehab?"

His answer is immediate. "Because you're better with him than I am."

In silence they loop up and over the canal. Even though it's concrete, even in the rain, the Canal Bridge, beautifully lit from below, gracefully arching over the narrow waterway, reminds Mia of Paris, a place she's always dreamt of living, although that dream feels pretty far off now.

They are almost across the bridge when the wiper blade on Michael's side flies off into the darkness. "Shit!" He pulls into the first free parking spot on Main Street, a metal arm—all that's left of the wiper—scratching away at the glass. He turns off the wipers; the windshield becomes a slide of water. Cursing, he climbs out of the Jeep and rustles through the trunk, but comes up empty. Beneath the back hatch, he tugs off a sock, rolls it into a ball and uses some dental floss Mia finds in her purse to tie it to the arm. He's soaked when he climbs back, but the low-tech, MacGyveresque fix clears an arc on the windshield just wide enough to see through.

As they cruise slowly home, the balled-up sock slaps back and forth like an angry foot. Mia can't help laughing.

"Jesus," Michael says. "People will think we hit some kid." Which shouldn't be funny, but is.

In their driveway, the engine ticks to quiet. The child's foot slides to still. Mia peers up at the house: the porch light casts a welcoming glow, but all the windows are dark. The front steps need painting. And she's been lazy with the flowerbeds, weedy and colourless except for a determined daisy and a few straggly poppies fallen over in the rain.

Michael takes the keys from the ignition. "When's his next appointment?"

"Friday morning. Ten o'clock."

"I'll take him."

"Great. And we have a meeting with David that day at eleven thirty."

"David." Michael scoffs the name, never mind the man worked pro bono half of March and all of April.

"I'm reminding you because you missed the last one."

"Okay, Mia. All right."

"Well, you did." She stares at the sock on the windshield. Without the slapstick motion, it's just a sad little still life, a skinny metal stick ending in a tethered lump, one side flattened wet against the glass.

FINN IS ASLEEP in the upstairs den, commercials flickering soundlessly over him. While Michael hunts for the remote, Mia rattles his shoulder. They go to and fro, mother gently shaking son—get up, honey, go to bed—son lazily fending off mother, until Michael steps in and yanks away the blanket. Fingers gripping fingers, hand gripping elbow, he pulls the boy to his feet.

Too rough, Mia thinks, but Finn is up and on his way to his room. She watches him stumble along the hallway, half-asleep, the clubby red end of his arm hanging limply from his sleeve. She imagines a wall encircling her heart—just a couple courses of stone, poorly stacked and readily crumbled, but still, the beginning of a boundary that's never existed.

Never mind him missing the last term of school. Never mind he barely even looks at that arm. Never mind that his life will be so much harder now, despite what she said in the car. Never mind, never mind, never mind.

I am separate, she tells herself. We are not one.

———

IN BED, MICHAEL tucks in behind her and starts massaging her neck. He tells her he just wants them to get along. She says that's what she wants too, but still she has to remind herself to breathe, to relax, to try to enjoy the back rub. But when Michael slips two fingers under the waistband of her underwear, she catches his wrist. She does not want this. Cannot have it. Neither her body nor her mind will allow it.

"I'm tired." Beneath the sheet, she returns his hand to him.

"You're always tired."

"Yeah," she says. "I am."

He huffs. Rolls away. Reaches for his iPad. They lie in the soft grey glow. She cannot.

HERE'S HOW IT GOES. How it's gone pretty much since the day Jess backed me into the bathroom. I set my alarm for 2 a.m. Sometimes I don't need it, but I set it anyway. When it goes off, I don't want to look totally desperate, so I'll wait a couple minutes before I pull back the curtain. Her bedroom window's right next to the fire escape on the second floor of the house behind ours. Her light. If it's on, I get up, check that my parents are sleeping and fumble on my lamp. If it's not, I let the curtain drop. On good nights, I tell myself tomorrow. Tomorrow, she'll be here and it's love that powers the universe. On bad nights, I bang my stump against the wall and punish it for her absence.

If I can't get back to sleep and I'm feeling really pathetic, I'll slide open the top drawer of my desk and check out the Ziploc. I don't take the ribbon out and fondle it or anything, don't usually even touch the bag. I just stare down into the drawer and think about how there was a little piece of her in the piece of me that got cut off that night and wonder if that means anything. If anything means anything at all.

Usually I just get up and grab the light blue Staedtler fibre-tip pen from the ten-pack my mom left on my desk, along with a new Hilroy notebook, so I could practise my amputee writing skills up here in private. Marker in hand, I'll stand on my bed with my feet sinking into my mattress and redraw the shorelines on the world map. National Geographic. Scale 1:24,031,000.

I don't remember how I even got started on the map, but it's mindless and monotonous and a lot easier than wobbling my name in the notebook. The shorelines are easy to follow and the blue is almost the same blue as the oceans, so unless you look really closely, you can't even tell Newfoundland's underwater and Iceland's pretty much gone.

While I shrink countries with my jerky left hand I remind myself of the rules: Jess is the one who makes them. I'm the one who obeys. No texting. Ever. No calls. Ever. Eric checks her phone. No likes, no comments, no tweets. All contact or signs of desperation forbidden.

What's allowed: I can wait for her to come to me. When she does, we can bang. We can laugh about stupid stuff after, when we're lying in bed. We can talk about when we were younger. We cannot say the word *love*. What we're doing? What we've been doing since she backed me into the bathroom? Just hanging out like we always have. Casually hanging out and fucking in my bed.

Tonight, the alarm chimes. Minutes troll past like dead-eyed fish. 2:04, I pull back the curtain. Her window's a bright rectangle lighting up both our backyards. I drop back on the bed, annihilated by relief. When I look again, Jess is at her window, a perfect silhouette.

Five minutes later, she's lying beside me. Her lips on mine, moving in slow motion, so we're kissing but also sort of breathing into each other, speaking a private breathy language. My good hand on the back of her neck, my bad arm tucked under my head. I'm careful with my positioning. But the smell is gone so I am no longer completely repulsive. And honestly? Almost four months out of the hospital and not that much has changed.

Jess still comes over two or three nights a week, same as before. Lately, she's been coming over a lot, so I'm not worried about that so much anymore. And I still wear plaid shirts over white tees only now I wear long-sleeved ones all the time. And jeans, the buttons and zippers are no problem—even belts are okay, necessary even, since I've lost some weight. And I mostly wear flip-flops since it's warmed up. One day when my parents were out, I picked up a hockey stick in the garage and tried taking a shot. The puck dragged across the concrete and stopped a couple feet short of the wall. So yeah, I only did that once. I did go spring skiing with Frankie, but I felt like an idiot because, well, one pole. And I'm kind of off video games. And school. Writing in public. Listening to people talk.

Jess pulls back a bit so I can almost bring her into focus. Your bed is super comfy, she says.

Your lips are super comfy.

Seriously. Why is your bed so amazing?

Memory foam? Bamboo sheets? Me?

She laughs. The sheets *are* soft.

You're soft. I stroke her neck. Your skin.

She sighs. Listen, she says, all serious. Eric's going to Vegas on the weekend.

Really? For how long?

Three days.

That's good, I say. That's really, really good.

This is good, she says, and rolls me onto my back. I slide the arm under my pillow as she swings up on top of me. I reach for her boob but she guides my hand between her legs and slowly starts rocking.

The 23rd

Michael hits the switch, the lights sizzle on, and like a moth to flame, the kid appears. No matter what time Michael shows up, from under the bridge he appears. Always alone. Always wearing the same stoner smile, the same baggy shorts, the same red running shoes. Tonight, almost without speaking, Michael and the boy head for the equipment shed and drag out the Arm. Both of them serious as they roll the old pitching machine across the damp dirt field, like wrestling some Eastern-bloc beast, five hundred pounds of blood-rust steel, five feet high and three feet wide, reluctant, utilitarian, without a whisper of grace to its line or form. This is no plastic-construct, whiny-engined, glorified leaf blower that farts out a ball with a suck and pop of forced air. The thing looks like it could drop from the belly of an old MiG-3 and land unscathed in any field of dreams, ready to rip one across home plate at eighty-five miles an hour.

The Arm, its name and patent number stamped into a small oval plate riveted to the frame. When Michael checked it out online, he'd been surprised to learn it had been manufactured in the 80s by a now-defunct company once operating out of Kansas City, Missouri—not in WWII Russia as the machine would want you to believe.

It had taken Michael a night of tinkering to get it in shape. Even when he had it pitching, and pitching hard, he'd had to keep adjusting the release mechanism with a sturdy pair of plumber's pliers after the thing misfired half a dozen times. The mechanical arm would ratchet back, gears clicking, springs compressing, until it was parallel to the ground. A ball would roll down the tubular feed and drop onto the end of the pitching sleeve. Fully cocked, dangerous with energy, there'd be the usual click, but no release, no small white missile launched. The kid or Michael would have to risk his neck tripping the arm, live with unsprung torque. The ball would fly wild into the backstop, and they'd both stare at it dropped in the dirt behind home plate like a live grenade.

While Michael lines up the throwing arm, the kid starts feeding in the balls. Two hundred baseballs clatter into the caged hopper, balls the boy pulls from an old army-green duffle bag they now stash in the shed, along with a couple gloves and a fifty-foot extension cord Michael found in his basement on top of a tangle of Christmas lights. He'd bought the balls with cash, no longer "spare," what with grocery bills and utility bills and lawyer's bills—Christ, *spare*—even the word sounds quaint. Regardless, Michael hadn't thought twice about spending the money. Still, he'd spread his purchases among various sporting goods stores across the city. He was probably just being paranoid, but in the back of his mind he knew some bylaw existed that forbade the breaking into of sheds and the unauthorized use of city lights and equipment and electrical power. Still, it was all petty stuff, nothing that would land them in any real trouble if someone started poking around. Besides, it's a risk Michael's willing to take.

Since finding the Arm, he feels a tug toward the diamond, like he did when he was a kid at school, daydreaming about the go-kart he was piecing together in his father's garage. It's given him a focus, something to look forward to, something he hasn't yet fucked up. After the rain kept him away yesterday, tonight he hadn't even waited for Mia to head upstairs before slinking out of the house. And really, he has nothing to hide. She hasn't asked a lot of questions, but she knows he goes out pretty much every night. She's seen the baseball bat.

"You up, Cheerio?"

"I'll catch, Dirk." It's what Michael calls him. A name he came up with to offset Cheerio, and the kid doesn't seem to mind.

Michael makes sure the boy is off to the side when he punches the red on-off button. The Arm chugs to life, the mechanical sleeve ticking up and back. The first ball drops and releases, hard and fast and inside. Michael grasps the metal frame and inches the machine left. The next ball flies straight over home plate.

The kid smiles as he steps in, the bat resting easy on his shoulder. A ball comets from the machine, a micro-planet of blasting white, catching the light, the eye, streaking toward the bat, the anticipation of connection, redirection, right field, left field, centre field, the sex-scream dream of the back wall, it's going, it's going, it's what they come for, it's what they come for every night . . . The boy swings, all shoulders and arms, a delayed lurch of his hips. The ball slams into the backstop and falls to the ground behind home plate.

The boy misses the next ball and the next.

If it were his kid up there, if it were Finn at bat, if such a thing were still possible, Michael would be getting tense, shouting instructions: time the pitch, shift your weight, keep your eye on the goddamn ball. But this kid, this bridge-dwelling perma-stoner, this shorts-to-the-ankle smasher of locks, this perpetual misser of balls, he's not Michael's responsibility. Let him struggle. Let him suffer his own weakness.

The boy swings again but the ball takes no notice of his flailing stick of wood.

"Fuck!" The kid lurches away from the plate. "Can you slow that bitch down?"

"Slow as she'll go, my gangsta friend. Slow as she'll go."

"Motherfucker." He glares at the Arm, which keeps hammering balls into the backstop. "Motherfucking fucker."

"I'm getting lonely out here, Dirk." Michael punches his glove.

The hopper's half-empty before the kid finally connects. And after he makes contact, he finds a groove, he figures it out, Michael can't get to the balls fast enough. He keeps slipping, the balls fall in front of him, behind him, small white bombs dropping into wet green grass.

"What do you think of that, Grandpa Cheerio," the kid hollers after he knocks one over Michael's head. "That's what I'm talkin' about!"

When there's a scatterplot of balls in right field, the kid bunts a few into the dirt ten feet in front of home plate. But it's only for show, because soon he settles in and does what he likes best, binging balls off the Arm, shivering its metal cage. Michael knows he should tell the kid to knock it off, but there's something deeply satisfying about the way the machine shrieks and shakes when a ball connects. Besides, the thing's a beast, built to take the abuse.

"Bitch!" The kid whoops every time he dings it. "*Bitch.*"

I DON'T KNOW what Jess is doing. Fourth night in a row she's in my bed. She's never come over four nights straight. And this time she brought a ten-pack of McNuggets. Which she's feeding me, because apparently I'm too skinny. I don't ask why she's not with her boyfriend on his last night in town. I don't give a shit about him. I hope his plane crashes on the way to Vegas. Or on the way back. Either's good with me.

Jess tears a McNugget in two, dips it into the little container of barbecue sauce that's balanced on my stomach and pops it into my mouth. Waits for me to swallow. Pops in the second half.

I lift my head off the pillow, grab a golden nugget from the cardboard package and try to feed it to her, but she turns away. They're for you, she says, tucking her hair behind her ear. She puts her hand on my chest, where it has always belonged. Slides her fingers along my ribs, following the grooves of my bones.

She feeds me another couple pieces of chicken. Greasy and bready. Pretty moist. As I chew, she licks crumbs off her fingers.

You sure you don't want one?

You need the calories, she says.

Yeah. I don't say anything about my knife and fork issues. Or tell her I don't really like McFrankenfood anymore. I lift my good hand and tease her bottom lip with my thumb. Let it rest, until she pulls it into her mouth and sucks on it, her eyes locked on mine. We're both kind of trembly when she finally stops. I drop the barbecue sauce onto the floor. She drops her head onto my chest.

Anda makan saya, she says, all her soft *a*'s warm on my belly.

Indonesian?

Yeah.

What does it mean?

You feed me, she says. You feed me what I need.

The 24th

Your mother says you need pants. My dad's talking to the windshield. I thought we'd go shopping when you're done. Since we're on this side of town.

I'm hanging out with Eli after.

Oh. The light ahead turns yellow. He hits the gas and we fly through on the red. How's it going, anyway?

What?

The psychologist. He frowns a bit when he says it, like he just swallowed a bug.

Fine. I'm keeping the bad arm out of sight, down low between the seat and the door.

Okay, he says, still frowning. If you say so.

What?

I just don't think you'd need new clothes if things were going fine.

I drop my head onto the headrest, stare out the window. It's not raining, but it should be. The blue sky and sunshine, the perfect summer weather, doesn't really fit the mood in the car. Why couldn't

Mom drive me, again? I ask. Does she have a meeting or something? Weren't you supposed to go with her? After that it's pretty quiet, just the two of us taking deep breaths and feeling like shit, so I don't even mention anything about him not working anymore or all the arguing they've been doing lately.

We pass the mall, a ton of cars in the lot. Pass Canadian Tire. Local Heroes, where I had a hockey banquet once. This one kid, Simon, choked on a chicken wing and the coach had to give him the Heimlich. We hang a left at Home Depot. Glenmore, the rehab clinic, is a couple blocks up, a two-storey jobbie, green mirrored windows along the upper level, lots of concrete below. I am very familiar with the building. My dad signals the turn into the lot, the sound of clicking loud between us.

At the front door. You sure you don't want me to come with you?

Positive.

Ask about the prosthesis, he says. I can't understand why they're not moving on that.

I will. And Eli's picking me up. You don't have to wait around. I get out of the car. Wave goodbye with my good hand, pretend to go inside.

BEHIND MIA THE door opens and David strolls back to his desk. Only a few inches taller than Mia's five foot six, he's not a big man but is one of those guys who look great with silvery hair. He's wearing it longer than when they worked together, and slicked back. He's slimmer too, trim from a cholesterol scare and his new habit of biking to work. The fact that he's recently single and probably for the first time making his own meals is probably also a factor.

"If you can get Michael to look this over"—he hands her a photocopy of the case chronology they've been working on, listing all the relevant dates and documentation—"and let me know if there are any inaccuracies, that would be great."

"Sorry he's not here." She doesn't mention the half-dozen texts she sent Michael before the meeting, all of which went unanswered, nor the words they had on the way home from the theatre.

"We're doing all right." David's easy grin contradicts his precisely cut suit. "Old hat for us, no? Working together on files."

"Yeah, although normally I didn't have to foot the bill."

"Peter will play his games, he'll drag things out, make sure Michael feels the pain financially, but he'll eventually settle. He won't want all the details of how he screwed his partner getting aired in court. And no one likes to be confronted with the reality that their partner's been ripping them off. Worse when it's a friend."

"It makes you question your own judgment," Mia says. "It makes you question a lot of things."

"Listen, what's happening here with Peter? It isn't unique. You know that. Majority shareholder gets what he can out of his minority partners, then convinces himself they're leeches, cling-ons, and promptly proceeds to deny them their share of the profits. Happens every day. Greed. The deluded belief that you deserve more than everyone else. It's fucked up, it's sociopathic, but it's what keeps me in business." David glances at his watch, perfectly at ease. Like he said, this is everyday stuff for him. "How about lunch?"

The thought of a restaurant, no doubt filled with half the men she used to work with, tires her. But so does the thought of going home and confronting Michael. Or sitting in this office one moment longer.

"How about the patio at Delilah's?" David says. "You love their salmon."

She does. And the slim asparagus, which she now avoids buying at Metro given the expense. The cold, crisp glass of pinot grigio. Unlike most of her business socializing, lunch with David always felt more like fun than work, or worse, a clumsy date with some man she would never choose to be with.

"You don't think Peter will be there?" She's a little jittery every time she leaves the house, but thus far, she hasn't bumped into either of them. She has spoken to Helen once. In late March she'd called the studio, and for some reason Mia picked up. The conversation had been awkward. Helen's brother, who neither Mia nor Helen particularly likes, had been diagnosed with testicular cancer. Frankie was struggling in math. She asked about Finn. Mia had offered a guarded update, but when Helen claimed that Peter had never meant to cut Michael out of the company, that it was all a big mistake, a mess-up in paperwork, Mia told her she could believe that if she wanted, she had to find some way to live with the guy, but they both knew it was complete bullshit, and the call had ended abruptly.

"You shouldn't be ducking around Peter Conrad." David leans over his desk and lowers his voice to a confidential register. "Just between you and me, Mia, the man does not have a lot of friends."

"*I* don't have a lot of friends," she says, feeling like a petulant child. "Peter and Helen were our default. It's pathetic. I need to join a women's group or something. A book club."

"You get along better with men."

"I don't even like men."

"Ah, but they like you." He grins. "Our Little Red Ferrari." Mia's nickname in the corporate world, never said to her face. She hadn't found out about it until after she quit, but apparently all the guys she worked with knew it. And the tagline that followed: hot, fast, and every man wants to take her for a spin. She supposes it was better than being the Rusty Beige Civic or the Blue Dodge Minivan, but still. She was a fool to think she could have ever been just one of the guys. Sure, she was good at her job, but she had hips and tits and a warm nook between her legs and no two ways about it, they all thought about fucking her. She'd come back from maternity leave, a new mom, soft with love for her son, her breasts swollen with his milk, and *hubba hubba*, they barely skipped a beat.

"Vroom, vroom," David says.

"It's not funny."

He laughs. "Come on," he says. "Lighten up. Come for lunch."

LISTEN, ELI SAYS, drumming the table with his fingers. I have to tell you something.

We're at Kettleman's. Having smoked meat sandwiches, our backs to the body ovens. When he glances at me, I see it right away. The apology that's coming. The mash-up of pity and guilt.

I toss my sandwich down. You've got to be fucking kidding, I say, and stab my pickle into the coleslaw. Don't, I say, threatening him with a limp cucumber and a bit of shredded cabbage. Okay? Just don't. We are not having some fucking talk.

He actually looks relieved. Usually things are chill with him. Usually he does not want to get into that night—what happened with Frankie in the laundry room, what happened in his backyard— which is perfect, because neither do I.

On the table, Eli's phone lights up. He swipes the screen. Oh hey, Jess, he says around a mouthful of meat. Yeah, he says. With Finn. He glances over, and his face is pretty much back to normal.

Put her on speaker, I whisper. He shrugs me off. I lean across the table. Smack him in the arm. Put her on speaker.

I quit my job. Her voice floats from Eli's hand. Come get me. I've got the whole day off.

FIFTEEN MINUTES later: I love the Caddy on days like this, Jess says, leaning forward, her arm dangling into the front seat. Feels like the first real day of summer.

Mostly I see her at night, in my room, and up close she's gorgeous and everything, but today with the top down and the sun blazing and her hair blowing in the wind she's *so* real and so right-out-in-the-open. Eli glances over at me, so I stop staring, and Jess, well, she fades into the back.

We head over the Canal Bridge, through downtown and north out of the city. Hit farm country, miles of flatness, before we start the climb into wilderness. Lots of trees and the occasional man-made cliff where the road got blasted through rock. Sheers of pink granite. Limestone—maybe. Some other sort of brown-rock rock.

Half-hour and we're in the Hills Provincial Park. Only a few paved roads, rolling bands of blacktop slicing through forest, and no cops around ever, so Eli drives fast through the park. A blur and flicker of sunshine and Jell-O green leaves either side of the car, the air fresh, recently cleansed by nature. And the Caddy's suspension is unreal. We float through the curves, roller-coaster over the rises, stomachs lifting, dropping as we cruise down the other side.

Jess rolls an elastic off her wrist and puts her hair in a ponytail while I fiddle with the radio, find a station we all like, then, yeah, I stretch my good arm along the seatback, so I can half turn to look at Eli, *hey dude,* look at Jess, *hey Jess, awesome day, right?* Just being friendly, singing along with Kanye, his god dream competing with the wind. Just letting my hand dangle behind the seat until Jess casu-ally reaches up and low-down curls her baby finger around mine for, like, a millisecond of contact.

We park in the lot beside the Parkway—a good ten-mile cut of forest road that's closed off to motorized vehicles.

You up for it? Eli says.

Definitely.

How about I go get us some drinks? Jess says. Eli tosses her the keys and starts rattling around in the trunk. She climbs over the seat. One long leg, then the other, one creamy-brown hand reaching for the wheel, her ass hovering above my head, a fantasy framed by blue sky.

The Caddy kicks up dust as she pulls out of the lot. I force myself not to watch.

Left this at my place last fall. Eli drops my longboard at my feet and hands me a helmet. New. Not mine. He gives me a slide glove, the left one, which also looks new, the thick, waxy pucks on the palm and fingers unmarked.

He waits as I work it on, pumping my hand and using my teeth at the wrist.

Where'd you get this stuff? I ask when I'm done.

Garage.

Looks new.

He just shrugs and holds out the other glove.

Seriously, dude?

You wanna tear that up?

He tosses the glove to me and I pull it on the short arm. The empty fingers flop back like some limp-dick joke. Eli positions the palm puck on the end, pulls a roll of duct tape from his pack, starts taping down the deflated digits. He doesn't look at me when he does it, doesn't ask if what he's doing is okay, he just tapes me up like he's been doing it all his life.

Let's roll, he says when he's finished, and pushes onto the Parkway.

The ride out is fine, it's good, I mean, I feel normal and the glove works and it's a sick day and the road's clean and smooth and dry and it's awesome to be out here, but halfway along, I tell Eli I've had enough. I make some excuse about being out of shape, feeling weak, I actually use those words, *feeling weak*. I tell him he should keep going, definitely, no problem, I'll hang with Jess, keep her company, or whatever, I'll just hang. And what's he going to say? I mean, I lost my fucking hand. It gives me some room to manoeuvre.

On the ride back, I surf the hills like an ultralight beam, tucking low and fast into the curves, barely using my hands, keeping the board right under me, pushing hard on the flats, the wind whipping past, the sun on my back and my plaid shirt flapping, feeling so good, so good, and at the top of the next big rise I swear to God a freaking owl swoops out of the forest, wings outstretched, shadowing the road, shadowing me, I can feel it above me, we glide down the long slope together, my trucks chattering, the owl drafting overhead, catching a current, carving higher, flapping silently away like it never even happened, and me down below, ripping along alone, every cell in my body lit, every atom thrumming with the speed and the heat and the bird and the slap of my sole on the pavement and Eric in Vegas and one last hill between me and the girl.

MIA AND DAVID stand side by side in the smooth drop of the elevator, face to face with their own reflections. "Handsome couple," he says, waggling his eyebrows. "Poster kids for Viagra."

Mia laughs, then runs her hands down her thighs. Paired with strappy sandals, her short orange skirt is barely passable as business attire, although her simple white blouse helps balance things out.

"No offence," David says, "but when I rebound, I'm going for someone younger. Much younger."

"Oh. How daring of you."

"Someone supple and tight and ready to please."

"Jesus, David, please don't make me hate you."

"Relax," he says. "I'm just trying to bug you. So tense, my friend, so tense. Maybe we should skip lunch. Go to my place and get high and fuck?"

"Ha! What are you, sixteen?"

"I may have had a reversion."

For a second, Mia considers his offer—made in jest, she's certain—and how easy it might be to set in motion. She could kiss him right there in the elevator. Push him up against the fake wood wall, grind her hips against his, lift his hands to her tits. It could happen. They get along. There's always been something between them. Mia wouldn't exactly call it heat, it's more like a vibe, a sense that they resonate at the same frequency, especially when it comes to having a good time. David's easy to be with. He expects very little from her. After what would only be described as a harrowing winter, she could use a little David right now.

So why not make it happen? There's a part of her that wants to. But honestly? David has never been her fantasy.

This is her fantasy: She walks away. Out of the house, down the porch stairs which need a coat of paint but she no longer cares about those steps, that porch, the door behind her, the people behind the door. She carries only her camera. She holds on to no one's hand. She boards a bus and lets it take her deep into the heart of nowhere. A scrubbed-clean motel room on the edge of a forest. A cabin on the shore of a lake. No need to share the bed with anyone, to spread her legs to someone else's hand, to rise to make another breakfast, to taxi to another appointment, to have even one more heartening talk.

A single pair of underwear drying in the bathroom. One soft pair of jeans. A roomy white T-shirt to sleep in. A television that plays only comedy while she laughs and eats crackers from a box.

The elevator glides to a stop. The doors open, four men in dark suits nod, she and David move to the back. A minute later, they all step out into the sun-bright lobby, soaring three storeys to a glassy atrium, so much space and light. The heels of Mia's sandals click on the polished marble as David guides her through the scatter of lawyers and bankers, admins and security guards, his hand resting light on the small of her back.

THE BARRED WHEEL on the screen of Michael's laptop spins. He logs on, navigates his way to LinkedIn's "Create a Profile" page. Until today, he's managed to avoid the whole internet networking thing, both corporate and personal. Fifteen years at the same company and with a wife who handled their social life, he didn't really need to be plugged in.

He pecks in his coordinates, confirms himself via email,

humbly informs the LinkedIn gods that yes, he's looking for a job—a worthy excuse for skipping the lawyer's meeting, since Finn blew off the shopping. When queried about his current state of employment, he gets up from the kitchen table and pours himself another coffee. In the front hall, he sorts through the mail. Bills mostly. An envelope from Glenmore. Some notice from the City. He opens nothing, but sticks a sheet of coupons from a local pizza joint up on the fridge.

Back at the computer, headlines of the day's not-to-be-missed LinkedIn stories have already popped up on his screen. "Why Leaders Should Always Make People Feel Like They're On A Winning Team." "Four Strategies To Renew Your Passion For Work." "Five Career Mistakes You Won't Survive." Michael's pretty sure he's already made a couple. And he wonders about the need for capitalization. Does Every Word Need To Shout?

He checks yes to linking up his email contacts, but immediately regrets it. Shit, will everyone now get some goddamn message informing them Michael Slate is on the hunt? He watches as a banner of polished people, a small sample of every person he's ever worked with, played golf with, told a dirty joke to, loads onto his screen. For the first time since leaving Conrad, he misses his secretary Bev. He doesn't even know how to put up a picture, although the site strongly recommends it; members with a photo get eleven times more views, and Michael's just a grey, jug-eared head.

And then, of course, there it is. Of course the platform has an algorithm that selects the people he's most connected to. Peter Conrad's grinning face. President and CFO of Conrad Management Group, with nine hundred plus connections. In the photograph, his long surfer hair doesn't even look to be thinning.

Christ.

Michael can't figure out how to abort. Delete his profile. Get the hell out. The last person in the world he wants to reach out to is Peter Fucking Conrad. The Guy Who Screwed Him Over. The Guy He'd Most Like To Punch.

He panics and shuts Peter down the old-fashioned way: presses the button at the top of his laptop and kills the power.

AFTER LINGERING OVER LUNCH, neither David nor Mia is in any rush to go back to where they belong. He calls his admin and clears his calendar and Mia, well, she turns off her phone. They decide on a drive, and at David's cajoling end up in Old Aberdeen, parked across the road from Peter and Helen's place. Mia leaves the Jetta idling, in case they have to make a getaway. Technically, they're doing nothing wrong, but it doesn't feel that way. The red flag on the mailbox is up; someone—Helen most likely—might come out for the mail.

David, however, apparently shares none of Mia's angst. In the passenger seat, he looks like a man setting out on vacation, his favourite hotel already booked. His hair, bright silver in the sun, his face tanned from biking or some recent winter escape. The sleeves of his shirt—purple and expensive looking; Mia has an urge to reach over and touch the fabric—are turned to his elbows, one of which is cocked out the open window.

"The property's impressive," David says, "but the house doesn't look like much."

Evenly spaced white tree trunks, undergrowth groomed back, a half-acre of mature birch trees separates the house from the road, and on either side, the neighbours are well out of screaming distance. A meandering laneway carves the manicured stand of birch in two, but it's hard to see much of what looks like a bluish-grey, single-storey rancher from the road. All that's really visible is the triple-car garage at the end of the drive, a recessed front entry, and Peter's BMW parked squarely out front.

"The lot drops down at the back," Mia says. "There's a walk-out basement, then another storey of windows overlooking the water. Terraced decks. A private dock." On hot days when they were stuck in the city, Mia used to bring Finn over to swim. One summer, a blue heron took to landing on the end of the dock every day around four, which, in the middle of the city, felt like some sort of blessing. On Christmas Eve, if the ice were good, Peter would shovel off a rink, although watching the kids skating on the river always made Mia nervous. Even in the coldest winters there were accidents, people and sometimes their dogs falling through.

"I did a search," David says. "The property's owned free and clear. No mortgage. No secured lines of credit. The cottage and chalet are in his wife's name, but they're also unencumbered."

"I figured." Which she had, although hearing it confirmed, she feels a little air go out of her—they are so much better off than she and Michael.

"Amanda's getting the house," David says, casually, no hint of bitterness in his voice. Amanda, his ex. Their home, as gorgeous as she is. "I'm sleeping on a mattress on the floor of an empty condo. But you know what? I wake up every morning and my first thought is, I'm free." He throws his head back and laughs. "I'm fucking free."

Mia's surprised and . . . what? A little envious? She'd imagined David would have a harder time losing half his assets, not to mention his picture-perfect wife.

He stares out at the house—perhaps regretful or contemplative—but when he turns back it's with a mischievous smile. "We should put a flaming turd in their mailbox."

"Do you have a flaming turd?"

"No. Not on me."

A small white rabbit jumps from the birch trees and hops languidly across the road, stopping on the dirt shoulder to twitch its nose at them. Mia watches it disappear into the long grasses on her side of the car. At this end of the island, the houses band the shore, but there are none in the middle, just a long, meandering meadow. The real estate people think it's the perfect spot for a luxury condo development, good luck to the bunny. So far the City does not agree. Years back, however, they did sell off a few acres closer to the overpass, so a private school could be built. Ferndale. Way back when, she and Michael went to an open house. The teachers were great, the class sizes small, but the parents all seemed like such snobs. And dressed in a navy jacket and school tie, crisply pressed shorts and white knee socks, the headmaster looked like an ass and talked mostly about making business connections. Which, when Mia thinks about it, would come in handy now.

"How about we drive up? Give a little beep. See who's home."

"David, no way."

"Might be fun," he says.

"Might not."

"I'm your lawyer. What could go wrong?"

"Are you trying to get me in trouble?"

"Maybe." He grins over at her. "Maybe not."

Mia's eyes widen as, over David's shoulder, the door of the garage starts gliding up. Together they watch the slow reveal: the long, tan legs, the short shorts, the bare midriff, the tight flowered top, the broad shoulders, the wild, auburn hair.

"Their daughter," Mia whispers, slightly relieved. Frankie isn't one to hike up a long driveway to fetch her parents' mail.

"Great legs," David whispers back.

Mia would smack him if she wasn't holding herself motionless in the car.

Frankie aims a hand at her father's BMW. The trunk jumps. She throws in a backpack and then leans up against the car, pulls a phone from her front pocket and begins thumbing the screen.

Mia hasn't seen her in ages. Not since before Finn's accident . . . the ski weekend at the chalet. She's watched Frankie grow up and always believed that she loved her. But if she had, if she really had, wouldn't she have found some way to keep in touch? Is the cast of her light really that small? She would never let Finn drift from her life for months, without so much as a phone call. She can't remember really even missing her. Over the past four months she's thought about Peter, viciously, and Helen, coldly and occasionally longingly, but she's barely considered their daughter.

Frankie slips her phone back into her pocket and, bracing herself against the trunk of the BMW, leans back and closes her eyes against the sun.

"Completely oblivious," David says. "Completely clueless."

"No." Mia jams the car into gear. "Trusting," she says. "And sweet. Like her mom." Easing off the clutch, she guides the Jetta onto the road. She almost wishes Frankie would look over, startled by the rev of the engine, suspicious of its source, but in the end, she's relieved they slip away unnoticed.

JESS RAISES A HAND and shields her eyes. She's sitting on the hood of the Caddy, one foot up on the bumper. Where's Eli? she says.

He went to the end. He'll be a while.

My feet are sort of numb from the vibration of the board, so I feel light and loose, like I've been shaken open a bit and have more room inside.

You want a drink? Finn? Stop staring and come here.

More room for her to come in.

I drop my board where I stand. Pull off my helmet and drop it onto the board. I use my teeth to work off the left glove. First the Velcro strap at the wrist, then the tip of each finger, the tough nylon fabric gritty where it touches my lips. It takes a while. It takes longer than it should. With my good hand free, I work the duct tape loose and yank off the folded-down glove. Give the cuff of my sleeve a tug, make sure everything's covered before I walk past her and hop into the back seat. On the right side of the car.

Finn? She turns around, a swing of high, black ponytail. I just smile. Through the back of my shirt, the press of sun-soaked leather.

Jess holds up a bottle of Vitaminwater. Light pink. I was going to get beer, she says, but this has electrolytes. Better after boarding.

Thanks. I stretch my good arm along the seat.

She finally gets up. When she leans in to give me the drink, I can see right down her shirt, her bra with the red cherries, their curved black stems.

I give her a smile and twist off the cap, drink half of the kiwi-strawberry in one long, thirst-quenching gulp. She's got dragonfruit, a dark reddy purple. Why don't you get in?

Jess stares up at the Parkway, its last, long hill. Eli might be—

It's not a crime to sit in a car.

She sighs and climbs over the side. I move my knees so it's easy for her to get by. She slides to the far corner, puts her legs up on the front seat so her feet are in the air. Her flip-flops. Toenails painted blue, lighter than the sky.

It's nice seeing you in the day, I say.

It's nice seeing you.

I stick the bottle between my knees so I can slide my hand across the seat, palm up, a thing I might do if this were, say, our first date. It takes a few seconds, but then just like I want, she reaches over and threads her fingers through mine. Holding hands—it's one of the things we skipped over.

How was your ride? she says.

Good. Her hand's small in mine, a perfect fit. Amazing day, I say.

Gorgeous.

I want to tell her so badly. Break her number-one rule. Maybe I can tell her I don't want to share her anymore. That I never wanted to share her and forget gravity, love is the most powerful force on the planet. Keep it light, Finn. Don't do anything stupid. I think about telling her about the owl, but I don't know, it just feels too fresh or something, too personal. First date, I remind myself, first date.

So, Vegas, I say, which is probably worse.

Yeah. Vegas.

You didn't want to go?

It was a guy thing, she says, lightly. Besides, Eric says he's been spending too much money on me lately.

Has he?

Probably. He's always kind of spoiled me.

Really? Even to me, my voice sounds hard. I have, like, two hundred bucks in the bank and a mason jar full of change in my room. I'm pretty sure my family is about to be poor. I let go of her hand and take another swig of sweetened water. Afterwards I keep a grip on the bottle, watch for Eric's brother to come cruising down the hill.

You know, Finn, my life isn't like yours.

I know.

No, you don't. Jess sounds tense all of a sudden, pissed off, even. You have a father who goes looking for you when you don't come home, she says. A mother who takes pictures for a living. Your family fits in. You are *in*. She takes her feet off the front seat, sits up straight so it feels like we're actually going to have a fight. About what, I'm not totally sure. I'm the brown girl, she says. The girl who lives in the *apartment*. The one with no father and a mother who's never around.

You're the beautiful girl, I tell her. The girl everyone wants.

Oh my god, Finn.

What? You are.

I'm pretty. Hot. Whatever. I've made the most of that. The world cares about that.

And you don't?

I don't know. She flops back against the seat, starts playing with the little silver ashtray on the armrest. My mother wanted me to be resilient. She uses that word a lot. *Tabah.* Resilient. She wanted me to grow up in a safe neighbourhood. She wanted to live by the water. That's what mattered. That's why we ended up in Old Aberdeen.

And that's bad?

No. It's not *bad.*

She shakes her head, all frustrated with me. But honestly? I don't know why we're talking about her mom. I watch her flip up the silver lid. Flip it down. Up and down, up and down, sharp metallic snaps.

I remember the first time I saw you, I say. In the crabapple tree.

Jess stops with the ashtray and stares down into her lap. I know she remembers, too.

You were barefoot. Squatting down on that big branch, with your arm around the trunk. When you jumped into our yard, your hair sort of flew out behind you and I thought wow. I clear my throat, take another chug of my drink, a little shaky, a little embarrassed. I was only like, what, six when you moved in?

Seven. Her voice quiet. You were seven.

Every time you came over I thought wow.

She finally looks at me, her eyes bright, squinting against the sun. What?

Even with the top down on the Caddy and all that blue sky overhead, the air in the back seat feels close and charged. Dangerous, even.

You make everything so hard. She tears a piece off her bottle's label, stuffs it into the ashtray. Gets back to not looking at me. You know what my mom does?

Works at Lee Valley?

Night shift. Extra shifts. Making fancy gardening tools. And we don't even have a garden. She's been trying to get an office job forever but they keep telling her her English isn't good enough. She's lived in Canada for twenty-five years. She has an accent. Her English is as good as it's going to get. Jess tears another neat paper rectangle off her bottle, stuffs it into the ashtray. Pretty soon, the whole label's in there. All those weekends you were skiing or playing hockey? I was standing behind a cash register scanning groceries, she says, and I feel my cheeks go hot. Student loans? They aren't even going to be a thing for you.

She holds the bottle out over the side of the car. Tips it mouth down. Drips of sunlit crimson fall from its clear plastic edge. That day your dad took those boards out of the back fence? For someone else it might not have been a big deal, but for me it felt like this huge gift. Just to get to come over to your house.

She drops the bottle onto the floor of the car. Nudges it around with her foot. Holidays? she says. New clothes? True love? Luxuries we can't afford. If we have extra money, we send it home to my mom's family. I want something else. With one flip-flop she stamps the bottle flat, that plastic, crinkly crunch.

I stare out at the rectangle of empty asphalt, the perimeter of trees, the hills rising from the parking lot like rolling green playgrounds. Nubs of old mountains worn down by twenty thousand years of rough weather after the ice age failed to crush them flat. I stare out at those mountains and I feel like an infant. Like I understand nothing. Like that whole thing with the owl was probably meant for someone else.

Hey. Jess smiles over at me, back to bright. Everything good, she says, right there on the other side of the fence. She taps the seat so I can't miss her hand. You. She taps the seat again. Right there.

And even though I feel like I'm on the most fucked-up first date ever, I finish off my sweetened water and drop the empty bottle onto the floor of her boyfriend's car and put the hand I've got left in hers.

You remember the night your parents took us to the Thunderbird Drive-In? We saw *Jaws*. Remember? You hid behind me when the shark attacked the girl.

I did not.

Yeah, she laughs, you did.

And then she tells me this story about when we were kids, and she was looking after me and we were at the park, in the little forest, on the path that cuts from the tennis courts to the swings—You remember that path, Finn?—Yeah, of course—and there was this group of girls, older girls, like high school girls or something coming the other way, really loud and laughing, and she tells me that when they saw me they just stopped and stared, sort of stunned into silence until one of them said, Look at him. Isn't he the most beautiful boy you've ever seen? And she tells me how much it bugged her when the girl said that and the way they were looking at me, so she took my hand and dragged me past them and pushed me for longer than usual on the swing.

Do you remember that, Finn?

No, I say.

And we're looking at each other now with our heads resting on the back of the seat and our hands locked together and the leather warm against my cheek and my lungs too confused to even try for another breath, my heart too messed up to beat, and she says, They were right, Finn. You are. The most beautiful, beautiful boy.

MIA DROPS DAVID off downtown and drives straight back to the river. The weather is so glorious, her mood so unguarded, she doesn't want anything to shift. And if she goes home, things will definitely shift. She ends up on the public dock across from the Kellys', shoes off, enjoying the breeze, dangling her feet in the sun-spangled water—cool at first, but she gets used to it. Across the slow drift of the river, through a lazy sway of willow branches on the far bank, Mia can make out one hoop of the Golden Arches—part of a strip mall that marks the start of the city's urban sprawl. Neighbourhoods of carport bungalows and split-level houses on 60s sized lots. A wide, practical main drag lined with autoshops, box stores, road-house-style restaurants Mia's never visited. Farther south, the real suburbs begin—old farm fields turned into subdivisions, grids of big oatmeal houses on streets with improbable names—Rocky Ridge Crescent, Sundance Circle, Great Plains Lookout. Mia rarely has occasion to drive out there, but Finn's rehab facility is over the bridge, a few blocks up from the water.

Not five feet in front of her, a pair of black swans glides silkily past, swivelling their necks in unison, checking Mia out. Beaks and eyes a deep, waxy red, feathers dense as matted fur, the swans are housed in a specially built sanctuary during the winter and released back onto the river in spring. Mia has never seen one without the other. She has never seen them trailing any young.

"I thought it was you down here."

She turns. Helen is standing behind her, in sandals and a simple white summer dress.

"Mind if I join you?" she says, a slight waver in her voice.

Even though Mia knew it would happen eventually, even though she braced herself for it every time she left the house, she just wasn't expecting it now. Today. Like this. Caught on the dock, shoeless, in the sunshine, in a pair of diva sunglasses.

Helen settles herself on the dock, lean and graceful. Frankie might get her big bones and her height from her father, but other than that, she's all her mom. They have the same long, slim legs. The same amber eyes, auburn hair, freckled skin that always appears slightly tanned. And beyond the physical they share a gentle nature. They both yield easily, forgive easily, are expert at keeping the peace.

Both are softer sorts than Mia, that's for sure. Helen's a kindergarten teacher. Mornings only. After Frankie was born, Peter wanted her to quit altogether, but she stood her ground; she was born to teach little kids.

"How are things at the studio?"

"Good," Mia says, although she never did reschedule any of the jobs she cancelled last winter and tells anyone who calls that she isn't sure when she'll be reopening.

Helen tries again. "I like your hair." Mia presses her hand to her forehead. To save money she's been trimming the bangs herself. "It's so cute on you. Short like that." Helen pulls off her sandals and dips her feet wincingly into the water; she's always preferred a heated pool to the real thing. "Listen," she says, "we should talk."

Mia considers her options, how gentle or snarky or careful to be. She decides not to make things easy. "I still have your casserole dish." Why should she make things easy?

Helen frowns. "Oh. Never mind about that."

"It's an Emile Henry."

"Mia, I don't *care* about a stupid casserole dish." Helen is easily flustered and hates confrontation. It was bold of her to even venture onto the dock. "How about we just sit here?" she says. "How about we just don't talk?"

Mia circles her feet, creating two tiny eddies in the water. She's fine with not talking. She hasn't really talked to anyone since Finn's accident. She glances over at Helen, looking forlorn in her white linen dress. Her hair's been cut too, just past shoulder length by someone who knows what they're doing.

"How's your brother?" Mia finally asks.

Helen turns her head and looks her squarely in the eye. "Impotent," she says. They can't help it. They each bluster out a laugh.

"How's Finn doing?" Helen asks, sounding more at ease.

Mia's feet go still. "Honestly? I have no idea." She's only slightly ashamed to admit this. But Helen understands; she has a teenager at home. Mia would like to tell her about Finn's hand lying on one of their recliners, how she sometimes imagines a wall circling her heart, her promise to Finn not to worry . . .

"What about Frankie?" she asks. "How was her math?"

"Seventy-eight. With a tutor. She's going out with Eli now." Helen hitches her thumb over her shoulder. "I just dropped her off. She's got two hours and we're dragging her up to the cottage."

Last summer they probably would have been hauling Finn up there, too. "Eli's a good kid," Mia says, her voice a little stiff.

"My husband doesn't think so."

Her husband. Mia's seen his signature scrawled on the bottom of so many damning documents. She watches the swans gliding downstream, those elegant, idiot creatures, heads so small their brains can't be bigger than lima beans. As if alert to her thoughts, they charge back upriver, hissing loudly, suddenly on the attack. Mia is about to scramble up, but Helen kicks water at the birds and shoos them away from the dock. Heads held high, red eyes arrogant and stupid, they gaze haughtily down their beaks, expecting what? To be admired? Fed? Driven to extinction?

Swimming in short zigzags, the swans do what they will to hold the women's attention. Growing impatient, one of the pair finally lets loose a raw, clown-horn honk.

"Apparently those things mate for life." Helen kicks more water at them.

"We should let them get close and wring their furry necks."

"Put them out of their misery," she says, and again the two women laugh.

Helen tips her head to Mia's shoulder, lets it rest, years of friendship fit into a second of contact, another second to recognize love, and then she bobs back up, restoring the careful distance between them, everything that's lost.

I KNEW THEY were going out. Still, it's surprising to see Frankie kiss Eli when she comes into the kitchen. Like full on. Like tongues are involved.

Frankie laughs when she finally comes up for air. What are you staring at, Finn?

I don't even bother answering. Don, Eli's dad—hammered because it's Friday, hammered because he's alive—shoves blender drinks into our hands and then pulls a pile of steaks out of the fridge. Tells us—wink, wink—that Eli's mom stayed behind in Costa Rica to make sure the pool boy was doing his job. But not to worry, he's working the grill, and Jess, Jess is making a salad.

She knows where everything is. The oil and the garlic, the lemon juice, the container of Parmesan cheese. I'm just leaning against the counter, drinking, watching her knowing where, like, everything is. The salad spinner in the cupboard by the sink, the tinfoil that Don asks for. The big bag of croutons.

And then I notice Frankie staring at me with this weird look on her face and Eli's staring at me, so I take a long, brain-freeze swallow of my drink and pretend I wasn't watching Jess and that I didn't see Frankie and Eli watching me and only once when Frankie's out on the deck setting the table and Don's at the barbecue and Eli's in the bathroom does Jess come over to my side of the kitchen. Stretches up onto her toes. Reaches into the cupboard behind me and rests her hand really lightly on my stomach—for balance, I guess.

Her palm just under my ribs. Her fingers trailing down my stomach. A force field of heat coming off her body, and I can't even touch her because I have a drink in my hand. I just stand there, pretending we didn't have an intense afternoon in the Caddy, that we don't fuck in my bedroom pretty much every night, that my heart doesn't throb every time it hears her name. When she bumps me in the head with the salad bowl, she says, Sorry, and it's just her handprint then, like a hot tattoo sunk through my T-shirt and onto my skin. Sorry, and she's back on the other side of the kitchen tossing lettuce into a bowl.

DON SLAPS A bloody steak onto my plate. I stab it with my fork and drop it back onto the platter. I don't eat red meat, I say, and Don's bleary eyes practically fall out of his head.

Since when? Eli says. Since lunchtime?

I concentrate on getting a baked potato out of the bowl, scooping up salad with one spoon.

Christ, Don says, hovering over the platter of meat, the pool shimmering behind him, the cabana. What's the world coming to? This is fucking filet mignon. He points his big barbecue fork at me. His cheeks and nose are a deep, ruptured red, wormed with tiny veins. Is that why you're so goddamn skinny?

Dad, Eli says. Just drop it.

What? Don stares from face to face. What? No one meeting his eye.

He drains his glass, plunks it down on the table. You should have told me, he says gruffly. I could have made you some chicken.

SO YOU AND ERIC have gone out since what? Frankie glances across the table at Jess. Since grade nine?

Ten, Jess says.

Wow. She cuts into her steak and the juices run. So, you've been together for, like, six years?

Almost, Jess says. She's sitting across from me and one seat over, but she's not looking my way.

You guys must talk about getting married.

Jess just shakes her head and I keep stuffing salad into my mouth.

Seriously? Frankie says. After six years, I think you'd talk about it.

Jess Kelly, Eli says. Not bad. Jess Kelly.

And I'm not a violent person, but I want to kick him in the fucking head.

DID YOU HEAR? Don says. Wednesday, I've got myself a new personal assistant. A gorgeous one, too. He slams a bottle of wine onto the table and gives Jess's shoulder a squeeze.

Wednesday. She reaches up and pats his hand.

Don lumbers to the head of the table and drops into his chair.

You're going to work for Don? I ask, trying to keep it casual, trying not to choke up my mouthful of salad.

Yeah, Jess says. Just for the summer.

Doing what?

Office work. Filing and stuff. Running errands.

I thought you were going to work at the hospital. So you'd have experience when you graduate.

That was her mother's idea, Don says. No money in nursing. Cleaning up after people. All those bedpans and shit.

Yeah, nurses are useless. Until you need one.

Don looks confused for a second, but then he decides to ignore me. Don't worry, he says, reaching across the table and grabbing Jess's hand. We won't work you too hard, Princess. He tries to give her hand a kiss, but she's still holding her knife and he practically pokes out his own eye.

LISTEN, JESS SAYS, scraping off the last plate. I've got to go.

But, darlin'! Don throws his arms wide. The night is young.

I'm going out with friends. She puts the plate in the dishwasher, throws in a cube of soap, flips the door closed with one foot, presses a button.

Girl friends, I hope.

Yes, Don. Girl friends. There's a low hum from the dishwasher, a gush of water.

Wouldn't want to have to put in a call to Eric.

Don't worry. I'll be good.

Come back later. He gives his hips a shake. We'll have our own little hula party.

I think they hula in Hawaii, Don. My mom's from Indonesia.

Well what kind of dancing do they do there?

I'm not sure. I've never been. She gives him a smile that looks about as fake as his hair. My mom left when she was seventeen so she wouldn't have to marry this old guy who offered her father a herd of goats for her.

I'm not sure if she's joking. I don't think Don is either.

Jess says a quick goodbye. Her eyes don't land on me a second longer than they do on him.

MIA IS UPSTAIRS in the walk-in closet stuffing a worn pair of cowboy boots into a garbage bag when Michael leans up against the door frame and crosses his arms.

"Your rodeo days over?"

Mia gives the dark plastic a stiff jerk. Caught on the lip of the bag, the boot drops onto a half-dozen pairs of old shoes. "Don't worry," she says, "I haven't touched anything of yours. I know you want to hold on to everything." His jeans and khakis and casual shirts jam the lower rack. His suits and dress shirts are above, and the shelf overhead is stacked with sweatshirts and sweaters.

Michael rattles the empty hangers on her side of the closet. "We don't exactly have the money for new wardrobes right now."

"I don't want a new wardrobe." Mia reaches up and quiets the hangers. "I don't want anything at all." She yanks a blouse from a hanger. The heat from the ceiling light, a bare bulb with a cheap pull chain they've never gotten round to replacing, beats down on her like a vindictive sun. A trickle of sweat slides between her breasts, and she is suddenly, desperately hot.

"You don't want to want anything, but you do."

She crumples the blouse into a ball, pressing back the knowledge that it's her Anne Fontaine, purchased a few summers ago on Rue Saint-Honoré, her favourite street in Paris. Marching bridal-like up long, elegant cuffs, the shirt's small pearl buttons feel like nuggets of treasure within the crush of silky cotton.

Michael nudges one of her Fly London sandals with his foot. "What's the rent on your studio these days?"

Her eyes jump to his. "I'll give blowjobs down on York Street before I get rid of my studio," she says, cramming the blouse into the bag.

"Is that where they're giving blowjobs these days?"

"I'm not sure. I'll find out." If she laughs right now, if she even smiles, she can end this. Michael's tone is lighter than hers. She can give him a break. Give herself a break. Get out of the inferno of a closet. He had dinner waiting when she got home, a store-bought rotisserie chicken, Greek salad, a fresh baguette. They'd eaten out on the deck under the trellis, threaded with white Christmas lights and heavy with wisteria, the pale purple blooms dangling over them like God-lit chandeliers. They'd shared a bottle of wine, avoiding any discussion of missed lawyer's meetings or where she'd disappeared to all day. She can't even remember how she ended up in the closet. She'd come upstairs for something . . . been drawn in by the half-empty garbage bag.

Michael hasn't moved from the doorway. He's wearing a retro CBC T-shirt and a pair of cargo shorts low on his hips. Like the rest of the family, he's lost weight over the last four months. His stomach is firm, his jawline sharp, and there's a new definition to his arms— no doubt from all the baseball. To look at him, handsome and fit and almost smirking, no one would guess there was anything wrong in his life.

Mia stares down at the jumble of shoes on his side of the closet and, despite all the purging, on hers. "You know we're almost eighteen thousand into our line of credit."

"Shit. That's a lot of blowjobs."

"Ha, ha," Mia says flatly. Between them, they must have sixty pairs. Tennis shoes. Golf shoes. Running shoes. A pair of silver heels Mia wore to Michael's Christmas party one year—she'd borrowed a shimmery bag from Helen to match. Two pairs of Fluevogs, from a weekend trip to Montreal. Football cleats Michael's had since high school, decades-old dirt still caked around the spikes. All of it excess. All of it weighing them down.

"David bought a two-bedroom at the Soho." She knows he's familiar with the building: Conrad manages it. Eighteen floors of luxury crowned by a rooftop pool. Michael negotiated the deal. "He asked me to do the interior. Which is good because I'll be making some money." Mia gives him a curt smile and reaches for another blouse, but Michael catches her, his fingers light around her wrist.

"Where were you this afternoon?"

"Where were you this morning?" She'd pull her hand away but she doesn't want to give him the satisfaction. "David and I had lunch." She doesn't mention meeting up with Helen, which somehow seems the greater betrayal.

"I know," Michael says. "I called his office."

"Then why'd you ask?"

"It was a long lunch."

He steps over the garbage bag, steps up close, so they're only a couple of inches apart. "You go over to his place? Check out his new bedroom?"

"Michael, grow up." Her disdain leaves no opening for the truth, that she'd considered, if only for a second, David's offer to "cheer her up" that afternoon. "Can you let go of me, please? I don't like being touched when I'm hot."

Michael uses his body, his bulk, the confines of the space, to march her farther into the closet. Empty shirtsleeves slap at her shoulder before he pins her against the wall. The buckle of a belt rests cool against her neck. His bathrobe lumpy behind her. The fingers of her free hand clutch at a silky dangle of ties.

He leans heavily into her. His chest against her chest, his forehead against her forehead, their breathing fast and uncertain in the glare of the naked bulb.

"Are you fucking him, Mia? Because you sure aren't fucking me." Michael sucks on her earlobe, draws it into his mouth, flicks it with his tongue, before he bites down hard. A gasp, her breath caught, all circuitry lineated to the pain, she whimpers as Michael lets go of her ear and snaps a tie from the rack. Works one end around her wrist. Steps back. He needs two hands to secure the knot.

Mia watches her husband bind her wrist. If she struggled, if she pushed . . . she lets him do it. She wills herself to be only here, no life beyond the closet. When he reaches for a belt, she offers her other hand willingly, an inverted fantasy, the opposite of walking away, a crueller escape from love.

He ties her wrists to the clothes rods. On his side of the closet, her hand is hidden in a thicket of suit jackets. On her side, empty hangers offer no camouflage for the green-and-red plaid of a Christmas tie, a gift from her son, one V'd end hanging long above a clutter of shoes.

"Turn off the light," she says, although the voice is not her own. "Shht."

Standing in the middle of the closet, Michael studies her. She's fully clothed, in the white blouse and orange skirt she wore to David's office, but still she has to force herself to meet her husband's eye. Stretched out and strung up, her arms ache. Sweat beads down her back. She is wet between her thighs.

Michael steps forward. Mia is ready for his fingers gripping her hair, his palm pressing her cheek to the wall, the full weight of his body upon her, but instead, starting from the top, button by button, Michael undoes her blouse. Runs a slow knuckle along the swell of each breast, tracing the line of her bra. Hooks a finger into her clavicle, gives a little tug.

"You like me anymore?" His eyes slide up to meet hers. "You like me even a little?" He slips her bra strap off her shoulder: a silky slither along her arm. Reaches in and cups her breast.

"Can I kiss you? Mia. Can I kiss you?"

This, this is not what she wanted. His body shadowing hers, charged inches between them, his thumb grazing her nipple.

They'd been on his dorm bed the first time it happened. The pure, hot bursting joy of it, cries of unexpected love between afternoon classes.

Michael kneels in front of her and lifts her skirt. Runs both hands up her thighs, catches hold of her underwear, runs his hands back down. A drag of wet cotton, one foot lifted, legs spread and his tongue between her lips, sliding inside her dark mouth, he kisses her gently, her little tongue, he kisses her.

YO, FINN! Eli yells up from the basement. Come on down.

Jess is gone. And Frankie's gone. Her parents took her to the cottage, away from Eli. Who'll want to keep drinking. Who'll want to get high.

I have to take a leak, I say, although I don't.

And I step out onto the deck.

The backyard's dark, except for the pool, glowing like a tropical night light in the middle of the lawn. I head for the shed, the scent of flame-broiled meat. I'm almost past the barbecue when I see the chunk of steak Don left on the grill—*fucking filet mignon!*—a fatty slice of bacon wrapped around the edge. When I pick it up a watery trickle runs warm down my arm. I lick it off before it reaches my sleeve, taste the salt and the juices.

Behind the cabana, I slurp the bacon into my mouth.

The first chunk of steak catches in my throat. I tell myself to slow down, but I'm half-starved. I am always half-starved. I'm seventeen and living on fucking finger food, salad and potatoes for dinner. I tear into the meat, tear and chew and swallow, tear and chew and swallow, Jess knows where the croutons are in her boyfriend's fucking kitchen, tear and chew and swallow, meat and blood and salt, crouched behind the shed, hiding, panting, idiot tears mixing with the juices that drip from my chin. I forget and rub it all away, messy and stupid, the empty cuff of my shirt, panting, the last mouthful of meat gone. Just gone.

Fuck! I hate being wimpy. I hate being weak. I force myself to stop crying, just fucking stop. I smack myself in the head a couple times. Order myself to *smarten up!* Force myself to lie down and assume the position. I move around until it feels close to what I remember.

Tonight, the stars are pale weak things. And the trees are just trees, hanging along the back fence, blowing in the wind every once in a while. Summer instead of winter, grass instead of snow, cool on my neck and arms. Prickly. The pool pump kicks on in the shed. A whiff of chlorine. Some guy laughing one yard over. Nothing dangerous. Nothing special.

I lift my arm and the plaid cuff falls back. Even in the flickering light of the pool, it's ugly. My brutal souvenir. A useless, clubby stump, scarred and red and ugly. I hate the way the bones stick out at the wrist. Hate the snake of stitches. The pocket of empty space, the phantom fist of nothingness ghosting the hacked-off end. The place my hand should be, my fingers, fingernails. The scar by my thumb where I cut myself one time when I used an X-Acto knife to sharpen a pencil.

I stare at my stump and I tell myself that maybe I'm a better person now, more enlightened or whatever, less afraid. Mostly I feel like that. Maybe not after that fucking dinner, maybe not right now, but mostly I believe that what happened out here was some kind of trade-off. My right hand to know, to absolutely know, what love feels like. So when I'm sitting with Jess in the back seat of her boyfriend's car and she tells me I'm the most beautiful boy, I understand what she's really saying, I under—

A door bangs open. Bangs shut—Don's on the deck, squinting into the yard. I lower my arm and press my body deeper into the grass and will him not to see me. He clomps down the stairs, scoops a leaf out of the pool, slams the barbecue lid shut and, with a grunt, reaches for the black cover lying in a heap on the ground. We are ten feet apart, max. He freezes. Motionless, except for the drunken sway. When his eyes meet mine, he lets out a scream—jerks up and smacks his head on the barbecue, the dull ring of bone against metal.

Jesus H., he pants, grabbing at his skull. He takes a long, raspy breath. You scared the shit out of me. He swears a bit more, then rattles into the shed. I use the time to sit up. When he slides down the wall beside me, he's clutching a fresh bottle of wine. It's a screw-top. A twist of his wrist and he's taking his first glug and his second.

I hear it was cold as a witch's tit that night. He runs one foot over the flattened grass, the imprint I left on the lawn, a chalk outline in dented green.

Yeah, I say, it was cold.

Eli said it was fuckin' forty below.

Something like that.

Kids, he says. Stooopid. He catches my eye as he passes me the bottle. I do appreciate your parents not suing.

Guess they can only handle one lawsuit at a time. I take a swig.

Dry and tart, but still it's cold, white, not nearly as bad as the red. It would be okay with some sugar.

Partners. Pain in the ass. Unless it's family, forget it. Even then, I got no use for partners. If your father had of asked me, I'da told him as much.

Peter started the business.

Peter Fuckin' Conrad. Any arsehole can see the man's a greedy son of a bitch. Now Eli's going with his daughter. The man practically shits whenever she comes here. Thinks we're a bad influence. How ironic is that? Greedy prick with his long hippie hair and his big place on the river, the cottage up there on Yirkie. Don plucks the bottle from my hand. You ever go to their cottage?

Yup.

Is Yirkie weedy? I heard it's weedy.

No, Don, it's not weedy.

Jesus. He takes a long swig, stares out at the pool for a while. I stare along with him at the glowing blue. We're not cottage people, he says. Too many bugs. Still, he says, she seems like a nice kid. Kinda big, you know, those shoulders—Christ, she could play football—but pretty. Pretty hair. And nice. She seems like a nice kid.

She is.

Good. I'm glad. Glad for Eli. I mean, let's face it, his brother got Dorothy's looks, God bless her down there in Costa Rica lovin' up the pool boy. I mean, who'd blame her, right? Don's face crumples and his eyes get all watery, and I'm thinking, great, now he's going to cry, but then he turns and bangs me in the shoulder. And you, he says. You handsome son of a bitch. You've got good, good bone structure there. You've got a face. Too fuckin' skinny at the moment, like I said before, but you'll put on the weight once you've stopped growing. How tall's your old man?

I don't know. Six, six one.

You'll be taller, he says, like it's all decided. Tall is good for business. Handsome is good for business. Still, I've done okay. He leans in close, his face right in mine. I'm pretty sure he doesn't floss. I keep it simple, he says. My place in Costa Rica. My place here. Real estate. Rental properties. Cash flow. Unless you got some inside info, stay away from the fuckin' markets. Bay Street. Wall Street. Biggest cocksuckers of 'em all. Sucking up everyone else's cash, sucking it from the bottom to the top and producing fuck all. Fuck all! Don takes a long, quivery breath and a gulp of wine to keep him going. What Peter Arsehole is doing to your dad? Don sweeps the bottle in front of him—there's not enough left to spill out. Just knocking him out of the way, he says. Like those bastards on Wall Street. Sucking up your dad's share and knocking him out of the way. Same thing on a different scale. You get it?

Yeah. Listen, I've gotta go.

Sit, he says. Sit right there. Look. Pool's pretty at night. Lit up like that. I like a pool at night.

When I go to get up, Don grabs my arm.

It's okay what you're doing there, he says, hiding it in your sleeve like that, but shit, Finn, we all know the hand's gone. He tightens his grip on my arm. A couple inches up from the end. Just above the knobby wrist bones.

What about one of those fake hands? he says. I saw one on TV the other night. The thing was practically bionic. I'll get you one of those. As long as your folks don't sue, I'll pay for the thing. I turn and stare at the fence, but Don keeps talking to the back of my head. Because I'm gonna be honest here, Finn. That stump? It gives people the heebie-jeebies.

He's squeezing now, squeezing with his big beefy hand, his fat fingers, squeezing so it hurts. I don't want to find you out here again, he says, feeling sorry for yourself, fucking away your life. You figure out what you want and you go after it. Don't let anyone stop you. That's what I tell my boys.

He stares at the pool and my eyes follow. He's right, a pool lit up at night is nice.

Don finally lets go of my arm. What are there? he says. Like seven billion people on the planet?

It's, like, seven and a half, but I don't tell him that. I just keep staring at the flickering blue.

I read the eight richest guys in the world have more money than the poorest fifty percent. The poorest *three and a half billion*. And there's probably a couple more being born right now. Like right—he snaps his fingers—now. He laughs. The idea of child-birth seems to amuse him. The Costa Ricans I know are good people, he says. Hard working. Friendly. And I mean, I like money as much as the next guy but eight to three and a half billion? That, that's a disease.

He drains the last of the wine and tosses away the bottle. You've been a good friend to Eli, he says. He looks up to you. Always has.

Don.

Don't kid yourself. He does. Don's face gets all soft again. His hands dangle loose between his knees. You wanna know why Dorothy stayed down south? he says. Come on, take a guess.

The pool boy?

Ha! He clears his throat, gathers phlegm, spits onto the grass, just short of the empty wine bottle, in the place where I lay—living, dying, like every other human being trying to survive love on this planet. There is no fucking pool boy. She's just had it with the drinking.

MICHAEL RETRIEVES A grocery bag of beer from the river. He'd tethered it to a rock earlier, in hopes of cooling it down, although the bottles still feel lukewarm. Regardless, he and Dirk lie on the grassy bank, well up from the overpass, and quickly down one beer and then another. The day was hot; the night feels even hotter. And the kid? Took one, maybe two turns at bat. It was Michael who'd pounded ball after ball into the outfield. Dirk just kept on running, catching, sweeping the field until the duffle bag was bumpy with balls that he plowed straight back into the hopper. The Arm barely had to pause; the kid only stopped to wolf down a handful of nuts he pulled from a pocket of his giant shorts. Michael was slick with sweat when he finally called it quits. He's slick with sweat now. The tepid beer offers little relief. Still, coming here, smacking balls—after the encounter with Mia in the closet, he had to get out of the house.

"A swim would be sick," the kid says.

"Current's too strong. Water's too weedy."

"Fuckin' weeds. Like swimming in snakes." Lying in the grass beside Michael, an emerald-green bottle of Heineken floating on the flat of his belly, the boy who chased down all those balls without one word of complaint? He might not look it, but after a dozen nights together, Michael figures he's not so bad. He's just a kid—with a gutter mouth, a questionable lifestyle and a propensity for small acts of violence and vandalism. Still, just a regular kid, replete with healthy snacks.

Michael drains his beer. "I know a place we can swim." He barely even hesitates. "Close by. Unless you have to get home."

"I'm good," the kid says.

"Your parents won't be worried?" It's the first time Michael has inquired about a family, which he assumes is deeply fractured, if not totally absent given the way the boy appears red eyed from under the bridge every night regardless of what time Michael shows up.

"Away for the weekend. Some medical conference thing. Besides, they know I'm totally nocturnal." The kid sits up, takes a last pull of beer, then tosses the bottle toward the water. It lands soundlessly in the tall weeds that fringe the shore.

Christ, who does something like that? Michael has to fight back the urge to tell the kid to go pick it up.

The boy pulls his knees to his chest, rocks back then forward and springs onto his feet. "Let's do this thang," he says. "I'm fucking hot."

Michael slowly pushes himself up off the grass. He doesn't believe the medical conference bit, but like the beer bottle, the profanity, the dinging of balls off the Arm, he lets it slide.

THE KID FOLLOWS Michael down the laneway, a gentle S-curve of tarmac carved through a forest of birch. On either side, trees rise like pillared ghosts and the canopy of leaves blocks out any ambient light. He and the boy shuffle near-blind up the long driveway. Ahead, the house is also dark, unplugged, as Michael thought it would be, and the asphalt pad in front, big enough to park a party of cars, is empty. When he steps into the clearing, the motion light over the garage snaps on. Both he and the boy throw up an arm to shield their eyes, like soldiers saluting the ray. They stand frozen, waiting, their long shadows stretching back, bending up into the trees. The house, its wood stained a cheerless blue-grey, shows no sign of life.

Michael moves quickly to the side of the garage, grabs hold of the window ledge and, toes scrambling for purchase, clumsily chins himself up. The BMW is parked inside, but the Escalade that Peter and Helen always take to the lake is gone. Michael drops down, brushes flecks of paint from his fingers, then follows the path to the rear of the property.

A sloping flagstone walkway, interspersed by six-foot-long stone steps, each weighing over a ton—Michael knows, since he helped Peter manoeuvre them into place with a rented Bobcat a couple of years back—leads to the water. Four greying Muskoka chairs sit horseshoed on the dock that stretches like a long finger into the river, so wide and deep and languid here, it feels more lake than river.

"Sick set-up," the kid says. "Like a cottage in the city."

"Weeds get cut back at the beginning of the summer. So it's good to swim."

"Sweet." Without asking whose place it is or whether they have any right to be there—he either lacks curiosity or has learned to hold his questions—the boy jogs to the dock and starts stripping down. Beneath the basketball jersey and the circus-sized jean shorts, he is narrow chested, narrow hipped, rib-thin, hairless. Without his swaddling of hoodlum gear, he looks no more than fourteen or fifteen years old. Michael's stomach kicks, remembering the beers he handed over without a thought.

The kid leaves his boxers on, and for that Michael is thankful. Following suit, he leaves his own underwear on, a fitted pair of black Jockeys, and joins the kid, standing with his arms crossed at the edge of the dock.

On the water it feels cooler, and the urgency of a swim has left him. The baseball and the beer are no longer buoying him up, they're all after-effect now, leaving him feeling tired, paunchy, middle-aged. Michael dips his toe into the water. It's cold and the blackness is unwelcoming, but he'd feel like an idiot backing out now.

"You wanna go on three?"

They count down together, leaning toward the water, but at blast-off neither one jumps.

"Fuck this." The kid turns to Michael. Takes a couple steps back and settles into a wide-legged wrestling squat, his shoulders hunched, his arms ape-low and reaching forward.

"Gladiator," he says.

"What?"

"Gladiator." The kid springs at him, catching him solidly in the chest with his shoulder, his fingers jammed up and under one arm. With his other hand he reaches round and grabs the waistband of Michael's Jockeys. The boy uses his legs to lift the man—stunned at the skin-to-skin contact, the intimacy of the embrace, how strong the kid is—and propels him to the edge of the dock. Michael is left hanging over the water, windmilling his arms, his body bowed backwards. If the kid gave him a nudge, he'd be gone. Instead Michael regains his balance, and a second later he has the kid, who is a good thirty, forty pounds lighter, in a headlock and is dragging him up the dock. It feels familiar, fun, he's done it a thousand times before, with Finn, with Frankie, battled them off the dock, squealing and laughing and begging for mercy. But this kid's scrappy, squirmy, all elbows and fists above the waist, all kicking feet below, he catches Michael hard in the back of the knee, collapsing his leg, and at the same moment wrenches free his head.

So the fight begins. Two Muskoka chairs are toppled, underwear is wedged up asses, both man and boy are scraped and clawed and panting by the time they fall. Head banging head, nose hitting brow bone, they sink in a tangle toward the mucky bottom, the fine hairs on their arms and legs, their chests and heads, aligned by the drag of the current.

I PRESS THE button for KHADIJAH. A second later the lock clicks and the buzzer buzzes. I jog up the stairs to the second floor. The door to her apartment's cracked open and the music's loud, so I stick the bouquet behind my back and walk right in.

Jess?

Beyoncé fading out. Mel?

I turn the corner. She's tipped into the hall, her hair hanging down in a long black gleam. I don't stop moving.

Finn! Her mouth drops open. What are you—?

I walk her backwards into the bathroom. Just like she did to me.

Finn, she says, her hand planted in the middle of my chest, her eyes stretched wide.

What?

She's got on a tight black dress. Low in the back. I can see it in the mirror. There's a radio on the counter, a bunch of makeup, a glass with toothbrushes.

Your mom here?

No. And I'm going out.

I can smell her. Citrusy. Fresh out of the shower.

I brought you this. I step back and offer her the bouquet. It looks worse than it did outside. Battered, half-dead, all broken stems and limp petals. Only the daisies look like they might, possibly, survive.

Jess doesn't take the flowers. She picks up her phone instead. Texts. Mel's on her way over, she says.

Mel?

Melanie. From my nursing class.

I'll leave in a minute, I say, and sit down on the edge of the tub, let the rejected bouquet dangle between my knees while Jess unscrews a tube and brushes black stuff onto her lashes.

I guess it was Don's pep talk that made me come over. To, you know, go after what I want. But it's hard convincing someone they love you. And I used up all my moves backing her into the bathroom. I should have gone home. Should go home now. Make Greenland smaller and bluer. Flood the Nunavut coast.

I'm sorry things have been hard, I say, finally. Like, with your mom. That stuff you told me in the car. I don't say anything about the herd of Indonesian goats.

Jess pauses mid-stroke to flash me a look in the mirror. Don't worry about me, Finn, she says. Or my mother. We're doing just fine, thanks.

It's just . . . I tap the bouquet against the tub. I don't know what it is. Petals start falling onto the tile between my feet, so I stop abusing the flowers. Blue petals. Brown tile. Countertop, cupboard, floor—all brown, brown must have been on sale when they built the bathroom—and there's this weird knitted thing on the toilet seat.

My mom should come over. She'd have some ideas on how to fix it up.

You know, Jess says to the mirror, he'll kill you if he finds out.

Yeah? What about you? Will he kill you, too, Jess? Is Eric the killing kind?

She gets busy screwing the brush back into the tube, extra hard. Then throws it into the sink where it clatters around a bit.

Why does it feel like we've been almost fighting all day?

I don't know, she says. It's stupid. I'm sorry. I'm just . . . I don't know . . . It's not easy being around you and them at the same time.

It sucks, I say, and hold up the flowers again. But I risked my life ripping these out of that garden on the corner. You know the one with the huge tree? The guy with that gold James Bond car?

How brave of you, she says. Randolph. He stopped me one day and asked if I knew anyone who might want to clean his house. She reaches out to stroke a daisy petal. Then rewards me by taking my stolen bouquet.

Careful, I tell her. Those big blue ones. I had to pull out, like, ten before I got one that didn't fall apart.

Hydrangeas, she says, and puts her foot on my knee. Like the rest of her, it is practically perfect. I wrap my fingers around her ankle so we are well attached.

Thank you. She rocks my leg with her foot. The flowers are beautiful.

Liar. I rest my forehead on her knee and stare down at the ugly tile. Are you going to marry him? I mean, seriously. Are you going to marry that fucking guy?

Shhh . . . She runs her fingers through my hair, lightly, her nails tingling my scalp. Like she used to when I was a kid. Shhh . . . I moan a bit and she laughs. Slips her hand onto my neck. Her fingertips creep under my shirt. You remember the night I came to the hospital?

I nod, and her leg wobbles. Like I could forget.

You told me when you were lying in Eli's backyard, it felt like it does when you're with me. The bouquet spins in her hand, one way, then the other. What did you mean?

How to explain it? How to explain it without breaking every rule? I close my eyes. The bathroom disappears. Walls have never been invented. Time is just a word in a book. I hold on to her. She holds on to me. We exist at the pressure points, a jangle of warm pieces. Hand neck forehead, ankle foot knee.

This, I tell her. It felt like this feels now.

"EPIC," DIRK SAYS, swiping at a slug of blood trailing from one nostril. He and Michael are collapsed in the two high-back Muskoka chairs that remained upright after the battle.

Michael can't miss the dark pinpricks tracking up the boy's skinny thigh.

The boy sees him staring. "Diabetes," he says. "Insulin."

"Right," Michael says. As if.

He takes a minute to catch his breath, then goes to the shed at the bottom of the property, and reaches under the eave for the key. He returns with two blue-and-white-striped towels, one of which he tosses at the kid.

The boy presses an end to his nose and, sinking back into the chair, drapes the towel lengthwise over his chest and knees. "This your ex's place?"

"No," Michael says. "I'm married."

"Yeah?" The kid pulls the towel back and examines the bloodstain. "So your wife," he says, "she hot or what?"

Michael snorts. Before he untied her tonight, he took her fancy blouse out of the garbage bag and hung it back up on her side of the closet. Told her he loved her. That he wanted her to love him back.

On the walk to the diamond—along Springfield, down Main,

up River Road, past the Kellys', across the soccer pitches—the chicken wire protecting the turtle nest now reinforced by a thicket of sawed-off hockey sticks, the old Asian guys still fishing near the public dock—Michael came to a decision: until she initiates contact, he's not going to touch her. He told her what he wants. If she wants David, fuck it, she can have him.

And yet. In college, before they'd started dating, tired from a long night of studying, she'd nodded off on his couch. He'd covered her with a blanket—stiff and smelling of closet—and carefully slipped a pillow under her head. He'd felt so undone just seeing her there, such an ordinary, extraordinary thing, that girl from class, Mia, asleep on his couch. Twenty-five years on, everything and nothing has really changed.

"You got any kids?"

Michael fixes his eyes on the boy. His hair hanging in wet strings, blood wet and slippery on his upper lip. "This is a friend's place," he says. "A former friend. A former business associate. Guy ripped me off."

"Big time?"

"Let's just say I probably paid for half of this place."

"*Sucks.*"

"Tell me about it."

The kid leans over and fist-bumps Michael's knee. "We should trash it," he says. "Like just rip it the fuck apart."

"Nah, I'm keeping things legal. Although the lawyer's getting expensive."

The kid grins, showing off his perfect teeth. "Don't tell me you haven't thought about it. Or like, kicking the total shit out of him or something."

"Nope."

"*Come on.* Tell me you haven't had any revenge fantasies. It's not normal. The cumwad totally screwed you over."

Michael *has* considered bashing Peter's mailbox in or slamming his head into his office wall, but other than that he's kept things locked down pretty tight. Tonight, however, sitting relaxed on the cumwad's dock, post-Gladiator wrestle, it doesn't take Michael long to come up with a few ideas. He could pay some guys—the kid's friends under the bridge—to tag the entire house, on a weekend when the family's out of town. Every window, every door, every square inch of siding obliterated by big cartoon cocks, a two-storey-high *fuck you* in giant, bulbous letters gracing the river view.

"If I knew I wouldn't get caught," he says, "I'd burn his boat. Twenty-five-foot bowrider, two-hundred-horse Evinrude. Bought it the first time he ripped me off."

The kid gives Michael's knee another bump. "We should do it, Cheerio. Burn the boat. Like a symbol. Or a message or whatever."

"It's at his cottage. On Big Yirkie."

The kid throws his head back and practically howls. "Big Yirkie? Are you fucking kidding me? That's hilarious. Dawg, we've so got to do this. You've got a car, right? We could go up—"

"Dirk, I'm not going to burn my partner's boat."

"*Former* partner's boat. Former Big Yirkie Douchebag's boat."

Michael laughs. "I did break a picture of it in his office."

"Oh fuck, I bet he's cutting you a big cheque right now. Pussy old man." He runs a hand under his nose, and his fingers come away clean. "Listen," he says, throwing the towel onto the dock, "I'm gonna head. I need something to eat."

The kid actually belts his shorts around his thighs before climbing into his bulky red high-tops. Back to hoodlum, he grabs the arms of the chair he'd been sitting in, lifts it awkwardly over his head and, with a grunt, tosses it into the river. The chair throws up a splash, then disappears silently into the water. Michael imagines its slow sinking, the wooden chair floating through liquid space, hitting the bottom, wedging deep in the muck, its exposed parts—half the slatted back, one sturdy arm, a leg—in a silty sway of chopped-back weeds.

The kid kicks in another chair, already tipped over near the edge of the dock. It disappears as fast as the first, burbling up a stream of bubbles that blister the water's dark surface.

He turns with a grin. "Your half of the furniture."

Michael knows he shouldn't, but what the hell. He raises a hand to meet Dirk's high-five as the kid shuffles past.

The 25th

All the legal documents, the financial statements, the photocopied emails are sorted into piles on the barnboard table in Mia's studio. Her camera bag is pushed to one end of the table, and the studio is swampy from the laundromat. Still, she's happier working here without Michael ambling around in the background, doing what-ever it is he does all day. A knock on the door, and Mia swivels round. She's expecting David—one more reason she chose not to work at home—but it's Frankie, her hair beaded with rain.

"Hey," she says timidly. "Is it all right if I come in?"

"Sure. Of course." She turns the document she was reading face down on the table: the legal action against the girl's father, thirty-nine pages—without appendixes—detailing his sins against them.

"How are you?" Mia climbs off her stool and steers Frankie away from the table. Her scent is light and clean, rain and some floral body spray. No adult ever smelled so good.

"You know," Frankie says. "Okay."

"You want to sit down?"

"No. Sure. No. I just came by to see if you had any of those pictures you took."

"Which ones?"

"After I got my nose pierced. Remember?"

"Yes. Right. Of course."

Frankie considers the settee for several seconds before plunking herself down. The front windows are grey with drizzle. Umbrellas bob on the sidewalk below, like gophers you smack down with a cushioned carnival hammer.

"It's my dad's birthday on Monday." Her knees jut coltishly above the crushed-velvet seat. She has one of those bodies; she'll lose her waist when she's older, but her legs will always stay slim. "I wanted to give him one."

"I haven't really done anything photography-wise since Finn's accident." Which is technically true; she'd had those pictures of Frankie printed before Finn lost his hand. "You want something to drink? Some water? Lemonade?"

"I just had a latte at Starbucks." Frankie sinks back into the couch. "I don't know what else to give him," she says sulkily. "He buys whatever he wants."

Yeah, with our money. Mia's spent most of the morning reviewing exactly when and how this girl's father diverted close to a million and a half dollars into Peter Corp. "Sorry," she says, "I don't have them." A small injury in the arena of the large.

"I guess I'll get him some golf balls or something lame like that." While Frankie studies her phone, Mia fiddles with the snaps on her camera bag.

"I could look at them early next week and have them ready, oh, I don't know, a few days after that."

"The party's tomorrow." Frankie turns her head to the window. "You guys used to come over for cake."

"We did."

"I don't really understand what's going on but I don't see why you just can't sit down and figure it out. I mean, whatever happened, whatever you think my dad did, like, it can't be that bad."

"It's complicated, Frankie."

"You guys are friends." The girl tugs her thin cotton sleeves over her hands. "Or you used to be, anyway."

"I know. I'm sorry. We'll work it out." Mia flips open the camera bag. Nestled between foam dividers, her Canon EOS and two spare lenses, a zoom and a fixed-length lens, which she uses for portraits. She bought it a few years back, without really much consideration, even though it cost more than she spends in a month now—excluding legal bills, which David has kindly agreed to defer until the case is settled.

The camera body, reassuringly solid, seductively smooth, feels good in her hand: her fingers curl around the barrel; the butt of her palm takes the weight. She twists the lens into place. A click signals the perfect coupling of metal ring to metal ring, optics to mechanics, the mated technologies of captured time and converging light. She flips the power switch with her thumb.

"Miracle of miracles." The screen grids with lines and numbers. "The battery's not dead." As she peers through the viewfinder, her blood slows. One deep breath and she settles the bull's eye on Frankie. Every freckle sharp on the bridge of her nose, every droplet of rain a mirrored bead in her hair. "Can I take a few shots? I've got a wedding coming up."

"You doing that again?"

"Just as a favour for one of Finn's nurses." She lowers the camera. "May I? It'll help me get back in the groove."

Frankie shrugs, a weighty shifting of her shoulders. She, of the selfie generation, pulls a tube from her pocket and glosses her lips while Mia adjusts the settings. Having her picture taken, especially by Mia, especially in the studio she's been coming to for years, is no big deal.

"Ugh," she says, checking herself out on her phone. "My hair doesn't even get wet right. I'm like a dog."

"You look great."

"Yeah, right," she says.

Mia stands a few yards back from the couch and starts shooting. Frankie doesn't smile or turn her way. She knows Mia wants her as natural as possible, so the first shots are of a slightly hostile adolescent, gloomily contemplating the rain.

"So, I'm going out with Eli now," she says.

"I heard. Can you lift your chin a bit? Sorry. There. How's that going?"

"Okay. I'm taller than him. And he's a bit of a fuckboi."

"A *what*?"

"I guess you'd say player. But it's more than that. You know, the internet. He's trying to get over it."

"I hope so." God. Mia checks her display: too dark. She changes the white balance to the overcast preset, and lowers the shutter speed. Eli's always been spoiled and can be pretty pouty when he doesn't get his way, but Mia can't imagine him as some sort of player.

Frankie turns to the camera, her eyes shining. "I miss you guys."

"We miss you, too." It feels right as she says it, although Mia has not been aware of missing anyone over the last few months. Even when she's alone, she feels surrounded, hemmed in by other people's needs. The shutter clicks harsh into the room.

Frankie holds up her hand. "Can you please stop?"

Mia keeps on. She knows without looking at the screen that it's a beautiful shot, or the next one will be, half of Frankie's face hidden by the palm of her hand, her hair sparking with rain, one eye bright with tears, a bruise of blurred velvet for a backdrop.

"Mia, stop!"

She lets her camera drop.

Frankie stands up. "I've gotta go," she says, staring down at the couch, searching the cushions for something she hasn't lost.

"Frankie." She's mad. At her. Mia doesn't think that's ever happened before. "Listen, I'm sorry."

"I *told* you to stop."

"It was a great shot."

"I don't care. I was trying to talk to you. I was upset. I don't want a picture of me looking upset."

Mia places a hand on her arm. "I'm sorry." There's a quivery vibe in the room. "I just remembered something. Wait here, okay?"

Frankie nods, biting the gloss off her lips.

It only takes Mia a second to find it. In the back room, in the file cabinet, in the A–E drawer. Frankie Conrad. Contact sheets chronicling her life. Eight-by-tens. If Mia flicker-fanned the edges, she could watch Frankie grow up all over again. Mia slips a photograph into a manila envelope and hands it to her at the door.

Frankie immediately slips it out. It's the one Michael saw the night they came to the studio to put up the sign. Finn was still in the hospital. Michael hadn't wanted her to give it to the girl. And today, she hadn't wanted to give it to her either.

"Oh wow," Frankie says, unable to hold back a smile. "I remember this. Your story. About your first boyfriend." Her eyes flicker from the photograph to Mia and back again. "You always make me look so good. My shoulders don't even look big."

"That's you, Frankie. You are that beautiful."

She blushes and reaches into her pocket. "My mom gave me money."

At the mention of Helen, her money, Mia suffers a prideful pang. "It's on me." She taps the photograph with her nail. "I liked your nose ring. It gave you a little *je ne sais quoi*."

"My parents hated it." Mia knew they would, their little princess, their only child. Like Mia, Helen couldn't have any more kids, another thing they had in common. "They thought it made me look tough."

"No, it didn't. You should push back a little." A hard edge settles inside Mia, the thrill of a little harmless revenge, nudging a child to defy parents who have hurt her own family, but she also loves this girl and believes Frankie has always been too compliant. "You should put it back in."

Frankie frowns. "I should."

"Definitely," Mia says. "I'd do it."

MIA STARES DOWN into David's kitchen drawer. "You have one knife."

"Yeah," he says, "but it's sharp." He sidles up beside her and considers the nearly empty cutlery tray. "What can I say? My needs are few."

Unlike every other man on the planet, Mia thinks as David hip-checks the drawer closed. "I do have wine. Or beer."

"Wine sounds good." Mia opens a glossy overhead cupboard. Inside, a kid's blue plastic cup and one white dinner plate. "How long did you say you've lived here?"

"Three months, twelve days, ten hours. Or something like that." David is lit by the open panelled-to-match-the-cupboards Miele fridge that Mia knows cost three times as much as she paid for her first car, a six-year-old Volkswagen Golf with a hole in the dash for a radio the previous owner had been too cheap to put in. "So . . . no wine," he says.

Feeling vaguely depressed, Mia shuts the cupboard; it swings with a precision soundlessness on perfectly engineered hinges. She retrieves a Moleskine notebook and churns through her purse for a pen. She's going to need a list.

"Guinness?" David says.

"Too heavy."

"That's all I've got."

"I'll just have some water."

"Come on. It's Friday night," he says and keeps rooting through the fridge.

Except for the electronic equipment on the living room

floor—TV, stereo, a clutter of speakers, a gaming console—and the mattress in the bedroom, the condo is empty. David has already given Mia the tour. He was obviously eager for her approval, and it was easy to be enthusiastic; the place is gorgeous, generously sized for a new build. Big, bright rooms, oiled hardwood, even the bathrooms are elegant: walk-in glass showers roomy enough for two, heated floors and teak vanities with thick composite countertops complete with sculpted-in sinks. It's obvious to Mia that David paid for the premium upgrades, and then some.

"You'll want some stools," she says, sizing up the kitchen island. "You need two feet per stool minimum, so you're not banging elbows. You could squeeze five in, but four would be better."

"Four's good," David says, returning with a can of Guinness, two glasses and an octagonal mustard-yellow tin scripted with Chinese characters. Mia jots in her notebook, putting the stools at the top of the first blank page, followed by the words *counter-height, rotating, industrial.* The living room has to be fifteen by twenty-five at least. She sketches an appropriately sized rectangle onto a fresh page and starts chunking in furniture: a large sectional, two accent chairs, Barcelona chairs or something more comfortable. A coffee table, at least one side table, a carpet, a couple of lamps, roller blinds for all—

When Mia looks up from her notebook, the tin is open and David is rolling a joint.

"Seriously?" she says.

"When was the last time you had a bit of fun?"

She studies the tiny furniture arranged on her page. Retraces the L of the sofa, darkening each line, pressing the tip of her pen hard into the paper, all those things she'll have to buy. She doesn't even like shopping. Hates it, in fact.

Beside her, David sweeps a scatter of twiggy stems and crispy flakes into his cupped palm, brushes them into the tin and snaps the lid back on.

"I haven't smoked in forever," she tells him.

"Like riding a bike." He slides open the balcony door. Behind him, a washed-pink sky spired by office towers all set to glitter as daylight sinks to dusk.

"David?" Mia says, and he pauses, one foot already out the door. "I'll have a puff but we're not going to, you know—fool around."

He laughs. "Of course we're not. I was just practising with you last week."

"Practising?"

"Recruiting. For the Cult of David. It's this new ladies' club I'm starting."

"Ha ha."

"Would you relax? I know you're a happily married woman," he says and steps outside.

She sets down her Moleskine. Clicks shut her pen. *A happily married woman.* She cuts away a word so the rest fit more easily into her head. *A married woman.* As she crosses the empty living room and follows David onto the balcony, she cuts away another.

MY MOM'S OUT, like usual, and it's already nine o'clock. So basically I don't have a choice. I find my dad's keys in the pocket of his jeans. Back the Jeep out of the driveway, nervous as shit the entire time. I only have my beginner's, so technically I can't be on the road without a fully licensed driver. And I've only got the one hand. And my dad has a temper. And generally doesn't like people stealing his car.

It's just a swing around the block to Jess's but I'm kind of all over the place. My stump's stumping around the centre console, nowhere to hide unless I stick it between my legs. Which I try. But it looks weird and while I'm staring down at my crotch, I almost run over a squirrel.

I have to reach across the steering wheel to put the Jeep into park. And of course, Jess looks gorgeous when she climbs in.

Hey Finn, she says, real casually.

Hey. I go over the curb backing out of her driveway, one wheel dropping down hard.

Should I grab a helmet? She reaches for the safety strap dangling from the roof. Joking, she says, looking over at me. Let's just have fun tonight, all right? Like we agreed.

Last night. In the bathroom. We decided to go out. Like a normal couple, doing a normal thing.

At the end of the street I signal the turn, it's easy, the lever's on the left side. The wipers would be trickier, but it's nice out, no chance of rain, the low sun turning the horizon a glowy pink. You have a good time last night with your friend?

Hard not to with Mel.

I wait for more but Jess just slides down her window and plugs her phone into the Aux cable. Starts bopping along to Beyoncé, getting all in formation in the passenger seat, with her hair blowing in the breeze, and for a second I think maybe this will work, maybe we can do this, be happy out in the world. But once we're out of Old Aberdeen, heading across town where I don't know the streets, it starts to feel more like a driving lesson than a date.

Jess turns down the radio. You're a little close, she says. Move into the left lane earlier. Give yourself time to turn. Yellow light, she says, yellow light!

My meat-stump practically resting in her lap.

In the lobby of Silver City, posters rectangled by Hollywood lights: a couple action movies, a few romantic comedies. Love complications, ha ha. I stare over at the concession line, a long straggle of able-bodied strangers. The smell of fake butter, the gross-out picture of the nachos and cheese.

In the arcade, some guy with a shaved head and a sleeve of tattoos is hammering the punching ball, taking two, three steps back and then coming at it, hitting it with everything he's got. There's a leathery smack and a loud metallic thump when the ball hits the back of the machine. Red lights flash, a siren wails. Smack, slam, wail. On the poster next to me, Margot Robbie looks cutely annoyed. Smack, slam, wail. I picture Eric punching me in the head.

What do you want to see? Jess is standing in front of a scruffy Chris Pratt.

You pick.

We should both pick.

I don't care. Smack, slam, wail. *Fuck.* I look at the guy hammering the ball, the lights around the movie posters, all those strangers, and all of a sudden what happens in my bedroom feels easy. This, *this* should be easy—going on a date, seeing a movie—but it's actually the other way around.

You okay?

Yeah. Even though I'm taller, she looks older than me. I feel people staring, at the skinny amputee, so fucking out of his league. They're not staring, but I feel them staring. Some guy bumps into me, I bump into Margot Robbie, her perky tits right in my face.

You want to go? Jess looks confused. She takes my hand. Crappy movies, she says when we're outside. She weaves us toward the car, the relief of fresh air and a dark parking lot and her hand in mine. We can watch them later on Netflix, she says, as if that's even possible. Or do ourselves a favour and skip them altogether.

"GOOD?" DAVID ASKS. He and Mia sit leaning up against the window, gazing across the condo into the far-away kitchen.

"I feel like I'm on vacation," Mia says. She now adores the emptiness of the space in front of her. The fact that there is nothing of consequence in the room. In the cupboards. A person can live pretty well on cold cereal and takeout. She'll buy David a bowl and a spoon and the place will be perfect.

He reaches over and for a second Mia thinks he's going to try to hold her hand, but instead he slides back the sleeve of her blouse. "An injury," he says. They both consider the band of reddened skin braceleting her wrist. "I saw it on the balcony."

Mia casually shakes down her sleeve. "It's nothing," she says, although she can't believe Michael's belt left that mark. Taking a page from Finn, she wore a long-sleeved blouse to cover it, yet feels remarkably unfazed by David's discovery. So what if she likes her husband to tie her up and get a little dominant? So what if she likes her sex a little loveless?

"Looks like rope burn."

"It's not."

"Ligature marks," David insists.

"Nope."

"Naughty girl," he says.

"No." Mia shakes her head. "Not me."

David bumps his shoulder against hers. "Fifty shades of Mia."

She just laughs and rests her head on the glass. She's tried not to think too much about what happened in the closet. Michael's pleas to kiss her. The way he so gently made her come. And afterwards, god . . . the blouse, his request to be loved.

"I want a pool table," David says suddenly, "and some really nice patio furniture. And one of those big stainless steel heaters so I can sit out there in the fall." He bangs her shoulder again. "We should go shopping," he says.

"*Now?*"

"Sure, why not?"

"We can't drive anywhere."

"There are places in the Market. We can walk."

"But . . . but I'm stoned." She wants to stretch out on the floor. Stare at the ceiling. Maybe eat something at some point.

"We won't be operating any heavy equipment." David works his wallet from his back pocket, slides a credit card from a tight leather slot and centres it neatly between Mia's bare feet. The rectangle of plastic shines up at her, a powerful pop of silver against the matte of the hardwood floor: the embedded chip, the raised numbers, the ghostly hologram, and AMANDA BARNARD embossed along the bottom.

"Wow," she says. "It's so beautiful. We should put it in a time capsule for future generations to worship."

David rolls up off the floor. "I changed her PIN. Sixty-eight forty-four. There's a thirty-five-thousand-dollar limit."

Mia peers up at him. Like the credit card in front of her, his hair shines silver in the light. "Take it," he says. He has full lips, a lovely shaped mouth. "For the condo."

He holds out his hand. It is close to her face, her shoulder. His nails are well tended. He wears no wedding band. "Come on," he says. "I don't want to start the cult on an old mattress on the floor."

JESS DRIVES. I sit in the passenger seat, feeling about two years old. If she's heading home, she's taking the long way. At one point she stops and goes into a little corner store and comes out with a bag she throws in the back. She checks her map app, takes a couple backstreets, then heads east out Number 7, a two-lane highway that connects the city to a strip of shitty little towns. Carp, Renfrew, Cobden. I played hockey in every one—their cold country arenas. Farmers screaming at farm kids, city parents screaming at city kids. At least that much is the same.

We drive along in silence for a while, fields of something on both sides of the car. Corn or wheat or canola, maybe—if I were older, smarter, knew anything about anything, I could probably identify the crop.

Want to know where we're going? Jess finally asks. We pass a junkyard, stacks of dead cars, then a gas station, two dark pumps out front, an old boat tipped against the side wall of the concrete-block garage.

The dump?

She ducks and points through the windshield. The movies, she says.

And right away I see it. Up ahead, on the left-hand side, the place my parents used to take us. The lights aren't working, burned out probably, or smashed out, but the sign's gotta be thirty feet high. Even with just the moon hitting it, I can make out the choppy edge of the feathers, the fade of the red and green and black paint, the letters totem-poled up the centre.

The parking lot of the old Thunderbird Drive-In is buckled and cracked and half covered over by weeds. Jess slows right down, but the car still bounces as we pull in. The chain-link gates are padlocked shut, and the ticket booths are falling down, but the board fence is still standing, and beyond the fence, I can see the top of the screen.

Outside the car, the shrill of crickets and the far-off smell of manure.

It doesn't take long to find a way in. Around the corner of the fence, a couple of boards lie in the long grass, rusty nails pointing skyward.

Do-do, do-do. Jess does the *Jaws* theme as we squeeze through the gap.

We set up thirty feet back from the screen. Jess has the bag from the store and I've got the blanket from the trunk. I stretch it out, a scrap of red wool in a coral of weeds and gravel. The windows of the concession stand are all busted. And the boxy metal speakers have been ripped out, but some of the posts are still upright, tipped and tilted and wires dangling, like a string of telephone poles in the wake of a natural disaster.

I lie down, and Jess sits cross-legged beside me. She opens a bag of Smartfood and starts dropping popcorn into my mouth.

Good? she says.

I lick the cheese off my lips and nod.

I also got root beer. A&W. Your favourite. We should drink it while it's cold.

I prop myself up on one elbow, take the bottle she pulls from the bag. I use my back teeth to unscrew it, spit the cap onto the gravel beside us, don't care about litter or being polite.

Sorry things aren't easy, she says.

I just shrug, like it's no big deal.

But you're strong, Finn.

You're strong.

No. She shakes her head. Not like you. I know how to take care of myself, but that's a different kind of thing. She stares at the screen, her legs tucked up, her arms hugging her knees. Remember the dancing drinks? she says. The wiener jumping into the bun?

I raise one eyebrow and take another chug, the root beer fizzing in my mouth.

What do you want to watch? The screen, greyed and warped from the weather, is cut by dark cracks where the plywood is coming apart.

Whatever.

She gives me a smile, so beautiful and simple out here where it's just the two of us alone. Something old, she says. Something we've already seen.

An Inconvenient Truth? Beasts of the Southern Wild?

Seriously, Finn.

I Am Legend, I say. Just a man and his dog playing in a boarded-up drive-in to a doomed audience of two.

No, Jess says. No end-of-humanity stuff. *Extremely Loud and Incredibly Close?*

Extremely Long and Incredibly Sad? Yeah, no thanks.

She stuffs more popcorn into my mouth. I hold her wrist and lick the powdered cheese off the tips of her fingers. It's the first time all night that I don't feel like a little kid she's being paid to look after.

Big Fish, she says, her thumb still in my mouth.

Okay. I let go. *Big Fish.*

The field of daffodils.

The old man dying.

God, Finn, do you have to be so grim?

She lies down and puts her head on my stomach so our bodies make a T. She's on my good side. I slip my arm across her. Just under her neck. She takes my hand so it's not on her boob. Her head rising and falling in time with my breath, our fingers laced. She turns so I can see her face, in the hollow below my ribs. The poet in the woods, she says.

The Asian circus twins.

Oh, you remember the twins. Every man's fantasy.

They were conjoined if you remember. Siamese.

Right, she says. Not so sexy.

I like it that she gets jealous of girls in a movie we watched when I was a kid. Somehow it makes things feel more normal.

But they weren't really, she says. Not in the end.

Nothing was the same in the end.

She squeezes my hand. Here's where I'd tell her. Here's where she'd tell me right back.

The big fish trapped in the pool, I say.

The house, she says, with the white picket fence.

MICHAEL AND THE BOY lean against the chain link of the backstop, arms propped on their knees. They're all set up, but tonight they pause to enjoy the view: the Arm parked smack-centre in the dirt, where the pitching mound would be if the diamond had one.

Michael reaches for the joint the kid offers, enjoying the sweet, earthy pong that clouds over him. The kid watches him take a pull.

"You know, everyone thinks you're a faggot."

"*What?*" he says through clenched teeth, barely managing to hold in the smoke.

"That you're going to ass-rape me one night or something."

Michael hacks up his lungful.

"Oh, yeah," the boy says. "You bet."

The kid's nodding as he pinches the spliff from Michael and takes a drag, perfectly relaxed. "Me? I think if you're going to do it, you're being pretty fucking patient." Michael laughs, barely. "But Rae Chan says we're all rapists. Just depends on the circumstances."

"*Christ.* Who is this guy?"

"Have to spread our seed, man. Survival of the fittest. Rae Chan's always talking about shit like that. Or how, like, you put a guy in uniform and he can just do it on command. Yes sir! Just following orders, ma'am! I mean, like, what's with that?"

"War. Men are killing each other. Lines are not clearly drawn."

"Yeah, but just physically, how does he do it?"

"I guess he'd get shot if he didn't."

"So he's scared into it?"

Michael doesn't want to think about it. Or himself in this context. Or Finn. Or any man he knows. Even the kid beside him. And he really doesn't have to: it's unlikely any of them will ever go to war. What Michael can't hold at a comfortable distance is the memory of pinning Mia against the bathroom wall, the fight that ended in a hard fuck on the floor. Or tying her up in the closet. He'd been gentle with her afterwards, but still, it wasn't what she wanted. Is it in him, declawed, half listening to reason, but there in his bones and blood?

"Maybe it's learned." He's talking to himself as much as he is to the boy. A we-don't-shape-the-culture-the-culture-shapes-us kind of thing. Michael read that once, in one of Mia's magazines.

"Learned?" The boy looks at him like he's crazy. "If that's learned, our dicks should get an A-plus." Dirk takes another drag—it's always a two-for-one thing with him—before passing the joint back to Michael. "But dudes whacking to hardcore? I don't care what anyone says, it's fucking shit up."

Jesus.

Dirk frowns out at the ball diamond, the grassy field. "Okay, like, say four bitches walk down that path, right now. Hot or just average or whatever. It's not like I'm going to get all rapey, but I'm like yes, yes, no, yes. It's that fucking simple. Couldn't shut it off if I tried." The boy's watching him again, but Michael keeps his head down, intrigued by the earth between his feet. "Don't pretend you don't know what I'm talking about," the kid says. "I mean I know you're old and everything, but you're still the same species. It's not like all of a sudden you're more evolved or something."

"All I can tell you"—Michael wants to end this discussion and move on to a lighter topic, or better yet, just get high and play some ball—"is I love my wife."

"Yeah. That's why you're here every night." The kid drops his head back against the chain link. From where he's sitting Michael can't see the river, but he can feel it, a fast, dark slide in the night. Thirty seconds pass before the boy blows out a long drift of smoke. "You wanna know what I think?"

"Jesus, Dirk, I like it better when you don't think so much."

"I think you come here every night because you're lonely and you're fucked up and you like baseball."

Michael snorts. His brain is losing cohesion, but still, the words feel close. Lately, he's not sure about much. He doesn't know if he's becoming more or less himself, if the guy lounging in the dirt of an old ball diamond beside a stranger kid with a bottomless supply of weed is a man he can trust. He knows he's fine with not working. And that when he's out here he doesn't feel stupid or angry or incompetent or betrayed. He feels good. Happy. He's happy now.

"What about you?" he asks. "Why do you show up?"

"My dad doesn't get me," the boy says. "At home—I drive him crazy." He stares out at the diamond and his mouth curls into a slow grin. "And it's a pretty sweet set-up, right?"

The brown earth, the heft of the pitching machine, the spread of the outfield, the belt of long grasses, and beyond it, the orange city glow hangs over the graffiti bridge like a primordial sunset. "Pretty fucking sweet," Michael says.

"My mom told me there used to be an access road but once that school there was built, the field got cut off."

"Makes sense," Michael says gruffly. Even stoned, mention of parents, a mother he talks to about this field, and no doubt about the lonely, fucked-up guy he plays ball with and, now, smokes weed with every night makes Michael a little queasy. The slippery stew of his brain starts sliding toward paranoid.

"Big Bill Brown wanted to come one night, but Rae Chan wouldn't let him."

"Big what?" Michael says. "Ray who?"

The kid laughs. Michael laughs, he doesn't really know who or what they're talking about, what came before that, the kid's mom, the school, that private school, Fern something. Ferncliff? Ferndale? He and Mia talked about sending Finn there, but then something happened . . . Does the kid actually have parents? . . . He met a teacher from Fern-fuck-whatever one night at some open house, blond, hot, she took off her sweater, her hair went up with it, out back by the barbecue, she had this little white tank top on and these huge tits—talk about instinct—he's pretty sure every guy waiting in line for a burger wanted to fuck her.

"Rae Chan." The kid thumps Michael's shoulder. "King of Paint."

"Is he the Asian one?"

"No, man. There is no Asian one. You're such a fucking lightweight."

The boy's up, halfway to the Arm when he stops and turns around. "You wanna know the real reason I come here every night, Cheerio?"

Michael stares at the kid, the amusing murk of him in the infield. "Tell me, Dirko."

"I wanna see what happens."

"What, what happens?"

"Whether you kill the guy or not. You know. Big Yirkie. You can't fool me. I've seen the way you slam those balls. I know what you're thinking."

"Dirk," Michael says, laughing. "I'm not going to kill anyone."

"We'll see," the boy says lightly, and Michael imagines him grinning, his sloppy stoner smile, but he can't really see his face given the darkness and the distance between them.

"You're an asshole, Dirk."

"That's what they all say." He gives the on-off button a smack.

When the first ball hits the fencing, Michael feels it in every part of his back. The impact thrums through the chain link, making the metal bite like a low-voltage shock. He leans forward, away from the fence, as the next ball sails toward the plate, but bat raised, the kid takes a smooth, easy swing, and the ball sails high and long.

He drives ball after ball into the outfield. Even when he misses, which isn't often, he misses well. Michael watches—stunned, mesmerized, stoned—and as he does, the ball becomes irrelevant.

The kid now holds the bat perfect off his shoulder. His stance is rooted but light, he steps strong into the pitch, rotating hips, torso, shoulders, sighting ball onto bat, which he propels forward with surety and speed. At the point of contact, his arms are fully extended, his upper body pulled round by the centrifugal force of himself. The boy finishes each swing one-handed, with the bat high and behind, his chest and hips open to the field, his eyes locked on the ball as it flies into the night sky's mandarin glow.

"God," Michael says. "You really are better when you're stoned."

"I'm ADHD. Weed steadies me. Weed," the kid says, "is my best friend."

The boy knocks another one into the night. The next ball rolls down the feed, drops, there's a click, but no forward snap, no rocketing round of white, no shiver of freshly sprung metal.

"I'll go." Michael pushes himself up and strides toward the machine, still marvelling at the kid's swing. He's never offered a word of direction, not a single piece of advi—

The arm snaps forward, bullets a fifty-mile-an-hour hardball into Michael's chest.

He drops to his knees like a man shot, mouth fish-holed, lungs locked. The arm ticks smoothly back, reloads and nightmares a ball at his head.

The kid hoots as he jogs past. Michael lies sideways in the dirt, the wind from the ball that would have killed him still shivering the delicate bones of his ear. Another couple fly past before the boy finally shuts the machine off.

"That was fucking funny," the kid says, standing over Michael, slapping his leg with a glove that once belonged to Finn. "You should have seen your face when that second ball dropped. I thought your eyes were going to pop out of your fucking head."

As the boy laughs over him, pitiless and mocking, Michael's mind pumps blood and fury and thoughts of killing other men.

WILL YOU DO something for me? Jess says.

Of course.

Sit up, she says. And I do. She kneels in front of me, slips both hands inside my shirt, onto my shoulders, and waits for me to look at her. Take it off, she says.

I stare up at the sky. Like I did that night. Instead of sliding trees and tripping stars, the big Thunderbird sign blocks out the moon.

Come on, she says. I'm almost a nurse. Please, Finn, she says. Take off your shirt.

I lean back. Anchor my good hand to the blanket. Work my stump into the gravel beneath the wool.

Jess slides my shirt down my arms, so the sleeves are bunched around my wrists, all ready to disappear.

Why are you doing this?

I just think we have to, I don't know, face up to things.

We?

Yeah, we.

I shake off one sleeve, set my good hand in hers. She kisses each of my fingers, five little pops starbursting in my chest. She returns my hand to me. Show me, she says.

Fuck, Jess.

You know we have to stop.

No. No, we don't.

This can't be my life.

Why?

I can't keep coming over. I'm coming over almost every night.

Why?

I don't know. But Eric's going to find out.

So? So let him.

She shakes her head. Finn . . . You're seventeen. I'm almost twenty-three. We have to be practical. We have to be realistic.

Realistic? You want realistic? I lift my stump from the ground. A net of severed nerve endings fires into nowhere, into nothing, electric and confused, always electric and confused. I lean forward. The puddled sleeve of my shirt falls away, that armour of plaid cotton, I move my right arm forward, it is lighter than my left, missing the weight of my hand, there has not been one minute since it happened that I am not aware that it is gone. The hand I used to touch her with. Everywhere, touch her. I don't give a shit about pens or forks or hockey sticks. I don't give a fuck about cutting up meat. This girl. *This girl.*

I place my stump in her hands. The bones of my wrist sticking out a bit on each side. The fleshy ridge of Frankenstein stitches just starting to turn white. If I drew on a pair of eyes, it could star in a Tim Burton movie. My heart could play the drums.

I want you to break up with him. I blurt it out. Even to me it sounds crazy. I want you to go out with me.

Finn, she says. We can't even go to the movies.

I love you, okay? Does that even matter at all?

She closes her eyes, a long blink. When she opens them again, it's like we're a million miles apart. Eric's coming home tomorrow, she says, and sets my stump on the ground.

I sacrificed for you, Jess. I fucking sacrificed.

No, she says, you didn't. You got wasted and passed out in the snow.

THE PROBLEM WITH making plans when you're high: by the time David and Mia walk to the Market, the trendy part of downtown, all the stores are closed. After some haphazard window-shopping—he picks out a king-size bed, she a $13,000 couch—David buys them dinner. Grilled sausages from a street vendor followed by a Smoke's poutine, eaten in the company of rowdy, alcohol-lit boys.

Mia calls home just after eleven, but no one picks up. Her text to Finn goes unanswered. She has no idea where he is or who he's with. Michael either for that matter, although she guesses he's probably playing ball with that kid in the clown shorts. She tells herself that they're okay, that tomorrow she'll make a big breakfast and get everyone sitting at the table together instead of standing at odd angles at the kitchen counter eating toast off of mismatched plates.

She and David end up riding along the canal on sturdy community-share bikes, something she's wanted to do since the city installed them last summer. A well-treed greenbelt separates the canal from Queen Elizabeth Drive and the rest of downtown: low, tightly packed urban neighbourhoods backdropped by city skyline, a glitter of high-rise condos and glassy office towers in the distance. On the bike path, warm air sweeps Mia's skin, soft along her arms, her shoulders, her neck. She skims along the band of twinkly water, beneath gracious branches, red oak, honey locust, cherry. Every push of the pedals raises a chant inside her—summer, summer, summer—like a blessing after winter's bitter choke.

"If you don't stop smiling," David says, coming alongside her, "you're going to swallow a bug."

They reach the Canal Bridge, a perfect arc of light, the water below doubling the beauty. Up and over and they're rolling down Main Street, its bohemian stretch, people streaming both ways across the bridge to enjoy their neighbouring territories. They pass the laundromat, Mia's studio above it, the House of Targ, a newish hipster place specializing in pinball and perogies. The Wild Oat—good coffee, healthy vegetarian food, and Kettleman's, its patio loud with kids. Closer to home, the Belmont, Von's, 4th Avenue Wine Bar, some of the fancier restaurants. The Wag, a posh café for dogs—it says so right there on their sign. The Italian deli. The French Baker. The billboard that advertised beach vacations this winter—a bikinied girl stretched in front of a blue sea—now flaunts air conditioners: a bikinied girl—the same one?—in mittens and a pompom hat bent over a streamered unit, butt a perfect peach, golden hair blowing in the breeze, nipples hardened by Freon and a one-word tagline, *HOT*. Mia has no idea how the billboard, an abomination in Old Aberdeen, hasn't been outlawed.

They swing off Main, onto one of the leafy avenues. There they have the night to themselves. David and Mia could be riding through an abandoned movie set, their tires humming the soundtrack. She lazy-loops her bicycle around puddles of street-light, rides straight and fast through the shadowy bands in between. They cruise the empty streets, glide past the silent houses. Mia risks a trip down Springfield, to marvel at Randolph's tree. She glides to a stop under its majestic canopy. It would take a quartet to hug the trunk. An Olympian to scale its branches. A magician to map its root system, stretching two hundred years into the earth, connecting to every other tree on the block. Sharing nutrients! Sharing sap! A community of trees—like friends—nur-turing each other!

She tells all this to David. He convinces her not to lie down under the big maple. He convinces her to get back on her bike and keep riding, away from the tree, which *is* great, past her own house, silent and empty like all the others—she waves—everyone out doing their own thing. By the time they reach the river, Mia is in love with the night.

They drop their bikes and stroll onto the public dock where she met up with Helen—was it only yesterday? It feels like some other life. The dock's a little tippy, a reminder that they are floating. Tonight, there's a perfect breeze and no swans honking, the water a dark, sensual slide holding the light of a half moon and a few deter-mined stars. From the bank, a bullfrog croaks. Mia turns and—

David's yanking his shirt over his head. He tosses it onto the wooden decking. Kicks off his shoes and start unbuckling his belt.

"You're not," Mia says. Apparently, it's her turn to be the sensible one.

"They swim a mile up." His shorts drop down his legs. "And somehow that's okay."

At Peter and Helen's place, well upstream, they used to swim all the time. But several of the city's old sewers overflow into the river between here and their property. Runoffs only happen after a major

180

snowmelt or downpour, but this week it's rained a couple of times. Mia mentions this to David.

"People swim in the Ganges, for god's sakes," he says with a shrug. "I don't think the Aberdeen River's going to kill me." He's still wearing his boxers, a fitted pair of white Calvin Kleins.

She has never seen David with so little on. His shoulders are broader than they look in a suit, his belly firmer, his legs leaner, but overall her impression is one of reduction, that there is less of him than she expected. She wonders what it would be like to press a hand to his chest, feel his heart beat beneath her palm.

David dips in a toe. "Hmmm. Pretty good."

And what the hell, Mia bends and undoes her laces. In a mismatched bra and underwear, she stands beside David, her toes curled over the edge.

He grins as he looks her up and down. "Good thing you didn't get hit by a bus. 'Cause those are some pretty shabby duds."

Another night, she might have been embarrassed, but tonight she reaches round, unsnaps her bra and tosses it into the water.

"Nice." David laughs as she kicks off her underwear, a beige twist that flies into the sky before disappearing—no splash, no slow sinking away, just gone into the dark.

For a moment Mia remains perched on the edge of the dock. It is a strange and glorious sensation to be standing naked in the city, on the river, never mind who's watching. Her nipples harden at the brush of the wind. She is eager for the otherness of the water. She clasps her hands and pushes off. Airborne, she remembers what it is to feel lucky.

July

The 20th

Two gloves lie in the dirt beside Michael, and the field lights are on, but tonight, the kid hasn't materialized—so much for his perfect attendance record. It's hot, humid. Michael doesn't want to wrestle the Arm out of the shed alone—if such a thing's even possible. And after having had the machine pitching to him for the last month and a half, whacking at balls he tosses into the air holds zero appeal. He's thinking about going home when he sees someone cutting through the grass field. At first he thinks it's Dirk, but the figure's wrongly proportioned, somehow both bigger and smaller than the boy. Michael's not sure when he realizes it's Frankie.

She's almost at second base when, with a low bend of the wrist, she waves. Her short, flowery top creeps up from the waist of her jean shorts, leaving her midriff exposed. "I thought it was you over here," she says, plunking herself down a few feet to Michael's right.

None of Dirk's buddies were under the bridge when Michael passed by a half-hour ago, but they easily could have been. They could be there now. Michael's unsettled that Frankie's out this late by herself, and that she's showed up here, at his diamond in a short top, with a baseball in her hand.

"You shouldn't be out here alone," he says gruffly.

"Don't get all parenty on me, okay? It would have been easier to just walk by." Frankie slouches against the backstop, and the chain link shifts under Michael's back. "I have to get home, you know." She stretches her legs out in front of her, long, bare, her feet slipped into black Converse running shoes, a smaller version of a pair Finn's given up on account of the laces.

"People might think it looks bad," Michael says.

"What?"

"Older guy. Younger girl."

"What*ever*." Frankie teases the ball's curve of red stitching with her nail. "You're like my second dad. Or you used to be anyway."

"Yeah. Sorry about all of that."

Frankie shrugs. "My father can be a jerk. So can you."

They both stare pensively across the diamond. The dark dirt, the cockeyed lights, the green of the outfield, the graffiti bridge in the distance, the city sprawling out beyond that. With traffic died down on the overpass and the pitching machine safely in the shed—no thunk of balls on metal sleeve, no snap of arm no crack of bat no bluster of boy—the soft burble of the river and the high beat of crickets act as accompaniment to the night.

Being out here with Frankie isn't as uncomfortable as Michael might have imagined. She's so low-key, no matter the circumstances, no matter how blunt her truths—even tonight her mellowness mellows him out. He hasn't seen her in months, and he realizes he's happy to have her sitting beside him.

Michael nods at the ball she's worrying with her thumbnail. "Looking for a game?"

"No." She tells him she's been at the Kellys' and that she found the ball in the field.

"I just broke up with him," she says, when he asks why Eli didn't walk her home.

"Oh. Sorry." Michael doesn't know what else to say. Teenage romance isn't his forte.

"It's fine." Frankie sets down the ball, picks up the smaller glove and starts slapping it gently against her leg.

"Finn's," Michael says, clearing his throat roughly.

"You waiting for him?"

"No. He can't play anymore. Not with . . ."

She runs her fingers across the worn leather. "If you ask me, he just seems to be ignoring it."

"That's what I think." Finally, someone who agrees with him.

"He'll figure it out though. He's an amazing person."

She's right, of course, although it seems to be something Michael's forgotten. Finn's a great kid. And given time, he'll be all right. It's what Mia's been saying all along. Still, hearing it from Frankie makes it feel real somehow.

"You coming to his party tomorrow?"

"Yup." She rolls her eyes. "Eli, too."

Again, Michael doesn't know what to say about that. He picks up the ball and tosses it into the air a couple of times. "Whaddaya think?" He gives Frankie a grin.

"Do I have to get up?"

"You feeling lazy?"

"Always," she says, slipping her hand inside Finn's old glove.

They stand centre field, thirty feet apart. Michael pulls back, and in one continuous motion swings his arm forward, steps onto his front foot, snaps his wrist and launches the ball. There's a sharp thwack when it hits Frankie's glove—"Ow!"—and she jumps her hips sideways.

"God, Michael," she says, shaking out her arm. "Take it easy. We're just two people tossing around a ball."

When he throws a second time, he stays on both feet, puts little weight into the pitch. He throws to Frankie gently. And she's a good catch.

A good athlete. Back and forth, back and forth, a smooth rhythm of catch and toss.

"I like being outside at night," she tells him, after they've been throwing easy for a while.

"So do I," he says, relaxing into his next pitch, launching the ball with only the slightest arc.

"I'm a fan of weather," she says. "Pretty much every kind. Every season."

"You like spring?" Soggy, colourless lawns. Pitted wastelands of snirt on every corner.

"Uh-huh. I love the rain. Although my hair goes crazy."

"Summers are getting pretty hot."

"Yeah, but this?" She cactuses her arms and lifts her chin, as if offering her whole self to the night. "It's like the tropics."

"Fall?" Michael asks, and her arms drop back to her sides.

"Come *on*."

"Winter?" Men having heart attacks shovelling. Drunk, drugged boys losing unprotected body parts.

"Skiing? Snow? Snowflakes?"

When she throws to him, the ball lands light and square in his glove. "I don't think I really liked Eli that much," she tells him.

Michael tips the ball into his hand. "Sounds like a good reason to break up."

"Still," she says. "I feel bad about it."

"Not every relationship works out." This time Michael throws high, a pop fly, an arc of white hooping through the night sky, never losing the light. Frankie raises her arms, takes a couple steps back and brings the ball soft into Finn's old glove.

TWO A.M. Her window dark. Our backyards dark. The gap in the fence. The tree. Dark for something like twenty-five days, give or take a couple seconds.

I let the curtain drop. Tell myself to get up, get over it, get productive. Tell myself it was never real. I grab a marker and trace some shorelines on my map. Head for the islands, the atolls and the archipelagos, low-lying, so it makes sense I guess. Oahu, Maui, Lanai. Swallow the Big Island's beaches, although inland, I figure the mouth of the volcano stands tall. American Samoa. French Polynesia. The Galapagos, which kind of hurts. Drowning exotic, endangered species unafraid of mankind. I traverse the Panama Canal and start on the Saints—Saint Martin, Saint Lucia, Saint Kitts. Puerto Rico. The Dominican. Haiti. One good thing: I'm definitely getting steadier with the left hand. Cuba goes under without a wobble. And just south, the Isle of Youth.

The 21st

While David's earning his $360 dealing with Peter's lawyer, Mia's earning her seventy-five dollar hourly wage at the condo overseeing the arrival of his new king-sized bed. The deliverymen set up the frame and the black lacquer headboard, but it's Mia, in a short, swingy pear-printed dress, her loveliest bra, her laciest underwear, who wrestles on the bamboo sheets and smacks life into the vacuum-sealed pillows. It's Mia who lies down first.

In her opinion, the bed takes up too much of the room, but it's quickly apparent that David, who picked it out without her, has exquisite taste in mattresses. Lying alone in the almost empty room, unfurled on the new pillow-top, memory-foam, coil-springed marvel, Mia feels almost weightless; even her heaviest parts, head, hips, heels and elbows, seem to float in a trickery of perfect support and suspension. From a rooftop air conditioner storeys up, cool air breezes soundlessly into the room, wafting the hem of her dress. Mia closes her eyes against the sunlight streaming through the glass—they'd called for rain, but apparently not at the Soho—and tries but cannot remember ever being more comfortable in her life.

And then, of all things, she thinks about Helen. About calling her up just to talk. She'd tell her about getting high and skinny-dipping with David, how she's been kind of turned on ever since, and she'd let that conversation unfold, leaving out the part about him being their lawyer. She'd tell Helen how quiet Finn's been lately, how down, she'd say heartsick if there were a girl involved. She'd talk to her about love and worry, love and sex, sex and security, about wanting to wall up her heart and turn her back on it all. She'd tell her about the big breakfast she made last Sunday, how she hollered upstairs but neither Michael nor Finn had come down. How she finally left for her studio at one in the afternoon, the scrambled eggs and bacon cold on the table, the fresh-squeezed orange juice grown thick and warm.

And for every story of hers, every confidence, every concern, Helen would have one of her own. Mia closes her eyes and tries to imagine the stories she'd tell, just the two of them together, chatting on the bed.

"I NEED A THIRTY." Finn dangles a pair of jeans over the top of his changing room door. "Or maybe a twenty-nine."

A twenty-nine? Christ, the kid's almost six feet tall. Michael keeps quiet as he takes the jeans. They've finally made it to the mall, while Mia's getting things ready for the party. Today is about Finn and regardless of pant size, money spent or the pound of the rap music—*I'm going to slap the fucking freckles off your face, bitch,* those can't possibly be the lyrics, that can't possibly be what he's hearing—Michael's going to stay friendly. Maybe take him for a beer in Quebec when they finish up shopping.

Michael relays Finn's request to the guy working the change room—tattooed and pierced, earlobes stretched halfway to his shoulders, good luck getting a real job—and sits back down. From his place on the bench, Michael has a good view of Finn's cubicle. Beneath the door, a pair of well-worn flip-flops and beside them, his son's size eleven and a half feet. Impossible. Yesterday, the day he was born, they couldn't have been more than two inches long. His toes, pulpy and black in the hospital, are now a healthy-looking pink.

Michael remembers wrestling on miniature socks. The terror of nail trimmings. Strapping his son proudly onto his chest and stepping out into a city grown suddenly dangerous—the sidewalks too narrow, the traffic too fast, the bridge railings precariously low.

On Finn's first birthday—the rapture of ice cream and chubby fistfuls of chocolate cake. Sometime during his second loop round the sun, the boy learned a new trick. He'd lie on Michael's chest and rub his face into his father's. A little drooly, a little rough, nose pressed flat, skin pulling skin, Finn would be giggly and glassy eyed with the fun. Such unabashed intimacy seems as impossible as inch-long feet now holding up a fully grown man.

He used to wrestle with his own father after dinner when he was little. There was no face rubbing, and he doubts the man ever changed a diaper or read him a bedtime story, but he was expert at tussling with a kid on a living room floor. When Michael left for university his dad shook his hand, pressing a folded fifty into his palm. He can't remember if he wished him luck or gave him any advice at all. He sure didn't tell him he loved him, not then, not ever: spoken aloud, those words would have embarrassed them both.

"Yo, bro." The sales guy with the earlobes slaps two pairs of jeans onto the cubicle door. Finn's hand pops up—"Lit, dude, thanks"— and the pants disappear inside. One pair slaps to the floor. Finn kicks his way into the other pair, his shins nearly as skinny as Dirk's. He pulls up first one side and then the other, awkward, uneven. Above the knee, behind the door, Michael can only imagine the struggle continues.

What with all the late-night baseball, he's been sleeping better and the nightmares of finding Finn in the snow have tapered off. Still, that moment is never far away. Waiting on a heartbeat, the whole world dead in the pause.

Finn steps out of the change room. His hair needs a trim, but the jeans look good on him. They fit him well. He pushes them lower on his hips, then turns and checks out his ass in the mirror. "What do you think?"

"Good. You should get a couple pair." He doesn't ask the size; the boy has another sixty, seventy years to fatten up.

"Thanks, Dad," Finn says as Michael slides his credit card across the checkout counter.

"You're welcome. You needed them." He claps Finn on the shoulder. "Happy birthday," he says to his son, eighteen years old and standing tall beside him, strong beneath his hand.

MIA HAD PLANNED to have dinner on the deck, but rain drove the party inside. They ate their spaghetti and meatballs at the rosewood bar at the back of the living room, which always feels more festive than the kitchen; the candelabra flickering, the silk chandelier dimmed and doubled in the old French mirror, the walls glowing a rich ruby red, a rebuke to the sullen sky beyond the sliding doors.

Michael's at the bar, fiddling with the iPod, and Finn and Frankie are sprawled on one couch, Jess and Eli on the other, when Mia carries in the cake. She'd fallen asleep in David's bed, barely waking up in time to get back to make it. The cake's still warm, the icing a little drippy, but she doesn't think anyone will notice, and if they do, well, she came home feeling light and well rested, looking forward to the evening.

They sing a sweet, off-key "Happy Birthday" to Finn, even Eli, who's been quiet all night, with a prickly edge to his glumness. He's barely even looked at Frankie, so Mia guesses his mood probably has something to do with her. In fact, all the kids were quiet at first, but two bottles of Champagne later, the others have brightened considerably. Finn looks happier than she's seen him in weeks; Mia curses herself for forgetting to stop at the studio on her way home to grab her camera.

When he leans in to blow out the candles, his beauty seems risen to the surface. Golden with light, centring the room, he draws them all closer, both concentrates and expands them. Mia's chest fills with the heat of eighteen tiny flames, the small fire celebrating this boy's life. Behind her rain beats on the glass, far off, hushed, an inconsequential patter.

"Make a wish," Frankie says, and Finn's gaze drops. In the candlelight, the shadows of his eyelashes fall long on his cheeks. Mia can see the way Finn holds Michael, too. Standing at the bar, near reverent, iPod forgotten, he watches his son consider how to spend his annual fling with magic.

Finn smiles over at Eli, at Jess, and a second later extinguishes the candles with a single breath. A light smoke rises from the cake, Mia blinks, Finn fades back on the couch, and the moment is over, if it ever existed at all. She sets the cake on the bar and starts plucking out the candles. Maybe the Champagne's made her romantic. Or the heart-twisting truth that Finn almost didn't make it to this day added a strange, gilded gravitas to the ceremony. Or maybe it was real. Maybe what rose in Finn also rose in them, a shared space, a common light, so for an instant they knew life to be both beautiful and good.

Mia expects groans from the kids, but Finn and the girls, chatting brightly, smile as Billie Holiday spools velvet from the speakers. One leg tucked up on the couch, his knee bobbing lazily to the music, even Eli's gloom seems to have lifted. He looks relaxed and only slightly pensive as he listens to the others talk.

When Michael comes for the cake Mia's slicing, she points her chin at their son.

"We did that," she says. "We made that boy."

"Yes." Michael leans across the bar. "I remember." And he kisses her, a tender, lingering kiss. Even with her eyes closed, Mia can feel the kids watching, embarrassed perhaps, perhaps not. It doesn't matter. Like the rain, they are far off, beyond the smallest circle.

The kiss ends. Michael delivers the plates. Finn and Frankie, Eli and Jess, everyone quiet in the wind-down, bites of warm chocolate cake, the clink of forks on good china, and only Billie Holiday singing magic to them now.

WHEN I COME out of my bathroom from taking a leak, Jess is in my room, looking kind of nervous, standing close to the door. She's already wearing her raincoat, zipped up and everything, a belt at the waist so I know she's not planning on hanging around.

Your mother said no presents but I brought one anyway. She hands me a rectangular package wrapped in light blue paper, almost the same shade as the stuff she puts on her toenails. No card. No "Love Jess." I lean up against my desk, fumble off the wrapping. Inside, a new plaid shirt.

To add to the rotation, she says.

Thanks. I don't say anything about it being short-sleeved. Or ask if her boyfriend paid for it. I don't tell her how I had to look away when she walked into the living room. That I didn't know she was coming and when I saw her, my heart went so raw.

New jeans? she asks.

I nod.

Nice, she says, and shoves her hands in her pockets. How are you?

I blow air through my lips, raspberry the nothingness in front of me, hold on to the desk with the hand I have left. Great. Fantastic. You?

I'm okay, she says, and I stare at the floor for a while. The bottoms of her pants are rolled up. Her feet are bare and still perfect. Unlike my mother, she's definitely not into shoes.

It was getting complicated, Finn, she says, kind of aggressive.

It was always complicated, I say, kind of soft.

Her foot brushes the hardwood. It was getting too intense.

It was always intense.

Listen, she says. I've gotta go.

No you don't.

She turns her head toward the wall and starts biting her bottom lip. Her hair a black blaze against the white of her coat. The white curved into a dream. She frowns. Walks toward me, past me, toward my bed, squinting a bit, her head tilted to one side.

What happened to your map? For a better view, she steps right up onto my pillows. I fiddle with the little metal handle on the desk. Open and close the drawer. Open and close. An inch or two, the tiniest bit. She licks her thumb and wipes the marker off the Indian Ocean. Stares at her new blue fingerprint. Shit, Finn. She swishes her hair over her shoulder and frowns at me. Bali? she says. Did you do that on purpose? You know I have family there.

Warmest July on record, I tell her. There. Everywhere. Ever. Till August rolls around. She licks her thumb and wipes off more of the blue. It's a shitty way to grow up, I tell her. And nobody's doing fuck all about it.

She turns away from my altered map. Don't be so fragile. Go chain yourself to a pipeline or something if you're worried. If you get into trouble, you have parents who will bail you out. She climbs down off of my bed. Fierce as she stomps across the room in her fancy raincoat and her bare feet.

I don't want her to leave mad. Don't want her to leave at all.

Hey, I say, hey, wait. I have something for you. And I open the drawer all the way. Pretty sure it's just one more dumb, pathetic thing I'm about to do. My hand shakes a bit as I pick up the Ziploc. My name on the side in Sharpie ink. A black velvet ribbon snaked at the bottom—her own small sacrifice to love. Or being wasted. I toss her the bag, kind of clumsy with my left hand. And the Ziploc's light, the air all resistance, the bag fluttery and falling.

Jess bends her knees, catches it low, just before it hits the floor. She takes a look. Her eyes get bigger. Her mouth goes serious.

The doctor found it that night, I tell her. At the hospital. In my hand. I was holding it in that hand.

Jess kind of tips back against the door, slayed by the weight of a ribbon.

I want you to have it. To, you know, remember me by.

She slips the Ziploc into her pocket. Doesn't even look at it. I wait for her to say something, to do something, but she just stands there, looking upset.

Why'd you even come over?

Your mother invited me.

You could have made an excuse.

I've been to all your birthdays, she says, her hand a fist in her pocket, her knuckles making bumps in the white. I didn't want to miss it. Her voice is unsteady. Her eyes bright and twitchy. And even though she never does, for a second I think she's going to cry. Like, actually. But she rubs her nose with the back of her hand instead and sweeps her foot across the floor again.

How about a kiss? She glances up and I risk a wanting smile, feeling a little brave after her rare display of emotion. I mean, it is my birthday.

I already gave you a shirt.

Ten steps. Maybe eleven. Whatever. It feels like a long way to the door. Okay? She nods and I unloop her belt. Unzip her raincoat. Slip my arms around her, pull her close, my chest tight lit at the centre, a spark about to jump.

I gave you what I could, Finn, she says, her breath warm against my shirt. Sometimes it felt like I was all I had.

I reach up and wrap her hair around my wrist, a beautiful black rope. Rest my fingers on the back of her neck. When she tilts her face up, her head gets heavy in my hand.

I take what she gives me. I give what she takes.

The 22nd

Good morning. My dad gives my shoulder a shake. Hey, get up, he says, you have an appointment. And today I'm going with you.

Which isn't ideal.

An hour later we're in the waiting room at Glenmore. He was chill in the car, but now, talking to the receptionist, he's getting a bit loud. Running his hand through his hair, forehead to neck, right up and over the top.

The receptionist slides a sheet of paper out of her booth. He leans in and lowers his mouth to the hole in the glass. What's this?

I've already explained. It's the bill for the missed appointments. The receptionist looks kind of happy when she says it. Your son has missed all ten of his appointments. We sent you a letter. She pushes through another paper. And this is the bill for the prosthesis that was never returned. She gives him a smile, the first one since we got here.

My father doesn't even turn around. But it doesn't matter. His anger's pretty versatile, capable of radiating in all directions. Even behind him, on the far side of the room, I feel his wrath.

He ends up going to talk to the psychologist without me, some expensive doctor I've never even met. I pick up reading material. *War Amps Monthly.* Holy fuck. I put it back down.

On the wall across from me, posters to inspire. The Canadian sledge hockey team cheering, their stumpy sticks raised. The Blade Runner crossing the finish line wearing his cool sunglasses and his fancy bouncy legs—they should probably take that one down.

A woman huffs into the waiting room, carrying a little girl on her hip. Both her legs are this unnatural tan colour and completely smooth and shiny. Even her running shoes look fake, although they're not, they just look fake because they're stuck onto the end of her fake legs.

The mother gives me a kind smile and plunks her daughter down at this table where she starts playing with these amputee dolls. In my new world, such things exist. Amputee magazines. Legless children. Families of mutilated dolls, floppy, woolly-headed jobbies, like something a Mennonite might make. And get this, the dolls are fitted with tiny prosthetics, except for the mother doll who just has two little stumps sticking out from under her dress.

The woman sits down a couple chairs over. She looks nice. She might be someone to talk to. Someone who might convince my dad not to kill me. This is my first Glenmore visit, I could tell her. Okay, technically it's, like, my eleventh. First time actually *inside*. Eleventh time onsite. This is where I'd want her to nod, to encourage me to keep going. The other times my mom or dad just dropped me off, right, and I'd pretend to go in but I'd actually go hang out in that little clump of trees at the edge of the parking lot, you know, where the smokers go to smoke. Why didn't I come in? Well, it's complicated. You know, the whole amputee thing. It's hard for someone my age. I know it's not great for your daughter either, but seriously, they strapped a hook on me in the hospital. And you know I can't, like, walk around with a hook sticking off me. I can't touch a girl with a hook, not that it's a huge problem 'cause the girl broke up with me. Yeah, it sucks. And heartache? It's a real thing, like someone taking a two-by-four to your chest. Pain. Suffering. Those might be the words. But she kissed me last night for my birthday. A pity kiss. A goodbye kiss. A kiss kiss. I don't know. Like I said, it's complicated.

The girl playing with the dolls looks about three or four or five, sunny-blond ponytail, cute I guess, except for the legs. She's thumping one of them against the table, plastic hitting metal, a hard, hollow beat. I try not to notice when she rips the prosthetic limb off the boy doll, a little BE dude like myself. So now his little meat-stump is poking out of his little plaid shirt, and I can almost feel his pain when she wrenches his arm backwards, dislocating soft limb from soft socket. Her tongue pokes out the corner of her mouth as she wrestles a figure-eight-type harness onto his shoulders—I recognize all the gear from the hospital—jams his tiny test socket over his tiny residual limb, fits his freaky little plastic hand onto the socket, feeds the phony cable from the shoulder harness to the hand.

Then she rips it all off and starts again.

And I want to yell, like, hey, why don't you play with your own doll, the mother doll, her legs are right there under the table. I'm half out of my chair, all set to yank the boy doll out of her hand and give her shit hollow leg a kick so she stops banging the table, I'm all ready to drop onto my knees and grab the mother's missing parts and shove them into her hand so she'll leave the boy doll the fuck alone, and I'm actually standing over her, I actually have hold of the doll when someone says, Finn. Really loudly. Finn. I look over and see my dad with this half-stunned, half-angry look on his face. Can you come in here, please?

Everyone's staring at me. The girl on the floor and her mom in her chair and the receptionist in her window and my father in the doorway and I'm like Sure, absolutely, no problem, so no one knows that the amputee boy standing in the middle of the room was about to yank an amputee doll away from a little amputee girl because that's just fucking nuts, you know? Like there's no explaining that to anyone. I mean, something like that? Something you can't even explain to yourself?

MIA POINTS TO the far end of the closet and David pulls the measuring tape to the wall. "Higher," she says, doing her best to ignore the ties dangling from the hanger behind him. "There. Just under the rod."

David's closet is bigger, wider—she just measured it—a wider stretch from bar to bar. Dimmable recessed lights strip the ceiling, Berber carpet cushions the floor—easier on the knees than hardwood. Michael's knees. David's knees. Her knees. My god, she has to stop thinking like this.

She thinks maybe the pot kicked something loose inside her. Or diving naked off the dock, the feeling of levity she'd had in the air, or, or . . . she doesn't know. She hasn't had sex in a while. Last night at Finn's birthday, when Michael leaned across the bar, she'd been ready for that kiss. But when she went upstairs later, in her swingy dress and her sexy underwear, he'd been snoring, his iPad fallen flat on his chest. And, well, here she is now, in another man's walk-in closet.

Thus far, the day hasn't been wonderful. On the way over, she'd stopped at Wild Oat, the vegetarian café near her studio. Treated herself to a coffee and a sandwich, thirteen dollars in total including tax and tip. But she'd forgotten to transfer money from the credit line into chequing, and when she tried to pay, her debit card was declined. Loath to use her Visa in case it too was rejected, she'd scrambled toonies and loonies together, while outside on Main Street a bylaw officer slapped a ninety-dollar parking ticket under her wiper.

Mia snaps the tape into its housing and scribbles the measurements into her Moleskine. They're doing built-ins in the closet. David's new king-sized bed takes up so much of the master, other than bedside tables and perhaps one comfortable chair, Mia doesn't want anything else cluttering up the room. Definitely no dressers.

"Do you need me to stick around?"

"No," Mia says, "of course not." She has a key to the condo, she can lock up . . . it's just she thought they might have a drink after she finished figuring out the closet. Grab some dinner. Get high. See what happens. It's Friday night, after all, and even though she should probably get home—she's shooting that freebie wedding tomorrow—she's in no rush.

Since arriving at the condo, Michael's phoned her twice. She let the calls go to voicemail. The one text she'd read in the lobby was enough: an incoherent rant about Finn's appointments at Glenmore, what she knows about his missing hand. What *doesn't* she know about Finn's missing hand? She looked after it for months. Wound Care 101. And the nurse, Cathy, was right. It got easier but it was never easy. Mia turned off her cell; whatever it's about, this latest crisis can wait.

David bends and retrieves a loosely coiled mat from the corner.

"Yoga?" she says.

"Hot yoga."

"Oh," Mia says, "the unpleasant kind." She begins fingering one of his ties, a rise in her chest, well aware of what she's about to do. Flirt, with a handsome single man, not thirty steps from his very comfortable bed. "I had fun last week. With you." Her eyes flicker to his. "Biking. At the river."

"I can't believe I never swam in it before. And you and that tree!" He laughs. "Once you ditched the ratty underwear, well, who knew my designer was such a hottie?" Grinning, David clutches the yoga mat to his chest. "Except for the old-lady bush."

"*What?*" Mia practically doubles over. "What did you say?"

"The old-lady bush. No offence, but these days girls are keeping things a little trimmer down there."

Mia whips her notebook at him. He bounces it away with his spongey mat and ducks out of the closet. He's lucky she wasn't holding the tape measure. She would have dinged it off his forehead.

"I've gotta go," he yells. "There's a razor in the bathroom. It's a straightedge, so be careful."

"Fuck off, David."

"I am. Right now. Fucking off. And congratulations. Peter's agreed to mediation. Date's set for September."

THE RAZOR IS in the top drawer of the vanity, next to a shaving brush and a crumpled tube of toothpaste. She flicks her wrist and the blade swings smooth out of the handle. She lifts her arm and presses the four-inch gleam of silver against her throat. Considers herself in the mirror. Maybe, she thinks. If she were a different sort of person.

She sets the razor on the vanity and lifts the front of her dress. Black silky underwear stretches low across her hips, all pubic hair hidden away by lace. She's been wearing pretty underthings all week. David shamed her into it, so he's part of the reason, but not all of it. Yesterday when she took delivery of his new bed, she'd put on her loveliest bra and panties knowing he wouldn't be around. Even just now in the closet, she had no real expectation he'd lift her dress. She's never cheated on Michael, and is pretty sure she's not about to start now.

So what's she doing in this sexy underwear? She isn't sure. All she knows is she likes the way it makes her feel: alive to sex, the possibility of sex, the way it brings sex closer. She can't believe all this yearning and confusion is about David. That he would have such power. Most of the time she likes the condo better when he's not in it.

Mia pulls her dress over her head. Tosses her bra onto the toilet. Wriggles out of her underwear. She picks up the razor and considers herself again, the inverted triangle of hair pointing like a furred arrow between her legs. When she stood naked on the dock, he'd been critiquing her. Even as she dove, joy-filled, into the water, what he saw was her old-lady bush. And what else? Her thickening thighs? The droop of her tits? The soft crinkle of her belly skin?

She should have masturbated in his bed, been the first to moan at his altar. She should have taken his credit card on a shopping spree, bought herself some shoes, a plane ticket to Paris. Instead, she ordered him a $13,000 couch. Digging through her wallet for change to pay for a fucking sandwich, that shiny rectangle of plastic looked mighty tempting.

Elbows jutting, Mia sweeps up her hair. The razor rests cool against the back of her neck. Her breasts rise. Her stomach stretches smooth. In the mirror, her areolas are plummy red, although still lighter than they were when she breastfed Finn.

Is she beautiful? What does it even mean? What does it even matter? She is forty-seven years old. She will be fifty-seven, sixty-seven, seventy-seven, if she's lucky she will be eighty-seven years old. What will they make of her then? She is dying flesh and brittling bone like every other person on the planet. She is a mother, a wife, a woman, an old woman with an old-woman bush.

She pitches the razor onto the vanity. It skids across the countertop and clatters into the sink. Chin lifted, she gazes at herself in the mirror. Fuck you, she thinks. She needs to find some women friends.

"SO, YOU KNEW about the prosthesis?"

Perched on the edge of their bed, Mia brings one knee to her chest, wraps her arms around her leg and starts undoing the long satin lace on her sandal. "Yes. I knew."

Michael paces in front of her, striding the length of the bed. "For how long?"

"Dr. Sullivan told me." Mia stops fiddling with the ribbon that wraps up onto her ankle. "When Finn was in the hospital."

Michael staggers to a halt. Seasons have changed, the planet has tipped closer to the goddamn sun, Mia's known about the missing prosthesis for—what?—five months and never said a word to him. And neither has Finn.

In the car on the way home from Glenmore, Michael hadn't raised his voice or confronted Finn in any way. He'd even been civil with the psychologist, a pink-haired twit without the brains to pick up a phone and call the parents of a freshly amputated kid who'd been AWOL since day one. But now, in his own bedroom, alone with his wife, he wants to let loose a swampy scream. *Five months!* The trip to the mall, the kiss at the bar, their entire marriage, all of it, everything feels like a betrayal. He wants to kick a hole through the roof, send shingles flying, tarry black rectangles that warn the neighbours: things are not right with the Slates.

"Finn said it was taken from his room," Mia says, switching legs to undo her other sandal. Michael watches the silky black lace slither loose from her ankle. David's no doubt seen those fucking shoes. "I thought it would turn up."

"Yeah? Well, it hasn't. Jesus Christ, Mia, what else haven't you told me?"

"Can you please stop yelling at me?"

"I'm not yelling." But he is. He knows he is. Christ, maybe Dirk's right. Maybe he is going to kill someone. He forces himself to slow down, to breathe.

"It was a hook, by the way," Mia says, kicking off her sandals.

"What?"

"The prosthesis the surgeon gave him. It was a hook. Like, you know, Captain Hook. At least that's how Finn described it."

Michael falters, tripped up by the image of a gleaming metal hook where his son's hand should be, his skin, his bones, his flesh and his blood. "That doctor was a fucking idiot."

"No, Michael, he wasn't. He just made a mistake."

"Why are you defending him?"

"Why are you attacking him?"

Michael reels again. His brain's a scramble—*Christ!* what are they even fighting about? Their son. He loves their son. He wants to protect him. Wants him to have the best chance at life. Why is that so hard to understand?

"Have you seen him? The kid is skin and bones. And today? He was fighting with some girl over a doll."

"*What?*"

"In the waiting room. At Glenmore. He was trying to rip this doll out of her hands." Mia gives him an incredulous frown. "I told you he was messed up. I told you we had to get involved."

She stands up, grabs her sandals by the laces and throws them into the closet. "Why don't you just go and talk to him. I'm sure he's as upset as you are."

Just go and talk to him. She makes it sound so simple.

Michael sits down on the bed.

It should be simple. Finn *is* upset. In the psychologist's office, he hadn't said a word. Looked like he was going to cry on the way home in the car.

Michael leans forward, elbows on knees, and grabs at his hair. Just go talk to him. And say what? That he doesn't give a shit about the bill—they'll figure out the money—but he is pissed off about the lying?

He tries to picture himself in Finn's room, maybe sitting on the end of his bed. Saying, saying—that what's most upsetting, Finn, is you've been going through some big stuff, and it's obviously been a lot to handle. Your mom and I are sorry we couldn't help you more. But you are the strongest person I know and you will make it through. No problem. I believe that with all my heart. Your mom and I will always be here for you. No matter what. You should never be afraid to talk to us. We're not perfect, but we love you.

It should be so simple. I love you. Michael exhales the breath he's been holding.

"Hey." Mia sits down beside him and, slinging an arm over him, drapes herself over his back. "It's going to be okay." He sniffs, twitches, lets go of his fistfuls of hair. "I'll go talk to him," she says, her chin digging into his shoulder. "You already kept it together in the car."

SORRY IF YOU heard that.

My mom's in my doorway looking really tired, like it's a ton of work to stand up. Even her weird bangs are crooked. I probably look just as bad, what with the meat-stump exposed. It's hot in my room, so I discarded the plaid. I think about sticking it under my pillow, but that feels like a lot of work.

Sorry about Glenmore, I say. I thought we had insurance.

We do. But you have to show up for the appointments. Or cancel ahead of time.

Sorry.

Sorry I've been such a shitty mother lately.

Sorry I've been a shitty son.

You haven't.

Neither have you. Although I guess she sort of has. Like, I told her not to worry about me but I never said anything about never being around. Or getting rid of everything in the house. The other day I opened the closet and there was, like, one towel on the shelf.

You know you can talk to me about anything. Or your dad.

I know.

She pushes her hair around a bit. Stares at the map over my bed. I just lie there waiting for her to notice, but of course she doesn't.

You know Cathy, the nurse who looked after you? I'm shooting her wedding tomorrow.

Yeah? I say, sounding as numb as possible.

Do you ever think about the hospital? What you told me about your hand being somewhere beautiful. About understanding things you hadn't before.

No.

Never?

No. Me, in the hospital. Ha. All pumped up on love and morphine. I don't say any of this out loud.

You want to get out of here? Go for a bike ride or something? Get some dinner downtown?

Dad ordered pizza.

Oh. Okay. She tries to smile, but it only makes things worse. She walks out of my room. I watch her heading up the hall. I hate her for a second because her feet are bare.

I didn't rip the doll out of her hands. It just comes out. I surprise even myself. My mom stops, turns partway around. It's just, it's . . . she was *mistreating* it.

And that bothered you? she asks.

Yeah, I say. It bothered me.

She comes back. Of course she comes back. Move over, she says. When she lies down beside me, my body tips toward hers. She lets out an epic sigh, then nudges my hand. It's possible—she's lying on my good side.

She hooks my baby finger with hers and gives it a squeeze. Shitty day, she says.

Shitty, shitty day.

The 23rd

I've managed to avoid my dad since the Glenmore debacle yesterday morning, but when I push through the swinging door, he's there, loading dishes into the dishwasher.

Hey.

Hey. He clatters in a handful of utensils, plunks in a couple of plates. Still lots of stuff on the counter. Apparently my parents were too busy arguing about me last night to clean up.

I grab a box of Vector from the cupboard and start making myself some dinner.

You just getting up? He's trying to sound friendly, but there's an edge to his voice.

No, I say. It's, like, six o'clock. I've been up for a while. A brittle tinkle when the flakes hit the bowl and me praying he doesn't ask about the fucking doll. Where's Mom?

Shooting a wedding. For that nurse. From the hospital. My dad swings the dishwasher closed. He splashes a pot into the sink and takes a scratchy cloth to it while I glug milk into my bowl.

I yank open the utensil drawer. No spoons, I tell my father. He jerks his chin at the dishwasher, sets the pot in the drying rack. I pull a dirty one out of the basket, some damp crustiness caked in the hollow. When I try to hand it to him, he steps away from the sink.

Go ahead, he says.

Like it's a big deal to wash a spoon.

I don't say anything. Just shove my hand into the soapy water and work the crap off with my thumb. My dad watches me, leaning back against the counter, trying hard to look relaxed. I keep a tight grip on the handle and my face completely neutral and just, you know, wash the spoon.

You miss playing hockey? he says.

I guess. It's summer, but yeah. I rub the spoon on the leg of my jeans. When I try to step around him, he blocks my way.

Why don't you do the rest of the dishes? That used to be your job.

I survey what's left. A pot, a bunch of rice stuck on the bottom. Doable, if I jam it up against the side. But the wine glass . . . that's risky.

My cereal will get soggy, I tell him.

It shouldn't take very long, he says.

Then you do it. I go to push past him but he places a hand flat on my chest. Light. Barely there. Like a force field barely there, a threat no one's talking about.

It's your job, he says, picking up the wine glass and holding it out. Just like I did with the spoon. Long, skinny stem. Shivery thin glass, the kind that sings when you flick it.

I'll do it after I eat.

Why don't you do it now?

We're eye to eye, my father and I, and I'm hanging in there, I'm not flinching. I downshift my energy, use calmness to brace myself against him. His anger, tamped down but ready to flare since that lady handed him the bill at Glenmore. Ready to flare since the day he was born. And his stubbornness. I see it in his eyes. There's no way he's backing down. He's got a dirty wine glass, and he's going to teach me a lesson. Thinks this is going to get me to slap on a hook.

He drops the glass into the water. A soft bump when it hits the bottom, a bump that sounds like an opening bell, I guess to him anyway, because all of a sudden he grabs my wrist and shoves my good hand into the water.

I tip my head away from him, but he's really close, his breath right in my face. He throws in a cloth. It brushes my fingers, like rough seaweed, before it settles onto the glass.

You can wash it, right? Or do you need another hand? It would probably be easier with two. And he grabs hold of my other arm and plunges it into the sink. Harder than he needs to because I'm not resisting. My stump slams into the bottom. The wine glass sideslips away, rolled by the violent current.

He's got me pinned. My plaid sleeves drawing water. His shoulder hard against mine.

You want me to get mad? I say. You want me to get mad like you?

I'm not mad. I just want you to do your job.

I stare into the sink, at my forearms bisected by a cloud cover of soap, and I think about how it felt when Jess and I were holding on to each other in her bathroom. How it felt when I was freezing to death in Eli's backyard. How everything melted into this big, borderless love-fest, and how right now it's like that, but flipped upside down. Everything getting smaller, not bigger. Not melting together but splitting apart. My father's hands might be clamped on my wrists, but we are completely separate, coiled tight around our own centres.

He starts fumbling in the water, chasing the soap-slick glass, trying to catch it between my stump and my fist. I let him drag my arms through the water, like two dead things. When he traps the cloth I pull back. An inch. A half an inch. One little jerk, a burst of resistance, of fighting back, of fuck you, of protecting myself from him.

I don't know how Mom even loves you, I say, and just like that, he lets go of my arms.

THE PLATES HAVE been cleared and the country club waitstaff slip between the ballroom tables, white thermoses in hand, whispers of *tea or coffee*. This is the part of the job that Mia dreads most. The dinner. The speeches. The wait for the bride and groom's first dance. She's seated with a mishmash of twenty-something singles who have been polite yet distant, more interested in checking each other out and defaulting to their phones when nothing comes of their lazy flirting than chatting with the middle-aged wedding photographer. Which actually suits Mia just fine. Her mind drifted through most of the dinner, and she'd slipped out for a quick walk when the best man got up to talk.

Now a stocky woman readily identifiable as the groom's mother clunks her way to the lectern. Not once did she smile in the family photos Mia took outside the church. And no mention was made of her husband; Mia presumes the groom's father is either dead or as good as. Despite the purple chiffon dress and floss of teased-up hair, the woman's bowed legs and thick body make it easier to picture her trundling toward a thatched cottage with a faggot of sticks lashed to her back than stepping up to the microphone at the Aberdeen Golf and Country Club. Mia fiddles with the sugar packet on the edge of her saucer. The last speaker. Please, God, let her be the last.

"Good ev-en-ing," the woman says. Her accent is thick, although Mia can't quite place it. Hungarian? Serbian? Czech? She can't recall the groom's last name either, although she'd seen it that morning, scrolled atop the invitation. "Thank you for coming to Toma and Cathy's wedding," the woman says, holding tight to the lectern. "And thank you, Cindy and William, for all your hard work." She nods solemnly at the bride's parents, then turning, finds her son at the head table: a barrel-chested young man with a dark line of facial hair delineating his jawline from the swell of his neck. Mia knows the thought is cruel, but unlike Cathy, who is a good forty pounds slimmer than she was the last time Mia saw her, he doesn't look like he starved himself for the big day. He smiles awkwardly at his mother, apparently, like Mia, willing this moment to be over.

"Toma," the woman says, gravely, "I'm supposed to say a few things about you." The woman is speaking with great care but her English is not good. Mia massages the sugar packet between her fingers. Inside the paper sleeve, granules shift and grind.

"Being a single mom," the woman says. "And a foreign mom? Is not so easy. In this world? In this country? Raising a strong boy? A tender boy? Is a tough job."

Tender. Mia hadn't expected that word. Finn is a tender boy. Vulnerable, Michael would say.

"Every day," the woman continues, "since Toma's a little boy I must teach him. Don't hurt the frogs. Help Mommy in the garden, help in the kitchen. Look after your things. Be nice to the old people. Be nice to the girls. They are strong," she says, "stronger than you, maybe, okay?"

Mia sets the sugar packet down as the woman raises a beefy, veined fist. "I tell him someone wants to fight you? Shake your head. Say no, no way." Her arm falls. Her fingers curl back around the lectern, looser now on the edge. "I tell him walk away. They laugh at you? They call you names? Doesn't matter. That's why we come to Can-a-da. So you can walk away. No one going to shoot you."

Bosnia. They're originally from Bosnia, Cathy had told her. Horvat is their last name.

"When Toma's a teenager"—the woman shakes her head—"man oh man. He's a stubborn boy. Doesn't want to listen. A *Canadian* boy. Tom, he tells me, now I am Tom. We have some hard times. Sometimes I think he is lost. Sometimes I think I am losing. One night, two nights, he doesn't come home. I ask myself how to love him?" Sitting in her hard-backed chair, Mia's heart flutters. "*How?* I am alone in this country. I am alone in this world. I keep trying. I keep talking. I say, Toma, you're a good boy. Remember you are strong. Yes?" At the head table, the groom's head is bowed; it is the bride who nods at his mother. "Cathy knows. Tom, my son, he is good.

"Look, I tell him. Look at the world. Full of problems. There, I say, there is your life. Go fix the problems. This will take a while." Some of the wedding guests chuckle, then fall silent again. The whole room silent and still. "Now he's a par-a-me-dic," she says, respectful of every syllable. "And Cathy is a nurse." And for the first time since she stepped behind the microphone she smiles, then seems to remember herself and pauses for a sip of water. When she puts the glass back down, her mouth is once more set in a serious line.

"Now Toma," she says. "I talk to you. No one else is listening." Her son lifts his head. Mia believes she can feel the life flowing between them, this mother and her son, like an invisible tether flung across the room. They belong to one another, are one another, as much as they are themselves. "Cathy"—she smiles again—"is a beautiful woman. She is now my daughter. So I tell you, love her like I love you. Forever. No matter what," she says. "No quitting."

MICHAEL GRABS A tea towel from under the sink and starts wiping the floor: the puddle near the stove where Finn's sleeves first dripped, across the kitchen, out into the hall. Michael follows the trail up the stairs. The droplets, like glistening demi-planets reflecting better worlds, will end at Finn's door. Not end—there will be more water on the floor in his bedroom, but Michael won't be going in to clean it up. Round one is over; he has shown himself to be a brutal father and been declared unworthy of love.

The towel is soaked before he reaches the landing. Through a thicket of banister spindles, at the end of the water-dripped hall, he can see Finn's door. Closed, which he knew it would be. He thinks about going in and apologizing, but doesn't trust himself not to get mad again. He gave it a shot in the kitchen and here he is, alone, sopping water off the floor. An epic failure. But he'd been waiting all day to talk to him, was already frustrated when Finn showed up at six p.m. and decided to be difficult. And the smirk on his face when he was washing that spoon, well . . .

In the laundry room, Michael opens the hamper, heaped with dirty clothes, and throws in the soggy towel. He grabs another one from the closet, is halfway out the door to finish wiping off the stairs when he turns back and takes another look in the hamper. Mia's pear-printed dress is on top of the pile, a pair of lacy black panties caught in its soft white folds. Michael reaches in and fingers the tiny bow at the front, runs his thumb over the lone rhinestone at its centre. It's been a while since he's seen her in something like that. Normally, she wears more comfortable underwear. Michael lets go of the panties, the small bite of the cheap stone, and flips up an edge of the dress. Underneath, a hot-pink thong, sharp and bright as a lie.

Michael drops the dress to the floor, yanks out the tea towel. Mixed into a tangle of dirty T-shirts and wrinkled shorts, flashes of minty green, baby blue, lipstick red, silky swatches of fabric, tiny hooks, crumples of see-through lace; it looks like the entire contents of Mia's lingerie drawer have been churned into the hamper.

Michael uses the wall to steady himself before he reaches in for the thong. It feels damp—maybe it's from the tea towel, but Michael doesn't think so. The thong was under the dress. He could be imagining things. Perhaps it's just cool. Or maybe all the clothes in the hamper are damp. He doesn't test the theory; he is unsure his heart would survive the result.

The thong weighs nothing at all. Still Michael hesitates, as if holding a great stone in his hand, before bringing the scrunch of silk to his nose. He inhales her scent, the ripe tang of her cunt. Not frigid, not sexless, no matter how often she's pushed him away. He inhales again, trying to discern someone else's juices, but all he can smell is his wife.

I HAVEN'T SEEN Eli since the barbecue at his place. And I told him straight up I didn't want to go out. That, seriously, I wasn't in the mood. But he was *so* hyper on the phone.

It's gonna be sick, he said. I'm coming for you, dude. Five minutes. I'm coming.

He'd been there in three. Edgy, like shotgunning a case of Red Bull edgy. Smacking the steering wheel with his hand. Snoop Dogg in the Porsche, it's the Porsche tonight, it's all niggas and hos *ce soir.* Two fuckbois and a bumpin' car.

I turn down the music. You okay?

Yeah, fuck I'm okay. Eli leans right into me. Big Heath Ledger Joker smile. Or Cameron Monaghan. He's so close it's hard to decide. Either way, I'm expecting blood around the edges. *You* okay? He screams it. *You? Okay?*

Maybe I should drive, I say. Like that's even possible.

Eli slams my shoulder, hard enough that I bounce off the door. Are you nuts? he says. My father wouldn't let you drive this car. He hits the gas, holding down the clutch so the engine roars. Slams the stick shift forward, yanks the wheel, and we're over the solid yellow line, rail smooth and rocket fast, tearing up Q. E. Drive, the canal ripping past on my side. The guy in the car ahead flips me the bird as we blow by. It's like we're in some video game. I'm hoping there are no points for pedestrians, and we've both got extra lives.

You on something or what? I ask when we're safely back on the non-lethal side of the road.

Finn. I'm disappointed in you. Good, clean fun, bro. Have you forgotten about good, clean fun? 'Cause tonight, my fucking one-handed wonder of a friend, that's what it's about.

He cranks up the music. Chance takes over. I hold on and say nothing. Me, the one-handed wonder. Eli slows down a bit after we pass a cop. Swings into a pull-off on the shoulder right before we hit downtown.

He throws the car into park and reaches into the back. Where we're going—he shoves a hangered shirt at me—they don't allow plaid.

What?

Put it on.

I stare at the shirt in my hand. Black, flat black buttons. Looks expensive. Feels expensive. Like nothing I wear. There's a dry-cleaning tag stapled to the label.

Where are we going?

If I told you, you wouldn't believe me.

I pick at the staple, work off the loop of numbered green paper. Dolce and Gabbana. Eighty percent Egyptian cotton. Sixteen percent Thai silk. Four percent elastodiene. No country taking credit.

Is this yours?

If it was mine, it wouldn't fit you.

Dolce and Gabban-a-na?

It's Eric's. Like a kick in the gut. Put it on, he says.

I'm not wearing your brother's shirt.

Trust me, he says. You'll want to put it on.

Trust me, I say, I won't.

And bam, just like that, Eli goes completely flat. Like someone just sucked all the hyper out and pumped him full of mean. A rush of passing cars, total silence inside, and Eli staring slit-eyed through the windshield, doing a pretty stellar impression of psycho. Heath, had he lived, might have given him a cheer.

Is Eric's shirt not good enough for you, *Finn*?

What?

Put on the shirt, *Finn*.

He's doing something weird to my name. I accept this because right now everything in my life feels strange and unreal. Why not twist my name around? Why not put on Jess's boyfriend's shirt?

If it means that much to you, bro, I say, trying to keep it light so *Eli's* head doesn't explode inside the car. I mean, guy's always been a bit of a dick when he doesn't get what he wants, but this is dickishness at a whole new level.

I shrug off the plaid, throw it in the back along with the hanger. I'm trying to be quick, my meat-stump's out, stumping around the Porsche, but the buttons are small, the front seat's small, I'm trying to get the thing around my shoulders.

Your T-shirt, Eli says, still staring straight ahead.

What?

You'll look like an idiot with that on underneath. The shirt's, like, fitted.

Fuck's sake. I throw open my door and tumble out, yank my T-shirt up my back and over my head so for a couple of seconds I'm shirtless on the side of the road. A station wagon drives by. A long beep. Some girl hanging out the back window hooting. Obviously, she missed the missing hand.

You makin' friends out there? Eli sounds happier now that I'm doing what he wants.

And it's easier out of the car, easier without my T-shirt sticking to it. And forget the cotton, forget the elastodiene, it's a hundred percent silk against my skin. Buttons like polished shells, they take a bit of work, but it's worth it. Fuck Eric, I'm never giving this thing back. I leave both cuffs undone—one I can't do up, and the other one is better like that, better to cover the arm.

I slide back into the car and Eli shakes his head at me, all disgusted.

What?

You look good, he says. He hits the gas and the Porsche fishtails onto the road. You look like a fuckin' rock star.

Two minutes later he slams on the brakes in the circular driveway of the Aberdeen Gentlemen's Club. The city's own little Playboy mansion. It actually sort of looks like a mansion. Lots of stone, big burgundy canopy over the front door held up by two brass poles, hinting at what's inside. The upstairs windows are painted black and I know there's a pool out back. If you walk down the alley behind the club at night, sometimes you hear girls laughing and splashing around. Eli and I used to ride our bikes downtown, press ourselves up against the fence and let ourselves get hard just listening to them.

Are you kidding me? I say. We're underage. We're—

It's taken care of.

A WWF fighter ready to Hulk out of his suit jacket jerks open my door.

Be cool, Eli says. To me—who's been sitting calmly in the passenger seat while he's been going all bipolar behind the wheel.

I get out of the car. The guy holding my door, his hand's as big as my head.

Eli swings alongside and tosses him the keys. We want valet.

Boys, he says, his fingers gently crushing the keys. Boys.

Kelly party.

The guy turns and signals one of his sparring partners guarding the front doors. George'll take care of you.

I try to saunter up to the carved double doors—George has one wrenched open—but I have all the swagger of a stick. And inside, the girl at the coat check isn't wearing a top, which is okay, I guess, because I'm not wearing a coat.

Summer, George hollers. Kelly guests. VIP room at the back.

Sure thing, she says, getting up off her stool. She's wearing a glittery skirt made of sequins that swish and sway when she walks.

No phones or pictures, okay? she says, pushing aside a red velvet curtain, looking over her shoulder, giving us a smug little smile, the profile of one perfect tit.

Coming, boys?

Yeah, Eli laughs, elbowing me in the ribs, we are.

THE JEEP BOUNCES along the rutted dirt track, and like a spring, Michael, who hasn't bothered with a seat belt, bounces along inside. He's driving fast, yanking the steering wheel only to avoid the deepest potholes. And he's late seeing the chain slung low across the service road. He stomps the brakes and grips the wheel with both hands as dust sweeps up and over the Jeep like a dirty dream.

Front bumper kissing chain, Michael throws open his door and steps one foot out. The churned road dust settles on his skin. He squints through the headlight haze at the scatter of kids under the bridge. All of them stare back, suspicious of the dramatic arrival. Flames flicker inside an oil drum, casting leaps of light and shadow on the dark underbelly of the bridge. Michael registers a girl in a bikini top and cut-offs bending down, a case of beer being dragged out of sight. Two boys with respirators and raised aerosol cans stand close to the wing wall; another wears a red bandana pulled up over his nose. They all look ready to riot, to do battle with police throwing tear gas and swinging heavy black batons.

"Dirk!" Michael yells. Music pounds in from the water, a party on the beach upriver, the far-off bass throbbing like blood at his temples.

The kid with the bandana yanks it down. "You wanna kill your lights, yo." It's clear he's not asking a question but giving a command.

Michael accidentally blasts the high beams for a few seconds—every kid wincing and swearing—before shutting them off. The under-bridge falls back to flame-lit.

"Hey, Bunner!" the kid calls. "Yo, dude, your boyfriend's here."

The kid sticks his head around a pillar, a grenade hanging like a silver sun just above his head. Michael climbs back into the Jeep and slams the door.

The boy clowns his way toward the vehicle, gives the hood a bang before he swings alongside. "Cheerio's got wheels." The kid's eyes are red slits, and a sweet pong follows him into the car. The kid must know he reeks. He hits a button and slides his window down. "No baseball tonight," he says with a smirk.

Michael slams the gearshift into reverse, backs up ten feet and charges forward. Two tires dip into the ditch, the Jeep tips left, the kid falls sideways, his head bumping off Michael's shoulder. Laughing, he grabs the safety strap and hauls himself upright. They bypass the chain, hit the gravel under the bridge, ghosting up a fog of fine grey smoke.

On the far side of the overpass the service road ends. Michael is forced to slow down. He plows the Jeep into the field of wild grasses like a scythe into wheat, the shoulder-wide footpath he normally walks each night centred on the hood. Struck white by the headlights, the grasses get chopped under the bumper, but whisper-slide the sides of the car in a defiant golden rush. The air slipping into the car is jungle-warm and prairie-scented and the night sky domes overhead, its darkness diluted by a full moon and the orange tinge of a left-behind city.

The kid sticks his arm out the window and without even realizing, Michael slows down again. "Sweet," the boy says. His fingers open and close, letting the feathery heads slip through his hand. "Sweet."

Michael watches him, his hand, the easy interplay of perfect digits and fleeing grasses, and for a second the tautness in his chest gives way and a great ache sweeps through him. He can suddenly see this moment from a different angle, in another time, when a ride through a midnight field with a kid in the passenger seat beside him might be fuelled by something other than anger or jealousy or reprisal. When, heart deep in the beauty of the world, this joyride night might be scored by something graceful and pure, untainted, like absolute forgiveness or love beyond its breaking point.

Beside him the kid shifts and rolls and is hanging halfway out the window. "Goin' to kick some Big Yirkie ass!" he hollers as the wind snatches at the snapback he's got cocked sideways on his head. "Goin' to burn us a boat!"

Michael grabs the waistband of the boy's shorts and hauls him back into the car. The kid just bangs him on the shoulder and laughs.

They come to a stop over third base. Michael scrambles out and into the shed. Returns with the bag of balls and throws it into the back of the car.

"Fuck," he mutters, "fuck, fuck, fuck, fuck, fuck." He's forgotten the bat. When he slams the hatch, the whole car shakes. Three strides and he's at Dirk's window. "Did you tell your friends we were going to burn my partner's boat? Like before you screamed it out the window?"

"No. Not really."

"*Not really*?" Michael glares at the boy. "For a kid who doesn't

220

talk much, you've got a big fuckin' mouth." His stupid hat. His stupid face. "Do you even know what day it is?"

"Saturday."

"Right. Saturday. It's the weekend, correct? So even if we wanted to, we won't be kicking Big Yirkie ass tonight."

The kid peers at Michael with half-mast eyes. "Well that fuckin' sucks."

Michael stands lost for a minute, unsure what to do next. Go back to the house and grab the bat? Throw the balls themselves? How long would that even take?

He gives himself thirty seconds to come up with a plan. In twenty, he yanks open the rear door. Flips down the back seat, considers the space. Roomy enough. He's squeezed in a double mattress before, hauled a load of paving stones up to Peter's cottage.

The boy turns in the passenger seat. "So what's the deal?"

"Get out of the car," Michael tells him. "Go get your friends. We're going to need some help."

THREE ABREAST, the boys lumber through the swath of grass flattened by the Jeep. With their low-riding pants, their shuffle, they'd be cartoonish but for the respirators pulled up onto their heads. The breathing vents point skyward, like blunted antennae. As they emerge from the field, they're end times threatening, flanking Dirk, who without the headgear looks like a child hostaged between men. Michael recognizes the one from the first night he came down to the river, the one who'd been smoking a joint with Dirk. Chubby, olive-skinned, Middle Eastern maybe, strands of long black hair escape the sides of his rubber mask like oil-slicked seaweed. The other one looks older, college age. And tougher. Tattoos crawl from his shirt and spread like blackened flames onto his skull where the ink blends with the thick straps of the respirator to form a new, more intricate pattern.

Neither of them even glances at Michael as Dirk makes the introductions. "Rae Chan, Big Bill Brown, Cheerio. Cheerio, Rae Chan, Big Bill Brown."

"Hey," Michael says. "Thanks for lending a hand." Christ, he sounds ninety years old.

Rae Chan pushes his respirator higher on his head as he considers the pitching machine, standing grim and graceless a few feet from the Jeep's rear bumper. He lays one hand, fingers capped with black paint, on the frame and gives it a push, testing the weight.

"Bunner," he says. His voice is surprisingly deep and rich, like an old-time radio announcer's. "In the back. BB, other side. You"—he nods at Michael—"same."

They take directions from the radio voice. They bend their knees, they lift on three, they watch their fingers, and the kid, Bunner, gets a grip—no not there, there—and pulls, guiding the Arm flat and square into the back of the Jeep while the others push. When the job is finished, he advises on how to best get the machine out of the car, then shuffles over to Bunner and sticks out his hand. "Give it."

The kid pulls a small Ziploc from the pocket of his jeans. He takes a long, appraising look at the tangle of mossy buds clumped in one corner. "Generous." He smiles widely as he tosses it over.

Rae Chan snatches the bag from the air. "Seriously?" he says. "Haze? That all you got?"

He's centre field when he turns, and for the first time lets his eyes rest on Michael. "Slow the fuck down under the bridge," he calls, resonant and booming, a profane god issuing commands from the outfield. "Your dust messed up my work."

Big Bill Brown fist-bumps Dirk before following Rae Chan through the field.

"He's a mover," the kid says. In the aftermath of the radio god, his voice sounds tremulous and light. "So he's, you know, good at moving stuff. And he's a killer tagger. And he's totally dope on drums."

There's no need to clarify who he's talking about. "We're all going to party at his cabin, next week. Should be sweet."

"I bet."

In the car, Michael roars the Jeep to life. When the kid turns on the radio, he doesn't protest the volume or the choice of rap music. He likes the pound of noise, the way it distracts. He drives slowly back through the grass field, the load taxing the engine, compressing the shocks. He slows down even more passing under the bridge. The gravel barely shifts beneath his wheels and all the dust stays low.

IN SUMMER, the laundromat turns Mia's studio swampy. It's one of the reasons she started shutting down in July and August. Even in just underwear and an old White Stripes T-shirt, she's hot. The air conditioner at the front rumbles loudly, but its putter of cool air doesn't come anywhere close to making it back to the mattress: David's old one, covered with threadbare sheets and a patchwork quilt originally intended for Value Village.

The bedding isn't the only thing Mia's rescued for the studio. On the counter, beside the coffee maker, sits an old toaster oven, like a block of darkness now. And the Anne Fontaine blouse Michael so pointedly rescued from the garbage bag dangles from the coat rack by the door.

Mia flops around on the makeshift bed. If she were in the mood, if she weren't so hot and twitchy, she'd get up. Turn on the chandeliers—she'd snapped on the goose-neck desk lamp when she'd come in, spotlighting a stack of *Slate v. Conrad* documents. She should get up and turn off the lamp. Turn off the air conditioner. So loud and useless. What she should do is adjust the lights until the room looks candlelit, and in that beautiful glow she should pull on the old Doc Martens she keeps stashed in the back and kick the fucking air conditioner out the window. Pitch all the legal shit through the hole it

223

leaves behind. Throw out the lamp once all the paperwork had landed.

Jesus. She never thought she'd end up like this. A frustrated woman. A distraught woman. Dependent on her husband for money and still counting every goddamn cent. A woman recently playing around at bagging a wealthy man with, let's face it, her waning sexual currency. If that's what she'd even been doing. Sometimes she thinks all she wanted was a bit of fun, freedom, easy sex that wasn't hurtful or complicated or loving.

Another thing Mia can hardly believe about her life: how easily she and Michael assumed their positions after she quit her job. Husband and wife, father and mother, man and woman—the only things missing were her apron and his goddamn slippers and pipe. She bought the groceries, looked after the house, cared for Finn, made ninety percent of the meals and did ninety percent of the worrying. At least she had, before her recent, unauthorized maternity leave.

And Michael. He'd made ninety percent of the money. Took out the garbage, looked after the cars, drove Finn to his hockey practices. She's a feminist, for god's sake! A feminist with a science undergrad and a master's degree in finance, a feminist decades before the internet twisted the word into a slander.

If they don't soon settle with Peter and Michael doesn't find a job—as far as she knows, he's not even looking—she'll have to go back to banking. Even when she'd been working steadily, her photography business never cleared more than $38,000. Hard to live on that. Impossible to stay in this neighbourhood.

She'll have to go back. To the world of men, that soulless business, because that's where the real money's at, her eighty cents to their dollar. She'll give the Little Red Ferrari an overhaul, get it back on the road. Put on her navy suit, her silky blouse, nylons, high heels, feign interest in golf scores and borrowing rates. Laugh at their jokes, curb her opinions, pretend she isn't just herself inside. Let them condescend, not take her seriously, explain things she already knows. She'll blow-dry her hair, polish her nails, harness herself into a pair of Spanx every morning for the next five thousand mornings of her life. Sure, they might want her brains, but that's just the beginning. Play pretty, play nice, play along. She wonders if it's too late to start sleeping her way to the top.

No quitting. Simple as that. Mia imagines Toma's mother, squat and resolute, fleeing her homeland so her son might have a better chance at life. A tatty suitcase, a warm woollen sweater, one sturdy pair of shoes. Mia has a hundred pairs, but not one that would carry her to the closest border, a child's hand in hers. She's too soft. Too spoiled. She wants to run when things get hard. Ran from the bank rather than fighting for more room at the table. Slapped her husband away well before their accounts were empty. Yanked Finn's sock off her hand after what? Five minutes of struggle? After a toothbrush tipped into a sink?

Mia flails about, kicking at the bedspread, unable to get comfortable. She will never, ever shoot another goddamn wedding. When she stopped to pee on her way out, there was a turquoise-gowned bridesmaid on her knees in a cubicle, the damp square of toilet paper spiked on her dyed-to-match heel shivering every time she retched. It was Mia's favourite shot of the night. A bead of perspiration tickles across her forehead, like a spider scrambling for her hairline. She swipes at her face, and as if on cue, the air conditioner starts thwacking.

In the cramped back room, she yanks on a pair of old jean overalls. Her elbow bangs the wall when she bends to roll up the legs. On her way down the stairs to the laundromat, her Docs hit every step hard.

SO MUCH TO look at. So much to take in. The girl circling the brass pole. The two tit-heavy blondes cat-crawling along the front of the stage. At one point, I slam right into Eli, who I thought was follow-ing Summer, her sequin skirt, but he'd actually stopped to watch the girl doing the splits up the pole. Legs so long I'm pretty sure she must be a high jumper. A thin gold chain dangles between her tits, and there's another one glittering around her waist, and yeah, that's pretty much it. Except for the gold heels, which look like they'd slit you to the bone if she dragged one down your shin.

Her hair is the only thing that isn't tight. It drifts out like a long black cape as she swings around the pole. Standing in the middle of the club, in a room full of dark tables and dark chairs and dark men in dark corners with dark fantasy girls, I think for a minute that I can actually smell it. Cutting through the stale, windowless air, the spill of beer, the men, their reek, their breath, their bodies, their drippy dicks, their spiced deodorant, the alcohol, the puke, the pissy washroom, the disinfectant, the soapy bucket, the industrial-strength air freshener, the pineapple wedges behind the bar, the smoke, the perfume, the girls, the girl on stage, her black hair clean and fresh and swinging at me like something out of a kinked-out, nature-dipped dream.

I think she sees me staring. For a second, I think she's dancing just for me.

Oh my fucking god, Eli says. I'm pretty sure she likes me.

Let's go, Summer says, her voice loud above the music. I drop my eyes and concentrate on her butt, the sway of glittery sequins slipping across smooth flesh.

A big dude standing V-legged blocks the beaded entry to a pri-vate room at the back of the club. He leans down and smirks as Summer whispers in his ear. Unless you have to piss—he jerks his head at us—you stay in here for the rest of the night because you look like children.

Fuck you, Eli says, slapping the beads out of his way. I slide in behind him and I have to admit, despite all the drama on the way here, I'm impressed with just how ballsy Eli's been since we arrived. And yeah. The VIP room is pretty all right. Low leather couches along the dark red walls—a colour my mother would like—with lots of hard little platforms between the cushions so the girls giving lap dances have somewhere solid to stand.

I don't recognize any of the guys in the room, but it's kind of hard with all that ass so close to their faces. A couple of vodka bottles decorate the low table in the middle of the room, lots of tall, ice-filled glasses. Eli grabs a bottle and sits down, but I just keep moving until I bump into the bar.

A girl in a black leather bikini with super-short blond hair who looks like she could be Swedish or, shit, I don't know, something, some blond nationality, asks if I want a drink.

Beer, I say, happy to get the word out.

You have a favourite? She smiles a perfect Swedish smile. Or you want me to pick?

I nod. She leans over so her black leather boobs are really close to the trough of beer and ice.

You like Stella?

Are you Stella?

She laughs. No, I'm Hannah, and she twists off the cap. Drinks are on Eric tonight.

Eric?

Yeah, Eric Kelly's picking up the tab. She gives her shoulders a little shake so her tits shake a bit, too. But we do appreciate tips.

I stuff my hand into the pocket of my jeans—of course it's Eric's party, of course it fucking is—and fish out a bill, a five, so dirty and crumpled it looks like I wrestled it off a junkie. I try to smooth it out on the bar, transform it into something worthy of a spot in a G-string, but it slips over the edge and flutters into the ice.

Sorry, I say, and Miss Sweden plucks it up with her long black nails and stuffs it into a big mason jar.

I tilt my head back and drain my beer.

Again?

Yes.

Don't worry about the tip, she says. It's been a long time since I've seen a guy blush.

I pound back two more beers before I work up enough nerve to turn around and check out the rest of the room. And fuck if Eli isn't sitting thigh to thigh with the girl from the stage. She tilts her head when she sees me and pats the cushion on her non-Eli side.

And I'm thinking about going over, I'm actually thinking about it even though Eli's not looking too friendly, and I'm thinking about the missing hand, whether or not she's noticed the empty end of my sleeve, and I'm thinking about how Jess would feel if she saw the way this girl was looking at me, when the beads on the door part and Eric steps in. A fading Vegas tan. He's shorter than me, but fitter, stronger, more ripped. Bulging biceps and shit. If I wasn't wearing his shirt he'd be way better dressed.

He raises his arms into a godlike V as he takes in the room. And the boys will play! He laughs. And the boys will fuckin' play! The guys on the couch cheer, a couple of them manage to free up a hand long enough to raise their glasses.

Eli's up off the couch, chest-bumping Eric.

Little brother, Eric says. Little brother's friend. He's right in front of me, grabbing my face, giving my head a rattle. Nice fuckin' shirt. He's behind the bar. You being nice to these boys, Hannah?

Very nice, she says. And this one here—she reaches out and strokes my arm—he's being very nice to me.

That one there? He's a nice kid. Right? Right, Finn? You're a nice kid. That's what Jess says, anyway. He winks at me. My heart jumps, organs slamming together on the far side of my skin. My stump bangs into the counter, fumbling for something to hold on to, bump, bump, *fuck*, too late, the blonde's eyes widen before I get it back below the bar.

Eric laughs. Too bad nice guys finish last, eh, Finn? His arm slung over Sweden's shoulder, his completely okay hand hovering over her perfect black leather tit. Have a shot with me, Finn, he says. Eli. Hannah. Have a shot.

There's a weird smile stuck to my face as I concentrate on picking up the glass.

To all the beautiful women, he says. We all love the beautiful girls.

The tequila—like gasoline all the way down. Eric sloshes up another round. We shoot it, my gut quaking and the room kind of quaking. I try to focus on something. The girl with the black hair's gone.

Hey Eric, Eli says, behind me. Show him.

What?

You know. Show it to him.

You think so?

Yeah, I fuckin' think so.

And Eric reaches into his pocket and pulls out a blue velvet box.

Oh, Hannah squeals. Let's see it.

Eric slides the box slowly across the bar, so slowly I have plenty of time to get sober. Completely sober and still. The whole world waiting for this frozen fraction of a second to skip forward. Waiting for the slow bang of my heart and the blue velvet box to collide.

Open it, Eli says, like I knew he would. Just like I knew he would. It's the reason he brought me here. So he could watch me open the box.

It's not that easy with one hand. I have to pick it up. Flip it around, grip the bottom with my palm, work my nail under the lid, while they all watch. I use my thumb as a lever, give a push, and the lid snaps up.

Oh my god! Sweden leans in for a better view. It's huge!

Two carats, Eric beams. Got it wholesale in Vegas. My old man set it up. He reaches across the bar, his hand heavy on my shoulder. What do you think, Finn?

He's staring at me, smiling and staring. I can't tell if he's fucking with me or not. I can't tell how drunk he is or how high, what he knows and what he doesn't, all I know for sure is that both of them, Eric and Eli, wanted me to open that box.

Big, I say because I have to say something.

Yeah, it's fuckin' big. But you know her, right? You know Jess. There's a weird flicker in his eye, and for a second he looks uncertain. Maybe a little scared.

Yeah. I know her.

So what do you think she'll say?

Eric's squeezing my shoulder, Eli's breath coming in hot from behind. The ring is in my hand. The biggest diamond I have ever seen. That Jess has ever seen. I think about all the stuff she told me in the Caddy, and how maybe what she was doing that day was preparing me for this right now.

What do you think she'll say?

I make myself look up. I make myself smile. I make myself say yes. Yes. And I hand Eric back the box.

"WE'RE NOT TOUCHING that one," Michael says, pointing high and right.

The boy follows the line of his finger to a window on the second floor. Like all the others—there must be twelve at least, plus the sliding doors—the window he's pointing at is dark and partially open. Its white sheers move with any breeze that finds its way into the house.

"That's his daughter's room," Michael says. "I want to keep her out of it."

"Whatever, man," the boy says. "Kid yourself if you want to. You're the one running the show."

And Michael has been. First he'd snuck up to the house on foot, alone. When he was sure the place was empty, he pulled into the driveway and parked the Jeep close to the garage. He and the boy had lassoed the Arm with the extension cord and, like a dog on a leash, they'd practically walked it down the paved path at the side of the house and onto the lower deck where it now sits, hopper loaded.

Next he'd stashed the Jeep in the parking lot at the private school. Plan B—if anyone shows up at the house, Michael and the kid will bail. Abandon the Arm and run or swim back to the car if necessary. Plan A is no one shows up, they blow out the windows. Michael gets the car, the kid collects the gear, they load up the pitching machine and take it back to the shed, leaving nothing behind but broken glass and a shitload of baseballs.

As Michael reaches for the on-off button, he feels the dark energy that has been coiled inside him for the last five months rise. He turns to share a complicitous smile with the kid, but the boy is no longer beside him; he's shuffling down the flagstone path toward the water. Michael watches, agog, as the kid drops into one of the two remaining Muskoka chairs that cast perfect shadows onto the ghost-grey dock. In the moonlight, the boy's high-tops are a dull red shine, the river a silver drift.

"What are you doing?" Michael hollers. Despite the fact that they're creeping around on someone else's private property, there's no need to lower their voices. Music throbs across the river, louder here than it was at the ball diamond. "Hey, Dirk! Come on. This is the fun part." But the boy flops back into the chair. "What the fuck?" Michael mutters as he trudges down to the dock. "What's up?"

"I'm tired," the kid says. "I'm takin' five." His face and arms are sheened with sweat.

"You hot? You want to jump in quick?"

The kid just shakes his head.

From the dock, Michael can see the amber leap of a bonfire on the beach a quarter mile upriver, can smell its woody smoke. A pack of dancing kids and what looks to be a half-dozen giant speakers ring the small crescent of sand. Michael checks his watch: 11:18. If the party is legit, if it's sanctioned by the city, which given the set-up and the volume of the music—louder than breaking glass—it probably is, it won't go much past midnight.

The boy stares up at him blankly. "You got anything to eat?"

"Christ!" Michael throws his hands into the air and the dock bobs beneath him. "No, I don't have anything to eat."

"I seriously need something to eat. I'm fuckin' shaky."

"Come on. Get up." He gives the boy's shoulder a shove and is jolted by the slick heat of his skin.

"I told you before," the kid says, "I'm diabetic."

Michael gives him a disbelieving look.

"What? I told you."

"I thought you were lying."

"Why would I lie about diabetes? It's not, like, something I go around bragging about."

The needle marks on the boy's thigh. Even after the kid said insulin, Michael had thought heroin, crack, cocaine, which he now realizes was stupid. He stares at the boy, collapsed in the high-backed chair, his stick legs connecting the tops of his fat shoes to the bottoms of his long shorts. "There were probably granola bars in the car. If you'd told me earlier . . ."

"I have a stash in the shed. At the diamond."

Goddamnit. "Listen, Dirk, we're all set up. I don't have time to go back."

The kid closes his eyes. His head falls sideways until it's practically resting on his shoulder.

"I could check the change room. There used to be a fridge in there."

"That would be good," he says without opening his eyes.

But when Michael feels under the eave, the key is gone.

"Juice," the kid calls over the music. "And cookies. Or a couple of crackers with peanut butter."

"YOU COMING FOR the show?" A block south of the laundromat, a dashing, dark-skinned young man smiles at Mia from a poster-plastered doorway.

Mia stops, momentarily disarmed. "I was just . . ." She points vaguely off down Main Street. She's seen this guy before; he's a doorman at the House of Targ, a barcade that advertises an eclectic mix of bands.

"Everyone's welcome," he says. "Everyone's friendly inside."

Mia cocks her head. "Yeah?"

"Yeah." His smile widens, beautiful white teeth, an award-worthy smile. She'd been planning to stomp around the neighbourhood, release some of her hostile energy through brisk movement, maybe go drown herself in the river if the stomping didn't work out. But the doorman has convincing cheekbones and soulful eyes, skin so beautiful brown it seems possible he was birthed from rich, fertile soil, causing no woman pain.

Mia motions to her overalls. "I'm not really dressed for the occasion."

"You look great. And things are pretty casual at Targ." He holds out his hand. "Mithoun. Engineering student by day, doorman by night."

His hand is warm and dry in hers, although its architecture feels finer and lighter than she imagined. "Mia. I'm . . . my photography studio's just over there."

"Cool." He lets go her hand and boldly holds open the door. A flight of stairs leads down into a low-ceiling basement, the bar bright at the back.

She and Michael have been once before. Last fall, when life still held grace enough to allow for a casual evening of drinking and dancing. It had been an alternative 80s night, lots of Modern English, and Bowie in the mix. They'd been two of the oldest people in the place, but it hadn't mattered. Like the doorman said, everyone had been friendly.

"Drinks are half price until eleven."

"You're very insistent. You get a cut of the door?"

Just the slightest flicker of his eye. "Tonight all proceeds go to the Acorn Women's Shelter."

"Ah." Mia presses a hand to her throat. "I apologize. I didn't mean to imply . . ."

"Better hurry," he says, graciously. "It's ten to eleven."

At the bottom of the stairs, Mia pays the eight-dollar cover, and instead of stamping her hand, a shaved-headed chick in a studded leather jacket pins a "Smash the Patriarchy" button on her shirt.

Mia's gin and tonic comes in a tall glass stacked with ice cubes and two twists of lime. She sips the drink, happy for the moment to be standing alone at the back of a crowded bar. It's not a cabin in the woods, but there's alcohol and no one knows her. A middle-aged guy with bushy sideburns and weepy, bloodshot eyes—Mia believes he's one of the owners—grabs a mic, and in his best Darth Vader voice announces that Koi Spice's perogies can now be picked up at the bar.

Pinball machines, lights flashing, bells dinging, line one wall. Facing off on the other side, old-school video consoles, race cars with plastic moulded seats, shooting games with wooden rifles tethered by flimsy chains. A small, low stage bumps out from the wall. An Asian woman sporting a velvet bustier and a tiny black thong hustles across the dance floor. She elbows her way up to the bar—even in heels she's a head shorter than Mia—picks up a plate, then hustles back across the room, her ass flat and pale and dimpled, a bit like the perogies she's carrying. Koi Spice, Mia assumes.

Mia takes another look at the crowd. Mixed in amongst the jeans and T-shirts, the plaid and the beards, are patrons wearing leather chaps, silky capes and tight vinyl dresses spilling off-the-charts cleavage and XL thighs.

"Kinky Burlesque Show starting in five," Darth Vader reverbs into the room.

Mia ends up leaning against a column, twenty feet back from the stage. As the dance floor fills, the spot to her right is claimed by a tall, curvy beauty in a red spandex dress, a pair of plastic devil horns flashing atop her head.

Mia takes a swig of her G&T and a brightness opens high in her chest, a sweet mélange of alcohol and expectation, or just marvel at how a block away from her studio she got so far from home.

HE SAID YES! Fuckleberry Finn said yes! He's gonna marry me! When Eric punches me in the shoulder I can't believe I actually felt sorry for him a minute ago when he was looking all frail. He slips a crisp twenty into Sweden's G-string—why don't you go give my little brother a dance?—and she slides out from behind the bar.

Hey, Eric says as I turn to follow her. I wanna talk to you. He grabs the bottle of gasoline, hooks a stool with one foot, drags it over, sits right down. Grab a seat, he says. He lines up two glasses and pours us both a shot. I take my time getting a stool. And I'm careful when I set it down. Leave enough space so I'm out of punching distance. Smack, slam, wail.

Eric pounds his tequila. I don't touch mine. From the corner of my eye I can see Eli on the couch, Miss Sweden standing over him, her legs spread, her leather-clad pussy at eye level. I keep my arms loose, the empty cuff of my shirt—*his* shirt—hanging between my knees. I smile. I pretend to be relaxed. I pretend to be fearless. I'm good at it; I've been pretending to be fearless for months.

But honestly? I didn't think I'd be this scared. I thought I would be madder. Raging inside. Like my father. But now that it's happening, now that I'm sitting face to face with Eric Kelly, I understand it doesn't matter how much I love Jess or who started it or whether it's over or not. The only way Eric's going to see it, if he knows about it at all, is like this: I've been banging his girlfriend, the one he wants to marry.

So, he says, did he tell you?

Tell me what, I say carefully.

That bitch broke up with him.

What?

Frankie. The fucking linebacker. Apparently she's *in love* with someone else.

Yeah? Every word careful.

Yeah, he says. But you know how fucking complicated these things are. He gets into spinning his shot glass on the bar, completely mesmerized, spinning it around like a clunky top, one way and then the other like he's forgotten I'm even there and the shot glass is the sickest thing in the world.

Like complicated how? I finally ask, because I want to get this—whatever this is—over with, and I can tell he's not done with me yet.

He waits until the glass spins itself out before he turns to me and says, It's complicated because even though she dumped Eli for this other douche, she tells him, get this, she tells him the guy doesn't even like her. That she's pretty sure he likes this other girl. This older girl, he says, staring right at me, but this guy is completely fucking deluded because this older girl's in love with someone else. And this guy, he's just a fucking kid, a fucking infant. I know, right? I told you it was complicated.

My smile is gone, but otherwise, I haven't moved. And I don't even blink when Eric pulls the box back out and pops it open. In case I missed it the first time. Rock the size of an ice cube. Even with the crappy lighting it sparks like sun on fresh snow.

Pretty sweet, eh? He plays with the box, flips it around a bit so the diamond keeps glinting in my eyes. I refuse to lift an arm to block the torpedoes of light.

Know what it cost me? Eric says. Eighteen K U.S. And that's wholesale. It would be twice that if you bought it retail up here.

Wow, I say, letting just a bit of the deluded infant creep into my voice.

You're fucking right, wow. Eighteen thousand for a fucking ring? But it's worth it. Because I know what I want, he says. And Jess knows what she wants.

I pick up the shot glass—I can move again, it was him saying her name—tip my head back, enjoy the distraction of the burn, a different kind of pain being inflicted. I consider telling Eric how I read this article about this Dutch guy who's figured out how to make diamonds out of smog—which we have a ton of—and how these fake stones are going to flood the market and make the real ones completely worthless.

Eighteen K wholesale? I say, instead.

You're fuckin' right. Eric takes another long look at the ring, snaps the lid closed and stuffs the box back into his pocket. Most of his friends have wandered out. There's just the bartender grinding on Eli's lap and this one other fat guy sort of passing out on the couch in the corner. Everything's a transaction, man. In this world? Give and take, give and take. Business. Marriage. Sex. This club. These girls. What we're doing here, you and me, it's a transaction, right?

I guess so.

You fuckin' *guess so.* He's sounding pretty hammered now, slurring a bit. Listen to me, he says. I give the club money, I get the room, I get the booze, I get the girls. Then I give it to you—the booze, the girls. Right? And what do I get in return? What do I get from you?

I don't know what you—

Respect! I get respect from you, 'cause I'm the fucking man, right? I'm fucking bringing it. And maybe Jess could do better. Better looking, better family, better fucking manners, smarter, whatever. But she can't do richer. Not around here. She knows it and I know it. And it doesn't even matter to me. I don't even want a fucking pre-nup, the old man's gonna insist, but I don't even want one. You know why? Because I love her, he says. You understand that? I *fucking* love her. You respect that?

Yeah, I say slowly. I respect that.

Good, he says. You better. You better respect that, you fucking child, you fucking amputee.

MICHAEL PUNCHES THE code into the glowing keypad and the garage door glides up. Before it's even waist high, he crouches down, shuffles inside and hits the button on the wall. The door pauses—a gear clicks inside the ceiling-mounted opener—and slides closed again.

He knows both cars are gone, he'd chinned himself to the garage window and checked it out already. He ignores the collection of thousand-dollar skis racked along the wall, the threesome of golf bags in the corner. He heads for the interior door, although neither Plan A nor Plan B had any contingency for breaking into the goddamn house for food. But when Michael had gone back to the dock with the news that forget it, he couldn't get into the shed, the boy had grabbed his hand.

"Feel this," he'd said and placed Michael's hand on his chest. Michael had pulled back quickly, but what he'd felt during those few seconds of contact, well, he doesn't know a lot about diabetes, but he does know no heart is meant to beat that fast. It had been his fear that the kid was going to go into some sort of low-sugar shock, have a diabetes-induced heart attack right there on the dock, that had pushed him up to the house.

Michael turns the handle—unlocked. A warning beep sounds. He strides up the hall to a glowing keypad, punches in a 2, a 0 . . . his own heart as wild as the boy's, he doesn't know what he'll do if the alarm goes off. Grab some food, race to the dock, shove it at the kid and get the hell out of here, with or without the boy . . . another 0, a 5 . . . the year they bought the house.

The beeping stops. Michael's heart eases back to a life-sustaining rhythm. The bastard, he thinks as he finds the switch and dims the hall lights, the bastard hadn't even bothered to lock the garage door or change the code on the security system. Peter believes Michael to be that harmless. He is that immune to guilt.

He walks to the back of the house, toward the kitchen, but is drawn to the living room's big picture window. They're definitely getting their money's worth tonight—and his—with the moon-lit river view. The dock's the brightest wedge on the silvery plate of water, the trees climbing the far bank a ghostly still of shadow and light. It's easy to forget the moon. Everything outside—even the squat un-beauty of the pitching machine—looks to be glowing of its own accord. Like the snow the night he found Finn. The whole backyard. Tonight, it's Dirk collapsed on a dock chair, his running shoes a bite of red in the monochrome.

Mia blames him. She withdrew. Lied to him about the prosthesis. Is probably fucking their lawyer.

On his way to the bathroom—he has to take a piss and has no plan to flush—he passes Frankie's room. The music from the river pounds in through the open window. When the curtains billow back, he sees the boy flat out on the dock. He rushes into the room, neat and white, and with one knee on the bed, yanks back the curtain. He's picturing flashing lights and paramedics, police with pencils and notepads, a dying diabetic boy.

The kid lifts an arm, brings his hand to his lips, and in the grey glow, a small, orange ember shines.

Christ! The asshole's smoking a joint. Michael pushes away from the window. As his foot hits the floor something sharp catches him low on the leg. He reaches down, grabbing for his ankle, but instead his hand meets metal, curved and cool and poking from under Frankie's bed. He wraps a finger around, what?—the prong of some garden tool?—and pulls.

His life. He no longer understands his life.

From beneath the bed, he drags a two-pronged hook, a bloodless metal hand trailing a bloodless plastic sleeve.

HONESTLY? IN ALL my fantasies, in every single one, I imagined the Aberdeen Gentlemen's Club would be more fun. A lot more fun. Not once did I imagine banging a handless arm into a bar. Not once did I imagine Eric Kelly shoving an engagement ring in my face. Not once did I imagine being eighteen and in love with my twenty-three-year-old babysitter who was going to marry some douchebag for his money. Not fucking once.

I was right about one thing. The washroom smells like piss. The door slams shut behind me as I wander up the hall. I'm not sure where I'm going, not back to the VIP room, not home—I'm too drunk to go home, have no money to get there—not anywhere near Eric and the blue velvet bulge in his pocket. Or his brother, the little fucking psycho. *Open it.* That crazy fucking voice. No wonder my dad never liked him. He *is* a bad influence.

I'm almost at the main room when the girl from the stage swings around the corner. Hips, hair, long gold chain, everything swinging now. She's got on a little white minidress but it's see-through, so it doesn't really count. Her face lights up when she sees me. Big, gleaming smile. Big, gleaming eyes. A swoop of black at each corner so up close she looks kind of Egyptian.

Hey, she says, I've been looking for you. A hand reaching up to finger one of Eric's buttons. With the high-jumper legs and shin-slitting heels she's a couple inches taller than me. Jess is shorter. I have to bend down to kiss her.

Aren't you the sweetest thing I've ever seen, she says. You old enough to even be in here?

Yeah, I say. No.

She laughs, her breath like cinnamon gum. I slip my arm behind me, try to make it look casual.

I saw it, she says. Before. Trust me. The shit I've seen in here, it's no big deal.

My fake smile frozen in place.

You want to go back? I'll give you a dance. Or we could go upstairs where it's private. See what happens. Eric's treat. Although you're so hot I'd take you up there for free. What do you think? You wanna go? I've got half an hour before I have to go back on. Hey, you okay? she says. You look a little pale.

I feel a little pale. I lean up against the wall. Close my eyes and let myself die a little right there in the hall. There is nothing good about dying in a strip club, nothing beautiful or expansive, no love or fearlessness anywhere nearby. Just my lungs collapsing and the reek of men and a nameless stripper reaching for my arm.

Shit, she says. Come with me. You look like you're gonna pass out. Don't pass out in here. The bouncers will freak. You have ID, right? Tell me you have ID.

She leads me through the main room and down a narrow hallway, pushes open a black metal door, and we're outside.

It's better outside. I can breathe outside. The un-pissy air. The un-Eric'ed space. Little waves slapping around a tiny pool. A concrete rectangle and a couple of lounge chairs around it.

She parks me by a potted plant. A tree, I guess. The leaves dark and waxy. A mini version of an actual tree. I hang my head and concentrate on dragging oxygen into my lungs.

The girl comes back with a glass of water. I drink it fast. The ice cubes frozen to the bottom let go and crack into my teeth.

Too much booze? she says.

Tequila, I say. Beer. Tequila.

You look better. She looks like a mirage, a porn-star Cleopatra. She has a bikini on under the dress, three tiny triangles of white cloth, a couple pieces of string.

I was worried there for a minute, she says. I thought you were going to drop.

My girlfriend broke up with me, I tell her. I guess it kind of hit me. I think it was kind of that.

Oh, poor baby. Well, you know what they say. The best way to get over a girl is to get under another one. Or on top, she says, taking my glass. I'll let you pick.

The curves of her body filmy under her dress. Those legs. The dark gap.

She was just fooling around with me, I say. Just using me, I guess. She didn't, you know— I reach over and puncture a leaf with my thumbnail, an ooze of whitish sap.

Bitch. She takes a step closer. I take a step back so we're both behind the plant, her body bumping against mine. Let me cheer you up. I still have time. Tab's basically open so we can do whatever you want.

Whatever I want.

I gather her hair in my hand, inhale. Christ, it even smells like Jess's. I want to run my other hand over her body, that's whatever I want, but I have to let go of her hair to touch her leg, that long, lean thigh. The brush of her dress on my wrist, her ass curving into my palm.

I want this. This easy thing, not love, not love, just this girl's ass in my hand and her body pressing into me and nothing else ever again.

You like to bang? she says.

Yeah, I like to bang.

I lift her leg and settle her foot on the planter. Her gold spiked heel right beside my hip, the same position we were in in the bathroom that first time. I pull her closer, watch her little G-string move against the outline of my dick, her ass rocking in my hand, she's reaching for my belt when something smashes into my face, the taste of blood in my mouth and a shriek from the girl and three of us stumbling around behind the planter. Me and the girl and Eli, *fuck*, Eli looking insane, panting, with blood on his knuckles—I don't even know how he did it, how he punched me so hard with the girl right in front of me.

You knew I fucking liked her, he hisses, drunk as shit and swaying, his fists up. His eyes swing between me and the girl, I can't tell which one of us he's going to hit next, and I'm pretty sure there's blood running out of my nose and I'm holding both arms out, like some perverted Jesus, holding Eli off, from the girl who got out of the way fast, a splatter of red on the shoulder of her dress.

Eli. What the fuck? Eli.

You guys are going to get thrown out, the girl says. You better fucking stop.

You knew I wanted her and you didn't fucking care. Eli all messy and pathetic and mean.

She's a stripper, okay. She's just, like, some, some prostitute.

The girl throws her shoulders back so she's about seven feet tall. You—she gives me and my missing hand and the rod in my pants a cold warrior glare. And you—she pushes past Eli and his fists, completely unafraid in her see-through dress. And your fucking perv brother. You're all cavemen. I hope you beat each other to death. Or the bouncers do it for you.

Through the leaves, the tick tock of her ass, the snap of her heels, the silent swish of her hair. The pull and slam of the metal fire door as she disappears inside. I'm still staring when Eli comes at me again. And because I can't quite believe Eli, my best friend, is actually going to hit me again, he manages to hit me a couple more times. Quick, hard punches, all on the one side of my face.

I finally get my arms onto his shoulders and wrestle him back, my stump pushing hard against another human being. I force him backwards, slam him into the planter until his knees give and he's deep in the branches, the snap of twigs and his body surrounded by leaves, his butt pressing into the dark, damp soil.

It takes him a good thirty seconds to fight his way out—it would be funny if he hadn't just punched me in the face. He doesn't even clear the twigs out of his hair before he throws the next thing at me.

I saw the way you were looking at her, he says.

Oh my god, Eli, she's a strip—

Jess, he snaps. I saw how you were looking at her. The whole time. In the car. In our kitchen. At your birthday. I don't know what the fuck you think you're doing, but Eric will rip your fucking heart out. I'll rip your fucking heart out.

Eli. I say his name firmly, loudly, so I don't sound scared. He's hunched up, panting over his fists. There's a slash of blood across his cheek. From a branch, maybe. A twig. We shouldn't even be here. We're not old enough to even be here. We should be in the forest. Cruising down hills on our boards past real trees. Sturdy trees. Owls flying overhead.

You think, Eli says, you think you can come into our house and steal our women.

Steal your women? Can you just lis—

Did you fuck her that night? In my house? Did you fuck her in my house?

No. What? No.

You're a piece of shit, Finn. His face is all twisted up, his eyes runny. You're a fucking piece of shit.

I didn't. It's harder now not to sound scared, with him crying and everything.

I *saw* you.

I swear to God, I di—

I saw you. He sways in front of me. His chest heaving, his fists dropped. And I turned out the light.

The air sizzles around us as if lightning has just struck close by. What?

You knew I liked her, he sobs, and you didn't fucking care. You can have any girl but you took the one I wanted, you took her into the laundry room and you fucked her in there and then you went into the backyard and I saw you and I turned out the light.

Eli says these things to me.

The branch behind him is broken. Dangling down. Dog-legged left. The leaves on it will die. Because I pushed him into the tree. Because he punched me. Because of what I did to Frankie. The leaves will die because of what I did to her. What Jess did to me. What Eli did. What we all did to each other.

You turned out the light?

I was mad, he says. I was wasted. He stumbles forward and takes another swing, weak and pathetic.

I go sit by the pool. Dangle my legs in the water. My jeans wobble. My Vans go extra-large. Carefully I roll up the sleeve of Eric's shirt, right up to my elbow.

My friend did this, I tell myself. Eli did this to me. But it doesn't make sense. I can hear him crying behind me. Can see him floating over me in the pool. My stump wavers on the water beside his wavering head. I lean forward. Watch the blood drip from my nose, dirtying up the blue.

DESPITE EVERYTHING—THE FIGHT with Finn, the sex-scented close-up with Mia's thong, the diabetic meltdown on the dock, the unplanned B&E, the goddamn *hand* that crawled out from under Frankie's bed—when the first window breaks, a thrill rips through Michael. Amped-up. High-voltage. And Dirk, or Bunner, or whoever the hell the boy is beside him, lifts his head to the sky and howls.

The kid is back to cocky after smoking a fatty, draining a glass of orange juice and wolfing down a piece of bread that Michael had slathered with peanut butter in the kitchen, his hand shaking so badly the knife had knocked out a tune on the inside of the jar.

"You get jumped by a ghost in there, or what?" the kid had asked when Michael handed over the food. And when the boy held out the roach, he hadn't argued. The wind swept the smoke downriver. Beside the dock, beneath twenty feet of water, two chairs buried in muck and weeds.

Before he'd smoked, Michael had actually been thinking of getting the hell out of there. Plan C, he'd say to the kid. Pack up and go home. The boy would freak, but Michael didn't care. He was that rattled by what he'd found under the bed. And his anger, or bravado or whatever it was that had brought him and his pitching machine this far, was gone. He hadn't even been able to look at the thing on his way back to the dock. Pointed at the house, its hopper choked with balls. Christ. It suddenly seemed so obscene. This was Helen's home, for god's sake. This was Frankie's home. Not to mention, this whole thing? Was pretty fucking illegal.

But now, now he can see the justice of blowing the windows out of a thieving partner's house. Now he can appreciate the power of the Arm and the rush that comes from breaking something beautiful, undefended, something that isn't yours but should be.

The boy nudges the back of the machine left so the next ball punches a second dark-holed sun through the glass just right of the first. It takes another blast before the pane shatters completely and slices of living room window starburst onto the flagstone below.

"Sick," the kid says. "So fuckin' sick."

Together they jimmy the machine this way and that, destroying all the windows on the upper level. They whoop, high and wild, after every direct hit. It's become a game of destruction. It's nobody's home, it's nobody's property, it's a shooting gallery of glass, *their* shooting gallery of glass. The music from across the river is still going strong, but it's been stripped back, it's all drums now, a frantic tribal beat, quick in Michael's chest, it makes him think sacrifice, a sacrifice going on upriver, an orgy, virgin blood being swallowed by sand, swept away by fast-moving water. He lines up the throwing arm with the sliding doors and punches the on-off button in sync with the bang of a drum. The arm ticks back, springs forward. There is a millisecond delay between the ball hitting the door and the glass blooming aqua green, another millisecond before it explodes into a million jagged pieces.

"Awesome," Michael says. "So fucking awesome."

"That bitch is tempered," the kid laughs. "That bitch knows how to blow."

THREE GUYS IN black shirts and jeans gyrate to "Pour Some Sugar on Me," one tall and skinny, one short and stocky, one built and buff. At the chorus, they rip open their shirts, revealing slatted ribs, wobbly man boobs, darkly oiled skin. Mia finds herself cheering along with the crowd. The men end on their knees, one behind the other, asses on heels, hips thrusting forward on beat.

Four gorgeous Middle Eastern women do an erotic belly dance without taking off a stitch of clothing. A crooner in an old-timey suit and a drawn-on beard sings a slow, sweet ballad. Male or female Mia can't tell, and the instant she stops trying to figure it out it becomes irrelevant. People, just people, of every shape and size flaunting their stuff on stage, flesh wobbling, whips snapping, genders blurred. Mia can't help but laugh. She feels glowy and bright-lit, with what? Amazement? Possibility? A spark of another kind?

She remembers how uncertain she'd felt standing naked, alone in David's bathroom. How critical she'd been, then defiant, then angry, hateful even. There is none of that here tonight. Even the S&M acts seem playful. And who is she to judge, anyway? Mia liked her husband tying her up in the closet, at least until he decided to be nice.

On stage, the Asian woman in the velvet bustier dances in the feathery shade of two Vegas-styled fans. The girl beside her leans in, green eyes glittering, devil horns strobing red. "Sexy, right?"

Mia shouts over the music. "They're all so confident. And uninhibited."

"I know! It's so empowering!" she says, as the next dancer steps on stage.

From beneath the hem of a leopard print coat, too large and hot for the season, come a pair of skinny legs, clad in knee-high gold boots. On top, honey hair teased to a froth, two feet wide and two feet tall. The dancer's makeup is all parody, sky blue shadow raccooned round big blue eyes, lashes drawn on like a Raggedy-Ann doll's, red lipstick lopsided, sexuality askew. Fast, plucky guitar chords twang from the speakers, turn snarly, the hard bang of a drum, and the performer begins lurching around the stage.

"Oh my god!" the girl beside Mia hollers. "PJ Harvey! Fifty Foot Queenie. I love this song." The act, the music, so different again from the rest. Raw and howling, this performer is a punk amidst coquettes, aggressively out of control, staggering like a drunken fawn. Metallic flashes from beneath her ill-fitting coat, the music a muddy, unrelenting rip of sound. The girl starts spinning, the tails of her coat fly out, only a shimmering miniskirt beneath, skin bronzed, a huge silver peace sign hanging from neck to navel, her tits riding its upper curve.

The dancer lurches to a sudden stop—a counter-point to the music—and, panting, tosses away the coat. It becomes a nothing cast-off, a shabby thrift-shop disguise. Arms wide, shoulders thrown back, she struts across the stage, long legged and high breasted, wild haired and crazed make-up, all awkwardness gone. She's swaggered into a fuck-you goddess, a warrior with no need for weapon or chainmail, a fifty-foot queen no one would dare jerk around.

When the song crashes to an end, the crowd whoops, but Mia is left breathless, heart banging, as if she's just sprinted a hundred miles into the heat of revelation. My god, if she stripped down now in David's bathroom, she'd do so joyfully. Put on some music—something fast and reckless—and shake her breasts at the mirror. Give her ass a happy slap. Worship the flesh that's blessed her with a child, pleasured her and a couple dozen men—Michael only one of the lucky.

When the house lights come up, the girl beside her is beaming. "Wasn't that amaze!" She takes Mia's hand and swings her arm gleefully. "Come meet my friends," she says, and starts leading her toward the back of the bar.

They're not even off the dance floor when Mia's cell phone shivers. She slips it out of her back pocket, the screen lit with the news that she has three new texts from Finn. She tells the girl she'll catch up with her, and standing in a jostle of people starts scrolling through her messages. *Can you pick me up?* Twenty minutes ago. *mom?* Six minutes ago. *can you come get me.* Fifty-seven seconds ago.

Mia keys in a reply. *Where are you?*

Finn's answer is immediate. *downtown corner of bank and powell*

You okay?

No

No? Finn is hardly one for dramatics. *What's up?*

please just come get me please

Hunched over the screen, Mia's face is cast in a lunar glow. *Stay put. Im coming.* And just like that, she's back in it, the thick of her life.

———

WHEN MIA PICKS Finn up, his jeans are wet to the knees. His mouth swollen, his lip split, he has blood on his face and on the front of someone else's shirt. When he tells her what happened his voice is flat. She thinks he might be in shock. She thinks he still might be in shock when she gives him a bag of ice and he lies down on his bed and, instead of the ice, puts his arm across his face and tells her he wants to be alone for a while. She says all right, honey, she says, you rest, I'll come check on you in a while, and she quietly closes his door.

The hall closet was one of the first she cleaned out so it's easy to find the bat. Propped in the back corner, beside a pair of tall yellow rain boots. She's relieved Michael hasn't taken it. She would have had to pillage the house for something else—a golf club, maybe. Or a hammer.

She tosses the bat onto the Jetta's passenger seat. Slides behind the wheel and backs fast out of the driveway. She is not in shock. She is thinking straight. At least she thinks she's thinking straight. She's got the bat. She's not driving recklessly. She's using her brakes and her blinkers.

She parks a neat six inches from the curb in front of the Kellys'. It isn't until she smashes out the red rocket lights on the fins of the Cadillac, Beyoncé-style, that she even starts breathing hard. There's a pop when each taillight breaks, a plasticky tinkle as the pieces fall onto the driveway: two scatterplots of red, small and dull against the asphalt.

She waits for something to happen. For a light to snap on in the house. For someone to shout. For someone to come running. The croak of frogs rises from the river across the street and a barely-there bass thuds like a faraway heartbeat, but otherwise the night remains calm. Mia moves to bash off the mirrors, but the sides of the Cadillac are clean. And bookending the toothy chrome grille, the headlights are small, sunken things; they lack the power to either amplify or dissipate—nothing will be changed with them gone.

She leaves the driveway and walks the path along the side of the house. Mia has not been in the backyard since the fall, the night of Eli's seventeenth birthday. Don had been pouring, and like most of the guests, she and Michael ended up drinking too much. At home they'd had clumsy sex, and Mia had woken next morning with her brain throbbing inside a freshly shrunken skull. That was the last time she'd been to the Kellys'. She'd seen no point in journeying back to the scene of Finn's accident. She'd wanted only to move forward, felt no need to look for someone to blame. But things are different now.

Now the grass is green and the trees are leafy and the pool is sparkling blue. Though the backyard is empty, all the loungers on the pool deck are empty, every light is on. The floods at the base of the biggest oaks, the small pots sunken in the pool's concrete perimeter, and of course at each corner of the cabana, tucked beneath the eaves, a spotlight, bright enough to save any boy, in any kind of weather.

Seeing them now, Mia is nearly overcome by the cruelty of what Eli has done. At the cabana, she stares up into the hot white glare until she is blind to everything beyond the light. She could be staring into the face of God or bearing witness to the end of the world as, two-handed, she raises the bat. Rage rises along with it, but also sorrow, so as she swings it is not a scream that escapes her but a sob.

The light explodes above her, loud and sharp. She tucks her chin to her shoulder to protect herself from her own violence and the place where she is standing falls dim.

"It was the other one."

She turns toward the voice, but the light has seared her retinas, made a negative of the world. Where there should be a man, there is only a black hole, fuzzy around the edges. "The other corner," Eli says. Eli at the centre. Footsteps pad across the wooden deck, barefoot and nearly soundless once he steps onto the grass. Mia blinks, trying to clear her vision. Eli becomes a stocky mass, featureless and faceless as he moves toward her, his one arm raised. "It was that one." He points behind her, at the far corner of the cabana. He is ten feet from her when she swings the bat in a wide, graceless arc.

"Stay away from me," she says. "I swear to God, Eli, you stay back."

"He was lying right where you are." He steps closer. Mia's ankle rolls when he presses the grass beside her foot. "His head was here, and his body was that way, by the wall."

Eli isn't even hurt. He has a tiny scratch on his face. A fight? It doesn't look like Finn even hit him.

"He was pretty deep in the snow," Eli says. He says, "It was cold . . . minus thirty, minus thirty-five that night."

This time Mia screams as she smashes the light. Severed filaments, like broken spider legs, shudder from the neck of the bulb.

Eli brushes shards of glass from his shoulder. "Someone would have seen him. If I hadn't turned it off." He looks empty. Mia goes empty, too.

"He was your best friend." Her voice icy. Minus thirty, minus thirty-five.

Eli is very close now, standing barefoot in a glitter of glass. She has known him most of his life. Photographed him, fed him, taken him on family vacations. She turns her head away. On the far side of the yard, the big oak is a lacework of leaves and branches. Furrowed by light. Gushing green. Horrible with beauty. Like the shimmering scrap of pool.

In front of her, Eli widens his stance. His arms hang loose at his sides. His hands are open. His whole body open to her.

"You hurt my son." She takes one step back, a crunch of glass, and brings the bat to her shoulder.

———

I COULDN'T SEE HER. My arm was over my face, but she sounded weird. I'll come check on you in a while, she said. Kind of flat but fake flat. Like she was lying. Like it was doomsday outside my bedroom and she had no plans for getting back. When the front door slammed I got up and went into her room, watched her back out of the driveway, the Jetta bouncing and jerking and then gliding smooth and slow up the street so I thought maybe she'd changed her mind and had decided not to be crazy. Thought it, but wasn't convinced.

It's the primal scream that gets me running, past my mom's car, along the side of Eli's house. They're by the shed. Under a busted light, standing in a patch of darkness. My mom's got a baseball bat on her shoulder, lined up with Eli's head. The weird thing is I'm not even that surprised. My life is that fucked up, everyone an inch away from killing each other.

I step into the backyard slowly, in case speed is the thing that trips the switch tonight. Not anger or jealousy or madness, just one body moving too fast toward another. When my mom sees me, her face softens. I watch her come back into herself, sane again, but spent.

When I'm close enough, she hands me the bat. I whip it away, a pathetic, wrong-handed toss. The bat wobbles through the air like a shot and falling bird, skids along the concrete. Barely a splash and it's floating quiet on the water, my father's Louisville Slugger in Eli Kelly's pool.

I sway on my feet for a second, trying to understand what's happening, what anything is about. Eli and my mom stare back at me, like stun-gunned children, like I'm the one who caused all the harm.

It's okay, I say. We're all right. But my eye's swollen shut and my face is kind of throbbing on the side where Eli hit me and my mother was going to hit him with my father's baseball bat and my hand is gone. My hand is gone and Jess is gone and Eli saw me, and he turned off the light.

We're okay, I say again. But I wonder. I wonder if in a moment of dying, or expanding into the universe, it's possible to be wrong. Like completely and totally wrong.

And I'm not sure why I do it but I have to do something so I step between Eli and my mom and I reach out and I put my stump on his forehead.

He leans back against the shed and closes his eyes.

I forgive you, I say. And I tap one of my Frankenstein knobs against his brow bone a couple of times. Harder, maybe, than either of us expected. More a knock than a tap. I forgive you, I tell him as I drag the brutal red hack of it around his face, the way my father dragged it around the sink. I slide my stump down his cheek like Eric slid the box across the bar, like Jess slid her hand into my pyjama pants the very first time.

Fuck sake, Finn. It's practically in his mouth. He looks like he's going to cry. I'm sorry, he says. Sounds like he's going to cry.

I've only cried once since it happened. Once in five fucking months. That time I was out here having a barbecue for one because I can't use a fork and a knife. I've taken my anguish out on a map. Told myself that what happened to me was worth losing a piece of myself. Knowing everything strips back to beautiful. Knowing everyone melts down to love.

I'm sorry, Eli says, and this time I put some weight into it, really press my stump into his forehead and kind of pin him against the shed.

I understand I fucked up that night with Frankie. And I understand Eli was drunk and he was mad. But I was practically dead when my father found me. It took the medics something like five minutes to find a fucking pulse.

Finn. My mom puts her hand on my shoulder. Hey. Finn.

I watch the bat bobbing around in the water, bumping against the side of the pool. I could go get it. I could go get it right now and I could smack Eli with it, turn his head to pulp. I could give it to Frankie, let her club me for being that kind of guy. I could admit that what happened to me out here was probably just a combination of insane jealousy and wicked weather, helped along by booze and drugs. That it didn't really mean anything, and I don't know shit about fearlessness or love. That Jess doesn't love me, never loved me, will never love me and I lost my hand because Eli and I both want girls we cannot have, we're all just cavemen like Cleopatra said.

Finn.

I could go get the bat. My father wanted to teach me the game he grew up playing. He wanted me to be just like him.

My whole body a shake and my stump pressing into Eli's forehead and tears running down his face and my mom holding tight to my shoulder. I almost died. Do you get that? You almost killed me. I spit the words at him.

Finn. Come on. Let's go home.

I forgive you, okay? I forgive you, you stupid fucking prick.

We leave him there, bawling under the busted-out light. We leave the bat floating on the water, by the steps, in the shallow end of the pool.

"YOU WANT SOME PIZZA?" Mia lifts up a flap and peers into a Domino's box at two waxy-looking slices, their edges curling away from the oil-stained cardboard.

"Do we have steak?"

"Really?" Mia straightens up out of the fridge. "Steak?"

Finn is sitting at the kitchen table, a family-sized bag of Green Giant peas covering one side of his face. When he lowers the bag, water drips onto the table. His top lip is split. His one nostril dark with dried blood. A smudged crescent of purplish black floats beneath his right eye.

She touches her fingers to her own mouth. "Will that even be, okay?"

"I want steak." Finn lifts the bag of peas back to his face, so his voice is muffled by plastic. "And a baked potato."

She finds a frost-fringed package of sirloins at the bottom of the freezer and thaws them in the microwave. The meal will take a bit of work, but at least she doesn't have to come up with a menu. After the surreal drive home from Eli's, Finn wanted to go straight to his room. She told him she'd make him something to eat, just to keep him downstairs.

From a bottom cupboard, she unearths a ten-pound bag of PEI potatoes. Uses a small paring knife to gouge the eyes out of a couple of the firmer ones. Gleams their yellow skins with softened butter. She pours olive oil into a copper-bottomed fry pan, adds a mash of garlic and salt, a few slices of onion. The steaks sizzle when they hit the pan.

She turns on the CBC. Instrumental music, long breaks between the announcer. Big band swings into the kitchen, then a flute solo of all things, Etude No. 5, a French composer she's never heard of. The music swells into her, like a hollow wind opening in her chest.

"Remember that scene in *Anchorman* with Will Ferrell?" Finn looks over from behind the frozen peas. "Would everybody love to hear Ron Burgundy play some yazz flute?" she says, in her best Latino accent.

"Mom . . . Please don't."

She plates the food and carries it to the table. Goes back for the butter dish and the salt and pepper. "I hope you're hungry," she says lightly, sitting down next to Finn, "because you know I hate cooking."

He smiles, barely, and she rests her hand on the side of his face, cold from the bag of peas, which now lies collapsed on the table in a pink-hued puddle of condensate. She runs her thumb across his eyebrow, the swollen corner of his lips. "Your beautiful face," she says, and his eyes flicker to the windows.

The outside lights are on. Tonight the world presses in. Wisteria hangs thick on the trellis, although its mauve chandeliers have fallen, as they should have by mid-July. A cloud of rusty red leaves hides the fruit ripening on the branches of the crabapple tree, and on the far side of their gap-toothed fence, the triplex's windows are dark. Unlike Michael, Mia's never really minded the added-on fire escape; she appreciates its light lines and the geometry of its structure, the fact it might save somebody's life.

The arm Finn's been hiding for months now lies undisguised on the table. Healed, but the end cap of skin still slicker and redder than the rest. It's better than the last time Mia got a good look at it, but it will never look great.

"Guess Eli's seen it now," she says.

"Yeah. And Dad's baseball bat." She feels Finn watching as she slices open a potato. "What if I hadn't shown up?"

Mia pauses, her knife and fork pointed into opposite corners of the room. "I don't know."

She'd taken the bat over to the Kellys' for a reason. Had she planned only on destroying property or had the property owners also been in play? Would she have clubbed Don if he'd staggered into the backyard? Would she have hit Eli if Finn hadn't shown up when he did? Eli wanted her to—maybe that's what saved him.

She'd like to think she had no intention of hurting anyone, but she can't deny the rush that claimed her when she smashed out the first spotlight. Just to hit something. To break one fucking light. The release she'd felt, the relief, the shameful satisfaction. Why, then, had she sobbed?

When Eli stood before her, eager for punishment, she'd thought of the dancer shedding her leopard print coat, stepping out as an emboldened goddess, her peace sign gleaming. She'd thought of Michael at the birthday party, the intimacy of their kiss. She'd seen Finn creeping across the lawn and a great relief had flooded through her. To see him alive in the place he might have died.

The crabapple's branches sway, and the fluttery leaves of the wisteria align with the breeze that's blowing in through the garden-room windows. Mia hadn't even realized she was hot until the night air reached her. It's late. After two in the morning. The coolest hour of summer.

"I wouldn't have hit him." Even before Finn got there, even empty, hostile to beauty, with a bat grown heavy on her shoulder, she'd been loath to hurt him. And when Finn pressed his stump to Eli's forehead—that had been hard to watch. When she gripped his shoulder, she'd felt his rage, how it shook him. How he had to battle back. Fight down his arm. Walk away one-handed.

My god—what Eli's done. What he has to live with. He's lucky, though. Lucky Michael wasn't the one holding the bat; man's been practising his swing all summer.

Mia slices into the meat and the juices run.

"You know that night, when I was out there in the snow?"

"Yeah." She cuts Finn's steak into bite-sized pieces, just doing what she's doing, so he can stare off into their backyard and tell her how the colder he got that night the more beautiful things got around him. The more connected. How it felt like maybe he was dying but also melting into something bigger. And love was everywhere and everything. *Love.* His voice tremors when he says the word; if her hand were still on his shoulder, Mia thinks she might feel a current.

She splits open a potato. Melts butter into its soft, white flesh. Wouldn't it be wonderful if it were true? Love powering the universe, dead centre of every chest. Ready to strike us open—the first piercing—setting loose what's already inside. What she has with

Michael is so much weightier. Love exposed to a steady light, stretched and thinned and emptied out, ignored, rejected, derided, and then maybe, maybe returned for another round.

"Sometimes it's hard, you know, to believe it," he says. "When it feels like no one else does."

Mia adds a dash of salt to the potato, dips her knife in for another dab of butter. Finn. Alive. Lying on her chest, clay blue skin, slick with afterbirth. The weight of him, still the weight of her. Lying side by side on his bed, their little fingers knotted. No wall strong enough to break their grip. And she and Michael—they've had a good life together. She wants not to fuck that up.

She pushes the plate toward Finn. "I think if anyone would know what love feels like it would be you," she says. "Eat," she says, and she hands her son a fork.

The 30th

It's been a week and so far nothing. No police have shown up asking if Michael knows anything about a house with all of its back windows missing. No write-up in the papers, nothing on the radio, no articles popping up online about the risks of riverside living in beautiful Old Aberdeen. No irate phone call from Peter and no retaliatory acts of vandalism have banged upon his door—Michael's beginning to believe he might just have gotten away with it.

He and Dirk agreed to lie low, but tonight, he risks a trip to the river. He reaches the water only to find the old fishermen gone, the graffiti bridge abandoned, the baseball diamond dark. When he wipes away the dirt and peers through the shed's back window, the pitching machine is right where they left it, a shadowy bulk of inert metal, like some decommissioned fighting machine left over from a long-ago war. Only the red extension cord he'd hung from the throwing arm, the one he once used to plug in Christmas lights, hints at more civilized times.

Michael's disappointed. He wanted to see the boy, ask him if there'd been any cops poking around. But mostly he wanted to talk about that night, laugh about it, the thrill of what they'd done. He still can't quite believe how easily he and the kid pulled it off. Plan A perfectly executed, at least once they started launching the balls. Michael might not have accomplished much over the last five months, but shit, blasting every window out of that scumbag's house with such skilful precision, now that had been a feat. At some point he and the kid had actually jumped around the deck arm in arm. Jacked on adrenaline, total He-Men, they'd hadn't even broken a sweat getting the pitching machine back into the Jeep. Christ, they could take their show on the road, hire themselves out to anyone with a major league grudge and an appetite for destruction. And the thrill of revenge, Michael hadn't properly anticipated the afterburn of that glory. Man, he'd felt good that night and would have given anything—*anything*—to see Peter's face when he got an eyeful of his new river view, unencumbered by glass.

But now, walking the path through the grass field alone, so still and so quiet, he feels left behind, the only person who didn't get the doomsday news at which all the other citizens fled. Even the chicken wire and hockey sticks have packed it in. Michael saw the emptiness between the goalposts when he passed by. He has no idea if the hatchlings made it back to the river. He'd marched along the edge of the soccer pitch, practically every night this summer, bat in hand, and never once bothered to go take a proper look.

And Michael doesn't know if it was Dirk or him, but that night in the delirium of destruction, the laughter and the whooping, Frankie's window got hit. He'd seen it when they were packing up the Arm. The sheer white curtains wafting from her room like twisted ghosts. High on adrenaline and a couple puffs of weed, he'd thought what the hell. I mean, who had he been kidding? The kid was right. Frankie was going to be impacted. Helen was going to be impacted. With all or most of the glass shattered, either way, they wouldn't have the luxury of feeling safe in their own home.

Under the bridge, he picks up a handful of gravel. Squats by the bank, between the main support columns, and one by one, throws the small stones into the rushing water. He imagines them spinning, mute and near weightless, rolled deep by current and gravity, bouncing off boulders and sunken tree trunks, their eventual landing soft, muddy, a puff of oyster ink where no light reaches, a hundred miles downstream.

The river is real. The river is always. The river cuts and carves, sweeps and swallows—anything weak, poorly attached, unable to resist its current. The canal: tidy stone walls and gentle waters, designed by men, built by men, controlled by men. Maybe that's what Mia didn't like about that dance performance. The column of rain centre stage, the conceit of the natural world harnessed.

Michael takes more time between throws. He tells himself he is a good man, that in his life he hasn't caused much harm. That it was only glass he broke. He tells himself when this handful of stones is gone, he'll go home. Let Mia know he's ready to start seriously looking for work. Tell Finn he's not mad anymore. They don't have to know how his anger dissipated, how he released it out into the world. They don't need to know anything about a back wall of broken windows or a diabetic street kid or an old pitching machine tucked away in a falling-down shed.

He misses the baseball. The exercise. The dope. The Arm rocketing a ball across home plate. The hard swing of the bat, the crack, the flight, the randomness of the boy. His energy. His foul mouth. His cockiness, a mix of vulgar and vulnerable. It wasn't always pretty, but Michael doesn't think the kid ever lied to him, and, well, that's something. Even the diabetes thing was real.

He pulls back his arm to throw another stone when a bright speck comes rushing at him, riding the fast-moving water. A brilliant purple circle, and quick, without thinking, he plunges in his hand and scoops it from the river. He lets the cool water drip onto the gravel before he uncurls his fingers. On his palm, a flower, smaller than a dime. Five cloverleaves of wet, velvety purple fanning from a drop of white. Michael nudges a petal with his fingernail and exposes an inch of stem, transparent green, thin as dental floss.

It's not a wildflower—too bright, too cultured, too cared for. It must have blown from someone's garden, carried by the wind, separated from a larger cluster. He doesn't even think about tossing it away or floating it back onto the water. It might be nothing, it might be dumb, but he's going to take it home. Tell Mia it's a gift from the river.

The 31st

Can you pass me the toast? My dad smiling at me like he actually means it. I put my juice down and hand him the plate. I'm at my usual place at the table, facing her house, so when she walks into the backyard I'm in position. But it's not her. It's her mom. Carrying a basket. Both my parents turn to watch her hang laundry on the line as jazz plays in the kitchen.

I barely ever see that woman, my father says as she snaps a pair of jeans from the basket.

She works all the time, my mom says. Nights still, I think.

She looks like Jess. But smaller, stiffer, still pretty though, and watching her—I can't help it—I start wondering again about the goats. If that story was true or Jess was just playing around with our ignorance.

She grabs a white T-shirt from the basket, gives it a shake, and pins it up beside the jeans. I don't recognize any of it. Nothing of hers. Maybe she got something new. It's possible. I haven't seen her since my birthday.

I ran into Jess the other day, my mom says, like it's no big deal, like she didn't just crawl into my head. At David's building. Apparently, Don has a unit there. She and Eric have moved in.

My bite of toast sticks in my throat. I breathe around it; there's no way I can swallow.

I wish her luck with that, my dad says. The radio song ends. Another one comes on.

She says they're getting married. Next spring. At a resort in Costa Rica. I think Don might own it. My mom takes a sip of coffee, while I die a little more. I mean, I knew. But still, I die a little more.

Christ, my father says. How old is she?

Twenty-three? Twenty-four? Old enough, I guess.

But Eric Kelly?

At least it's not some sixty-five-year-old with a potbelly and a yacht. My mom sets her cup back down. Jess is a survivor. She'll figure it out.

You know I saw her that night. My father raises his eyebrows at me. The night I went looking for you.

I take a glug of OJ, swallow hard, work the soggy lump of toast and peanut butter down the narrow pipe of my throat.

She was drunk, my father says, sick, half passed out on the bathroom floor. He starts buttering his toast, dragging the knife across the bread, making that dry, scraping sound, scraping it down to its core. It's a relief when he sticks the knife back into the butter.

She told me she loved you, he says.

I stare at the table. At the shot glass in the middle. A miniature flower floating in it. Purple. Impossible. A bouquet for an elf.

I was asking her if she knew where you were, if she'd seen you, my father keeps talking, buttering more toast, the knife gliding easy now, and she said, I just love Finn.

Jess has always been crazy about you, my mother says. Right from the beginning, she was . . . Hey, honey? Finn? Finn!

But I'm already gone. Out of the kitchen. Up to my room. So I can lie on my bed. And close my eyes. To be alone so I can feel the truth, like a miracle rushing in.

MIA FROWNS INTO her coffee. "That boy."

"He's coming to grips with losing his hand. It's got to be tough." Michael picks Sunday's *New York Times* off the chair beside him. He hands Mia the magazine and starts thumbing through the sections.

She flips to the table of contents. "He's been so quiet all week."

"He's got an appointment with his psychologist tomorrow," Michael says. "If you want, I can take him."

"It's my turn. I'll go. Maybe I can get him to open up in the car."

And Michael's not exactly sure how to go about it, but he's going to get him "to open up" about the hook he found under Frankie's bed. He'll think of something—the thing's worth twenty-five hundred bucks. And he knows Mia would never agree, but he thinks shoving Finn's hands into the sink that day might have done its job. Made him face up to the reality that the way he is now, he can't even wash a wine glass. Sure, it was rough, but as a kid, Michael saw far worse. Maybe it did wake Finn up, might even be the trigger that has them all moving forward again, slowly, as a family. Sometimes softness works, sometimes you need a shakeup.

Michael doesn't really understand what happened between Finn and Eli, what their fight was about. A girl, apparently. Finn wouldn't say more than that. He's looking better, just a scab now, matting his one eyebrow. There are things about him, about Mia, that Michael will never know. That it's probably better not to.

Mia liked the flower. Laughed when she saw it lying bright on Michael's palm. Tiny but tough, capable of surviving a fast river ride, a journey through the city in a loosely coiled fist, in two ounces of tap water, afloat on a kitchen table. Out the back windows, summer sunshine and freshly hung laundry. Today, even the shitty fire escape looks alright.

In the kitchen, the Sunday-morning radio show breaks for the hourly news. Michael tunes it out. He opens the sports section, but only grazes the pages. Things are better. Easier between them. He and Mia are being kind to each other. They've both been sticking close to home. Last night, up in bed, it felt as if they reached for each other at the same moment, finally, after so many months. Their lovemaking like a return from exile. His body wrapped in her arms. Her body welcoming his. *I know you.* Bracing himself on his elbows, he slid lightly into her. *I know you.*

"What did they say?" Michael lowers his paper. Watches Mia take the two steps from the back room into the kitchen, her eyes fixed on the radio, on the counter, beside the stove. "Something about Big Yirkie. A break and enter. A boat being set on fire."

"What?" Michael mouths the word.

Forearms on the counter, Mia leans in and turns up the volume.

"Four males, ages estimated between sixteen and twenty-five, are being sought by police on charges of breaking and entering, arson and the sexual assault of a minor. Police are asking for the public's help. Please go to our website at—"

Mia turns down the radio. "You don't think . . ." Her hand floats to her throat. "No, it can't be."

No. It can't be. Of course it can't.

August

> For every action, there is an
> equal and opposite reaction.
>
> NEWTON'S THIRD LAW

The 1st

Mia takes the casserole from the oven, puts a bottle of Pérez Cruz in a canvas shopping bag along with a fresh baguette, and totes it all out to the car. On the drive over to Peter and Helen's, she stalls the Jetta twice—once at the stop sign at the end of her street, once when she pops the clutch at the four-way pulling onto theirs.

Despite Frankie's age, bits of the story have trickled out—a minor whose name cannot be released sexually assaulted by four boys while her mother played bridge at a neighbour's cottage and her father stood guard at the family's recently vandalized home. The news moves in Mia like a poison. Her hands tremor, her stomach cramps. She wakes to her own cries, the sheets damp and Michael gone from the bed, the room hot with the aftershock of nightmares and humid summer air.

In the car, Mia flogs herself with the memory of the day Frankie came looking for a birthday present for her father. Upset. Needing to talk. And Mia had upset her further. She hadn't lowered her camera when Frankie asked her to stop. All for the sake of a photograph. Or was it a hit of power, having power in that moment over a vulnerable girl? Mia no longer gives herself the benefit of any doubt.

269

And the rough sex she and Michael had when Finn was still in the hospital has shaded to a darker hue. The thrill and relief in that game of control and submission, the fight and the yielding, feeling she'd made some sort of escape. But an escape from what? Being a wife? A mother? A responsible, loving woman in a world written by men? When Michael strung her up in the closet, she'd had no desire for tenderness. She'd wanted him to be a harder, more powerful kind of man. Lying so still on the bathroom floor, with his full weight upon her, she'd thought not only *danger* but *security.* Which feels like nonsense now. An old fairy tale seeped under her skin: man as conqueror, protector, king. Fifty shades of bullshit. Delete the money, scratch out *yes,* and what's left of the fantasy? All humanity diminished by what four boys did to a girl.

Mia parks the car alongside the stand of birch trees, at the far edge of the Conrads' driveway, a respectful distance from the door. When she sets the bag with the bread and the wine down on the front porch and waits for her knock to be answered, she remembers being this frightened only once in her life. When she and Michael followed a nurse down the hallway in the ICU before the doctors would say if Finn would live.

Footsteps clack inside the house, grow louder, stop on the other side of the door. Mia senses she is being watched through the peephole, her head fish-eyed, her body warped to small. In her mind's eye, only the red enamel casserole dish she holds in front of her maintains its proper proportions. Warm vapours waft up from the pot—creamed mushrooms, chicken juices, garlic fried in butter.

The door cracks open. Helen's face is slivered between it and the wall. And in that sliver, wreckage. Their eyes lock, Helen reaches through the narrow gap and seizes Mia's arm, gripping, squeezing, *my god, my god, Frankie . . .*

She steps onto the porch. Her hair is loose and unkempt, her long legs bare in a pair of navy shorts. She seems skittish. She seems to have lost inches of height. Behind her the hallway tunnels dark to the back of the house.

She takes the casserole dish from Mia and sets it on the bench beside the door.

"Chicken and mushroom," Mia says, swiping at her eyes. "Your recipe. Your pot."

Helen remains hunched over the bench, as if she's forgotten the mechanics of straightening her spine. Mia places a hand lightly on her back. Like the aching apart of continents, a deep whimper escapes Helen before she turns and presses her face to Mia's shoulder.

In Mia's arms, her frame is so much smaller than Michael's or Finn's. Holding Helen is like holding an elongated bird—the flightless wings of her shoulder blades, the light tremble of haunted bones.

"Helen?" Peter calls from somewhere inside. "Helen!"

With the front door open, Mia has a sightline straight to the back of the house. She can't see Peter, but the living room is even darker than the hallway, as if every curtain has been drawn against the light. But it's not the curtains. It takes a moment for Mia to realize the windows have been boarded over, as if braced for a storm that has already hit.

Peter appears in profile at the far end of the hall, a tall silhouette. It's been so long since Mia's seen him. He stares into the living room and then swivelling his head he finds them, framed in the doorway in a bright rectangle of sunshine. Helen and Mia are no longer embracing but they are still entangled, their arms slung low across one another's back.

He strides toward them. Almost to the door, his leg knocks against a lumpy garbage bag slouched against the wall. With a plastic crinkle, its load shifts, and one, then two baseballs thud onto the floor. Mia blinks as each one falls. Baseballs. A whole bag full of baseballs.

Helen steps away and lifts the casserole dish from the bench.

Peter stares at Mia from just inside the doorway, the balls rolled up close behind him. White with red stitching; they could belong to anyone. Peter's hair has been cut short. He looks older, balder, a new hollowness around his eyes.

"Mia brought us some dinner," Helen says. He glances at the dish in her hands, then back to Mia.

"Get off my fucking property," he says, and for a second Mia is too taken aback to react. "Stay away from my fucking wife."

Helen turns away from them both.

Mia's almost to the car when something heavy smashes onto the driveway—Helen's casserole dish. Fresh mushrooms and heavy cream, puréed broccoli, garlic, lots of pepper and a half cup of shredded cheese. Three chicken breasts cut into cubes and cooked until the juices ran clear. A meal they used to share at the cabin after a day of skiing, comfort food now splattered across the asphalt and the backs of Mia's legs.

The 3rd

Twice in the past three days, Michael was sure he was having a heart attack. After recovering from the first, he looked up the symptoms online and ticked off every box. But when the next one hit—when his chest tightened and his jaw ached and he could not draw air into his lungs for the pressure—he could not bring himself to tell Mia or call 911. And both times when he lay down the symptoms slowly passed. While a spastic, blood-sputtering muscle would be one way out, lying on the bed sweaty and terrified as his heart rate fell back to normal, Michael is ashamed to admit that first and foremost, he was thankful to have survived.

He keeps the radio on at all times now, his eye on news websites, the television, the front door, the windows, but so far, none of the boys have been found. Yesterday the descriptions came out. For the most part vague, heights and weights, skin and hair colour. There'd been nothing about perfect teeth or skinny ankles or puffy red running shoes, but from only a few brief words in the paper, Michael had known them all. Anyone who'd seen him would recognize the tattooed guy. If they're caught, when they're caught, Michael has no doubt he'll be picked up and taken in for questioning. Charged with breaking and entering, destruction of property . . . and all the rest. He has an alibi, he was home with Mia that night thank god, but obviously none for the one he spent blowing tens of thousands of dollars' worth of glass from the victim's riverside home.

Frankie's home. His son's friend. His once friend's daughter. A little kid wrestling him off the dock in a striped bikini. A teenager flashing him an après-ski peace sign. A beautiful broad-shouldered girl with her arms raised, sighting a ball into a glove.

Michael tortures himself with the details. That's what brings on the heart attacks.

Rae Chan would have decided, his cold blue eyes upon her. His capable, paint-stained hands. His deep radio voice issuing impossible commands.

He would have been first to rape her.

Maybe when he was finished, he told the boy to go next.

Take that, you bitch, he'd said, every time he nailed the pitching machine. No, no, no, yes. Pussy old man. All the little abuses Michael let slide; he would never have done that with Finn. Thinking his responsibilities ended at his own front door, looking out for himself and his family and to hell with everyone else. Thinking they lived in some bubble. *Christ!* There is no fucking bubble! Everything leaks out, everything seeps in. Give it time and the shit always rises to level on both sides of the divide.

He should have made the kid pick up the beer bottle, given him hell about the pitching machine, told him to watch his goddamn mouth. Better yet, he should have called Peter on his bullshit the millisecond after the bookkeeper talked to him, demanded he sell the boat then and fucking there. Just that and none of this would have happened.

What had he been *thinking*? Taking that kid to their house, throwing a stone in their little money war, too arrogant in that moment to acknowledge the likelihood of collateral damage. Pretending that glass broken, revenge exacted, all ripples would cease. But when has life ever been that simple or history writ a violence so neat? Twenty dollars, thirty-five thousand dollars, a million and a half dollars. Picture frame, dock chair, window. Stone, stone, stone.

What had Frankie called him? Her second dad? With two hands he rips at his hair, bangs his head into his pillow. He can no longer claim to be a good man, worthy of a decent life. The worst has happened. He deserves every consequence coming his way.

He gets out of bed. He no longer sleeps. The clock reads exactly 4 a.m. While Mia tosses under the covers, he dresses in the dark, then goes and gets the green duffle bag from the garage. Empty, except for two baseball gloves, one man-sized, one slightly smaller. He rummages through the front closet but cannot find the bat. He searches the house, the garage, the Jeep, under the seats, in the back. He goes over everything in his mind. Did he leave it in the shed? With the extension cord? Not that night, he didn't. But before? He's sure the bat's not there, and he's not going to check. When he pictures the shed, he pictures it staked out, a SWAT team horseshoed in the long grass beyond the outfield, boots and bellies and the butts of assault rifles pressing into the dirt.

He knew. He fucking *knew*. Lugging the pitching machine out of the backyard with some white trash stoner boy, he'd seen the curtains wafting from Frankie's window. Maybe his imagination was too narrow, too cinctured by privilege to ever take the real nightmare scenarios seriously or conjure the exact nature or extent of the horror—not him, not his kind—but he knew what he'd put at risk. And the missile that dropped him to his knees at the ball diamond? The hook that scratched at him from under the bed? It's not like he hadn't been warned.

In the driveway, Michael's bowels turn liquid. He barely makes it to the toilet to shit out his insides. After he cleans himself up, he carries the duffle bag to the river, the gloves bumping against his legs. The bat should be in the bag, too, but instead, it will be one more thing that keeps him up at night.

Near the spot where the old men fished, Michael squats and begins filling the bag with rocks from the riverbank, wet and heavy and slick. Early August, the tang of spring rot has been replaced by the fragrance of summer. The air's cool and fresh near the water and Michael is completely alone. It's too late for anyone honourable to still be out, too early for anyone lucky to have risen.

Reaching for another rock, his hand dips into the river. The water pushes warm against his palm. His fingers have to work to fight the downstream drift. Michael turns his hand sideways and the pressure eases, a dark, easy flow splitting around his wrist. He reaches deeper for a bigger rock and something—slippery, scaly— brushes against his fingers. He jerks his hand away as a clawed limb rises slowly from the water and slaps onto the rocky bank, inches from his foot. A leg. A lizard leg. Michael scrambles up onto the grass behind him as the thing drags itself from the river.

Head like a prehistoric cock, thick, slit-eyed, breathing in and out of a wattled neck. A giant plated shell, green with algae, stuck with mud. At the lip of the bank, the snapping turtle reaches up a stumpy leg and a fleshy membrane stretches from its soft underbelly. Oblivious to Michael, it hulks onward, in the direction of the public dock, its dinosaur-spiked tail dragging slow over the grass. Twenty feet downriver, the turtle vanishes into the murk of a willow tree, under a long sway of dark branches.

Quickly, before he loses his last wisp of courage or decides what he's doing is insane, which it is, Michael lugs the duffle bag, bumpy with rocks, up onto the overpass. Six lanes of traffic and not a car in sight. In the middle of the span, he drops the bag into the deepest, fastest water, and in an instant it is gone.

He forces himself across the road, onto the abandoned sidewalk. Grips the railing and presses his forehead to its concrete cap, like a man in desperate prayer. A minute, two minutes pass, before he lifts his head. The ball diamond is just beginning to lighten along with the sky, the chain link hinting at silver, mist weeping from the blue-black earth.

Even now, even after everything, Michael thinks it's beautiful, this perverted field of dreams. He longs to have stayed right there, tinkering with the pitching machine, slamming balls into the outfield, hurting no one, breaking nothing, just releasing steam until fall came, winter came, his anger cooled, the case settled, Mia forgave him, Finn got better, Peter paid in full—the happy ending everyone thought was deserved.

It could have happened. It was so easily possible. Better actions, better outcomes. Simple as that. The motivational posters aren't always wrong. Brave now, because you don't get to go back for another round.

And Dirk. He could have stayed a lost boy, an outsider even among outsiders, stumbling around in his red high-tops, stoned and harmless, trying to catch balls in Finn's old baseball glove. For a second, Michael lets himself wonder where he is. If he's even still alive. He doesn't know. He shouldn't care. The boy has done unspeakable things. It's better if he's dead, if all of them are dead.

The cabin where they'd been staying has been found. A search confirmed that the property across the lake from Peter's was owned by an old widow, and that the boys who'd broken in really liked their porn and their booze and their drugs.

From his bird's-eye view on the bridge, it's apparent there are no robocops in the grass field, no guns trained on the falling-down shed. Michael's seen too many movies. When they come for him, it'll be some old fart with a paunch who slaps on the cuffs. His will be a civilized takedown, as he gets yanked from his civilized world.

Michael holds tight to the railing, the concrete cap cool beneath his palms. He narrows his eyes and sees her on the field, beneath an old floodlight he had no right to turn on. Cut-off shorts, a flowered top, a slip of skin anchored by bellybutton. She scowls up at him, shocked and indignant, as she shakes out her arm. *Take it easy, Michael. We're just two people tossing around a ball.*

If he weren't such a coward, he'd go drag the Arm to the river and drown it alongside the bag. Burn down the shed. Pave over the ball diamond. Destroy that piece of himself. He imagines the graffiti grenade hanging high up on the main support column finally detonating, the whole bridge crumbling, his body crumbling along with it, dropping in dusty chunks into the water, the cast of a modern man, chipped from million-year-old stone.

If he were a better man, he would do it. If he were a bigger man, he would jump.

The 4th

Birch trees pole past as I longboard up the driveway. In front of the house, a truck I don't recognize. Humphrey's Glass and Mirror—I read the name through the panes clamped along the side.

No one's really seen her since it happened, but we've been texting a lot. She knows I'm coming over. I'm not sure about her mom and dad. I pick up my board and the front door opens. Two guys in white overalls push past me, hustling for the truck. Then Helen is there, on the porch.

Finn, she says, with a busted smile. It's been a while. Frankie will be happy to see you. She keeps her eyes off my missing hand.

I follow her into the house. A breeze blows up the hallway, flapping the sleeves of her blouse. At first I think the back door must be open. But then I see the big, empty rectangles framing the backyard. In the living room, a leaf, fresh and green, tumbles across the carpet.

Helen doesn't say anything about the missing windows, and I don't ask. With one knuckle, she taps on Frankie's door. Finn's here, she says, poking her head into the room, the door tight to her shoulder. Okay? And then she lets me in.

Frankie's curled up on the bed, her hands tucked between her knees. The door clicks closed behind me. The curtains flap over her like the sleeves of her mother's blouse. The wind and the sun and the river are inside the room, too.

Frankie looks the same as she always has, only a fallen-over version of herself. She doesn't move and for a long time I don't move either. Finally I go and put one knee on the end of the bed, so I'm kind of kneeling, and I rest my hand on her ankle.

Is this okay? I ask. She doesn't say no, so I crawl up behind her, six inches behind her, and shape my body to hers, six inches of air between us. I have to tip my head back because of all her hair. Then we just lie there and listen to her parents fighting out in the hall.

Her father wants me out of his goddamn house. Helen tells him to think about Frankie for a minute. She tells him to smarten up. She tells him over her dead body. Footsteps slam away, going in opposite directions up the hall.

My father's gone crazy, Frankie says.

My father went crazy, too, for a while.

My dad thinks your dad broke our windows.

What? I lift my head. A piece of her hair tickles my nose. No way he'd smash up your house.

I know, she whispers. But somebody did it.

Somebody did it. Somebody did a lot of things. Maybe they blew out the windows first. Howling as the glass broke. Howling as they tore her open.

I don't want to be a coward. I don't want to pretend it didn't happen. I'm sick of pretending things didn't happen. And I want to tell her I'm sorry about what I did in the laundry room. That it was shitty and hurtful, and because it was shitty and hurtful it caused other shitty, hurtful things to happen.

And then I want to tell her something about love. That it exists. That it's real. That it's what we're really made of and who we really are. I want her to believe that. But I'm afraid that she won't. That she can't. Because sometimes when I think about what they did to her, I can barely believe it myself. Love. What they did to her. What they did.

I'm tired, Frankie says. I just want to sleep.

I go to get up, but she reaches back and takes my arm and pulls it around her. Then she knots up her hair so I can move in closer. So our bodies can touch, and we can lie together in the sun and the wind, listening to the river and the curtains flapping lazy into her room, and she can cup her hand over my stump and hold it to her chest so I realize, suddenly, that I am tired, too.

September

The 1st

My dad's got his head in the fridge when I tell him Peter thinks he broke their windows. He pauses, his hand frozen in the veggie drawer. *What?*

I explain about the windows, but he still doesn't exit the fridge. He lets go of a tomato, shuffles containers of yogurt, a block of old cheddar, the milk. It takes a while before he swings the door closed.

That's awful, he says, giving me a grimace. But I don't know a thing about it. You want some breakfast? he says, and holds up a carton of eggs.

I can't tell if he's lying. The carton's so steady in his hands.

He fries the eggs, chewing on his lips and looking a little wrecked, which is pretty much his natural state now. My mom's at her studio like usual, and there's no bacon in the house, so I just do the toast.

You've seen her? he says, so stiffly I can tell he had to make himself ask. And he knows I go over there.

Yeah. Pretty much every day.

How is she? He flips the eggs, breaks both yolks.

Brutal, I tell him. Scared. Angry. Quiet. Tired all the time. I glance over, but he keeps staring into the pan. She told me you guys played baseball one night this summer. She said you had a good time.

We did. He swipes hard at his nose, nudges the eggs around the pan.

I don't tell him that whenever we played together I always felt bad about myself after. Like I'd never make him happy. Like he was big and I would always be small.

The toast pops. I go get the plates. When I turn back, my dad's hunched over the counter, the spatula hanging limp in his hand.

It takes me a while to ask. You okay?

He turns his head, and I see he's crying, just all these tears running down his face.

Get her outside, he says. Get her out into the sun.

The 12th

David and Mia shake hands, rather formally, Michael thinks as the bell for the elevator dings. All business now, their lawyer holds open the door, thanks them for coming, offers reassurances that he'll do all he can to fix another date for the mediation. He reaches inside his suit jacket, pulls a slim white envelope from his breast pocket and presses it into Mia's hand. It's an awkward exchange—his arm practically caught by the closing doors—but Michael doesn't feel he has the right to ask any questions.

"Last cheque," Mia tells him, as if sensing his reluctance to pry. "For the condo."

"It's done, then?" He leans forward, thankful for a relatively neutral topic of discussion. The lobby button lights at his touch.

"I'm done." She slides the envelope into her purse and snaps the clasp shut. "David's new girlfriend is finishing up. Tiffany. His twenty-six-year-old yoga instructor." The elevator begins its descent from the thirty-sixth floor. "She bought some paintings at HomeSense," she says. "They match the living room."

"Sounds awful." Michael chuckles, in sympathy, pretending he is still half of the couple he and Mia once were, the one everybody believed in, the one everyone thought would last. He holds himself upright, squares his shoulders. He put a suit on for the meeting. Mia wore a dress.

"The space was beautiful," she says, with great seriousness, "and now there's shitty art on the walls."

The elevator glides smoothly downward, 25, 24, 23 lighting up the panel. Michael experiences a moment of vertigo, the elevator dropping faster than he is, leaving the soles of his shoes light on the floor, his insides pulling upward by a false reversal of gravity. He rearranges his facial features in an attempt to look steady beside his wife.

She's been spending most nights at her studio. When he took lunch over for her the other day, he saw the bed she'd made for herself at the back. Their old toaster oven on the counter, her toothbrush in a glass by the sink. She's leaving him, slowly, probably with Finn in mind. She is standing a foot to his left, falling along with him, and already she is gone.

"We should have expected it," Mia says.

"Yes."

"That Peter wouldn't come."

"Yes," Michael says again, realigning his thoughts.

"What he's going through?" Mia says. "What they're all going through? It's no wonder he didn't show up." They conduct their conversation via the gleam on the elevator doors. They need not turn their heads to face one another directly. The ceiling is low, the walls panelled in dark wood, the lighting dim. In the doors, their reflections are blurred around the edges. "We'll look ruthless if we push him into mediation now," Mia says. "And no one's going to have much sympathy for us if we take him to court. Nor should they."

"We'll have to wait it out. Like David said."

She shakes her head, unconvinced.

"We can't walk away with nothing."

"We owe sixty-eight thousand in legal fees," she says flatly. "With the mediation delayed indefinitely, the partners will be looking for payment. Our credit line's up to thirty-nine thousand. The property taxes are due."

Jesus. "I'm meeting Clint Sheppard Friday about a job."

"Clint Sheppard? I thought you couldn't stand him."

"He's looking for a VP of sales and marketing."

"'Drop the *n* and even the dykes love me.' That's how he introduced himself at one of those industry parties."

"Witty," Michael says. "A real charmer."

"I've put out feelers," Mia says. "To see if I can get some consulting work for the bank."

"What about your photography?"

"A hobby," she says dismissively. "No money in it. Besides, I can't take pictures of people right now."

"Don't lose heart, Mia."

She turns so she is no longer conversing with his reflection. "How can I not?"

He would pull her to him if she'd allow it. He would hold her in the elevator. Remind her how simple it can feel. "I'm telling you," he says. "Do not lose heart. Leave that for other people."

"I've been shooting outside. Trees mostly. We live in a ridiculously beautiful neighbourhood." She adjusts the strap of her purse so it sits squarely on her shoulder. "I'm better when Finn's around."

A smooth upward pull glides the elevator to a stop. Michael steps disoriented into the lobby, sunshine pouring in through the atrium's glass, business people rushing by, suit jackets slung over their arms, highheels clacking. He and Mia move against the crowds returning from lunch.

"You want a lift? The car's parked downstairs."

"I brought my bike," she says.

"How about grabbing a bite?"

"We probably shouldn't spend the money."

Through the revolving doors, Michael follows Mia onto the sidewalk. He watches as she works the lock on her fancy Dutch bike. Pale yellow with an internal hub so the gears never slip and the chain never falls off, the bike had been her fortieth-birthday present. He'd filled the front basket with flowers, set it up on the deck for the party, hired a band, a caterer, they kicked off their shoes and danced in the living room after all the guests had left.

She steps over the crossbar and is about to prop herself on the seat, she is about to ride off—Michael grabs hold of her handlebars. "Will you just talk to me for a minute?"

"About what? The boy you played baseball with all summer? The one who fits the description in the papers?"

Michael's knees go weak, his grip on her bike all that's holding him up.

"What? Did you think I wouldn't worry? Sneaking out of the house every night with that goddamn bat?" She leans in a little closer, so her face is not far from his. "Did you take him over there? Tell him about their cottage? Talk to him about their daughter?"

He squeezes her handlebars. "All we ever did was play baseball. I swear to God, that's it."

She raises her arm, shielding her eyes from the sun. "So it was just you, then, breaking all those windows?"

Michael looks up the sidewalk, into the madding crowd. He might have fooled Finn the other day in the kitchen, but he stands no chance with his wife.

"We have been so careless. Such careless, selfish people." She lifts his hand and returns it to him. "Chasing after money. Being stingy with love." She slides the strap off her shoulder and sets her purse carefully in the front basket. "I feel like I have failed her," she says.

"Mia. No. Listen, Peter—"

"I'm telling you how I *feel*, Michael. At the deepest, most fundamental level, I feel like I have failed her. That we have all failed her. You maybe most of all." She kicks her pedal into place and settles onto the seat. "In her most intimate moments, I believe it will be hard for her not to be scared."

He stares down at the sidewalk. His polished black shoes. His navy suit pants. The front tire of Mia's bike. It's my fault. He should say it. I got mad. I wanted to get even. I took that boy to her house. I didn't know who he was. We smashed all the windows. What happened? What happened to Frankie? It was my fault. He lifts the toe of first one shoe and then the other. If he says these things, who will he be? Who will he be to Mia? The man that he is, for the rest of his life.

He glances up. Mia's holding tight to her handlebars, looking sad in her pretty dress. "We're not that different," he says.

"I know, but we're different enough." She pushes off. "For one thing, I'm a better talker."

She is a block away when a driver in a parked car throws open his door. She shrieks as she swerves to avoid it, in front of a minivan, brakes screech—Michael loses sight of her—she wobbles across the yellow line, heading straight into oncoming traffic. Horns blast, Mia steadies the bike, swings back into the proper lane, pedalling away, on the far side of the street.

The 26th

Mia is pushing her shopping cart up the aisle at Metro when she sees Dr. Sullivan coming toward her. In sharply creased khakis, a white golf shirt and a matching cap, he looks decidedly more relaxed than he did when he was caring for Finn. He moves slowly down the aisle, carefully reading labels, adding a can of something to his basket, a bottle of Worcestershire sauce. Like hers, his cart is small. When he is close enough, Mia says hello. He nods formally, ready to push on, then his eyes light. He parks his cart next to hers, so the romaine lettuce and the roast chicken in his upper basket are jockeying with her giant box of Frosted Flakes.

"Your son . . ." he says, uncertainly. She is about to jump in but he holds up a hand. "No, wait," he says. "I'm picturing his chart." He closes his eyes and rolls his wrist, as if wafting the bouquet of a fine wine toward him. One roll. Two rolls. "Slate!" he says. "Finley Slate." He beams at her, those old, crooked teeth and behind his heavy glasses, his sharp brown eyes.

"The BE amputation," Mia says. "We call him Finn."

"Yes. Of course. Finn. The Slates. The modern Stone Age family."

"That's us," she says. "Mia."

"August." He dips his head at the introduction. "Gus to my friends. You reminded me to be polite that day in my office."

"I don't know where I got the nerve," she tells him truthfully.

"I appreciated it."

"And I appreciated the cookies. You gave me three, if I recall."

"Arrowroots," he says. "They're practically calorie-free." Then his face grows serious. "So, how is he, then? Your boy."

"He healed well. Like you said he would. And it took a while, but he finally found that prosthesis."

Dr. Sullivan, August, *Gus* lowers his voice to a gossipy register.

"God almighty! We tore the hospital apart. He was so convincing about it having been taken."

Mia almost laughs, something she hasn't done in a while. But this escaped-from-the-hospital version of the doctor is so animated. She'd judged him so harshly that day in his office, had been unable to imagine him young. She leans in, as if she's about to share a ripe secret. This man does not know Frankie, or how they are connected. "Stashed under a friend's bed," she says, and for the first time since it happened, she sees Frankie as just that. A friend helping Finn out.

"Well," Dr. Sullivan says, "it had to be somewhere."

"He's not wearing it yet. But he's seeing his psychologist."

"Dr. Zappia? She's really something, isn't she? With her pink hair and her hula hoops and whatnot."

"She calls me dude."

"Me, too!" he says, delighted.

"Finn seems to like her."

"That's the important thing."

They shake their heads and then stare off down the aisle as if expecting a familiar face to call them away. They barely know one another. And yet, they linger.

Mia inches her cart closer to his, giving a man with a seated toddler—elbow-deep in a box of Goldfish—room to get by. "You've retired," she says. "That's why you're so relaxed."

"After thirty-two years, I finally have the luxury of sleeping nights. And my replacement is an excellent surgeon. And so much younger than me. Good with names, proper bedside manners and all that. Dr. Whetung. I feel very good about having left things in her competent hands." Mia was right; he was in no hurry to get away. "My partner and I are living up at the lake full time now."

"Big Yirkie," Mia says, her voice weighted.

"You heard what happened, of course." The furrows in

Dr. Sullivan's forehead that Mia remembers so well return. "A horrible thing," he says. "It makes one wonder. It really does."

The story has slipped to the middle of the local papers, been relegated to the edges of the screen. Last week Mia saw a headline that read, "Cottage Community Still Shaken by Sexual Assault." As if it were the community that had been attacked, the cottagers victims for having to lock their doors at night and install alarm systems. Frankie's become a footnote to the story, the assailants' descriptions unworthy of mention. It's only been eight weeks. Eight weeks because she's a rich white man's daughter and a rich white man's boat got burned. If she'd been otherwise, if it had happened to Jess, the story might never have made the front page.

The furrows on Dr. Sullivan's forehead smooth. His face brightens. Mia can almost see him shaking off the horrible thing that she will carry with her—forever, she believes—like a water sack sloshing inside her, upsetting her balance, making it difficult to draw breath. She imagines the doctor's resilience is what allowed him to carry on as a trauma surgeon for so long. All those nights, and all those boys, and all that damage done, right here in good Old Aberdeen.

He is an old man now. Past seventy, she guesses, and only just retiring. *I hurt no one*, he'd told her in his office. *I compromised nothing in myself.*

Mia cannot say the same. She hasn't even called the police about the boy.

People always said she was strong, but in truth she needed to be stronger.

Dr. Sullivan gives his black hipster glasses a push. "If all that hasn't scared you off cottaging completely, and it isn't too bold of me to ask, perhaps you and your husband would like to come up to the lake for a sail sometime. Finn, too, of course."

"That's a lovely offer." Mia's cheeks warm. "But unfortunately my husband and I have separated."

"Ahh," Dr. Sullivan says, as if the news, sad as it is, comes as no surprise. "Trauma to a child can be hard on a marriage."

"Life can be hard on a marriage. And I am an unforgiving person." She is surprised at the bitterness in her voice. In her studio, she moves from settee to table, from table to bed, from bed to settee, lost in one room, adrift on a second floor. Missing him, a man who offers her a pair of socks warmed by his own body or ferries her safely home in the rain with just one. Kisses her gently on the lips. Makes gifts of river flowers. Not missing the dark shadow of that love. Unaccustomed to real difficulty, God forbid anything go wrong; all the people burned to the ground and the houses still standing, an old dream turned to a nightmare.

"There are things that are difficult to forgive," the doctor says, softly. "Differences we cannot easily reconcile. I guess we've been lucky in that regard."

Lucky. Mia used to think they were lucky. But things changed so quickly, like a mountain range erupting around them, and she and Michael faltered on the climb. They forgot they loved each other. They failed to take care, made mistakes, got tired, got greedy, got mad, did damage, so much damage that when they tried to find the path back to the lucky times the path was gone.

They could have done so much better. They had every opportunity. Every privilege. Lose a bit of money, a bit of compassion, a little piece of yourself and someone's going to get hurt. Someone vulnerable, someone they helped make vulnerable, hiding in plain sight.

"I have an apartment," Mia says, clearing her throat. "Finn's slowly moving in."

August taps the box of Frosted Flakes. "That explains the sugar cereal."

Mia has to smile. "It's across the hall from my studio. You should come by. I'll take your retirement photo."

"Oh, this old face," he says.

Mia remembers how unkindly she'd first framed him, and is again embarrassed by how vindictive her thoughts had been that day. "You should mark the occasion," she says. "I'll make you look good."

"I suppose we could staple my lips shut," he says. "And Jay. He might like a photograph."

Mia had wondered. Perhaps it's another reason the doctor had sidestepped the draft, that culture of manly men harnessed to fight. "I could take his picture as well. Take the two of you together."

"Beauty and the beast—well, I'll think about it." But he's stiffened up, drawn back, and she can see that he won't. Two women turn into their aisle and glide quickly toward them, their shopping carts loaded. Big families, Mia thinks. Lots of children. She wants to reach out and seize their arms as they pass, tell them to pay attention, to be diligent, to never stop talking to their sons, to teach their girls to roar. No quitting, she wants to tell them. No quitting on the kids.

Dr. Sullivan edges his cart forward and says a polite goodbye. He negotiates his way smoothly past the women and their rolling hillocks of food while Mia remains rooted in place, in front of the canned vegetables. She glances at her watch. Finn will be waiting for her.

His new bedroom overlooks a parking lot, complete with dumpsters and a teetering stack of tires. Mia's bleached the mould from the bathroom tiles, but there wasn't much she could do with the banged-up cupboards or the yeasty smell in the kitchen. She's been keeping the doors open between the apartment and the studio so the upstairs feels better connected, more like a home. Still, at some point she'll have to look for something more suitable—she knows Finn's going to hate it—and cheaper, unless her new consulting business takes off, which she half hopes it doesn't.

One thing is certain: she doesn't want to be dependent on Michael in any way. She will not go back to what they had. They'll sell the house. She'll take her half of the equity and use it to move on. Find a place she feels good in, a space just big enough for herself and Finn—that cabin on the edge of a forest, a motel room with two clean beds.

But why? Why should she creep away to the margins, dragging her son along? Why can't she find a way to be new here? Crack open the centre, create more space, so it's safe in the shade of the old trees, surrounded by fresh water. Isn't that what everyone wants? She'll volunteer at the women's shelter, work up her own burlesque act—a slow-motion striptease to Billie Holiday—befriend the Bosnian widow, take photographs of kids climbing trees, say hello to Jess's mom next time she's hanging out laundry.

And what about Frankie? What if instead of telling her amusing anecdotes about falling in love, Mia had told her other stories? About the boy who threw her on the couch and wouldn't take no for an answer. How she'd had to fight her arm free and punch him not once, but twice in the mouth. How at fourteen, she'd had to draw blood to make him stop. How her head hit the taxi window when a colleague wrestled her onto the back seat after a friendly night at a pub. How next day at work, they said a stiff hello and then for years acted like nothing had happened. What if she'd told her about the Saturday night at university when four guys she didn't know walked drunk into her boyfriend's dorm room and tried to pull her, naked, from his bed. How that time it had taken both of them to save her.

Would those stories have changed anything for Frankie? Or just made her unnecessarily afraid? Mia doesn't know. The love stories should have been enough.

When she was growing up, no one talked about any of it. There were no trophy pictures posted online. Now legions of women tweet out the details of their assaults, and still the questions get asked: what was she wearing, how much did she drink, how many guys has she slept with? Good swimmers are released after serving a couple of months in prison, if they're white, if the girl even goes to the police, if the guy gets charged, sees trial, ever gets convicted. Keep your knees together. Wear a longer skirt.

She should have toughed it out at the bank. Clawed her way to the presidency, just to prove she could do it. Used her new-found power to give every customer a rebate, her microphone to discuss the currency of radical kindness.

Dr. Sullivan has almost disappeared from the aisle. Mia surprises herself by calling out. "You still killing the planet with that capsule coffee?"

He turns, one hand holding on to his cart. "We've found a good bean at Wild Oat," he hollers back. "Grinding our own. We have the time now."

She swings around. The front wheel of her shopping cart pulls hard to the right; she has to fight to keep it moving in a straight line. "Maybe Finn and I can come up to the cottage sometime for a cup." She doesn't have to shout now, although she feels a little desperate, chasing after him like this.

"That would be wonderful. To tell you the truth," he says when she reaches him, "we're a little lonely up there by ourselves. We'll have lunch. And afterwards I'll take you for a sail." He fishes into his shirt pocket and comes up with a pen and a neatly folded square of paper. Using her cereal box as a table, he writes down a rural address and phone number.

"I'll call you," she says.

"Do. And tell Finn his surgeon is very pleased he found that damn hand."

Mia slots the paper into her purse. Into the zippered pocket, where hopefully it won't get lost.

———

"I'M GOING NOW, DAD."

Michael looks up from the newspaper he's been pretending to read: forcing himself to the end of a sentence, a paragraph, he couldn't say what any of it's about.

Finn is standing in the doorway of the kitchen, holding tight to a suitcase.

"Mom's waiting outside."

Michael pushes his chair back and rises from the table. Once standing, he finds he has to pause. Whatever it is that strings him together, whatever it is that makes him a man, has come unbound. He is not certain he can walk the ten steps from the table to the doorway. He is not certain his body has anything to do with his mind. He is not standing paralyzed at his own kitchen table, but alone in a wind tunnel, the cords that tether soul to skeleton, skeleton to earth, flapping wild.

His son sets down his suitcase. It is Finn who comes to his father, the boy who walks toward the man.

November

The 19th

Beneath the graffiti bridge, Michael nods at the kids circled around the old oil drum. He doesn't recognize any of their faces. A new batch, huddled close to the fire. They barely acknowledge him. Still, he forces himself not to rush.

As he plods into the field of wild grasses, bleached of colour, flattened by fall rains, he turns up the collar of his coat and jams his hands into his pockets. Not yet used to the idea of another winter, his gloves are still boxed away. He hadn't bothered to look for a hat.

Close to the ground, on either side of the path, the grass stalks have begun to rot, and despite the cold, there's a swampy tinge to the air. The sky's overcast, black, the moon and stars buried by clouds, yet as Michael steps onto the outfield, he feels spotlit. He glances over his shoulder. None of the kids are watching. Old man—he has already been forgotten.

Spread before him, the ball diamond is little more than a dark clearing in the night. The backstop a flickery shadow, the shed a line drawing knocked askew. Michael's told himself he came for the extension cord. That he'll be damned if he doesn't put lights up for the holidays. Finn's made it clear he's not crazy about living part-time above the laundromat. He and Mia haven't discussed it, but Michael assumes they'll spend Christmas Day together as a family, at the house, which will be properly decorated.

Still, he had no good reason to come here. He's working again, on a three-month probationary contract. He's paying the bills, covering the mortgage, insisting Mia take enough to meet her next month's rent. They haven't made a dent in the legal bills, but David says the mediation will happen—sometime—and twenty bucks to plug in some Christmas lights wouldn't have mattered a bit.

Michael came to the diamond because he wanted to. On nights when Finn's with Mia, he works late, happy to lose himself in the mundanity of his job—bids for snowplowing services for the apartment portfolio, a graffiti abatement proposal for the city's public spaces. When he does go home, he eats microwaved burritos standing over the sink and drinks one too many beers. He gets out of bed in the middle of the night to piss and ends up roaming the house. He doesn't even have to pull the chain on the bulb to see the left-behind hangers dangling on Mia's side of the closet. He'll push open Finn's door and make a study of the empty bed.

That's why he's standing on the edge of the outfield. He came because he needed to remind himself that he deserves his loneliness. That he's right to be scared. That the details he imagines are real even if the tremors in his heart always pass. Sometimes he wishes they'd just come for him—the police, Peter, the guy with the tats— spare him another night of wandering a ghosted house. He's tired of just holding on, of existing on love's fringes.

He has made a decision. A pledge, he might call it. A pledge not to get mad. No matter what. He's prepared to do whatever it takes to excise that emotion from his repertoire. Anger management classes. Meditation. A sweat lodge. Whatever. He will send no more fury out into the world. He plans to get so Zen he'll make Gandhi look like a thug.

The padlock still hangs on the door of the shed. Like he has dozens of times before, Michael uses his nails to pry back the hinge, pulled loose from the rotting frame. He gives a shove and the door swings open. The pitching machine's still there, a blackness in the dark interior, but the smell is what hits him first. Sharp and pissy, sour and unwashed. He turns his head away and steps back from the door, thinking coon, wolf, street person cloaked in duct tape and garbage bags.

He pulls his phone from his pocket and slowly sweeps the shed. The extension cord lies just inside the door, moved from where he left it. He travels the beam up the Arm. The small round of light dissects the machine into a horror show of toothy gears and wire cages, well-oiled chains and trigger-tripped coils. Michael imagines the arm snapping back, springing forward, rocketing one last ball at his head. With his light, he follows the electrical cord across the floor. Unplugged. Nowhere near the outlet.

He bends for the extension cord and something moves in the shed. He skitters the beam around until it grabs at a scrap of colour on the floor. Red. Red high-tops, the laces dark with dirt. No socks. Twigs for ankles. Skin filthy as the shoes. He travels the light up. Baggy jeans, chest concave, face . . . skeletal. There is no other word. All bone and teeth and eyes.

"Cheerio." The boy's voice thin as the rest of him.

Michael grabs hold of the door jamb. Glances back at the bridge—no one is watching—and steps inside. He fumbles his light off, lets the smell become familiar and his eyes adjust to the dark.

A nest on the floor. The kid is standing in it. Pieces of flattened cardboard, a foul sleeping bag. Bottles of water. A box of Ritz crackers and a jar of no-name peanut butter set between two wall studs.

"Where are the others?"

"Gone," the boy says.

"Where?"

"You think they'd tell me?" It's so cold in the shed, the kid puffs smoke when he talks. His hair, longer now, is pulled back in a greasy knot. He leans up against the Arm, his forehead pressing into the hopper's metal cage.

"You never should have been with them," Michael says. "You should have been with better people."

The boy snorts. "I don't have better people."

"You have parents."

"I go home, my father kills me."

Michael picks up the extension cord and starts trying to organize it into some sort of coil. He forces himself to loop it carefully. He can't let himself get soft. He puts words into his head. White trash. Animal. "I should kill you," he says, but he's shaky, shaken, there's no heat to the threat.

The kid manages a smirk. "I always said you were going to kill somebody."

Rapist. There. *Rapist.* "My friend's daughter."

"Your *friend*." A flash of teeth, still perfect and white. "Fuck you, your friend. He's no friend of yours." The boy folds skinny arms across skinny chest. "I need insulin. Food. Money."

Michael squeezes the extension cord, thick now across his palm. Here in the shed, with this kid, his pledge is unnecessary, without meaning. He doesn't even have to struggle. Anger? Rage? Infantile emotions from a simpler broken place.

"You have to get out of here," he says. "Go somewhere else."

"I've got nowhere else." The boy's voice breaks. "I don't even have a fucking coat."

Michael drops his head, steels himself, turns and opens the door.

"The boat. Your partner's boat."

Michael stalls. Past the frozen ball diamond, the field of rotting grasses, the river edge will be sculpted by fragile ice, layered and carved by the fast rush of water, frozen to a crystalline lace. Michael closes his eyes. He should have taken up fishing. Brought a pole down to the river instead of a bat. Befriended the old Asian men in their rubber boots and bucket hats. Even the fucking turtle knew enough to head for calmer waters.

From behind him, mingled in with the sour, comes a whiff of fermenting fruit.

"We floated it away from the dock," the boy says. "It was like something you'd see in a movie. Like the sweetest thing in the world. That boat burning on the water." The air wobbly with heat, bright with flames. What Michael had wanted all along, a beautiful revenge, an exact and fiery justice that would just sink away. As if such a thing were possible. As if the scorch and smoke weren't real and dangerous and the beginning of something else.

Michael yanks his wallet from his pocket, throws all of his money, five twenties, to the floor. The boy scrambles up the cash, and when Michael hands him his coat, he scrambles it on—so big on his starving frame, he looks like a child playing dress-up in his father's clothes.

"Thanks, man," the boy says. They are closer now, the pitching machine no longer between them, the sweet smell of fermenting fruit grown stronger. "Thanks for saving my life."

Michael steps away, closer again to the door. "I'm not coming back," he tells him.

"You have to man. I'm dying here."

"I'm not coming back."

Huddled inside Michael's coat, the boy falls still. "We had no plan. We just looked up and she was standing in the window."

Now it's Michael's turn to freeze.

"You *know*," the boy says, his voice suddenly fierce. And the way he's looking at him, his gaze so sure, turns the cold inside the shed to a chill that seeps through Michael's sweater, into his bone marrow, his DNA, nipping away gene combinations that might allow him to recognize warmth in the future. Michael has to clamp his jaw shut to stop the clatter of tooth knocking against tooth.

"That night at your buddy's house? All that glass right there in front of us? No one watching." The boy reaches sideways, threads his fingers through the mesh of the hopper. Michael's hand follows. He clings to the caging, the metal biting his fingers. The boy's eyes shine wet and bright above the dark hollows of his cheeks. His scent foul, his breath like rotting apples. "It felt like we were powerful. Like we had a right."

"You had no fucking *right*."

"Neither did you."

The boy is staring at Michael. "My name is Connor Tucker," he says, holding tight to the cage. "I am sixteen years old." The boy is staring at Michael, and he is crying. "I like playing baseball. Same as you, Michael," he says. "Same as you."

The 21st

My mom gave me the address. And the name's right there on the board. KELLY 1634.

When I reach for the button, my backpack digs into my shoulder.

A second later—Hello?—Jess's voice buzzy through the intercom.

Hey. It's Finn.

Finn. Then a long stretch of nothing.

Can I come up for a second?

Sure, she says. Of course.

The elevator rockets to the sixteenth floor. The doors fly open. When I get off, she's in the hall, her arms crossed in front of her as if she's protecting herself from the cold. Even though we're pretty far apart I can't really look at her. When I follow her into the apartment, I stare down at her feet—bare, of course.

Inside, huge windows, a river view, a couple big couches out on the balcony, all ready to party.

Wow, I say. Pretty sick.

We still need to get more furniture and stuff.

She looks around the room—a sectional, she says, a coffee table—and I risk it. She's wearing skinny jeans and a big beige fisherman's sweater, which might be his. She looks skinnier than before. And her hair looks shinier. In the craziest, most delusional part of my brain, I thought she might be wearing the ribbon. Maybe it's stashed somewhere in the condo. Maybe not.

How are you? she asks, when she's done fantasy decorating the condo.

Good. I fake a smile for one beat. Except my parents split.

I know. I can't believe it. You think they'll, like, get back together?

I clunk my backpack onto the kitchen island. Instead of collapsing, it stands up tall and green. My mom's got the hydro bill pinned up with a Smash the Patriarchy button, I tell her, so, yeah, it's not looking good.

Shit. And Frankie, Jess says. Oh my god.

Yeah. We've been hanging around a lot.

That must be good for her.

It's good for both of us, I say, letting my voice get a bit hard.

We've started a late-night texting routine, Frankie and me. It's something to do when we're lying awake at 2 a.m. After school we walk around. Out by her place, mostly, away from people, in the field across the road from her house, looking for wildlife—there's a ton of rabbits. The other day we saw a wild turkey. Sometimes we go down to the river. Stomp on the shore ice. Scream along with the crunch and the crack, our voices echoing back across the water. Ice therapy, we call it. On bleak days I think about inviting Frankie over to work on my map, but yeah, that's not going to help anyone, so we usually just watch movies in her room, lying on her bed, propped up by lots of pillows. Her mom brings us popcorn and grapefruit juice, which is actually a pretty good combination.

Do you want something to drink? Jess heads for the fridge.

No, thanks. I take off my jacket—still the life-saving blue—and hang it on the back of a kitchen stool. I'm wearing a long-sleeved shirt, but it doesn't totally cover my stump.

I could make you something to—

I didn't know how to touch you with it, I say. I make myself say. The thing I came here to say. I didn't want to touch you with it.

Jess stops, kind of stranded half out of the living room, halfway into the kitchen. She reaches for the counter, but it's too far away so her arm just kind of stretches in front of her. Her hand. The big, sparkly ring.

And that's all we really did, right? Touch each other. Hook up. Bang.

It was more than that.

Probably the closest she'll ever come to saying it. She can't say it. My father had to say it.

You think it was easy? Her arm floats to her side. How could it be easy to walk away from you?

Or maybe that's the closest.

I couldn't wait for you to grow up, she says. And I didn't want anyone else to have you. Her face is all serious. It was selfish. It was wrong.

It wasn't that bad, I say. I mean, all that sex and everything. I'm thinking she might laugh a bit or something, smile, whatever, I'm trying to cheer her up, which is kind of messed, but she just turns her head and stares out the windows. Across the water, a flat run of frozen farm fields and way in the distance the rise of the Hills, a dark, rolling line on the horizon.

Nice view, I say.

It is, she says. It really is. I feel lucky every time I look out. Against her leg, she spins the diamond. It appears, disappears, appears again.

I've seen it, I tell her. Your fiancé showed it to me one night at a strip club. Right before he called me a fucking amputee.

Jess's eyebrows move closer together. Over the last year, I've pretended a lot of things, but I've never pretended I don't hate that fucking guy.

And Don? I say. He told me my arm gives people the heebie-jeebies. I spare her the details of how her soon-to-be brother-in-law tried to cull me from the pack. For now, forever, that's staying between me and Eli and my mom. I see him at school. We are no longer friends.

Costa Rica, right?

Yeah. She nods. In May. First time seeing the ocean. And next fall we're going to Bali. Kuta, actually, but no one's ever heard of it.

Show off the new husband?

No, she says, I'm going with my mom.

Oh, I say, feeling stupid again. Spoiled. Small. And then because it costs me almost nothing, I give her what my father gave me. That night at the strip club? Eric told me he loved you. Sounded like he meant it, too.

He does. In his way. Please don't worry about me, Finn. I'm happy. I know what I'm doing. She pulls the arms of her sweater down, so just the tips of her fingers are sticking out the ends. And I know they can be—she takes her time picking out the word—insensitive.

But they're right. I mean, I'm kind of getting used to it, I say. And I lift up my arm and slide my sleeve back to reveal the stump. My stump. My nub. My unhand. I don't want to be like this, I say. I mean, who wants to be like this? I can't do anything like this.

I pin my backpack to the counter and jerk open the zipper. The sleeve and hooks slide right out, but the cables and harness get caught up so I kind of have to wrestle with them a bit.

Then I just hold it all in my hand. Except for the hooks, it's pretty light. The sleeve's plastic, and the harness is this kind of black-netted material that runners would probably love. The cable hangs off it like a depressed antenna. Sometimes I think it looks like something a complicated insect sloughed off. But right now, with Jess standing in front of me, all I think is that the hooks look really hard.

Stainless steel, I say. To match your kitchen.

She doesn't even smile. She heard my voice shake. Sees the way the whole thing's kind of shaking in my hand.

I know it's pretty brutal, but my doctor—I can't say psychologist, not to her, although we talk about Jess a lot—tells me I have to get Zen with the Claw. Later, I say, I'll get a better one.

I could get Don to help pay for it. You got hurt in his backyard.

That's okay, I say, because seriously, I don't want either Eli or his dad anywhere near my life. So I tell her about the guy who designed this 3D printer and how he makes these spare limbs and sends them over to Africa. I tell her I'm going to email him. Get him to print me one up.

Then I hold the whole thing a little higher. I hold it out to her. You're almost a nurse, right?

Graduating next June, she says. Maybe I'll look after you one day.

I can't wait to get sick.

Finally she smiles. Motions at the stool. Sit, she says, and I do.

I guess I was more fucked up than I realized.

What happened to you? she says. It wasn't small. And she comes and takes the prosthesis from me. Over or under your shirt?

Over, I say. Although I'm not sure. I've never even put it on. But I can't take off my shirt. Not in front of her.

But I let her stand next to me. I let her move around me. And I love how her voice sounds when she asks me to lift up my arm. How she touches me, I love how she touches me. Her hand on my shoulder. My back. Her fingers trip my skin when she slides on the sleeve, a new kind of electric shock. And when she picks up the hook, I love how she leans in and kisses me, once, before she fits it onto my arm. How she touches her lips to mine, so for a second, a half second, I am both living and dying, letting her love me—because she does, we both know she does—and saying goodbye at the same time.

When she's done, I reach out and I touch her with it. Her soft skin. Her long, beautiful neck.

The 23rd

Coming to the Mekong for lunch hadn't been Michael's idea. Halfway through his third pint, he's still jumpy every time the front door opens. But like Peter Conrad—who hasn't shown up, thank god—apparently Clint Sheppard also enjoys two-for-one Asahis and solicitous Asian waitresses on Friday afternoons.

Clint, tie gone and top button open, leans across their table for two. The quarter pound of gold ring he's wearing clunks against his wedding band as he taps his index finger on the table. This isn't their first lunch together. Michael's been working for Clint for over a month; he knows all about his glory days as a safety for the Western Mustangs, how they blew out Saskatchewan thirty-five to ten in the first-ever Vanier Cup to be played at the Toronto SkyDome. Michael's done some digging. Found out Clint was third string, and despite his stories, Michael doubts he even played in the championship game. His new boss. So far it's been an uncomfortable fit. He'd been his own man for fifteen years. Or so he'd thought.

"You realize we have an opening," Clint says, his tapping finger paused.

"An opening?"

"What happened with Conrad's daughter?" He is not a discreet man, but he has the decency to lower his voice. "It makes people uncomfortable. They'd rather not deal with the dad."

Michael doesn't flinch, but something, a flicker in his eye, an involuntary micro-contraction of his brow muscles, gives him away.

"What?"

Despite all the beer, Michael's mouth is dry. He can only shake his head.

"You think it's ruthless?" Still tipped across the table, Clint points at Michael. "It's not ruthless. It's life. It's business. There's an opportunity, you take it. You know that. I mean, we all feel bad for the girl, horrible, but after the way Conrad fucked you over, I didn't think you'd have a problem going after old clients. Am I wrong, here?"

"No."

Clint leans back in his chair and picks up his glass, too tall, too elegant for his beefy hand. Eyeing Michael over the rim, he takes a slug of Asahi, then lowers the glass, empty except for the drifts of foam slipping down the sides. "People *like* you, Michael," he says. "Peter's always been a prick to deal with."

"There's no problem, Clint. I'll make the calls. I'll get it done."

"Good. Because that's why we brought you on." He signals their waitress, who bobs her way to their table. Kimmy. Michael knows her, from all the other Fridays. Originally from Taiwan. Has a young son at home. Has never mentioned a husband. Can't be more than thirty, although it's hard to tell. When Michael came in, she gave him a warm welcome back.

She takes their order—two more beers—and they watch her slipstream between tables, making her way to the bar. "They should put *that* on the menu," Clint says, "instead of fucking coconut ice cream."

Michael forces himself to laugh.

"That's what you need," Clint says, still staring across the room. "Time to climb back on."

They watch her. Michael watches her. Her narrow waist, the swell of her ass, her small hand circling the tall pull on the beer tap. When he finally looks away, it's Clint who laughs.

Michael picks his knife off of the table, tilts the blade, one way then the other, the handle cool and heavy in his hand. "Last thing she needs is some old fuck like me." He glances up from the knife just to watch Clint's laughter fade. "A couple more years, I'll probably be fighting to get it up."

It's the phone that saves them, vibrating next to the boss's plate. He picks it up and starts thumbing something in. Michael says a quick thank-you for them both when Kimmy delivers their beer. He checks his own phone. Opens a text from Mia, clicks on the breaking news link.

The boy has been found. Fallen through the early-winter ice. Miles downstream from Old Aberdeen. For millennia, the river has carved rock, cleaved land, carried flowers, but still refuses our sins. Police recovered the body this morning. It's early going, but at this point there's no evidence of foul play. People walking their dogs by the river have been interviewed and it's unanimous—everyone's happy Connor Tucker is dead. Except for his parents: a dentist and his wife, a dental assistant. Michael finds this news staggering. They're quoted as saying Connor was a good kid who struggled with health and learning issues, a loner who never managed to fit in. They apologize to the Conrad family, although they believe in Connor's innocence; they know their son would never do the things he's accused of.

Michael texts Mia back. *Thanks for sending.* He struggles to find the right keys. *Heavy news*, he types, and something breaks hard in his chest. *I love you.* As he hits the last letter, he isn't certain he hasn't sobbed.

"You all right?" Clint frowns across the table. "Christ, buddy, you're scaring me. You're making me worry."

Michael sets his phone on the table. He cannot hold it in his hand, waiting on a reply that may never come. To be loved. To be forgiven. To be worthy of either one.

He takes a long second to draw himself back. Another few seconds to find the strength to reach up and loosen his tie.

His friend, the rapist, is dead. And Frankie, afraid to fully live.

He tells Clint the one about the camel. Tells him the one about the hat. Asks how his daughter's getting along in first-year engineering. How the renos are going. About the vacation he has planned. Clint scrolls through his photos, so his new VP of sales and marketing can marvel at his beautiful life.

Michael does it. He nods. He smiles. He sits back and he lets the man talk.

ON THE TABLE, his screensaver pops up. Finn in that ugly brown ski tuque, his guileless smile, the gracious truth of him. Michael picks up the phone. Sends his son the same message he sent his wife. A second later, a dotted grey text bubble blooms green.

Hey thanks! Love you 2 dad!

Easy. It can be as easy as that.

The 24th

Sitting at the high table in her studio, Mia flips through the photographs she's finally had printed, the ones of Randolph's tree. Lying on her back, she'd shot up through the foliage in September and October—a lift of staggered greens turned to autumn golds, interlaced by dark branches. In the chill of November, a vein work of wood above her, each sturdy limb mother to slimmer limbs, curving higher, dividing into outstretched arms and twiggy hands. She loves the tree bare, the architecture of its branches. While she wouldn't dare mention it to anyone, and isn't sure why she's skipped over the photographers, Mia's been studying Van Gogh's olive groves for inspiration, Monet's last blind water lilies, Pollock's cosmic *One*, hoping to use her lens to reveal a beauty both new and infinite, the secret of a grand survival, converging light and capturing time via leaf and water and wood.

So far the old maple hasn't given up much. The pictures she's taken are static, everyday—she knows Finn's not impressed. He thinks she should get back to people and portraits, but she's looking forward to a good windstorm to bring the century-old limbs into motion. Come spring she'll take action shots, the unfurling of tender new worlds. She'd like to burrow underground to photograph the hidden cathedral, rooted deep in good earth, tethered to bedrock, in community with all its neighbours. If she can't get the tree right, she'll go small. Lying flat on her belly in the long grasses, she'll photograph the souls of crickets, the dusty sex of wildflowers.

Of course there are no shots, will never be any shots, of what happens when she lowers her camera and presses her palms to the trunk. Creeps her fingers into the woody grooves and rests her cheek on the bark. She's not sure how long she communes with the old beauty, doesn't care if anyone's watching. With each breath she draws in the tree, wills it to calm her, to fill her with some ancient grace, a divine truth she didn't know she'd forgotten.

"Mia."

She sets the photograph down slowly and swivels carefully around on her stool. In the doorway, Frankie stands stiff inside a navy coat, unbuttoned, her hands buried deep in the pockets. Mia recognizes it; an old peacoat of Helen's.

She forces herself up. Takes one step forward and then another. Frankie turns her head sharply to the left. Her nose ring's back in, her hair's lassoed into a ponytail and her face is lightly tanned—Finn says they've been walking outside a lot.

Mia cannot understand how foolish she'd been to have thought a slim hoop of gold through one nostril gave Frankie some kind of edge; frail decoration, her skin would be torn if someone yanked it from her nose.

"Finn's not here," Mia says, finally. "He's at home." She corrects herself. "He's at his father's."

"I didn't come to see Finn. I came to get the pictures you took of me. The ones you got printed."

"Oh. Okay."

When Mia returns with the folder, the door is closed, the turn-piece on the deadbolt horizontal. Seated on a stool, still huddled inside her coat, Frankie nudges Mia's photographs around the wooden table.

"Is that the big maple? On the corner of your street?" Mia nods and sets the folder down, within easy reach. "Does that guy even let you on his lawn?"

"Technically the tree's on city property. Or part of it anyway. Randolph's been surprisingly good about it. Told me the tree was the reason he bought the house in the first place."

She glances up. Not directly at Mia; her gaze drifts toward the back of the room. "I've always loved that tree."

"You can have these if you want." Flustered, heartsick, clumsy, humbled, Mia can't say what she is as she gathers the pictures, babbling nervously—"I'm just starting out. Sorry. Hopefully they'll be better next time."

When Mia offers the photographs, Frankie slides them into the back of the folder, centres the folder in front of her, and starts slowly flipping through.

Every shot, Mia remembers. She has known Frankie all of her life. A newborn, red faced and furious, tiny hands balled into fists.

An eight-month-old, propped in a pumpkin patch, embroidered snowflakes decorating the sleeves of her sweater. Her chubby arms clutch at the pumpkin settled between her legs. In the low autumn light, her hair fizzes a sunstruck bronze.

"We were at Sanders' farm," Mia says. "You kept falling over. Your mom had to prop you up."

"I was so fat."

"You were so sweet." Frankie and Finn just babies and she and Helen so young, faking their way into motherhood. "How is she? Your mom."

"Destroyed. She misses you."

"I miss her."

"So call her, then," Frankie says, and flips the picture down. As she moves through the stack, the girl in the photographs grows up.

"Finn told me you're back at school," Mia says, softly.

"When I walk down the halls I feel like a ghost. No one's supposed to know, but everybody does. Most people won't even look at me."

Mia's heart stalls. "Finn—"

"Finn's different," Frankie says. She glances at the stool beside her. "Could you? Standing behind me—"

"Oh. Oh sorry." Mia sits down, clumsily, and not too close.

Frankie stops flipping. She has sprouted up. Four feet tall and skinny now, wearing a red dress, the hem just above her knees. She wasn't happy about the dress, but loved the backpack humped at her feet. Helen had helped her embroider her name on it, *Frankie*, hooped above the zippered pocket in thick yellow thread.

"First day of school. I came to your house to take your picture."

"Grade three." Frankie frowns. "We had Mr. Jensel. He used to touch my hair."

Through the floorboards, Mia can feel the shiver of the washers and dryers. The sweet smell of laundry soap wafts up the stairs. "Maybe you and your mom can come here." She floats the idea carefully, her voice soft, the offer light. "We could have dinner with Finn."

"Maybe," Frankie says. Maybe. The buttons on her sleeve scrape the table as she drags two photographs from the folder. Mia took one of them last winter. Frankie casting a long stare into the camera, the day they'd talked about boys. So open in that moment. So unafraid to show herself. The other shot was taken at the beginning of summer, when she came looking for a present for her dad. Half of her face, half of her plea to stop, hidden behind the bright, big palm of her hand.

"I knew you'd get this one printed."

They both stare at the pictures lying side by side on the table. A lump has set high up in Mia's throat, but even if it hadn't—what is there to say? She swallows hard. "I'm sorry. I shouldn't have taken that one."

Frankie taps the photograph. "This," she says, "this is nothing." She says, "People keep calling them animals, but they're not animals. They're men." She says, "I want you to take my picture," and she stands up and shrugs off her mother's old coat.

Underneath, black leggings and a loose black sweater that hangs halfway to her knees. She moves inside the sweater as she moves across the room. She sits down on the settee at the front of the studio. Behind her the windows frame a sky thinned to winter blue, beautiful and clean, as if it doesn't read the papers, as if it never got the news.

Mia opens her camera bag. Couples body to lens.

Through the viewfinder, Frankie comes up bright against the crushed purple velvet. Her hair packed away. Her chin lifted. Her eyes closed. The studio buzzes with silence, the soft grief of a dryer thumping downstairs.

"Talk to me," Frankie says. "You know me. You know who I am."

December

(epilogue)

Where the myth fails,
human love begins.

ANAÏS NIN

I stand inside the dark cottage and watch the men untie the ropes. Flames flicker low in the boat as they push it away from the dock. It glides into blackness, stops thirty feet from shore, quiet for once, its engine off. The boat floats on its own reflection. A lifejacket bursts to orange. The flames spread and climb. The captain's seat becomes a pyre, the windscreen a warp of gold.

Together, we watch the boats burn, one up, one upside down. The water so calm it's hard to tell which is real and which is not. If the men are cheering I cannot hear them. They stand motionless on the dock. They are not drunk or high or dangerous. They do not turn around. They do not see me standing half-asleep in the front window, the wild outline of my hair. They do not see the black bears printed on the nightshirt I've had forever, the finger-sized hole near the neck, the pulled threads. My breasts underneath, the right one a little smaller than the left. My not-so-flat belly. My private girl parts, what I'll need to make a new life. They say pussy. They say cunt, slut, bitch. I say clitoris. I say womb. I say earthling. When I press my hand to the window the glass is cool, the heat of the flames far off.

My mother will be happy. She never liked the boat. One night, their fighting woke me. She was crying, pleading with my dad to get rid of the fucking thing, him yelling *he would not*. It was a long time ago, but I still remember the shock of hearing my mother swear.

In the reflection, my father is a generous man. He gives his money to charity. Orphans come to live with us. My mother teaches them to speak English. We have a houseful of people and no boat to burn.

Michael knows how to handle my father and is always kind to his son. He is not the type to throw balls at other people's houses. My father is not the type to throw casserole dishes at women.

Eli asks me to go to the movies and I say okay, but just as friends. I never kiss him in the kitchen trying to make Finn jealous. I am not the kind of girl to do something stupid like that. I do not lose my virginity to Eli on the floor in his basement, just to get it over with. He does not pound into me because he knows it's my first time. I tell him it's my first time.

When I walk home alone on a hot summer night, I am not thinking about my tight top or my short shorts or my long legs. I do not look down at the gravel as I pass under the bridge. I do not make myself small. There is no reason to be afraid of those boys.

My mother frowns when she sees my new nose ring, but she doesn't make me take it off. She listens as I tell her it's my body and I can do what I want with it. Later, when my dad freaks about the piercing, she tells him to back off. I tell him to back off.

When Mia asks if I've met anyone special I say, yes, I've known him all my life. When I ask her about a birthday present for my father, she offers the photograph of me laughing and it is already framed.

When Finn turns around in his chair at the party he's happy to find me standing behind him, and we are both only pleasantly lit. He takes my hand and leads me out of the kitchen. We put our boots on in the laundry room, zip up our coats, dig through the hats and mitts and find him a glove that fits. We slip out the side door together and clomp into the backyard where we throw poorly packed snowballs at each other, like couples in those rom-com movies who are just about to kiss.

This is the story I choose. A fun, easy night, fooling around with Finn and the possibility of love in the distance. The generous choices. The good people. The girl I am, the girl I was, safely back in bed and the canoes headed home with their crews of righteous men, their paddles dipping soundless into the water.

ACKNOWLEDGMENTS

I wish to gratefully acknowledge the financial support of the Ontario Arts Council and the City of Ottawa.

They say it takes a village to raise a child, and I guess I'm still growing up. Biggest thanks to:

My agent, Samantha Haywood, and my editor, Nicole Winstanley: for keeping the faith, for pushing for more, for seeing this work so finely into the world. Jennifer Griffiths: my heart lifted the first time I saw your cover. Emma Ingram and Deborah Sun de la Cruz: for all you have done for the novel.

My Bennington family: Victoria Whitaker Clausi and Dawn Dayton: for wrangling me across the border. Esteemed teachers Rachel Pastan, Bret Anthony Johnston, Jill McCorkle, and soul sister Lynne Sharon Schwartz. The entire class of June 2014: our time at Bennington was both beautiful and insane. My tennis partners, Keith, Tara, Bridget, Major, Susan, Rachel, and Phillip Lopez. Every workshop buddy, dance partner, pool player, and late night end-of-the-world drifter. I loved it all.

For the pages: Corina Zappia, Bridget Sampson. For Finn: Libby Flores, Simon Proulx. For Michael: Keith Lesmeister, Martin Proulx. For Mia, sanctuary in New York, and letting me rip off your haiku: Jennifer Miller. For the whole damn thing: Jay Hodges (!), Denton Loving (!), Erin Kate Ryan (!). You lifted me higher.

The gracious and gifted poets Cassie Pruyn, Emily Mohn-Slate, Jennifer Miller: for welcoming this lowly prose writer into your hallowed circle.

My Algonquin students: for believing in love and teaching me about life and writing.

Madeline Hennessey: for the sex talk. Ash Nayler and Jayne Guertin Schlott: for the photography lessons. Chantal Proulx: for the medical bits. Patrick Boyle: for the playlist. Jana Gannon: for the day off in Malibu. Jodi Anderson: for the laughs at the water cooler. Walter Robinson: for the joke. Steve Ellis: for the story. Tami Galili Ellis: for the artful conversations. Bob Lloyd: for dealing with the mice, warning me about the bears, and Dawn Lloyd, for sending over the flower. Gord Walker: for digging me out and letting me steal your power. Stephane Delillo and Carrie-Lee Brown: for keeping in touch and the weeks in Paris. Chris Burke and Charles Bristow: best Zen cop, bad cop, finance whiz team ever? Jaqui Cadieux: for the yoga lessons, and the gifts of food and friendship. You helped see me through.

Simon, Sophia, Elise. Cody, Brady, Behn: a prouder mother you will not find.

Martin: Gawd. Sorry. You took the brunt of this one. I owe you life, my darling.

My parents, Mary and Mike Vasiga: one day I hope to write a story worthy of the love you have shown me.

A NOTE ABOUT THE TYPE

The body of *We All Love the Beautiful Girls* has been set in a digitized form of Bembo, a typeface based on an old-style Roman face that was used for Cardinal Bembo's tract De Aetna in 1495. Bembo was first cut by Francisco Griffo in the early sixteenth century. The Lanston Monotype Corporation of Philadelphia brought the well-proportioned letterforms of Bembo to North America in the 1930s.